# THE BELOVED

## ONCE LOST SERIES BOOK TWO

KELLY HARREL

*To all the parents of prodigals.*
*Keep praying. Keep believing. Keep loving. Keep trusting the Lord.*
*Because that's what love does.*

*And to Donny Dee and the staff of the San Diego Rescue Mission.*
*What a blessing it is to see the lives changed by your ministry. May God pour His blessings upon you for being His hands and feet.*

Now rescue your beloved people. Answer and save us by your power.

Psalm 60:5

# A NOTE FROM DANNY MORTON

THIS IS NOT YOUR TYPICAL FEEL-GOOD CHRISTIAN BOOK WHERE everything is perfect. The truth about sin is it leads to death. The way I see it, you experience two deaths. First comes spiritual death. When you don't walk with God, you think it's no big deal. I mean, you've existed without God, so what's the difference? But with spiritual death comes darkness. Lack of hope. Eventually, utter despair. It doesn't come all at once but in waves—over time. The second death is that of your hopes, dreams, of who you're meant to be. This is ironic because when we choose sin, we might think we'll gain more. We think we'll achieve our dreams, success, happiness. At least, that's what I thought.

This is the period of my life when I was consumed by sin. I didn't care. I turned my back on God. The darkness can overwhelm us as we look back, tempt us to fast forward through it. But I write it in hopes that, as you read, you will see how He never turned His back on me. He sent His people to love me though I mocked them. He continued to provide for me despite stupid choices. While I wallowed in the filth, I was still His beloved. I write that you may realize His love for you is just as strong, regardless of what you've done. God is always with us. Watching over us. Loving us. Waiting for us to call out to Him so He can save us from ourselves.

Because there are two sides to every story, my sister Lydia has come alongside me to share the hell my family went through while I was away. One person's decision always affects others, but as Romans 8:28 says, *"He works all things for the good of those who love him and are called according to his purpose."* Things may not happen the way we want them to, but it's for the good of those who love Him. Because He is good. Even when we can't see it.

Perhaps, although things aren't hunky-dory, this is your typical Christian story. After all, everyone has sinned and fallen short of the glory of God. Some of us just fall harder than others.

*Danny*

# CHAPTER 1

## DANNY

I'M FREE.

The cold night air stings my face as I ride down the street on my skateboard. I shiver but resist the urge to put on my jacket. The chill in the air both relaxes and exhilarates me. I'm no longer under my dad's roof, his authority. I'm off to start a new life.

The life I was meant to live.

Finally.

I power up my phone and plot my next moves. Brett's house, the bank, somewhere to sleep. I'll look for a car later today. Something cheap that'll make it to LA.

The time flashes on the screen. 12:03.

I text Brett. *You up?*

The reply comes a minute later. *Not really.*

*I need my stuff and whatever you have.* My fingers fly across the keyboard. *Rolled. I have cash. Meet you outside your house.*

*Go to sleep, Danny. I'll bring it to school tomorrow. You don't need to get high tonight.*

Now I'm heating up. *I won't be at school tomorrow. I need to get it now.*

*Why aren't you going to school?*

I cuss. Seriously, Brett? You get all curious at midnight? *I'll be at your house in ten.*

*Ok*, he replies.

I jog up the steps to Brett's porch. The front door swings open. Brett exits barefoot in flannel pajama bottoms and a T-shirt that barely covers his belly. Bob, his pathetic mutt, races out. She does her business, scurries back up the icy steps, and slides on the last one before bolting past us into the house.

"Where you goin'?" Brett glances from the duffle on my skateboard at the bottom of the steps to the backpack over my shoulder.

"Out of here." No way am I bringing Brett into this. My sister Lydia knows we're friends and have lockers beside each other. She already suspects we do drugs together. My parents will be all over him when they find out. "Whatcha got?"

He pulls the prescription bottle I lifted from Mrs. Dossle's desk from his pocket along with four joints. "That's it. Thought you just bought some."

"I did." I take out my wad of twenties. "How much?"

"What are you doin'?" Brett scratches his head.

"Leaving." I replace the drugs in his hand with two bills. "Running away."

"What?"

"I'm done with my dad. I'll never be able to do what I want at home."

He looks to my duffle. "You're sleeping on the streets?"

"Whatever it takes. Thanks for this." I stuff the bottle in my pocket and start down the stairs.

"Wait!" Brett shoves the money back into my hand. "I won't take this."

"No, I want to—"

He moves back. "Stay here 'til things blow over. My mom hates abusive guys. She'll protect you. I'll kick my brother out of his room. You can sleep there."

I grin. Funny that this guy, who I put down in my mind for years, wants to help me. He might be my only friend. "Thanks, but I can't stay." Grabbing my bag, I get on my board. "Take care, Brett."

"You too, Danny," he says as I skate down his driveway.

The night is quiet as I roll through the deserted streets. The further I go from Brett's, the more the reality of what I'm doing sinks in. I thought I was trapped in that school for two more years. Adios, Dillinger. This happy truth is sinking in when a parked police car on the city street comes into view. If a cop spots me, he'll take me back home for breaking curfew.

At the corner by the jewelry store, I peek around at his car. His head is down. My bank is beyond him. The wind kicks up, cuts through my clothes. I pull on my jacket and zip it. Various options run through my mind when another cop parks beside him in the middle of the street. I speed down the street perpendicular to the one they're on. My GPS tells me the closest bank is two miles away. Not the best start to my adventure.

Exhaustion sets in about the time I roll up to the ATM outside First National. My body reminds me I've been awake over eighteen hours. There's an office building next to the bank. Hopefully I'll find a place to crash there for the night.

I slide my card, enter my pin, then choose "withdraw." I push "other amount" and type 1-0-0-0. Though I have three times that, it's a start.

The machine informs me the amount is too high. Let's try five hundred.

Denied.

On the previous screen, the highest denomination for withdrawal is three hundred. I pick that. It processes the request. The machine spits out twenties along with a receipt. Two thousand, nine hundred, forty-five dollars remains. Super. I only need to do this ten more times.

With the cash in the pocket of my backpack, I begin the entire process again. After I hit "withdraw," a new message pops up.

*"You have reached the daily limit for withdrawal. Another withdrawal can be made after 24 hours. Contact the branch during business hours if you feel you have received this message in error."*

I slam my hand against the machine. I need this. I really need this.

Hours of operation are nine to five. Guess I'm done until tomorrow.

The building next door is pitch black inside; the front doors are locked. Can't a guy get a break? My bags feel heavier than a coach's equipment bag, my eyes feel scratchy like they're filled with sand. I skate around the building. There's gotta be an open door.

No such luck.

A larger complex in the distance has dim lights on the bottom floor. Lights might mean someone is inside.

Which could mean an unlocked door.

A security truck is parked close to a side door. Not too worrisome, since the building is at least eight floors. Plenty of floors to get lost on.

A small side door pops when it opens. I freeze, count to ten.

My heart pounds.

Am I really breaking into a building?

I reach ten without an alarm sounding. No guard appears. I step in, quietly close the door behind me. A sign that says Security points to my right. The light is dim, but I make out a few domes on the ceiling.

Cameras. I hadn't thought about those.

To my left is the stairwell. Probably my best option.

Arm against the wall, I inch my way around the perimeter of the room. My gear grows heavier by the minute. I breathe a sigh of relief when the door clicks shut.

It's as cold in the stairwell as it is outside. Once my eyes adjust to the fluorescent light, I see my breath in front of me.

There aren't any cameras that I see. Although the light is bright, a shadow falls behind the stairs. I situate myself under the first flight with my stuff pushed as far forward as possible. Minutes after I settle into my sleeping bag, fully clothed, my jacket zipped up all the way,

I feel warm for the first time in hours. It doesn't matter that the cement is hard, that things haven't gone smoothly or that I'm exhausted.

I'm free.

I'm finally free.

---

## LYDIA

*Danny and I stroll down the beach, and the sand squishes between my toes. Salty breezes blow my hair—mostly in my face—but I don't care. As he tells me about his new play, my attention shifts between the storyline and his goatee. When did my brother grow a goatee? I have to feel it because I don't believe it.*

*Danny laughs and pushes my hand away. "You'll be at opening night?"*

*"In the front row. If you're nice, I might share my popcorn with you."*

*"Don't think they sell popcorn in the playhouse. Maybe M&Ms." He leans into me. "You've always been the best part of our family, Lyd. You know that?"*

*Cold water rushes over my bare feet. Chills run through my body. He has a pained expression on his face. I don't understand why sadness fills his eyes.*

*"Danny!" Dad's voice carries down the shoreline.*

*Danny sprints out of sight.*

*"Come back!" I try to scream, but the words don't escape.*

"Margaret! Margaret!"

I bolt up in bed. Why is Dad screaming for Mom? I rub the sleep from my eyes and giggle at the thought of Danny's goatee. If he didn't shave for a year, he still wouldn't have that much hair on his face.

Dad flings my door open. He's fully dressed and frantic. "Where is he?"

"What?" I pull my covers around me.

"Danny's gone." His eyes are wild, like those of a madman in a horror movie. "Do you know where he is?"

"No." The beach dream fades, and yesterday's real-life nightmare slaps me in the face.

*We found marijuana and pills in your brother's room*, was how Dad greeted me when I walked through the door after work. *Do you know how long he's been using?*

I was shocked until I thought about how distant my brother has been lately.

"Lydia, did he say anything to you?" Dad is in my face. "Did he wake you?"

"No." I scoot back, afraid he might grab me. "I studied before bed." I lift my American Government notebook from my nightstand to prove it.

But really, I couldn't focus enough to study. For over an hour I stared at my notes, thinking about Dad taking Danny to the teen rehab center this morning. My prayer was the same—*God, work out this mess. Take care of my brother.*

By the time sleep came, my head and eyes hurt from crying.

"Chris," Mom calls, "I found a note."

We race down the hall to Danny's room. Mom's in front of his desk with a piece of notebook paper in her hand.

"What does it say?" Dad tries to grab it, but she blocks him.

"'Mom, sorry I hurt you,'" she reads. "'I've gone to live my life; the life Dad won't let me live. Please don't call me. I'm never coming home.'" She whispers the last part, the color drained from her face. "Oh, God. No."

Dad rushes from the room. Mom's cheeks are wet and shiny, and she clutches the paper to her chest. I shift my eyes to the hole in the window where Danny threw his autographed baseball out after he fought with Dad. A heaviness builds in my chest at the thought.

I step toward the window. Glass pokes my foot. The framed team photos Mom took pride in hanging each year are in a broken heap on the floor. All this as a result of his rage against Dad.

Careful to avoid the glass, I kneel to lift the frames to the desk. At the age of five, a smile spread across Danny's face. The smile is just as wide at six, though his front teeth are missing. Oh, that toothless grin.

By twelve there's no smile.

The biggest change has been since his fifteenth birthday. Apathy replaced joy. His jokes became hurtful, sarcastic comments, like on his birthday when he lashed out at me. That's when he stopped talking. He wanted to quit baseball to focus on his new passion of writing. Dad pushed with extra practices, rigorous workouts, and insisted he attend every team event. It broke my heart that Danny blamed himself for the season ending poorly. Dad made Danny work at his sporting goods store like a punishment for not making it into the state championship. Since Super Subs where I work is across the parking lot from Dad's store, I asked Danny to have lunch with me when we had similar shifts. He said if Dad gave him a break, he spent it doing homework. I blamed Dad for pushing him too hard. Now I blame myself for not standing up for my brother.

Collecting the broken pieces of glass in my hand, I think about how I tried to get Danny to talk to me last night. We used to lie on his bed for hours talking about school, our family, sometimes God or faith. If the discussion turned heavy or I got upset, he'd make a joke, so I'd laugh. We have a special bond I never had with my sisters. Maybe it's because we're the youngest. Mary left for college years ago. Anna started working when she turned sixteen. The two of us were left at home to watch Mom's anxiety grow with the increase of Dad's dictatorial side. I prayed that with Anna going to college this school year Danny and I would reconnect, yet this summer he started to lock his door at night. I'd press my ear against it, trying to hear if he was awake. There was only silence. Last night his face was emotionless as he packed.

"I know what I need to do now," he said. "I'll be okay. I'm moving forward. In a good way."

*Oh God, what's happening? What has he done?*

"Did you know?" Mom's staring at me. "Did he tell you?" Her pleas are filled with genuine concern, not anger like Dad's.

Tears come to my eyes. "No." I stand, place the glass I've gathered on the top picture. "I had no idea. I would have done something if I'd known."

Mom's lip quivers. "My baby," she whispers. "My baby's gone."

I wrap my arms around her. I want to take away her pain. I wish I could tell her everything will be okay, but none of this is okay. Nothing has been okay in this house for a long time.

Dad rushes into the room, waving his phone in the air. "I texted him. He keeps saying he's not coming home. He dropped my call."

Mom brushes her tears as we break our embrace. "Please, Chris. Please be gentle with him."

"Gentle?" The way he growls the response is anything but. "He's a drug addict, Margaret. We're way beyond gentle." He steps toward me. "Where would he go?"

*God, help me. Where could he be?* I take a deep breath. The face of his druggie friend pops into my mind. "Brett's! He has a locker next to him. The kids Brett hangs out with look like they do drugs. That's probably where Danny got stuff."

Mom and I hurry to either side of Dad when he begins to text.

*Where are you? Brett's house?*

*I'm not coming home*, Danny replies. *Leave me alone.*

Dad's hands tense. *Son, we need to talk.*

*You've done enough talking. I'm not coming home. You've controlled my life long enough. Leave me alone.* I hear Danny shouting the words in my mind. He's finally snapped.

*You can't do this*, Dad types. *We will find you and take you to rehab.*

My stomach rolls. I've never seen my father so blinded with rage.

Dad cusses when his reply won't send. "He blocked my phone. Margaret, where's yours?"

Mom rushes from the room with Dad right behind her. Something brown in Danny's trash grabs my attention. My heart sinks. I lift Danny's leather Bible from it to my chest. *God, he's given up on You, too.*

We have attended Sunday school, the main church service, and midweek service every week for as long as I can remember. Mom encouraged us to begin serving in our teen years. People always smile at us. They comment on how neat it is that we still squeeze into one pew. Once upon a time I thought we were a great Christian family. I've tried to ignore the growing chaos in our home—the way mealtime prayers more often feel like lip service than true gratitude; the fact that we never talk about God or what we learn at church anymore. Deep down I convinced myself that if I grew my own faith, that would be enough. Now I realize I was deceiving myself.

"Please, God." I hug Danny's Bible while I walk downstairs. "Let us find him."

## *CHAPTER 2*

### *DANNY*

I SWITCH MY GPS ON. SINCE MY DAD HAS SO RUDELY AWAKENED me, it's time to find some caffeine. That will hopefully dull my headache. A twenty-four-hour fast food place is a seven-minute walk away. I'm at the light when my phone rings. My mom. I reject the call. Another immediately follows.

"Mom, I'm not coming home." I skate when my light turns green.

"Danny." It's my father's voice. "Where are you?"

I should've known. "I'm not talking to you. I'll only talk to Mom."

"You can talk to her when we pick you up. Where are you?"

"I'm leaving town. Don't worry, you'll never see me again." Ending the call, I block my mom's number as well.

The smell of fried food and coffee greets me when I open the door to the restaurant. First, I go to the restroom, then I order. Hash browns, breakfast sandwich, and a soda. Extra-large soda. Until I can get more cocaine, I decide to compensate with caffeine.

I write during breakfast. Joe the Barista needs a new adventure. The world is filled with tons of people who don't drink coffee. Time he met some of them.

*AT RISE: JOE and AMANDA are behind the counter. Another guy around AMANDA's age, PETE, is with them. A banner that reads "GOOD LUCK JOE" hangs in the background.*

JOE. So, Pete, you feeling comfortable on the bar?

PETE. Yeah, man, I think I got it. It ain't that hard.

AMANDA. (*Frowns at JOE.*) I can't believe you're leaving.

JOE. I know. Seems like I've been here forever. But it's time to move on. I need to explore the world while I can.

AMANDA. Where's your first stop?

JOE. The Great Lakes. I've lived this close to them for six years but never visited them. Lots of hiking and fishing in store for me over the next week.

AMANDA. How long until you need to be on the west coast?

JOE. I told my parents I'd be in Oregon in two months. I can find and lose myself a couple times over.

AMANDA. (*Wraps her arms around his neck.*) I'm going to miss you.

JOE. (*Returns hug.*) I'm going to miss you, but I've trained you well. (*Takes off his apron as they break from their embrace, folds it, then hands it to AMANDA.*) You'll be fine if you remember the most important rules.

AMANDA. (*Puts up a finger with each point.*) Consistency, tell them what they want to hear, and make them feel special. (*Smiles.*) Everyone likes to feel special.

JOE. See, you got this. Now I'm off to learn the rules of the real world.

AMANDA. Keep in touch, 'kay?

JOE. I'll send you pics of all the interesting stuff along the way.

I head to the restroom once more before I leave. It's a hassle with my stuff—a duffle, backpack, skateboard, and huge jacket. I barely fit through the door. Ridiculous is how I look and feel, but it won't be for long. Soon enough I'll have a car.

I squeeze back through the restroom door on my way out. I freeze at the sight of my parents at the counter talking to the cashier.

How did they find me? I didn't tell Brett. I grab my cell phone from my pocket. That's right. My mom made me download a family GPS app when I started to drive.

The employee points to the opposite end of the restaurant where I ate my breakfast. I bolt for the exit. The minute I'm outside I leap on my skateboard.

"Danny!" I hear my mom scream seconds later.

The desperation in her voice sends chills up my back. Head down, I pump faster. A bus is loading across the street. I might die getting to it, but that's better than going home.

I bolt into the street between oncoming traffic. Horns honk, my dad screams my name. My legs feel like jello. I jump the curb as the last person loads. I have to make it—

Dismounting my board, I scoop it up then sprint like I'm trying to beat the ball to home plate.

"Wait!" Sweat drips in my eye when I leap the stairs. The bus doors close behind me.

"Just in time." The driver pulls from the curb. "Pay up and have a seat."

"Thanks." I drop ones in the jar.

Sinking into the front seat, I glance back. My dad is on the sidewalk, bent over. My mom is beside him, weeping. For a moment I regret my decision. I regret the pain I've caused my mom and Lyd. I regret not trying to make things work. Maybe—

My dad kicks at the ground, then turns toward my mom, hands waving in the air. She covers her face.

Satisfaction settles deep inside me. He lost. He finally realizes he can't run my life. It was never his to control. I'm free at last.

---

*LYDIA*

My parents race out the door after a quick lesson in using the family locator to find Danny. Pacing the family room gives my worries time to multiply. What if Danny hitchhikes? Some crazy person could pick him up. What if he gets ahold of more drugs? He might OD. Praying with someone would calm me down, but my sisters will freak if I call them. They'll blame Danny for everything because Dad does no wrong in their eyes. I need someone who will be supportive and sensitive to what I'm going through.

Jason.

Jason sat behind me in English freshman year. He's so cute I was always too nervous to say anything except hi. In October, I struck up a conversation with him that ended with me inviting him to Bible club. He showed up that Friday, sat next to me, and talked to me like we'd been friends forever. We've had lunch together almost every school day for three years. He's on the varsity baseball team with Danny, but I know he won't judge him.

"Hey," Jason answers on the second ring. "Funny you called. I was thinking about you. Wanna meet for coffee? I was up past midnight studying for Precalculus. I need some serious caffeine before class."

"Danny's gone!" Tears come the minute I speak.

"What?" he asks.

"When we woke up this morning, he was gone. He left a note for my mom saying he ran away." I fall to my knees. *Oh God, he ran away.*

"Why would he do that?" Jason pauses. "Does this have anything to do with him not showing for practice yesterday? Coach was fuming."

"He's on drugs." My stomach flips. "He got called to Mr. Ward's office. Mrs. Dossle accused him of stealing pain medication from her desk. The school security didn't find anything on him, but Dad found marijuana in his room along with a couple of their prescriptions." I rub my temple. "I kind of knew, Jason. I didn't see him do anything, but I had a feeling something was wrong. Allergy medicine and cold meds kept disappearing from our bathroom when no one was sick."

"He drank a lot at the parties last year. That was one of the reasons I wanted them to end. He wasn't the only one, but he could outdrink most of them. I just couldn't support it."

"Dad was taking him to rehab this morning. Danny was packing when I got home from work last night. I begged him to tell me what was going on. He said it was okay, that he knew what he needed to do."

Jason sighs. "I'm sorry. What can I do?"

"We tracked him with the GPS app. My parents are on their way to him. I just...I just..." I close my eyes. "Can you pray?"

"Absolutely." Jason takes a deep breath. "God, we pray for Danny. Bring him to a place of clear thinking. Help him to know You love him and that his family loves him, too. Show him how getting involved with drugs and alcohol has pushed him away from You."

My tears fall faster.

"We pray for wisdom for Lydia's parents. We pray they would find him so they can get Danny help. Bring him home to his family—and You. In Jesus's name, amen."

"Thank you." I wipe my face with my sleeve.

"How about I come over? I don't need to go to school today."

"Finals start tomorrow. Go so you can share your notes with me. I couldn't study last night even though I tried." I stand. "They'll find him. I'll probably be there by second period."

"Okay," Jason says. "I'm praying for you. And for Danny."

I crawl to the coffee table, place my phone in front of me, and open the GPS app. Mom's and Dad's pins are together, closing in on Danny's. "Oh God, please. Let them get him. Let them bring him home."

All movement stops when the pins end up in the same location.

"Let Danny know we love him, God. Keep Dad calm. Help Danny to see—"

Danny's pin moves away from them.

"No, Danny. Stop running. Stop—"

My phone plays Mom's ringtone.

"What happened?" I ask.

"He's on a bus." Mom's voice shakes. "He skated across four lanes of traffic to run away from us."

Dad curses in the background.

"We couldn't get the number," Mom cries. "We don't know where he's going."

I switch my phone on speaker to check the GPS. Danny's pin is stopped. It says 'GPS is off' next to his name.

"Can you follow the bus?" I ask. *God, there has to be something we can do.*

"We'd have to go two lights down to make a U-turn. The bus turned. We don't know what direction it went—"

"Lydia!" Dad screams into the phone. "Get ready. We're coming home. I froze his bank account. I want you to go with us. You've always been able to talk sense into him."

"Okay," I manage to say. "I'll be ready."

I pull on jeans, a sweatshirt, and a hat. Then text Jason.

*Danny ran when he saw them. We're going to try to get him when he withdraws money from the bank. Please pray.*

*I am,* his response comes, along with Isaiah 26:3. *"You will keep in perfect peace those whose minds are steadfast, because they trust in you."*

*I trust You, God.* I sit on my bed. *Bring him home.*

# CHAPTER 3

## DANNY

I RIDE THE BUS TWO STOPS, THEN BOARD ANOTHER TO HEAD TO A bank outside our city. Once I settle into the back, I text Amano, my cocaine supplier.

*Need fresh powder. 8:30?* I add the address of a coffee place beside the bank.

His reply comes as I get off the bus. *You don't think others sleep?* My phone reads eight o'clock. This from the guy who texts me three, four, five times a day when I go more than a week without contacting him?

*Sorry, headed out of town. I want double my normal.*

If the fact that I'm leaving town doesn't capture his attention, maybe my manners will. Drug dealers care about that, right? He should definitely care about making twice as much off me.

I'm at a table in the corner of Mocha Mania with my caramel macchiato, extra shot, extra caramel, when his reply comes.

*8:45.*

Oh well, at least he'll come. Gives me time to write my next scene.

*AT RISE: JOE walks into a coffee shop before dawn, dressed in jeans, flannel shirt, and a fishing hat. One middle-aged fisherman, ROD, is in line in front of him, two people are at the handoff bar. After ordering his drink, JOE waits by ROD at the handoff bar.*

ROD. (*Looks JOE over.*) You going out today?

JOE. Sure am. First time since I was a teen. You fish at the lake often?

ROD. It's my favorite pastime.

JOE. Any advice?

ROD. There are three keys to being a successful fisherman. The first is patience. You can't rush the fish. If you're anxious, you'll be miserable, and they'll never come.

JOE. (*Chuckles.*) My dad always said, "Sit still, Joe. You're scaring away the fish."

ROD. I've told my own kids the same. I use the time to appreciate the beauty around me. If you stop everything, pocket your phone, and look, you'll see sights more gorgeous than any pictures or paintings.

JOE. Sounds great. What's the second?

ROD. (*Picks up drink when barista calls his name.*) You never see the best ones coming. Big ones go deep. You have no idea they're there until they almost pull you in. A fifty-one-pound catfish almost yanked me off my boat last year.

JOE. (*Eyes huge.*) Fifty-one pounds? You're kidding?

ROD. Not at all. The biggest fish caught in the area was a one hundred, ninety-three-pound sturgeon in the late seventies. That one would have pulled me in. (*Takes a sip of his drink.*) I doubt they saw it coming.

JOE. (*Grabs his drink.*) Crazy.

ROD. (*Both walk toward door.*) The last is, some days things don't turn out how you want them to. When that happens, find gratitude for the little stuff—a day off work, beautiful scenery, a day without the wife nagging—and determine to try again. It's easy to quit when you come up empty handed, but if you do, you could be missing out on the biggest fish of your life. It could just be a few trips away.

JOE. (*Extends his hand to shake with ROD.*) Thanks, Rod. I appreciate the tips. Now to go freeze my butt off. (*Smiles.*) And have a great time doing it.

Amano parks his Cadillac in a handicapped spot at eight fifty-four. One of his philosophies must be "always keep them waiting." Dropping my stuff next to his passenger-side door, I lean inside the window.

"What you doin' out here?" he asks. "Where you goin'?"

"Out of town for the holidays." I don't know why he cares, but I definitely don't want him to know. "What'd you bring?"

"Two eight-balls." He takes two baggies from his pocket. "Three hundred."

I grab the wad of twenties from my pocket. He tries to take me every time. I'm not one of his stupid executives who pay whatever he demands. "Two sixty. That's fair." I drop the bills on the seat and stick out my hand.

"Only for you, Danny." He slams them down. "Merry Christmas, kid. See ya in the new year."

"No, you won't," I say under my breath as I walk away.

The line at the bank is five people long when I enter. The overweight, bald security guard at the front door and a young male employee at "new accounts" wearing a suit two sizes too big glance toward me. I rub my palms on my sweats, push my duffle forward with my foot as the next person goes to the teller.

Three more customers stand between me and my money.

A commercial for mortgage rates loops on the huge screen on the front wall. The handsome man in his polo shirt slips an arm around his Barbie wife's shoulders while the blonde-headed kids ride their bikes around the cul-de-sac. Yup, that's the perfect family. All they're missing is a Bible in their hand or a sign on their yard that reads "Jesus Loves You."

"Can I help you?" The red-haired teller resembles a strawberry with her red shirt. She stares at my duffle the entire walk to her. Now her eyes dart from my backpack to my face.

"I need to withdraw money from my account." I pull my debit card from my wallet.

"Please swipe your card." She stares at the screen. "It seems you withdrew the max this morning."

"I'm buying a car." I wipe my palms again. "I need to withdraw the rest of the money from my account."

"Oh." She leans closer to the computer. Her mouth opens, then her lips shift to an awkward smile. "If you have a seat in room three, the bank manager, Mrs. Jarvis, will be right with you." She motions across the room to an empty office with a "3" on the glass window.

Something is very wrong; my gut tells me on the way to the office. There are two burgundy chairs in front of the desk. I sit in the one closest to the door. The teller is on the phone, her mouth shaded. When she hangs up, she makes eye contact with me.

*You've blown it,* a voice inside me says. *She's calling the cops. You'll be locked up in that rehab center by noon.*

*What have I done?* Rubbing my temples doesn't relieve the stress. *I just want my money.*

*You're a screw up. Always have been. You hurt yourself running to first base, then you lose the chance of going to state finals by diving with your eyes closed. Of course, they caught you taking the drugs from your teacher's desk. If you get caught with cocaine in your pocket, you'll end up in prison, not a youth facility. You can't do anything right—*

"Thank you for coming in, Mr. Morton." The manager's gray hair matches her skirt suit. "I'm Mrs. Jarvis, the bank manager."

"Is there a problem with my account?" I move to the edge of my seat.

"I need to verify a few things. Can I see your card and a picture ID?"

I pull both from my wallet. "I don't understand—"

"It should only take a minute." Mrs. Jarvis clicks away at her keyboard. Her eyes narrow with confirmation of my social security number, and address. They widen with my full name. She scribbles on a piece of paper before sliding my cards across the desk to me. "I'll be right back."

I crane my neck to catch a glimpse of my dad's name and cell number on the paper. I'm stuck.

With a deep breath to clear my mind, I assess my surroundings. Pillsbury Dough Boy outside the front door doesn't stand a chance at catching me. Mrs. Jarvis would do a face-plant running in her spiked heels and skirt. A well-plotted escape will leave them in the dust.

The center has two driveways. One is close to another strip mall with a construction store. The other leads to a hill. A hill that heads to...

A mall.

Lots of people. Lots of stores. Lots of buses.

That's where I need to be.

The manager hangs up the phone. She walks to Strawberry Shortcake. Her hand blocks both their faces. This is my opportunity. I speed walk to the exit. The minute my skateboard hits the pavement, I'm off. The manager runs out when I'm four stores away. The security guard makes it about ten feet. I'm speeding down the hill to the mall, he's hunched over panting.

The bus is loading as I skate up. Dropping in my fare, I hurry to the back. My entire body shakes. Pulling up my dad's number, I push call.

---

*LYDIA*

From the time Mom and Dad pick me up from the house we sit in silence. Dad decides to park by the freeway, so we don't waste time. Dad seldom speeds, yet the minute the bank calls, he's driving like he's in the Indie 500.

Then the manager calls again saying Danny ran. Dad screams words I've never heard him say.

My heart stops when Dad's phone announces a call from Danny.

"Hello," he answers on the car's Bluetooth.

"What'd you do with my money?" Danny asks.

"It's time for you to come home."

I'm thankful Dad's not yelling, but his voice lacks any emotion.

"What'd you do with my money? It was mine." Danny's volume shifts from screaming to barely above a whisper.

*He must be in public. God, where is he?*

"I froze your account. You can't get any money out or use your debit card."

The determination in Dad's voice gives me the chills. Danny worked hard for that money. It's rightfully his.

"The manager at Greenwood said you ran. Are you at the mall near there?" Dad asks.

"I'm not...coming...home." I can tell by the pauses in his sentences Danny's trying to calm down. "I want my money. You have no right. I earned it. I worked my butt off—"

"I didn't take it. I simply froze your account. Go through detox and you can have it. I'll hand you the cash myself after you finish."

I stare at my father, his expression so determined. Is this about helping Danny or getting his way?

"Danny, please stay there," Mom pleads. "We're on the way."

"You can't do this!" Danny screams. "It's my money!"

Mom begins to weep.

"I reported you as a runaway." Dad's voice turns firm. "There's no point in continuing this. The police are looking for you. If you get caught with drugs, it'll be worse. You've proven your point. You hate baseball. Stop this drama and come home."

"No, Dad, it's time for you to stop. You can't run my life. You can't control me anymore."

I hate that Danny is doing this, but I'm proud of him for standing up for himself. I've wanted that for years.

"Come home for your mother. For Lydia. We all want you to be safe—and sober."

The statement cuts me to the core. My baby brother's a drug addict.

"You can't always get what you want," are Danny's last words.

A stream of bad words comes from Dad. Mom clutches her chest, weeping.

*We've lost him.* I lower my head. *We've really lost him.*

"Call him!" Dad yells at me. "Tell him I'll cut off his cell service next."

"That won't make him come home." Mom hangs on his arm. "We can't leave him without a phone. What if something happens? He won't be able to get ahold of us."

"He doesn't want anything to do with us." He slams the palm of his hand against the steering wheel.

"He might come home when he calms down." Though I don't believe it, I'm desperate, like Mom, not to lose Danny completely. "What if he promises to contact me weekly to let us know he's okay? Maybe in a few weeks he'll come home." *Please God, let him come home.*

"Please, Chris," Mom begs.

He stares at her with narrowed eyes. "He doesn't deserve—"

"For me," Mom sobs. "Please."

"Call him," Dad says. "If he doesn't agree, I turn off his phone today."

*C'mon, Danny,* I think as his phone rings. *Please answer.*

It goes to voicemail after the third ring. I immediately send a text. *It's me, not Dad. Please call.*

I stare at the screen. *Please, God. Let him call.* I've started to give up hope when it rings.

"Hey. Where are you?" I ask.

"I'm leaving. I'm tired of him running my life."

I hear other conversations in the background. Is he at the mall or maybe a bus?

"We both know this is the only way it'll stop."

The truth of his words breaks my heart, but I won't give up. "Come home. We can figure this out."

"It's too late for that. I'm done with him." He takes a deep breath. "I need my money, Lyd. I earned it. I deserve it for what I put up with. I need a car."

Mom is staring at me. Dad adjusts the rearview mirror to see me. I lower my head.

"I can't help you." *God, I want to, but I shouldn't.*

"Yes, you can. Talk to Mom." He's talking fast. "She's on the account. She can lift the freeze."

"They won't—"

"Take his phone. Open the bank app. It'll only take the touch of a button."

"We want you to come home." I close my eyes to hold back my tears. "You don't need to do this—"

"Thanks a lot. I thought you were different."

A tear falls. "Danny—"

"Don't ever call me again."

"Wait!" I yell. "Don't hang up."

"I have nothing left to say."

"Dad wants to disconnect your service. Mom convinced him not to because this is the only contact we have with you but—"

"I blocked their phones." He sighs.

"Dad says if you reach out to me once a week, he won't turn off your phone." I swallow hard. "He wants you to come home."

"He wants to control my life."

"I want you to come home. Please, Danny."

"You're the only person I text. On Mondays. I don't want to hear from Mary or Anna. Ever. If they try to track me, I'll sell my phone and never speak to any of you."

"Okay." I know what I need to say, because it won't leave my mind. I don't want Danny to be mad, yet I've always been honest with him. *Please, God, let him accept it.* "It's best if you get clean. Even if you don't come home, will you give up the drugs?"

He doesn't say anything, which tells me everything.

"I text you. You don't text me. Or call. Agreed?"

"Yes." I sigh. "I love you."

He hangs up without a response. The heaviness that built in my chest all morning crushes my lungs.

*He's gone,* I text Jason through my tears. *We couldn't get him.*

There's no answer. He's in class. I should be, too, since finals start tomorrow. Even if I go, I won't be able to concentrate. Not with everything that's happened.

"I'll call the school when we get home," Dad says. "They should be able to give you his locker combination. Clean it out. Bring everything home. I need to go through it."

"I don't think I can go today." I wipe my tears.

"It's finals week. You have to keep your grades up to get that academic scholarship to the Ozarks. What did you need? A 3.75 GPA? If you let your grades drop, we lose money. I won't let your brother's irresponsibility and selfishness ruin your scholarship."

I gaze out the window to avoid looking at my father. He's definitely the master of making everything about him—and against Danny.

# *CHAPTER 4*

## *DANNY*

I PULL MY HOOD UP AND TAKE A FEW DEEP BREATHS. PEOPLE ARE glaring. If I come off as an out-of-control teen, I'll be reported and picked up by the cops.

Now that I can't pull out my money for a car, time for plan B.

My instinct is to get the heck out of Indiana, but I need to keep my eyes on the end goal: Make it to the west coast.

I search 'bus stations near me.' There's a large one in Bloomington, an hour away. That gives me space. I can also get to California from there. It'll take four different buses and three hours to get there. Gotta love public transportation.

The next issue is money. I'm at two hundred and change. I silently curse my dad for freezing my account. My mom wouldn't be as spiteful. He's such a—

Deep breath. The fact is I'm putting miles between us. He has no idea where I'm headed. Right now, that's what matters.

After I switch buses, I open my backpack for a book. I knew they'd come in handy. Huckleberry Finn is the most appropriate in this situation. I haven't read it for years. Maybe Huck will give me some tips for living on my own.

"That's a good one."

I'm still on the first page when the gray-haired lady with glasses in front of me makes the comment.

"Yeah." I grin at her then return to reading.

"I don't see many kids like you reading classics."

I shift my eyes to her. Like me? I start to get offended then realize my hood is still up. Sliding it off, I smile at her. "My mom raised me well."

"I'm lucky if my grandkids will read comic books." She shakes her head. "Such a waste of good minds."

I stare at her for a few seconds, clueless as to what to say. Then I lower my face in hopes—

"Shouldn't you be in school?"

Yup, just my luck to sit behind the most curious person on the bus.

"I finished my finals early. I'm headed to California to see my grandparents for the holidays. They're all alone out there. I'm the oldest, so Mom agreed to let me go."

"She did raise you right!" The woman purses her lips. "Mmmhmm. That's a good grandson."

I settle back in my seat impressed with my storytelling ability. I assessed my audience to create a relatable story that gained acceptance. That's definitely a gift. Time to share it with the world.

Two more buses, and identities, later, I arrive at Bloomington. It takes patience and balance to maneuver through the crowded bus station with all my crap. I bump into an elderly couple, sideswipe a guy busy on his phone, and almost take out some boy while he argues with his sister. Exhaustion has set in from this morning's chase. My back throbs. I can hardly focus. First stop after I purchase my bus ticket is the restroom to do a line of coke. That's the only way I'll make it through this day.

"One ticket to Los Angeles, please," I say to the girl behind the counter, who strangely resembles Dorothy from The Wizard of Oz.

She looks beyond me. "Are you alone?" The tone of her voice tells me I shouldn't be.

Maybe if I ask her where Toto is, that'll distract her. "My mom's parking. I'm headed to California to visit my friend."

"The next bus for today is sold out." She clicks on her computer. "There's a seat for tomorrow, nine o'clock?"

That's not what I want, but what choice do I have? "How much?"

"Three hundred forty-five dollars."

I pull the wad of cash from my pocket. "Excuse me?"

"A one-way ticket is three hundred forty-five dollars," she says.

I glance at the cash and back to her. "For a bus ticket."

"Prices go up around the holidays. Mid-January is when they drop."

"Do you give a student discount?" She doesn't need to know I'm now technically a drop-out.

"We do." She types on the computer. "With a student discount it's three hundred twenty-five dollars."

I shove my money into my pocket. "Thanks for trying."

"I thought your mom was coming?" She raises an eyebrow. "Won't she give you the money?"

"I...I had to save it myself. I don't have that much."

"Come back after January 14th," she calls.

January? What in the world am I supposed to do until then?

A sandwich shop is a five-minute walk down the street. When I get there, I do some coke in the restroom. While this might not help me think straight, it'll make me feel better for twenty minutes.

I slide into a booth with my foot-long Italian sub. When I pull out my wallet to put away my money, a blue card behind my student ID catches my eye. It's the credit card Mom gave me when I got my permit.

"If you find yourself in a predicament, you can use this," she said.

This qualifies as a predicament. I don't know a ton about credit cards, but I overheard Dad explain them to Mary and Anna.

"The bill comes the fifth of every month. Be responsible and pay it in full. You need to track your spending through the month, so you don't get in over your head."

By my calculations I can charge whatever I want, and he won't know until I'm on the west coast. This makes my entire day. I search on my phone for hotels. Not cheap one- and two-star ones. I look up three and a half to four-star ones. They're a little farther out, but a good night's sleep is worth it. Time for Dad to pay back the money he took from me. To pay for the crap he's put me through. He owes me.

---

## *LYDIA*

*I'm sorry.* Jason's text arrives when I exit the office with Danny's locker combination. *I'm praying. I'll come over this afternoon with notes.*

*I'm at school,* I type. *After I get Danny's locker combination, I'm going to clean it out before class.*

*You didn't need to come. Your teachers will understand.*

*Dad made me.* I shake my head. What kind of father makes his daughter go to school the day her brother runs away? A cold wind sends a shiver through my body. It's almost freezing, and Danny is out on the streets. The pressure in my chest increases.

Another text arrives from Jason. *Where's Danny's locker?*

*In the science hall,* I text back.

*K. I'll meet you there.*

My instinct is to cover my ears when I enter the science building. I usually love crowds, but today the noise is too much. Even the lights hurt my head. There's no reason for me to be here. I should have stayed home.

Straight ahead, that druggie, Brett, opens his locker.

"Hey." I run to him. "Hey, Brett."

He hikes his jeans over his butt before he turns. "Hey." His smile fades when I get closer. He shoves a book in his locker.

"It's your fault," I say. "I know all of this is your fault."

He shakes his head. "Nah, it's not."

"Danny got his marijuana from you." I poke my finger into his chest. "He's been going to your house to party. He goes over there every day after school—"

"I help him with math." His face is expressionless. "Ask his teacher. He has, like, a B in the class. No way he could get that on his own."

"But he drank—"

"The baseball players taught him to do that." Brett points behind me. "Ask him."

I glance around to see Jason approaching.

"By the time Danny came to me, he could drink us under the table."

I cross my arms over my chest. "The marijuana—"

"Was to escape your dad. He sounds like a real..." Brett pauses when Jason stops beside me. "Something's wrong at home for Danny to run." Brett scratches his head. "He came over last night—this morning."

"You saw him?" Jason asks.

"Yeah. He came to my house to get..." He stops. "I told him to stay with me until stuff blew over. My mom wouldn't care. She hates abusive men."

I shake my head. "My dad didn't abuse him."

"Right." Brett laughs. "He just forced him to play a sport Danny hated, then wouldn't give him the money he promised for a car. Worked him like a dog on the field and at his store. My dad gave me physical scars. Your dad gave Danny mental ones." He shuts his locker. "Danny's a great guy. If he comes back, I'll try to get him to stay."

Jason wraps his arm around my shoulder. Does he know I want to rip this guy's throat out? This slob disgusts me with his ripped T-shirt and worn jeans that can't stay around his waist.

*Why would Danny hang out with him?*

The answer comes immediately. They were both trying to escape their fathers.

*God, forgive me for judging him.*

I scribble my number on a piece of paper and place it in his hand. "If you see him, call me. Please."

He glances at it before he shoves it back at me. "I'm no traitor. I don't turn on friends."

My eyes follow Brett down the hall. The one person who knew my brother, who could have contact with him, is gone.

"Did you get the combination?" Jason's voice breaks my trance.

I hand it to him. Am I a traitor for wanting Danny home?

"They must have told his teachers." Jason's stuffing things in Danny's workout bag. "Coach got a message halfway through last period. He stormed from the workout room cussing."

Danny's hoodie still smells like him. Part BO, part fresh mountain breeze. *God, please bring him home.*

Jason shuts the locker door. "My next class is by the gym. I'll put his bag in my locker until the end of the day."

I frown. "You came all the way from the gym back here?"

"I wanted to help." Jason places his hand on the small of my back. "I'll walk you to fourth period."

"You'll be late."

He starts toward the social studies building. "Don't worry about me, Lyd. You've got enough on your mind."

Tears rise inside me at the door of American Government. *Keep it together.* I take a deep breath.

"I'll meet you at the cafeteria at lunch." Jason gently pushes me in the room before heading down the hall.

"We have lots of work to do, people," Mr. Nash announces from his podium. "Sit down and listen up!"

"You okay?" My friend Katie rests a hand on my shoulder when I sit in front of her. "I was worried when I didn't see you in Precalc. Jason wouldn't tell me what was happening, just to pray."

I shake my head. If I open my mouth, I'll cry.

Writing down everything Mr. Nash says doesn't keep my thoughts from wandering. By the time class is over, my head hurts from trying not to think about my brother. Quiet would help, but Katie won't stop talking on the way to lunch.

"That super cute guy, Jonah, sat next to me in Precalc. I think I'll talk to him after our final. Maybe tell him we're going to the mall Friday. Would you go? I won't be as nervous if you're there. Maybe Jason, too. It'd be like a hang out—"

"Danny ran away." I stop.

"What?" Katie pauses.

"He ran away last night. Or early this morning. We tried to find him but couldn't." I start walking again, my hand pressed against my head. Everything is spinning. If Jason were here, he could help me feel better.

"Lydia. Wait." Katie runs to catch me. "I can't believe it. Why would he do that?"

I think about Danny on his birthday, happy after he spent time with his friends. Did he drink and smoke marijuana that day? He cut school, not even caring.

"Lydia?"

I stare at Katie. We've been friends since junior high. She loves my parents. We joke about how she's the fifth child in our house during the summer because she's over constantly. How can I tell her my family is a complete mess—

"Hey." Jason puts an arm around my shoulder, holding me up.

"Jason, what's going on?" Katie asks. "Lydia told me Danny ran away."

My eyes plead with Jason's to tell her what I can't. He does as we head to the cafeteria, so my only focus is walking, not falling over.

*My brother's gone. I can't believe he's gone.*

"What are you having?" Jason asks when we get in line.

"I can't—"

"You need to," he whispers. "I'm sure you didn't eat this morning. You need to eat lunch."

Jason knows my past struggle with anorexia and cutting. I thought I'd put it behind me in junior high, but stress over my grades and finals freshman year brought back those feelings. When he wouldn't let it go that I skipped lunch two days in a row, I shared my struggle. He didn't look down on me; he started looking out for me.

"Pizza or turkey sandwich?" Jason asks.

"Really, I'm okay."

"Choose one or I'll buy both—and watch you eat them."

"Sandwich." I fight the smile at his joke because, though it's funny, I know he's not joking. "I'll have a sandwich."

Jason meets me after each class to walk me to the next. I'm grateful, because my head is so foggy, I don't always know where I'm going.

He follows me home after school. Without a word he takes Danny's bag to my dad's office and shuts the door. Mom's at the kitchen table staring into a glass of water. She doesn't look at me until I kiss her cheek and tell her hi. Her swollen red eyes tell me her day has been as hard as mine. She goes to her room and shuts the door when she sees Jason.

I enter the dining room with two bottles of water. Jason's math study guide is in front of him.

"In problem three we need to solve for the cosine."

Jason explains each problem, yet my mind runs through the events of the morning. I think of Danny's Bible in his trash.

*God, You did let him down. Before state last year when he missed the play, Dad making him go back to baseball and not letting him have a car. Things just kept getting worse.*

"I'm sorry, Lyd."

"It's not your fault." I brush tears from my cheek. How often did Danny say that when I apologized for something Dad did? I sigh. It is all Dad's fault.

"I'm sorry you have to go through this. I'm sorry Danny's bad choices hurt you—"

"His choices? It's Dad—"

Jason shakes his head. "Your dad may have pushed, but you can't blame him."

"It is absolutely his fault!" How could he take my father's side? "Dad pushed him into varsity last year. Danny wanted to be done this year. He wanted to take drama instead."

"Why didn't he?"

"My father wouldn't let him! He controlled Danny's entire life. Danny wanted to go to USC. Dad refused to consider anything except one of the top ten baseball schools."

"That doesn't make sense."

"Everything in this house revolved around baseball. If Danny played well, we celebrated by going out or with steak. If he didn't, we had chicken or pork chops. Something he hated. Dad would ignore him during the entire meal."

"I don't think he'd intentionally—"

"I saw it, Jason! We all did. None of us did anything. We sat around this table and said nothing. No one stood up for him. I guess we're all to blame."

Jason leans forward. "Danny made bad decisions. First drinking, then drugs. He's spiraling out of control. You can't take the blame for that."

Looking at him will bring back tears so my focus remains on my math book.

"What you can do now is pray God will turn Danny from his sin and bring him home."

I want to agree, but the truth is if Danny comes home now, I'm afraid things will get worse for him.

# CHAPTER 5

## DANNY

The lobby of the hotel has blue and orange furniture scattered around this waterfall that comes from the ceiling into a pool the size of a jacuzzi. If I had my suit, I'd jump in. The entire room smells like chocolate chip cookies. I snag two from a plate on the way to the check-in desk. They're as good as my mom's fresh out of the oven. Yeah, this is going to be an awesome night.

"Can I help you?" The guy with bushy hair and a gray suit at the counter stares over his glasses at me.

"Checking in. Morton." I toss my license and credit card in front of him.

He clicks on the computer. The squirrel man examines my cards, and sizes me up. "Christopher Morton is—"

"My father." I nod toward the door. "He went to park."

"Only one night?" He raises an eyebrow.

"Yup. We head out in the morning."

Paperwork prints as a line forms behind me. "Well, I need his signature—"

I scribble *Chris Morton* by the x and grab the keys in the paper envelope marked 407. "Thanks."

First order of business is to fill the ice bucket. Mom insists that's what you do when you walk in a hotel room. After all the running I've done, it sounds good. Once my glass is filled with ice, I inventory the minibar. Since I usually drink beer, I don't know much about the various liquors. There was a senior on the baseball team who only drank rum and Coca-Cola. It's worth a try.

Next it's time for room service. I skip the burgers and salads. Tonight is steak night. Prime rib medium rare is the perfect meal to celebrate my last night in Indiana. All those years of baseball, Dad had Mom reward me or punish me with the meal she served after a game. It was twisted. He succeeded in making me feel like a loser with his prayer of chastisement and pork so tough you could hardly cut it with a steak knife. Tonight, I'm the winner. I showed him for sure.

I add on garlic mashed potatoes, broccoli, and a piece of chocolate cake for dessert. Dad complains broccoli smells up the house, so Mom never makes it although it's one of my favs. And cake is only on my diet when it's someone's birthday.

Flipping on an R-rated action movie, I prop pillows against the wall and sink into the soft bed with my drink while I wait for my food to arrive.

My mind wanders back to home. Though shots are being fired on the screen and profanity is shouted, Mom and Lydia come to mind.

*"Please, Danny, come home. You don't need to do this."* I hear Lydia pleading.

Then it's my mom. *"Please, if you can't do this for yourself, do it for me. I need my son back. I miss you."*

I add more rum to my drink.

*It's too late. You can't go back. If you do, you'll be stuck forever, living a life you hate.*

Next they're on the couch, my mom and Lyd, holding each other and asking "*Why?*" Why I left, why God didn't stop me, why their prayers were unanswered.

*They don't care about you. They only care about themselves. It's about the appearance of the perfect family. You've never fit into their family.*

I shake my head at the thoughts. They're true, just like unanswered prayers are a part of life. That crap about God giving us our heart's desires? It's another sentiment to give the down-and-out hope when there is none. If God cared about me, I wouldn't have been forced on the baseball team again by my dad. I would have been in drama. Everything would be different.

The drink slips down easier as I imagine my teachers' responses. Math and Chemistry probably won't notice until the final when they have to give me an F. Mrs. Dossel, AKA Mrs. Fossil will realize that yes, I took her pills. Perhaps my health teacher will celebrate my uniqueness. Coach Peck? I top off my drink with the last splash of rum.

"Here's to a fabulous season." I lift my glass.

I wash down a pain pill and am taken to that state of not caring. Yes, I've disappointed a ton of people. But I'm done with that. Time to move on. Tomorrow begins a new life on the west coast.

---

## *LYDIA*

Mom comes out of her bedroom at five thirty.

"She's not making dinner, is she?" Jason asks at the sound of cupboards opening and closing.

"Probably. Dad will be home after six. Dinner needs to be on the table." I walk into the kitchen to find her filling a pot at the sink. "Mom, don't worry about dinner. We can order something."

"It's fine." She wipes her sleeve across her eyes. "It's Tuesday. I'm making spaghetti."

I pull out my phone. "That Italian place down the street delivers. They have a Tuesday special."

"No!" Mom grabs my phone. "The entertainment cash is gone." She sets it on the counter. "I don't want to upset your father more."

*Oh God.* I press my palm against my forehead. *Danny stole money?*

"Food will be here in forty-five minutes." Jason walks in. "Lasagna, garlic bread, salad, and a pepperoni pizza."

"You didn't need to." Mom runs her hands over her face and then her hair. "I'm fine cooking."

"It's okay, Mrs. Morton." Jason smiles. "Go relax. Lydia and I will let you know when the food arrives."

Her eyes glisten with tears. Several times she opens her mouth but says nothing.

I gently rub her back. "We'll take care of setting the table."

She nods, kisses me on the cheek, and returns to her room.

"I have cash." I walk toward my backpack.

"My dad sends me a check every month." He places a hand on my arm. "I've got it."

"You don't need to."

He smiles that smile that has melted my heart since freshman year. "I want to."

"Thank you." A hug isn't enough to repay his kindness, but I give him one anyway.

When his strong arms surround me, peace fills me. For the first time since I woke this morning, I feel like I can breathe.

The table is set about the time dinner arrives. Jason offers to leave, but I insist he stay. He sits beside me. His knee touches mine, telling me he's there for me.

The silence is comfortable. My mom and I are both broken, and we don't need to pretend. I pray we'll finish eating before Dad gets home. Unfortunately, he walks in ten minutes after we start.

"What's this?" is Dad's greeting. His eyes are fixed on the food in the middle of the table.

"Hello, Mr. Morton." Jason stands. "Lydia and I were studying for finals. I know it's been a hard day. Ordering dinner was the least I could do."

My dad's eyes meet Jason's.

"Hopefully you don't mind," Jason says.

"That's very generous of you." He nods, then glares at Mom. Her gaze doesn't leave her lasagna.

"You ready for finals?" Dad cuts a huge piece of lasagna for himself, then piles a piece of pizza and garlic bread on top.

I stare at my own plate—the lasagna has two bites missing, my salad bowl is half full, the garlic bread is completely whole. *How can he have such an appetite when Danny is missing?*

"I think so." Jason pats my knee under the table. "We both have Precalc and English tomorrow."

"I'm taking all mine tomorrow." I lift my garlic bread.

"Why would you do that?" Dad asks.

"To look for Danny." My eyes meet Mom's. "If I finish them tomorrow, I can go out the rest of the week to hang up flyers."

"That's absurd," my father says. "You will finish your finals this week as they're scheduled—"

"No." I glare at him. "I've studied. I'm as ready as I'll be. I won't waste any more days. I should have been out there today looking for him."

"Your scholarship—"

I raise a hand. "My grades won't drop. If they do, you don't have to pay for my college."

That look he had this morning when he discovered Danny was missing returns. He shifts his eyes to Jason and back to his food. Jason's hand slips in mine under the table.

"How's business?" Jason asks Dad.

Dad clears his throat. "Busy with Christmas coming."

A half smile forms on Mom's lips when she mouths *thank you* to me. It's going to be a hard road, but at least we have each other.

The minute Jason leaves, I go to bed. The day has been long and exhausting. My eyes are raw from crying. My heart is crushed. Two days ago, everything was fine. Finals and what I should get Danny for Christmas consumed my thoughts.

*God, it's not okay. I don't understand. Why did he leave? Why didn't you—*

The phrase 'free will' comes to me. The serpent in the Garden of Eden whispered to Eve, tempted her to eat the forbidden fruit so her eyes would be opened. That's what destroyed her relationship with God.

*God, what tempted Danny into a world of drugs and alcohol? What are the lies Satan is telling Danny? I want to understand.*

Faces come to mind. Willow, Brett, Coach Peck, Anna. Most of all, my dad. Each had a part in Danny getting to this point. Even myself. I should've pushed him for the truth. I should've spent more time with him. I should've—

*It's too late.* The lies Danny's listened to come to me with every inhale and exhale, each one piercing my heart.

*You can't go back.*

*You'll be stuck forever, living a life you don't want.*

*They don't care about you.*

*It's all about the appearance of the perfect family.*

*They only care about themselves.*

*You've never fit in.*

Free will.

Jason was right. Danny made the choice. He believed the lies.

"God, take away the lies." My pillow is damp from tears. "Show him the truth. Please bring him home."

# CHAPTER 6

## DANNY

THE DAY STARTS AT SEVEN A.M. WITH A SHOWER AND TWO LINES OF cocaine. After a free continental breakfast, I head to the bus station. It's only half as full as the day before. For five minutes I watch the ticket sellers. The gray-haired guy who makes little conversation with customers seems my best bet. In and out. That's what I need.

"One ticket to LA, please," I say. "My mom's parking."

He types on his keyboard, not even a glance my way. "The nine a.m.?"

"Yes, sir." I pull out my wallet.

"Sorry, it's sold out."

"Yesterday the lady—"

"Completely booked." He types some more. "In fact, all buses to LA are full for the rest of the week."

The station is half-full. How can that many people from Indiana want to go to LA?

"We have some for the twenty-eighth, starting at $385."

I cuss. "You're kidding!"

The man shrugs. "Lots of people travel over the holidays. Did you want a ticket for the twenty-eighth?"

"No, thanks."

I take my stuff to the nearest plastic chair. Unbelievable to be that close yet not able to leave. There has to be another way to LA. It would be nice to fly, but with security what it is and me under eighteen, I'd be reported and get caught.

Goal #1: Not to end up back home.

Rideshare could be an option. With Dad's card, it doesn't matter the cost. I download an app. Current rate is almost a dollar a mile. At two thousand miles...

*Are you over eighteen?* The question pops up immediately. Strike two.

I doubt you can buy a used car with a credit card if you don't have an ID that matches.

A woman at the door of the terminal catches my attention. She's wrapped in a tattered quilt with plastic bags beside her. The sign she holds says, "Homeless. Please help." Some guy drops a dollar in her lap. She shoves it into her blanket. This brings about my next goal.

Goal #2: Make money

Even when I make it to LA, I'll need cash. Maybe the best idea is to hang out for a couple weeks, increase my cash flow while living on my parents' credit. Imagine if I made enough to buy a car.

Time to find a place with lots of generous people. I search 'malls near me.'

An hour later I plant myself inside the warm mall beside the coffee shop with my cardboard sign—*Headed to CA for Christmas. Anything helps.* If people will drop five bucks on drinks they don't need, maybe they'll give me a dollar or two. 'Tis the season, right?

"Merry Christmas." I smile at an elderly couple.

"Merry Christmas." The woman nudges the man. He reaches in his pocket, takes out two ones.

"Thank you, sir." I slip the money in my pocket, turn to a mom with toddlers in a stroller. "Merry Christmas."

She glances at my sign without slowing down.

So it goes. Five people pass before one hands me money. Usually when that person does, it's more than a dollar. Some give a handful of coins. I compliment people's Christmas sweaters, comment on their packages, wish them a Merry Christmas and happy holiday. People seem more comfortable dropping money inside an empty water cup. I'm okay with that as long as they're giving.

"What are you going to California for?" one middle-aged man asks.

"Visit family." I figure that's a good angle with a guy his age. "I'm out here going to school. My mom's all alone. We don't have much money, but I want to surprise her by getting a bus ticket."

That earns a twenty. The story about my elderly grandmother later in the day gets a five. My lie about a reunion with my long-lost father only snags a couple ones.

Hunger sets in about the time a security guard walks up.

"What are you doing, son?"

"Nothing much, officer." I fold my sign and grab my stuff.

"Panhandling is illegal, you know," he says.

I wave. "Enjoy your coffee break."

The booth at the far end of a burger place is secluded enough to count my income. Fifty-seven dollars and seventy-two cents. Not bad for an hour. I search nearby hotels while I eat my double cheeseburger meal. Since it's illegal to panhandle, it's best to move around during the day. If I switch up my location every hour, I can stay around the mall today and head elsewhere tomorrow. I reserve a room at a 4-star hotel downtown for a week. Math isn't my strongest subject, but fifty bucks an hour will bring in three hundred a day, over two thousand in a week. That will definitely get me a car.

The entrance of the largest chain store is my destination after lunch. The foot traffic should be highest there.

"Merry Christmas." My sign in one hand, I hold out my hat to a woman. She doesn't glance my way. The next three hurry by. I switch it up from "Merry Christmas" to "happy holidays." Nothing. Finally, after twenty minutes, a guy drops something in my hat. A quarter, dime, and a gum wrapper. Nice.

"Help a kid out," I call as people walk by. "Trying to get home for the holidays."

"Your family is in California?" a tall woman with a long, designer leather jacket and huge designer purse asks.

"My mom." I play the mom card, hoping for a twenty.

"Why are you here?"

"I live with my dad." I shove my hat closer.

"Does he know you're out here?"

I stare into this lady's face, cautious of my answer. "They don't get along. That's why he left her."

She tilts her head. "You're running away?"

"Nope. He told me I could visit if I raised the money. Could you spare a couple bucks?"

Her drawn on eyebrows rise as she squints her eyes. She digs in her purse and produces a dollar. With a 'thank you,' I hurry away. People who ask questions are not good. That location yields three bucks and change. At the sight of security, I move on.

I check into the hotel after three o'clock, feet tired, face chapped from the cold wind, and only a hundred and six dollars richer. Twenty bucks an hour isn't awful, but it's not the fifty I started the day making. Once the ice bucket is full, I search drink recipes with the contents of the minibar. I sip my vodka tonic while I write my next scene.

AT RISE: *Stage left is the cafe. AMANDA is at cash register. Stage right is a sandwich shop. JOE is at a table with his lunch in front of him as he writes a postcard.*

AMANDA. (*Calls to the customers at the table in front of her.*) Hey, guys, we got a postcard from Joe!

CUSTOMER 1. Oh yeah? What does it say?

AMANDA. (*Reads postcard while JOE is on the other side writing.*) Hey Amanda, all is well here in South Dakota. This is The Corn Palace. Who would have thought to decorate the outside of an arena with corn and grains? Wouldn't that be cool if there was a Coffee Palace?

JOE LAUGHS

CUSTOMERS LAUGH

AMANDA. (*Reads from postcard.*) I got more mosquito bites than fish at the Great Lakes. The four presidents are looking good. I tried climbing up them, but apparently that's not allowed. The scenery is amazing. Better than the inside of the cafe. You can't beat the peace and quiet. No whining kids and screaming parents—

(*Action in Cafe freezes.*)

(A family enters sandwich shop, three girls and a mom and dad. Through the window of the restaurant you see the boy who was walking with them stop to pet a dog on the patio with its owner. Family doesn't realize the boy doesn't come in with them.)

MOTHER. (*Turns to FATHER.*) I'm thinking if we get a couple foot-longs we can split them—

OLDEST GIRL. (*Hurries in front of FATHER.*) Dad, did you hear what Amber said? She said South Dakota is not nicknamed the Mount Rushmore state, but I saw the sign that said it is.

AMBER. (*Crosses arms over chest.*) No, I said its motto is "Under God the people rule." Isn't that cool, Daddy? Their motto has God in it.

FATHER. That is impressive, Amber. Very observant of you, Mindy, but let's not fight.

YOUNGEST GIRL. Yeah, you guys. We're sisters. We need to get along.

FATHER. Order what you want. (*Motions for them to go to the counter.*)

MOTHER. (*Places a hand on his arm.*) Honey, we'd save a lot of money if we shared sandwiches. Mindy and Amber could share. Drew and Lizzy like the same and then you and I—

LIZZY. (*Looks around.*) Where's Drew?

(*Switch back to Café.*)

AMANDA. (*Still reading letter.*) I'm thankful to not have to deal with ridiculously high maintenance customers.

(*Back to right side.*)

FATHER. (*Motions with hand.*) I don't want to bother with that. Let's just order what we want. (*Steps forward to read the menu.*) I'd like the Italian sub, but can I have regular bacon instead of Canadian bacon? I also want the Italian dressing, but the kind from the packet, not from that squirt bottle you have...

(*FATHER continues to order high maintenance sandwich. Two older daughters join in.*)

MOTHER. (*To LIZZY*) Have you seen Drew?

LIZZY. (*Confused look on face.*) Did he go to the bathroom? I thought he came in with us.

(*The volume goes off on right side of stage while MOTHER and LIZZY frantically look for boy. FATHER and other girls continue to order, oblivious that the boy is missing.*)

AMANDA. (*Reads aloud.*) It's also great to not deal with frantic customers who lose their kids or oblivious ones who let their kids do whatever they want in the store. (*AMANDA raises eyes to the corner table where two moms are sitting. One toddler is standing on the chair, the other is running around the store.*) That would be awesome. (*Returns to reading letter.*) Overall, I'm enjoying myself. Vacation is everything I hoped for.

(*MOTHER and LIZZY discover the boy outside. After smothering him with hugs, the three of them enter the restaurant.*)

AMANDA. (*Reads aloud.*) Hope all is well there. Say hi to everyone for me.

CUSTOMER 1. Sounds like Joe made the best choice by quitting. Good for him.

CUSTOMER 2. Great to hear he's happy.

AMANDA. (*Turns postcard over in hand.*) Yeah, I'm glad he's having fun. I just miss him.

(*Left stage lights dim. Bring up right stage lights.*)

MOTHER. (*Approaches FATHER at the cash register.*) Did you order?

FATHER. The three of us did. It was ridiculously expensive. Maybe Lizzy and Drew should share a sandwich. And you can have half of mine.

MOTHER. (*Forces a smile.*) Sure, dear.

Ice clinks in the bottom of my empty glass. My next goal comes to mind.

Goal #3: Forget about my father.

Maybe once I'm out of this state, when I move on to the life I'm supposed to live I will. I grab the room service menu. Until then, I'll run up his credit card. A few thousand dollars is a small amount for him to pay for the years of abuse I endured. I smile at the wine selection. No doubt an entire bottle will help me forget him tonight.

---

## *LYDIA*

The tears start by the time the shower heats up. I woke every hour during the night to the same thought.

*My brother's gone.*

Once my hair is dry enough it won't freeze, I pull it into a ponytail. I wear jeans with the sweater Danny gave me for Christmas last year. Makeup can't fix my swollen eyes, so what's the point of putting any on?

Mom's at one end of the kitchen table, twisting her robe around her finger while staring into her coffee. Dad's at the other end, news blaring on his tablet. His plate is filled with scrambled eggs, toast, and bacon, just like every other morning.

Two bananas on the counter have small black spots. Since Danny's the only one who eats them, I grab one. It's probably best for Mom's sanity if they're gone.

I kiss her cheek. "Bye, Mom."

She dabs her eyes. "Did you get breakfast?"

"I'm good." I hold up the banana.

She frowns then hugs me. "I love you."

"I love you, too." I squeeze her. "I'll go downtown after school."

"Thank you," she whispers. "Text when you're on the way home."

I'm almost to the kitchen door when Dad yells, "Do well on your finals!"

My Government teacher not only agrees to allow me to take my final at lunch, he says he'll be praying for my family.

"Lydia?"

I turn from putting my books in my locker to a girl from my English class. "Hi. Robyn, right?"

"Yeah. I just wanted to say I'm sorry." She bites her lip. "I heard about your brother."

He's gone twenty-four hours and the whole school knows? "Thanks." I shut my locker and walk towards the math building.

"My friend who works in the office overheard the secretaries. She wasn't gossiping, it's just that she knows I get it. I lost my brother two years ago."

I stop. "You did?" My throat tightens.

She nods. "Cancer. He fought super hard for a year."

"I'm sorry." I hug her. We aren't even friends, but we have a connection. She does understand how hard this is.

"If you need to talk or text, well, I understand." She backs up. "What's your number? I'll send you mine."

I tell her and she texts me.

"Maybe we can have lunch sometime, if you want," she says.

"I'd like that. I go to Bible club on Fridays, if you're interested in coming."

"Maybe." She pockets her phone. "We haven't been to church since Mike got sick. My parents were so upset after, they refuse to go."

I think of how I wrestled with God last night. "It's hard to make sense of it all, but I'm praying he comes home."

"I hope he does." She nods. "See you this afternoon in class."

The text from Robyn is simply a heart with her name.

*God, thank You for bringing someone who understands.*

"You okay?" Jason asks when I walk into Precalc two minutes before the bell rings.

"Exhausted from waking up every hour last night." I sit in front of him. "But Mr. Nash said I can take my final during lunch."

"Good." He places a hand on my shoulder and bows his head. "God, be with Lydia. Clear her mind as she takes her finals. Help her to do well and bless her efforts as she searches for Danny. In Jesus's name, amen."

"And help the rest of us to not fail," Katie says from in front of me.

"Amen." I chuckle at her comment. "Thanks, guys."

"I'll bring lunch to you in Nash's room." Jason squeezes my shoulder.

Tears almost come, but not from sadness or frustration. An overwhelming thankfulness has grown inside me. God is gathering people around me to support me. This isn't what I want, but He'll provide what I need.

Jason meets me at the parking lot after our last final. He has a stack of flyers in one hand and a soda in the other.

"I'll go with you, if you want." He hands me both.

"You've done more than enough."

"Whatever you need, Lyd. I'm happy to do whatever."

We stop by my blue Camry. "I know." I wrap my arms around him. "Go work out and study. I know you need that academic scholarship along with the baseball one to attend Texas Christian in the fall."

"But if you need anything—"

"I'll call. Promise."

He opens my car door. "How about we meet for coffee in the morning? You only have one final, right?"

"Yeah. I'd like that."

The outside of the bus station is dim. It doesn't help that the building is gray or that storm clouds are gathering.

*I need to be here to look for Danny.* My pep talk doesn't settle my stomach.

A man with thin hair sits beside the door, a brown blanket around him and a tiny sand-colored dog so skinny its ribs show curled up on his lap.

*My brother is on the streets, homeless, like him.*

I take a deep breath to focus, but the smell of urine makes me gag. Inside, people are rushing around. There are several windows open to purchase tickets. I head to the one with the shortest line.

"How can I help you?" the overweight lady with a stubby ponytail asks.

"I'm looking for my brother." I set a flyer in front of her. "Have you seen him?"

"Runaway, huh?" She squints as she reads.

I swallow back my tears. "He left home yesterday. Have you seen him?"

"Nope." She flips the paper at me. "Sorry."

None of the workers recognize Danny. My heart sinks when I post a flyer on a wall among a dozen others. *God, I don't want him to be one of many runaway teens.* My hand glides over his face. *Bring him home.*

Most of the business owners downtown are kind enough to take a flyer, yet none have seen him. After four hours I'm left with sore feet and a crushed spirit. The last place I want to go is home, yet I head that direction.

The house smells of pork chops and gravy, same as it does every Wednesday.

"Did you work after your finals today?" Dad forks his last bite when I sit.

I take the smallest piece of meat from the platter. "I went around town to put up MISSING flyers."

A thin smile appears on Mom's face as she shifts her eyes to her almost full plate.

"I don't want you doing that," Dad says.

I pause, the mashed potatoes spoon in midair. "I'm trying to find Danny."

"By plastering our personal information all over the city?" He shakes his head. "I won't have it. Tomorrow you'll take down the posters you put up."

Mom wrings her napkin.

"No." I plop potatoes on my plate. "I won't."

"You will." Dad slams his fist on the table.

"Chris!" Mom grips the tablecloth. "She's trying to find our son. If someone has seen him—"

"We don't need our personal information out there."

"I put *my* number on the flyer." I pull up the document on my phone. "See?"

He looks it over, shaking his head again. "The world is full of crazy people. Now they have your number. I don't approve of this."

"I'm sorry you don't approve, but I will continue to look for my brother. I love him and want him to come home."

Dad stares at his empty plate, lips pressed together.

I cut my meat into tiny pieces. My stomach turns, but I hear Jason's voice in my mind. *You can't skip meals, Lyd. Not because you're upset. You need to treat your body like the temple it is.*

Dad excuses himself, leaves his plate on the table, and heads to the office.

"Thank you." Mom dabs her eyes. "I reported Danny missing today."

"But Dad said—"

"We had to wait twenty-four hours. I went this morning." Her lip shakes. "The police said if he left the state there's nothing they can do. Most runaways either return within forty-eight hours or are never found."

I'm done pretending like I'm strong or that any of this is okay. I go to her and we hold each other as we cry.

"I'll keep looking," I say between sobs. "And we'll keep praying that God will bring him home."

# CHAPTER 7

## DANNY

EACH DAY IS FILLED WITH FREEDOM AND POSSIBILITIES. THE freedom to do what I please, the possibility to bring in a wad of cash to get me closer to my goal.

Friday is my third day making the rounds—popular malls, tourist attractions, movie theaters—any place with a crowd. I plot out my route, don't stay at one place longer than an hour to avoid a run-in with security. I recycle through stories and find there's no pattern that produces the most money. Average daily intake is one hundred fifty. Not super, but not bad since my current expenses are zero. In another week I should have enough money for a car. West coast, here I come.

I ran into a drug dealer on the streets the night before. They're easy to spot—a shady looking person on the street late at night who mumbles names of drugs as they pass people walking alone. The free sample of his coke isn't nearly as good as Armano's. He didn't like it when I said that. I managed to get enough to carry me into the new year for two hundred. That'll hold me until I'm settled in LA.

It's easiest to order food to-go from places via mobile apps. They don't ask for ID with the credit card. Friday, I search the shelves twice without luck.

"Can I help you?" a girl who works there asks.

"Mobile order for Morton."

She gives the shelf a once over. "I'll be right back."

My palms sweat. The order went through fifteen minutes ago, plenty of time to make the sandwich. Something's wrong—

"Hi there." A woman in a skirt suit with "manager" underneath her name greets me. "I'm sorry. There seems to be an issue with the card linked to your app."

"Oh?" I rub my hands on my pants.

"Did you have another form of payment?"

"Sure." I dig into my pocket. "I have cash."

My heart races as the cashier rings me up. If the card was declined, that means the hotel could know also.

Skating as fast as I can, it still takes fifteen minutes to get to the hotel. I have no energy to climb the stairs, but I can't show my face in the lobby. I need to get to my room before they lock me out.

One flight of stairs is hard. By the seventh I'm out of breath.

*I'm almost there. I've gotta get my stuff.*

A final burst of energy comes over me, and I sprint down the empty hallway to room 715. I wave my key in front of the sensor on the door.

Red light.

"No, no, no." I wave it again.

Red light.

I wiggle the handle. Nothing.

*You've done it now. You've lost everything you own. It's time to stop playing this game. Give up this façade and surrender. You know you've lost.*

Deep breath. I slowly pass the card over the sensor.

*C'mon, c'mon.* I shake the handle. Nothing.

Hopefully they found out less than an hour ago. Maybe they only deactivated my key. They want to force me to go to the front desk to give a new card for payment. Even if they reported it and my parents are on their way, they won't get here for at least fifteen more minutes. There's gotta be a way.

I head down the hallway to the vending machines for water. On my phone I search "how to break into a hotel room." Surely there's instructions somewhere on the internet about that.

The elevator opens. A Hispanic maid with a big chest and big hair rolls out her cart of cleaning supplies. I smile.

"Hi." I wave. "I left my key in my room. Do you have a master key to let me in?"

"You no have key?" she asks.

"Yeah. My parents are out, and I forgot my key."

"What room?"

"715."

She speeds off. I actually have to jog to keep up. "Key in wallet. No lose," she says.

"Great idea. I'll definitely do that."

The minute she waves her key, the green light goes on.

"Thank you." I rush by her.

"Mmmhmmm." She continues to the end of the hall with her cart.

In five minutes, my clothes and the entire collection of bottles and snacks from the minibar are in my duffle with washcloths and a towel to pad them. I snag a pad of paper and pen from the desk. I laugh at the Gideon Bible in the top drawer of the nightstand. How many people truly have a "come to Jesus moment" in a hotel room? I'm grateful to be done with that.

The maid's cart props open the door two down from mine. She sings completely off pitch to Mexican radio at the top of her lungs. I glance at the contents of the cart as I crawl by. Dozens of tiny alcohol bottles line the bottom row. The hall is still deserted. I watch her make the beds while I grab three bottles at a time—between my fingers to make sure they don't clink—and set them in my backpack. Over a dozen are in my pack when she spins to sing at herself in the mirror. I crawl one door down before I exit to the stairs.

Relief comes over me when I burst out the stairwell.

"Hey. Hey, you."

A twenty-something guy in a suit is leaning against the building smoking. "Aren't you the kid in 715?"

My board hits the ground and I'm off.

"Hey! Hey, stop!" He runs after me, cigarette between his fingers. "Hey, kid, where's your dad?"

I gain speed down the driveway. He stops at the top, screams threats of calling the cops. I salute with a swerve to the right. Two blocks away I board a bus. I kick it in the back with my sandwich. GPS says a mall is twenty miles away. Far enough that if my parents look for me, they won't find me, and hopefully enough people that I can finish the day with a decent take.

Two bus changes and an hour later, I arrive at Herrington Mall along with the rain. I stand under the canopy outside the door to the mall for thirty minutes and get nothing. I grab a coffee to warm up, do a line of coke in the bathroom, and take my place inside the mall outside the door to the coffee shop.

"Merry Christmas," "happy holidays," even "stay dry," are a few of the ways I greet people, my sign in one hand and empty cup in the other. Two bucks is my take for an hour. Reality hits. My credit limit is gone. The rain will make for an awful night on the streets. If I use my cash on a hotel, there's no way I'll ever be able to purchase a car.

"Sorry we're late." A woman with a little girl sits at the table of a lady with a stroller. "Samantha left her jacket at school. We're headed skiing right after Christmas. There's no way I was buying her a new one."

"How'd you get in?" the other asks. "Hasn't school been out for a week?"

"We caught the custodian before he locked up. Good thing we went. He starts his vacation today. No one will be there until January 3."

January 3? I smile. Plenty of time for the weather to improve. Time to earn more money. Bus tickets will even be lower by then if I don't have enough for a car. A brilliant idea indeed.

A search of "elementary schools near me" brings up Parks Elementary less than five miles away. Awesome.

I stop at the store to purchase groceries for the week. A loaf of bread, a box of cereal, some granola bars, a jar of peanut butter, and some bananas. I've always liked bananas, but Mom only buys them occasionally because no one else eats them. I also grab a couple slices of pizza from the deli for dinner.

It's not easy to balance on a skateboard with a backpack, a duffle bag, and groceries, especially in the rain, but I make it to the school at sunset. A parking lot is along the side of the school. The fence to the playground is about ten feet from the parking lot. I stash my skateboard under bushes, transfer breakables to my backpack, then launch my duffle over the gate. I begin my climb. It's not awful, even with the rain, until I get to the top. My jacket gets caught on the chain link. Then the clouds open up. My patience gone, I rip my jacket to free it. I descend as the rain increases. Three feet from the bottom I jump, scoop up my duffle, and sprint across the field. The closest classroom is a portable on the edge of the playground. My guess is if the school has a security system, the main buildings are wired but not the portables. If I'm wrong and an alarm is triggered, I'm screwed. There's no way I can scale the gate in this rain.

A zigzag ramp leads to the door of the classroom. I inspect the windows. The latch on the last one is up. The screen pops off easy, although it's thoroughly bent. I push the window and it slides open. No alarms go off. When I grab my duffle from outside the door, I notice the sign on the door.

*Welcome to Mrs. Crew's Kindergarten Class!*

A colorful bouquet of balloons carries a giant teddy bear into a cloudy sky. Somewhat creepy, but little-kid cute.

The tables are low to the ground. I feel like a giant. The chairs are comical. When I sit in one, my knees are up to my chin. They work fine for me to drape my wet clothes and damp sleeping bag over. Once the heat kicks on and I'm in dry clothes, I warm up. My pizza is soggy, but whiskey mixed with Coca-Cola compliments it. Laptop open, I create Joe's next adventure.

*AT RISE: JOE walks into a dimly lit bar. A few couples are scattered around the room, a small group of guys in the corner watching a baseball game. One woman in a sundress sits at the end of the bar with a drink. JOE approaches the bar.*

BARTENDER. Hey there. What can I get for you?

JOE. (*Sits on stool in front of bartender.*) Vodka tonic.

BARTENDER. You from out of town?

JOE. Sure am. What gave it away?

BARTENDER. (*Chuckles, points to JOE's baseball hat.*) You're far from Cleveland, my friend. Thankfully all the mellow sports fans are here tonight, or I'd have to ask you to remove that.

JOE. (*Laughs as bartender places a drink in front of him.*) Point taken. Thanks.

BARTENDER. Passing through or relocating?

JOE. Passing through on my way to visit my parents in Oregon. I'm taking my time getting there.

BARTENDER. Good for you. I always thought we had this retirement thing backwards. Why wait until you're too old to travel? Best to do it at your age when you can enjoy it.

JOE. (*Raises his glass.*) Agreed.

(*BARTENDER walks away. Woman in sundress moves next to JOE.*)

SCARLETT. Hi. My name's Scarlett.

JOE. (*Extends his hand*) Joe.

SCARLETT. So, you're passing through?

JOE. Yeah. Thought I'd head up to Yellowstone, then to Jackson. Might hang out a couple days if something grabs my attention. You live around here?

SCARLETT. I do. Have my whole life.

JOE. Then I guess you'd be the person to ask. What's there to do around here?

SCARLETT. (*Raises glass.*) You're doing it. (*Laughs.*) There's a movie theater that plays second-run movies. If you've been traveling a while, there might be something you haven't seen.

JOE. It has been a while. (*JOE's eyes shift to the ring on her left hand.*) And where's your husband?

SCARLETT. Ex. Left me four months ago. (*Wiggles ring finger.*) I wear it when I go out to keep guys from hitting on me.

JOE (*Laughs.*) Yet you feel comfortable hitting on me?

SCARLETT (*Shrugs, finishing her drink.*) You seem like a nice guy. Passing through means you don't care about a relationship. And you're cute. You meet all my standards.

JOE. Whatcha drinking?

SCARLETT. Midori sour.

JOE. (*To bartender.*) Can we get another midori sour?

SCARLETT. (*Eyes and smile widen.*) And you'll buy me drinks. That's a bonus.

I pull my dry sleeping bag to the book corner after nine o'clock. Two bookshelves jam-packed with picture books and easy readers section off the area with eight large, colorful pillows. It only takes five pillows to make a lumpy mattress. It's not a queen-size bed but it's better than the wet concrete. A book hangs out of the shelf—*The Very Hungry Caterpillar*. My mom read it to me often as a kid. I always thought it would be cool to be a caterpillar and eat as much as I wanted. I switch off the classroom lights. It's my mom's voice I hear as I read the book with my flashlight. I smile at the thought of the inflections of her voice, the excitement on her face as she flipped to the last page—the beautiful butterfly.

"We're like butterflies, in a way," she always said at the end of the book. "God wants us to feast on His Word to fatten up." She would always poke my belly. "Then trials come. We might feel like we're lost in the darkness, but we're covered by God's love while we're in the chrysalis. In the darkness He makes us stronger and grows our faith. In His time, we burst out, full of life and color as beautiful as can be." Then she would kiss my forehead. "God has great plans for you, Danny. I know He does."

I shove the book to the side. I don't know who I'm more mad at—God because He didn't do anything, my dad because of his determination to destroy my mom and me, or myself because I miss Mom. I want to run without looking back. That's harder than I thought.

---

*LYDIA*

"Mom! Mom!" Anna bursts through the front door, dropping her duffle in the hallway.

"In the kitchen," Mom answers from the sink, where she's doing dishes.

"Oh my gosh, Mom." Anna wraps her arms around Mom's neck. "I hardly slept last night. I couldn't believe it when Dad called."

Her hair is perfect, makeup done.

"Are you okay?" she asks.

Mom lifts the corners of her mouth wearily as they part from their hug. "Well, you know."

"I can't believe it. I mean, how awful." Anna shakes her head. "It's just like Danny to be totally insensitive—"

"Hi, Anna," I say from the kitchen table. I won't allow her to bash our brother.

"Oh, Lydia. How are you?"

More drama, more hugs, but she doesn't talk bad about Danny.

"When will Mary be here?" Anna asks.

"Soon." Mom doesn't turn from the dishwasher. "Dylan is coming too."

"Good." Anna sits across from me. "That's what we need. The entire family together to make a plan and pray."

*Because Mom's and my prayers aren't enough? Because it's not enough that I've traveled an hour radius in each direction the past three days hanging flyers and talking to people?*

Dad insisted on waiting two days to call my sisters because they had finals. Anna wanted to drive home as soon as Dad told her last night. He forbade her, so of course she obeyed. She's always been the favorite. She'll do anything he says and agrees with his perspective about everything. I also think he didn't want them to come too early because he wanted to work. Heaven forbid he miss a day, especially close to Christmas.

Anna drones on about the awfulness of the situation, how it has affected her. She's a mini-Dad.

Mary and Dylan arrive around noon with sandwiches for lunch. Dad shows up a while later. The minute we say "amen" for our meal-time prayer, the discussion about my brother begins. Dad tells them the details starting with the school visit on Monday through to the chase the next morning. Mom and I stare at our food as we are forced to relive the worst twenty-four hours of our lives.

*God, how has it only been five days since this nightmare began? It feels like an eternity—*

"I think Danny was using cocaine," Dylan says.

My heart sinks.

"Cocaine?" Mom gasps.

"I noticed signs at Thanksgiving. Jittery, bloody nose."

"Why didn't you say something?" Mary asks.

"I confronted him when we were alone. He snapped back, almost taunted me to say something. I was afraid of being wrong." He looks at the rest of us. "Does he have money?"

"He stole two hundred and withdrew three hundred," Dad says. "I froze his account to prevent him from withdrawing more."

"Do you think he has any drugs?"

"Not that I know of. I took what was in his room Monday night."

I don't want to be a snitch, but we need to put the pieces together to find him. It's time to be honest. "He got something from Brett. Plus, maybe the painkillers from the teacher's desk."

"This is such a mess!" Anna throws her hands in the air. "He needs to hit rock bottom. We can't help him if he's not willing to get clean."

"I'm sure the painkillers hooked him in the first place." Dylan finishes the first half of his sandwich. "It's a danger among teens, especially if they take them with alcohol. I assume he drank as well?"

"Jason said he did with the baseball team." I rub my forehead.

"I think he did at Willow's house," Mary says. "I questioned him about it, but he argued with me." Mary shakes her head. "I can't believe he did drugs for almost a year and we didn't know. If he shows up, you won't let him stay, will you, Dad? You'll force him into rehab, right?"

Dad glares at her. "That's what we were trying to do, Mary."

"If Danny spent most of his money on cocaine, that doesn't leave him much to travel on," Dylan says. "Especially this time of year. My guess is he's still in the state."

Dad pauses, sandwich in front of his mouth. "But we don't know."

"It wouldn't hurt to make flyers, a video, maybe even contact local TV stations." Dylan kisses Mary's hand. "We can find him."

"I've hung up posters." I'm thankful someone else wants to do something. "Maybe we can make a video after lunch."

"I'm not okay with our personal information on the internet." Dad crosses his arms.

"We can use my phone number." I glance from Dylan to my mom. My allies. "I used it on the flyers. I don't mind."

Dylan nods. "You should probably be the one to talk, Lydia. He seems closest to you."

Surveying the faces of my sisters and father, I'm saddened at the truth of his statement. Hard times should bring a family together, but somehow, I feel this may divide us.

"Sure." I push my sandwich aside.

My sisters' remarks while we film give me a headache. I'm thankful Dad gets a call before we start and doesn't come back. If only my sisters would leave too.

"You're being overdramatic," Anna says when I get choked up on the first take.

"She needs to show concern," Mary says, before adding, "We need to get him home and into rehab."

Dylan finally convinces them to keep their opinions to themselves. Once we upload the final product to Danny's video channel, I share it on social media. Then it's on with life. Mary and Dylan will both stay the week with us. Dad insists Dylan stay in Danny's room, which causes an argument that ends with Mom in tears. The guys end up reclining on the sofa watching football. Dad hangs on every word of Dylan's medical stories. As I climb the stairs, I try to remember the last time Danny and Dad had a conversation that wasn't centered around baseball. I can't.

"What if we take out half his clothes?" I hear Mary say to Anna from Danny's room. They went in there to change the sheets. "We could fold them, put them on the shelf in his closet. That's fine, right? Then Dylan can hang up his."

"Good idea," Anna says. "I mean, we're just moving them out of the way."

Tears threaten to spill over as I shut my bedroom door and flop onto my bed.

What's happening to our family? Where is the love, the compassion we're supposed to show one another? My heart breaks for my brother's pain and disobedience, but it seems everything continues to unravel despite my prayers. My efforts aren't enough to change him or bring him home.

Mary knocks, then opens my door. "We leave in an hour." She looks me over. "You might want to shower and change. Dad said he'd take us out to dinner."

Of course. Anything for the two of them. I roll away from her.

"C'mon, Lyd." She sits at the end of my bed. "Don't be like this."

"Like what?" I snap. "Missing my brother? Worried for his safety? I love him. How can I not be like this?"

"We love him too, but we can't let it consume us. It's his choice. If you ask me, he seems to want to hurt Mom and Dad. That's not okay."

I turn toward her. "Dad pushed him. He didn't want to do baseball this year. Dad made him give up drama—"

"Don't make excuses for him." Mary holds out a hand. "He's sixteen—"

"Did you know Dad forbid him to buy a car?" I sit up. "He was mad at the conflict Danny had with a customer on Black Friday—"

"Another example of how out of control he is."

"You have no idea how bad it is around here. You've been gone three years. You haven't seen—"

"What's going on?" Anna enters.

"Lydia's making excuses for Danny." Mary rolls her eyes.

Anna sits at the head of my bed, running a hand over my wrinkled bedspread. "Danny is a drug addict, and he's run away. Statistically speaking, he's more likely to end up arrested than back home."

I narrow my eyes. "He's only been gone a few days. Have you really given up on him?"

"I'm being realistic." Anna's voice is eerily calm. She places a hand on my arm. "You need to accept the fact that he doesn't want our help."

"No." I yank my arm away. "You need to stop being judgmental and pray for him."

"I prayed the entire drive here. That God would convict him, for him to hit rock bottom, and for God to strip him of his pride. I prayed for Mom and Dad as they go through this trial. I can't imagine how difficult it is for them."

I cross my arms over my chest. "It was ten degrees last night. Did you think to pray that Danny wouldn't freeze to death? Have you prayed that he would realize God's love rather than simply feel God's conviction? Have you ever prayed he would achieve his own dreams, not the ones Dad has for him?" Tears come to my eyes. "Don't tell me to forget our brother and let go of my hope that he'll come home. I've been praying for his faith since I saw a change in him last year. Now I pray for his safety, for him to give up his addictions and to truly come to Jesus. If you really love him, you'll pray the same."

I run to the bathroom, locking the door behind me.

# *CHAPTER 8*

## *DANNY*

I head out on Christmas Eve to tug at some heartstrings. It's at the grocery store that I make the most money. The parking lot is almost completely full. I stand by the front door with my sob story.

"I'm trying to get enough cash to visit my mom in prison. All I want for Christmas is to see my mom again." I consistently earn five dollars or more.

Only one person asks why she's incarcerated.

"Embezzlement." I say the first thing that comes to my mind. The woman walks by without giving me a dime. Can't say I blame her.

I splurge on a rotisserie chicken and mashed potatoes for dinner. Marijuana is my dessert. It's truly amazing that you can find anything on the internet if you know how to search. "Slim," as his friends call him, refuses to negotiate a decent price. I feel cheated, but decide the overpayment is my Christmas gift to him. Even drug dealers deserve Christmas gifts, unless you believe in that whole naughty and nice philosophy. I suppose this year I crossed over to the naughty side myself.

Back at my classroom I enjoy dinner at sunset. Though I don't want to, I think about my family in their pew at church. In O *Come*

*All Ye Faithful*, Dad will fade out during the third verse. The girls will sing *Silent Night* with their eyes closed and hands raised. Mom will tear up at the beginning of *God Rest Ye Merry Gentlemen*. And Lyd would have slipped her hand in mine at the first notes of *What Child Is This?*

I miss Lyd the most. If I were at home, she'd wrap my presents for two dollars each, including her own. My gift to her this year was a sweatshirt from the College of the Ozarks. It probably arrived this week. Hopefully my mom intercepted it. No doubt my dad would throw it away to spite me. I need to text Lyd since it's Monday. According to our agreement, that's when I'm supposed to text.

*I'm alive,* is what I send. There's no way I can have more contact with her. Not while she's under their roof. Maybe next year, when I'm in LA and she's at college, we can talk again. She warned me not to allow Dad to get the best of me, so hopefully she understands.

I blare rock music to drown out the Christmas songs in my head. I don't want or need that remembrance. None of it. I open two mini-bottles of wine from my hotel stash along with my computer to see what trouble Joe is finding himself in.

*AT RISE: JOE and SCARLETT are in the parking lot of the bar. SCARLETT laughs at something JOE said.*

JOE. I had a great time tonight.

SCARLETT. Me too. Thanks for the drinks.

JOE. My pleasure. (*Stuffs hands into pockets and lowers his head.*) I guess I should get going.

SCARLETT. (*Steps forward until she almost touches JOE.*) It's still early.

JOE. (*His eyes follow up SCARLETT's body, stop at her face.*) You know, you're pretty gorgeous.

SCARLETT. (*Presses her body against his.*) And you're pretty cute.

*JOE and SCARLETT's lips meet in a passionate kiss as the lights go off.*

"Cheers." I raise a bottle to the computer screen. "Here's to your happy ending tonight, Joe. Don't worry, tomorrow it'll fall apart."

I head outside to smoke out. Don't want to trip any alarms or sprinklers in the classroom.

The cold bites at my face. The full moon lights up the entire playground. The sky night is speckled with stars. I lose myself in the beauty.

*Whatever is good and perfect is a gift coming down to us from God our Father, who created all the lights in the heavens.*

A chill comes over me. I thought Willow was a gift. She ended up being a cheat. If I believe Lyd and Mrs. Del Pizzo, my writing is a gift. But if it came from God, why won't He let me use it? Why couldn't I be done with baseball? If my dad hadn't pushed me into baseball this year, I'd be home right now. The school would perform my play this spring. That would be good and perfect. This is just screwed up.

*And we know that God causes everything to work together for the good of those who love God and are called according to His purpose for them.*

I can't help but cuss when the next verse comes, especially since I hear it in Anna's voice.

I scroll through my albums. The Doors. Perfect. Jim Morrison became an icon of mine this summer after I read his biography. I search quotes by him and download a couple of memes with my favorites.

*There are things known and things unknown and in between are the doors.*

*Expose yourself to your deepest fear; after that, fear has no power, and the fear of freedom shrinks and vanishes. You are free.*

And my favorite—

*A friend is someone who gives you total freedom to be yourself.*

I wonder if I'll ever find that person. Lyd came close, except she couldn't accept me not being best buds with Jesus. To her, He's still a superhero. In fact, I bet she's praying right now that He'll bring me back home. I imagine her voice in my mind—

*"Please, Jesus, bring Danny home. I know You can. I trust in You."*

"Sorry, Lyd," I say once I exhale. "I'm never coming home."

Closing my eyes, I allow Jim and the drugs to usher me into the state I've grown to love—that of not caring.

---

*LYDIA*

Having both sisters in the house exhausts me. After my meltdown their first day home, they don't put Danny down. They don't mention him at all, which hurts almost as much.

Mary insists we make and deliver cookies to the neighbors on Christmas Eve like we do every year. Mom bakes with us, tears in her eyes the entire time. Though I don't want to go, Anna drags me from the house. I follow without singing. The neighbors who have been on the street as long as we have frown when they open the door to Mary and Anna singing *Joy to the World.*

By the time we get to church that night, I need a break. I excuse myself to go to the restroom and end up in the deserted youth room reading my Bible.

"Hey, Lydia." Pastor Mark walks in a few minutes before seven. "We're in the sanctuary tonight. I came to grab my Bible."

"I know. I can't."

"Can't what?"

I take a deep breath as the tears rise. "I can't sit in that pew like nothing's wrong. Everything's a mess."

"I know." Pastor Mark sits. "Do you want to talk about it?"

"Dad is over the top angry, Mom's crushed. Anna is convinced Danny will end up in jail, and Mary is disappointed because he's wasting his potential."

Pastor Mark grabs a box of tissue from beneath the seats. "And you?"

"I miss him." I take a few to dry my tears. "I miss his jokes and sarcastic remarks, our talks before bed about school, books we read, movies. He's one of my best friends." I blow my nose. "I'm worried because it's cold. I hung up missing posters this week at the malls, bus stations, and coffee shops. I'm not sure it'll do any good. I pray, but..."

"God hears your prayers, Lydia. But Danny has free will. And his relationship with your dad is so strained he may not have any desire to come home."

I stare into his eyes. How does he know?

"It's my job to read kids. I had a difficult relationship with my own father, so I recognized his struggle. That's why I offered to meet with him. I hoped to help him through it." He sighs. "I'm sorry I didn't reach out after Danny left. Your dad told Pastor Raul that he appreciated prayers, but you guys needed time to process what was going on."

It's been so hard, why would Dad say that? We needed help—

My phone buzzes. *You coming?* Mary texts.

"Things aren't the same, Lydia. It's not okay that Danny's gone." Pastor Mark's acknowledgment somehow lightens the burden in my heart. "Don't feel the need to pretend. I've always appreciated your genuine faith." He leans forward. "This is an awful situation. Take your questions and hurts to God. He's there for you. Lean on Him, believing Him for a miracle."

I can't stop the tears.

"The good news is God is a God of miracles. Christmas is proof of that." He stands. "How about we focus on the miracle of Jesus tonight? Rather than pretending you have it together, rely on Him to hold you together."

I nod. On our way to the sanctuary, a text comes from Danny. My heart races as I open it.

*I'm alive.*

No "Hey Lyd" or "Merry Christmas." Just "I'm alive." I can't wipe the tears fast enough.

*God, he needs a miracle to turn his life around. I'm trusting You for that.*

From the back row with Pastor Mark, I watch my family. Anna seems oblivious to everything, arms high in the air. Mary glances at her phone. Dad sings every other verse. Mom's head is down, and she continues to dab her eyes. I text Mary to tell her where I am. Inside I feel so broken it almost hurts to breath.

Pastor Mark's right. Church isn't about traditions and appearances. It's about worshiping God, being moved by His Word. I can bring my brokenness to Him. There's no need to pretend.

New realizations come to me as the pastor reads the Christmas story. There was no room in the inn, but God provided the shelter of a manger. The angels chose to share the good news with lowly shepherds. Mary and Joseph bring Jesus into the world without a home but with love. God used the less-than-desired circumstances for His glory.

*God, can You use this mess for Your glory?*

The girls and Dad talk the entire way home. I stare out the window at the stars. My eyes fix on the brightest.

*I wish Danny would come home.*

Using the excuse that I'm tired, I hurry upstairs as soon as we walk through the door.

I pull the new sweatshirt Danny bought me for Christmas from my closet. It arrived two days ago. Mom cried when she opened the package. I wear it tonight to remind me to pray for him.

Prayer can change things. I want to believe it can change this horrific situation, but that doesn't seem to be how this is going.

*I love him...*

If he had been home, he would have paid me to wrap his presents. It's never been about the cash. Two dollars a gift isn't enough to make it worthwhile. I do it because I love him, because he asks me to. Every year I laugh to myself at his ability to distract me enough that I don't know when I wrap my own gift.

*What I'd give to have him home.*

What would I give? I'd give up my car to give him his own. I'd give up going out with my friends to visit him in rehab. I'd give up the School of the Ozarks to be home for him. I'd give up my own life to have him home safely.

*God, why does it need to be this way? I don't understand why You took him from me. I don't understand why You won't bring him home.*

God is silent. Tears fall on my pillow. There's no explanation, no promise or relief. There's only a pain in my chest that grows.

"Please, Jesus, bring Danny home. I know You can. I trust in You." But even as I speak the words, I fear He won't do what I want.

# CHAPTER 9

## DANNY

I AM THE KING OF MY KINDERGARTEN CLASSROOM. IT'S BELOW freezing and raining outside, but the thermostat is set at a cozy 72 degrees. Peanut butter sandwiches and cereal are my main nutrition with alcoholic beverages to wash them down. Cocaine gives me an awesome burst of energy. I type so fast my mind can hardly keep up with my fingers. When inspiration ceases, watching movies on my phone gives me a mental break. Sometime after one a.m. when exhaustion hits, I wash down a couple pain pills with some booze.

Mrs. Crews has a nice collection of read aloud novels, including the Harry Potter series. My parents forbade them because of the "witchcraft." Were they worried I'd run away to wizardry school? Much better that I run off to Hollywood.

The mall seems a good place to go the day after Christmas. My new sign reads *Earning money to start the new year in CA. God bless!* I hate the "God bless." It feels very Anna-ish. But 'tis the season. I need to maximize my potential income.

Two hours at three different locations bring in five bucks. It doesn't even pay for my lunch. Guess the season of giving is over. Today's about being selfish.

" 'Earning' money?" one guy my dad's age says. "How exactly are you 'earning' money? By standing around holding a sign?"

"By putting up with opinionated jerks like you." Well, I didn't exactly say jerks.

"Kids like you are the problem with society." He sticks his finger in my face. "You feel self-entitled, like the world owes you everything."

"Actually, it's idiotic fathers like you who ruin the lives of kids like me." I point to his sweatshirt. "I suppose you went to the University of Texas and that's where your kids are going."

Insert profanity. "It's a great school."

I narrow my eyes. "Did you ever ask them where they wanted to go? What they wanted to do with their lives? My guess is you pushed your college and your beliefs on them."

The man laughs in my face. "If you were my kid, I would've thrown you out a long time ago."

My cup crumbles in my hand as he walks away. I flip over my sign and write—*Following my dreams to CA. Anything helps.* Thirty bucks comes my way in an hour. Guess since Christmas is past, people are over God.

Lunch is a philly cheesesteak sandwich at a fast food place while I write until the rain passes.

*AT RISE: JOE, fully dressed, sits on the edge of a bed, pulling on his shoes. SCARLETT, under the covers, stares at him.*

JOE. So, that's what you do for entertainment around here?

SCARLETT. (*Grins.*) Only when I've seen all the movies that are playing. And I meet a cute barista from out of town who doesn't mind getting me drunk.

JOE. (*Chuckles.*) Best fifty bucks I've spent in a while. In fact, I'd be willing to buy you breakfast, too.

SCARLETT. (*Takes phone off nightstand.*) Can't. I need to call my husband before I go to work. I'm free for dinner tonight.

JOE. Ex-husband, right?

SCARLETT. (*Rolls her eyes.*) Technically we're still married. He deployed four months ago.

JOE. (*Pauses tying his shoes.*) You said you were divorced.

SCARLETT. He refused to sign before he left. I was done when I caught him sleeping with the neighbor. He convinced me to wait until he comes back. If he gets killed, I'll receive his pension. (*Laughs.*) After three years with the jerk, I figure I deserve at least that.

JOE. (*Shakes head.*) You used me to get back at him?

SCARLETT. Not entirely. The sex was awesome.

JOE. (*Finishes tying shoes.*) Glad you enjoyed it.

SCARLETT. (*Wraps a blanket around herself and crawls over to JOE.*) Hey, don't be offended. I like you. (*Kisses JOE's neck.*) You said you'd be here a couple days. Let's make the most of them. We're both adults. We have the right to fill our days with a little fun.

JOE. There's something wrong with it if you're married.

SCARLETT. Today I'll talk to him about the paperwork. I swear. I mean, we're practically divorced. (*Nibbles on his ear.*) Come over tonight. I'll make you dinner to celebrate.

I scan the restaurant. There's a family of four across from me, each on their phones. At the table next to them, a mom ignores her three loudly obnoxious kids while she chats with a friend. In the corner of the restaurant, an obese man devours his super-size combo with an extra-large soda. Once upon a time I might've thought my story was far off, but not now. The world is full of self-absorbed people. Instant gratification is as American as apple pie. The mom with the kids prayed with them before they started to eat and now yells at them to shut up. The husband in the family asked at least four questions of his kids that have gone unanswered. And the fat guy heads to the counter to order dessert. People don't care about values anymore. They want to feel good. Which is to my advantage. Definitely easier to find drugs.

---

## *LYDIA*

Super Subs has been my work home for about nine months. The manager, Mr. Dannenberg, treats us all like family. It was a lot to ask for so much time off during the holidays, but he understood how hard it was when Danny left. Now it's time to get to work.

*You can do this;* I tell myself on the way. Unfortunately, my anxiety isn't listening.

I'm about to turn off my engine when a familiar song comes on. It's from the Christian album I bought Danny for his fifteenth birthday. Memories of that night come like a flood. In his room after dinner he shared how he stood his ground with Willow to be pure sexually. It meant a lot that he made a choice to glorify God and keep the purity commitment we both made that summer at camp. I prayed God's blessing over him, that he would remain pure and devoted to the Lord. It was the best day of the entire year.

My heart is torn in two. How can I get on with my life like everything's okay when I've lost my brother, my best friend?

"There she is!" Mr. D says from behind the cash register. "So glad you're back." His smile shifts to a frown when I stop in front of him. "Lydia, are you okay?"

"I'm sorry." I hand him my apron. "I can't work right now. I hate to leave you short-handed." Tears fill my eyes again. "I just can't..." I bite my lip.

"I understand." He walks around the counter to give me a side hug. "If you ever want to come back, call."

I make it to my car before the tears start again. Though home is the logical place to go, right now there's no comfort there. Twenty minutes later I'm knocking on Jason's door.

"Lyd, what's wrong?" he asks the minute he sees me.

"I think I quit my job." I frown.

"You think? You don't know?"

No words come, only sobs. He leads me to the family room sofa where I collapse in his arms. "I had to go to work today. I mean, I'd been off since..." I take a deep breath. "A song by Caffeinated came on before I got out of the car."

Jason sighs. "Danny listened to them, didn't he?"

I nod. "I can't handle the memories, Jason. They rip me apart. One minute I'm doing okay, the next I can't handle the pain."

"I know, but you can't stop living your life. God doesn't want you to give up everything."

The words cut me. I thought Jason understood. Why am I here—

"Lydia!" He grabs my arm before I make it out the door. "What are you doing?"

"Leaving! I thought you'd understand. Obviously, you don't."

He shakes his head. "I hate to see you giving up things you love when Danny couldn't care less."

"What?" The air is ripped from me.

"He only cares about himself right now. He doesn't care how this is affecting any of you."

"Danny's not that way."

"The old Danny, maybe. But he's on drugs. He's doing them to forget in hopes of stopping the pain. I was in that awful place the first several months of my parents' divorce. I drank and smoked out, to leave my problems behind."

How have we been friends three years, yet I didn't know this? "What got you out of it?"

"I came to Christ the summer after eighth grade. Freshman year I met an amazing girl who was on fire for God. I was insecure because she was out of my league. Then she invited me to Bible club on Fridays." He smiles. "I knew you wouldn't have anything to do with me, even as a friend, if I didn't clean up and develop a real faith."

Now it's clear. It's not that Jason dislikes Danny; he actually identifies with him.

"I can't get over this." I swallow back the tears. "I can't pretend like nothing's wrong."

Jason takes my hand and leads me back to the sofa. "You don't need to. I know how much you love him. That's one of the reasons I love you."

I lift my eyes to his face.

"Take it day by day. Pray for him. Cry when you need to. Just don't give up your own life. I'm headed to Dad's tomorrow, but I'll help you hang posters today. Then let's go to the movies after." He gently caresses my face. "Don't let it consume you. Do what you need to do and leave the results to God."

"You'll go with me?"

"Yep." He tugs on my visor. "I'll even buy you a sandwich for lunch."

I sigh. "I probably shouldn't have quit my job."

"Call Mr. D. Ask for a couple more weeks off. He gets it."

"I don't have any more flyers."

He hands me his laptop from the coffee table. "Sign on to your account. We can print them before we go."

I call Super Subs while Jason prints flyers. Mr. D agrees that I can start back mid-January, or later if I need to.

"I pray for your family every day," he tells me.

We start at the train stations, then the mall. Jason talks everywhere we go. I make it through the entire afternoon without tears. We're even fifteen minutes early to the new comedy I wanted to see.

Popcorn and soda between us, the movie trivia challenge is on. He wins two out of three. His comments about the movie facts have me laughing.

"Music to my ears." He grabs a handful of popcorn. "Glad you let me help today."

I lean against him. "I'm thankful you did. I'm thankful you're my friend."

The lights dim with the first preview.

"You will get through this," he whispers, "with the help of family and friends."

*And the grace of God.*

# CHAPTER 10

## DANNY

It will take six hundred and eighty hours to walk to LA, and probably a dozen pairs of shoes. Hitchhiking is free, but I'm not a fan after watching a criminal drama where a serial killer scouts the highways for his next victims. Kills over fifty hitch-hikers in a year. It's important to show up to California alive. Of course, Thoreau, van Gogh, and Dickinson were dead before they became famous, but where's the fun in that?

It's not easy to bathe and wash clothes in the classroom sink, yet I do it. On the thirty-first, I head out in clean clothes, my still-damp hair combed. First stop is the gas stations.

"I'm on my way to California," I say while I wash people's windows.

My story is adapted from there depending on their age, sex, and marital status.

"You're kidding?" one young woman asks after I tell her my twin was raised ten miles from me and I didn't know he existed until last year.

"Totally. Could you help me out with a couple bucks to get to California?"

I score a ten from her.

By noon, I reach a hundred bucks. A writing lunch break seems in order.

*AT RISE: JOE stands on porch (STAGE RIGHT), flowers in hand while he paces. Audience can see SCARLETT (STAGE LEFT), while she cooks inside kitchen.*

JOE. (*Runs hand through hair.*) What am I doing? (*Looks at flowers.*) She's married, Joe. Ring on her finger, husband in the military, married. (*Sighs.*) She said they're going to sign papers, but they haven't. Not yet. That means she's committing adultery. This is wrong. (*Turns to door.*) Then why does it feel right? (*Pushes doorbell and takes a step back.*)

(*SCARLETT pauses in the kitchen. Her smile grows as she crosses the family room, straightening her skirt. Right before she gets to the door, JOE walks down the steps.*)

SCARLETT. (*Flings door open.*) You came!

JOE. (*Glances over shoulder.*) I did. But I shouldn't have.

SCARLETT. (*Hurries to him.*) Yes, you should have. (*Takes flowers and links arms with him.*) Come in. I just finished the risotto.

JOE. (*Follows her to the kitchen.*) You talked to your husband today?

SCARLETT. For a few.

JOE. And he's signing paperwork?

SCARLETT. (*Laughs, reaches for vase out of high cupboard.*) Not today. Today he invaded some middle-eastern city or something.

JOE. But you guys are officially separated?

SCARLETT. You could say that. I mean there's several thousands of miles between us.

JOE. (*Frustrated look on his face.*) Seriously, Scarlett.

SCARLETT. (*Saunters over to him.*) Seriously, Joe. (*Runs her hands up his chest.*) All I ask for is dinner. Sit down, keep me company while we eat. There's nothing wrong with having dinner, is there? (*Massages JOE's shoulders.*)

JOE. I guess not.

SCARLETT. I have some steaks, a bottle of wine, and maybe if you feel like it for dessert—

The screen goes black. Guess Joe's fate needs to wait until I get back to my computer cord. On the way back to the classroom, I open my music app.

*Account not found,* it says when I try to log on.

After a second and third try, I open my movie app.

*Account not found.*

I text Lydia. *Did Dad cancel the music and movie accounts?*

*Yes, sorry,* is her reply.

It's just like my dad. Cancel the two things he can take away from me. If I could afford to, I'd dump my cell phone to end his control over me. One day I'll make it writing plays or movies. I entertain myself by thinking of what I would say, or write to him, when I do.

The gate from the parking lot to the campus is open. A green Honda is in the lot. Definitely a stellar day.

A woman in the driver's seat is on her phone. With the bushes to hide me, I make my way to the gate. Stashing my skateboard and backpack under the last bush, I sprint through the gate.

The door to the classroom is unlocked. Of all the teachers to come in on New Year's Eve, Mrs. Crews had to be the one. Yup, that's my luck.

Like a contestant on some show running to win a million dollars, I weave between tables grabbing my clothes off the backs of chairs where they were drying. Hopefully she just got here. The cops could be several minutes out. I cram them and my sleeping bag into my duffle, race to the door. It swings open. I'm face-to-face with a petite Asian woman in a black raincoat, jeans, and black boots.

"It's you!"

"Sorry. I'm leaving." I shift to the right.

She spreads her arms to fill the doorway. "No, you're not! The police are on their way."

"Which is why I'm leaving." I nod to the door.

"You broke my screen!"

"Sorry about that." I'm a few feet from her, but she doesn't budge. Does this tiny chick, who I can toss across the room, think she's going to stop me? "Please move."

"Why are you here? I know you didn't take anything. Except my goldfish crackers. And my soda."

She was in the classroom long enough to notice those were gone? "It's freezing outside. I needed somewhere to stay."

Her eyebrow rises. "You're homeless?"

"Yeah." I glance at my stuff. This is my chance. I need a good story to stir up sympathy to get out without hurting her. "My parents died in a car accident last month. I'm only seventeen. The state wants to place me with a foster family." I step forward. "My grandma lives in LA. Bus tickets cost a lot this time of year."

"Oh." She folds her arms over her chest. "Why didn't your grandmother come get you? Or go to the funeral?"

Good question. "She's not healthy enough to travel. I don't have her number, but I remember where they lived before Grandpa died."

"You don't have any other relatives?"

"Dad's family are missionaries in Africa." I didn't see that coming. Pretty impressive.

"Wow." She unfolds her arms. "You're Christian?"

"Yeah." It's not a total lie. I used to be.

"I'm sorry." She lowers her arms.

"You have a nice classroom." I'm inches from her. "Great library. I probably would have liked kindergarten if you were my teacher."

A smile appears on her face. "Thank you. Your name is Danny?"

I stare at her blankly. How does she know my name?

"I saw your notebooks on my desk." She leaves her post and picks them up.

"Yeah. I was transcribing my play."

"These are plays?" She flips through the notebook on top.

"Hopefully I'll sell them in LA. Make some money to live on." I take the notebooks and jam them in my duffle. "Sorry again about the mess and inconvenience."

"Oh." Her eyes widen. "The police are on their way."

"Right. I need to leave." I run down the ramp.

"Wait!" She chases me, money in the air. "Take this. For your bus ticket."

I pause. She has at least three twenties. Such easy cash—but my conscience kicks in. Yes, I still have one.

"Use it for new goldfish. Or soda." I speed away.

---

*LYDIA*

Mary's birthday falls in January when she's back at school. I'm an awful sister for thinking it, but I wished we could just not celebrate it. When Dad insists we celebrate on December 31st, I have hopes going out will distract us from our normal New Year's routine of fondue and game night; however, at breakfast Mary announces Dylan's parents and younger sister want to come celebrate with us.

"Could we please have fondue and play games?" Mary asks. "I told Dylan about our tradition. He thinks they'll love it."

"Sounds great," Dad smiles.

Tears well in Mom's eyes. "I don't have anything—"

"If you make the list, we'll go to the store," Anna says.

"Of course, we'll do it here. That's what Mary wants." Dad doesn't even look at Mom.

Without a word, she leaves the table, scrapes the rest of her breakfast in the trash, and starts the dishes.

*God, I shouldn't hate him, but how can he just disregard Mom's feelings like that? Why do they continue to act like nothing has changed when everything is different?*

Our kick back day turns into non-stop activity. Mom and I bake and decorate the cake in silence. Once the girls return from the store, prepping for the fondue begins. Dad and Dylan only leave the TV at 3:00 p.m. to run out for more sparkling cider. Every time I pull the brick of cheese across the grater, I think how Dylan's entire family will be here but ours won't.

"Do you think Dylan will propose tonight?" Anna asks while she cuts celery.

"I don't know." Mary looks up from slicing cucumbers. "It did seem weird his parents would come to town when we're headed to their house tomorrow. I would think if he was, he would've asked permission."

They turn towards my mom.

"I haven't heard anything." She continues to cut pineapple.

"Maybe that's why he went with Dad to the store!" Anna slams the knife on the counter.

"Would he really propose in front of us?" I ask. "Shouldn't that be a romantic thing for the two of you?"

"He's all about family. I'm sure he'd love to have everyone here."

"Everyone?" How can they ignore the fact that our brother is gone?

Mary turns to Anna. "You think he's asking Dad? Right now?"

"Probably." They squeal and hug.

Danny is on the streets with temperatures below zero. I want to point out the weather forecast is snow, but they're too wrapped up in their own little world.

My phone buzzes with a text from Danny. It's Monday, his day to text. The minute I open it, my heart sinks.

*Did Dad cancel the music and movie accounts?*

Dad announced last night he wouldn't renew the subscriptions this year. It was up to us if we wanted to purchase individual accounts. Was his motivation simply to take it away from Danny?

*Yes, sorry.* I wish I could say more. I want to, but there's nothing to say. Even 'I love you' probably doesn't mean anything to him.

I close my eyes to hold back my tears. *God, please protect Danny. Take him somewhere safe and warm. Watch over him...*

*"For the angel of the Lord is a guard; he surrounds and defends all who fear him."*

The verse repeats in my mind. Where is it located? I search "he surrounds" on my Bible app. It takes me to Psalm 34. Verses four to seven settle my anxiety.

"I prayed to the Lord, and he answered me. He freed me from all my fears. Those who look to him for help will be radiant with joy; no shadow of shame will darken their faces. In my desperation I prayed, and the Lord listened; he saved me from all my troubles. For the angel of the Lord is a guard; he surrounds and defends all who fear him."

*Yes, Lord, free Danny of his fears. As he turns to You, may he find You. Meet his physical needs.*

"You okay?" Mom rubs my back.

I push my phone toward her. "Praying verses four to seven for Danny."

"Mmmm." She kisses my cheek. "Those are good. Eight to ten as well. I'll add them to my list."

I continue to read the next three verses.

*"Taste and see that the Lord is good. Oh, the joys of those who take refuge in him! Fear the Lord, you his godly people, for those who fear him will have all they need. Even strong young lions sometimes go hungry, but those who trust in the Lord will lack no good thing."*

I exhale slowly. *God, I know he's not doing what's right, but I pray You would not withhold any good thing from him. Bring him to a place of trusting You again. May he see You and experience Your love in the midst of the darkness he's in.*

# CHAPTER 11

## DANNY

I SEARCH "SHELTERS NEAR ME." ONE COMES UP.

"Women and children only, no teenage boys." That's nice of them.

Though I panhandle four more hours, fifty is all I bring in. The cheapest one-star motels in the area have raised their price to eighty bucks for tonight. If I shell out that kind of money, I'll never get to LA.

The couches scattered throughout the mall prove comfy enough. It's so warm I use my jacket for my pillow. A security guard wakes me shortly after I hit my REM state of sleep.

"You can't sleep here." His belly hangs about six inches over his belt.

"I'm waiting for my mom to finish shopping." I sit up.

He glances at my bags under the couch. "Up and out of here, kid, before I call the cops."

The wind howls, the cold bites my face. This was why I hid in a classroom. I consider going to another school, yet figure police may have an eye out. Business high-rises are in sight. It worked my first night. It's definitely worth a try.

The hike across a deserted field is longer than I calculated. My flashlight goes out a fourth of the way across. My phone battery is at five percent. Getting stuck midway would be awful. Back toward the city I go.

"Hey, kid, got a light?" The man is half hidden in the shadows of a doorway. The half I see is his tattered jacket and gnarly teeth.

"Sorry. Know any places to sleep where the cops won't bug me?"

"Fifteenth and J are quiet." He points the way I'm headed. "Well, no cops at least."

A few blocks away is a liquor store. A guy in his twenties is headed towards the door.

"Hey, bro," I call.

He turns.

"Would you get something to warm me up? I gotta sleep outside tonight." I offer him a twenty. "You know, something to take the edge off?"

He sizes me up then nods. "I got you covered. Wait here."

The gravity of my situation comes over me. I'm about to spend the night on the streets in subzero weather. This just might kill me. Fun.

"Here you go, kid." The guy exits with two brown paper bags and hands me one. "Happy New Year's."

I open the bag to a bottle of fireball, a shot glass, and a bag of hot Cheetos.

"Don't drink the whole thing tonight or you'll puke your guts out!" he says.

"Thanks." I wave. "Happy New Year's."

The farther I go down fifteenth, the darker it gets. Not only because of the lack of streetlights. I no longer pass people in their New Year's party attire. I'm among the homeless. The down-and-out. The scum of the street.

A woman in a faded gray parka paces in the doorway of a closed Italian deli.

"What do you want? I can't do any better. I did what I could." She reaches the wall and turns. "Of course, you can. You aren't trying. You never try. You're lazy and stupid. I always knew you wouldn't amount to anything."

Her voice fades two doors down. That's where I spot a lump covered with holey blankets. It's curled up in the corner of the jewelry store's doorframe. I wouldn't think it was actually a person except for the moan. The deep moan that sends chills up my spine.

I glance down a narrow alley to find a guy urinating on the wall.

"What?" He glares at me. "You got a problem?"

It's not his words but the way he growls them that makes me increase my speed.

A figure, probably female because of the pinkish ski cap and dirty pink mittens, pulls something straight from the trash, smells it, then eats it. I'm close to puking in a trash can.

Once across J Street, I duck in the closest empty doorway and spread out my sleeping bag. I pull on another sweatshirt along with sweatpants. Layers are good with this weather. With my duffle as a pillow, I climb into my sleeping bag, jacket on.

The first shot of fireball burns, the second warms me from the inside out, and the third numbs me. My head spins. The hot Cheetos are stale and have a nasty bite, but it's true—beggars can't be choosers.

The sidewalk smells of urine and dirt. How many people, or animals, have peed where I lie? The thought makes me gag. I attempt to breathe through my mouth instead of my nose. Cold air stings my throat.

In the distance, a man screams one profanity after another in an angry voice. Dogs bark. A woman shrieks. Finally comes "the preacher." At first the murmur is low, muffled. The longer he speaks, the clearer it becomes.

"Then I witnessed in heaven another significant event. I saw a large red dragon with seven heads and ten horns, with seven crowns on his heads. His tail swept away one-third of the stars in the sky, and he threw them to the earth."

The darkness not only surrounds me but cuts through me. I close my eyes to escape it. A deeper darkness comes—one that chokes out all rational thoughts.

*You're nothing.*

*You'll never amount to anything.*

*You know you'll freeze to death out here.*

*What were you thinking?*

*You've screwed up your life for good.*

Pressure builds in my chest. I gasp for air. My mind is a fog. Not like an easy-going smoke-out fog but an anxious I-can't-think-straight fog. Between the flood of insults, the same thought repeats.

*I've done this to myself. I chose this darkness.*

A part of me wants to flee. I want to go back to the light. I want to be right again. In my soft, warm bed next to Lyd. I'd give anything to listen to her talk about school, her friends, even the Bible. I want to be done. Done with drugs. Finished with disobedience. But that means going back to his house to be under his rule. I'd enter back into the life I hate. A life of constant criticism where I'm forced to push myself and my body to play a game I despise. I'd have to give up my dreams for the future—

*"For I know the plans I have for you."* I hear Anna quoting the verse. *"They are plans for good and not for disaster, to give you a future and a hope."*

If I go back, I give up everything I want. They'll lock me in rehab, tell me what I did wrong, lecture me about mistreating my body. I'll be forced back into baseball, to work for my dad, and to sit in that ridiculous pew on Sundays pretending to care about a God who hates me. What kind of future is that? There's no hope in something that goes against who I am.

"I'm done being someone I'm not." I don't know if I'm talking to myself or God. "This is my life. I'll live it the way I want."

"Then I saw a beast rising up out of the sea. It had seven heads and ten horns, with ten crowns on its horns. And written on each head were names that blasphemed God—"

"Shut up!" I scream, along with profanity. "Shut up!"

Silence. Only for a moment.

*You're breaking.*

*You can't handle it.*

*You're just a kid.*

*What were you thinking?*

I pull my head into my sleeping bag to drown out the insults. I will survive. I will succeed. I've worked too hard, come too far to lose now. I deserve to win. I deserve better. I repeat my truths hoping to drown out the preacher's distant voice, yet somehow it comes through loud and clear.

"For the accuser of our brothers and sisters has been thrown down to earth—the one who accuses them before our God day and night. And they have defeated him by the blood of the Lamb and by their testimony. And they did not love their lives so much that they were afraid to die."

*I don't want to die,* I think. *I didn't come out here to die.*

---

## *LYDIA*

"The last time we went to Africa on a missions trip, we had the opportunity to build houses," Oliver, Dylan's dad, says while we stand around the cheese fondue. "Well, mud huts, really. We gathered sticks and mixed together this tar-like substance..."

He continues on and my attention is drawn back to how he and his wife Christy match—her in a maroon skirt and black sweater and him with a maroon long sleeve shirt and black slacks. If ever there was a perfect Christian family—

"You're a senior?" Jenna, Dylan's sister, is beside me with her plate of cheese-dipped bread and veggies.

I nod, pulling my over-soaked bread chunk from the fondue pot. "And you?"

"I'm a junior. You know, you kind of inspired me."

I go to open my mouth, but it's cemented shut by the cheesy glob I'm chewing. I rest a hand on my chest.

"Yes." She giggles. "When Mary visited over the summer, she told me how you went to a Bible club during lunch. I decided to start one at my school. We have over twenty kids come each week."

I'm at a loss for words, plus I'm still chewing. Me, an inspiration? My life and my family are a wreck. If I'd met Jenna a month ago, we might have become friends. Now I have bigger things on my mind than Bible study and missions work. I wonder if Dylan's family even knows about the crisis we're going through. They smile and talk like everything is fine.

"This is wonderful, Margaret." Christy dips broccoli in the cheese. "I don't know that I've ever had fondue as a main course."

"It's our New Year's tradition." Mom glances outside the dining room window. The branches of the tree are white with snow.

"Well, thank you for including us," Oliver says.

"Glad you could join us," Dad says. "Good thing you beat the storm."

I twirl another piece of bread in the cheese. What about Danny? How will he beat the storm? *God, please be with Danny. Take care of him. Surround him and protect him.*

"So, Margaret, Mary told me you were involved with women's ministry?" Christy asks.

"That was a long time ago. A very long time ago." She looks to Christy with a smile. "Do you volunteer at church?"

"We lead a weekly home group. I serve on the women's leadership committee."

"That's nice." Mom twists her napkin. Her eyes wander back outside to the now rapidly falling snow.

"It was important for me to have everyone here tonight." The room silences at Dylan's comment. He places his hand around Mary's shoulder. "You all know how much Mary means to me. In fact, she's second only to God." He drops to one knee and pulls a box from his pocket.

A chill runs up my spine. Here, in the midst of all of us, Dylan proclaims his never-ending love to my sister. I glance from my mom, who's on the verge of tears, to my dad who's across the room, a wide smile on his face.

My phone vibrates. *Severe weather warning*. The tree in our front yard is whipping back and forth in the wind. I push back the tears, trying not to let my thoughts run wild. Too late.

*No one can survive that cold.*

*Hypothermia has probably set in. He's been on the streets too long.*

*He's so strung out on drugs it's doubtful he's taking care of himself.*

"Yes!" Mary says. "Yes, I'll marry you!"

Applause and cheers fill the room. Tears fill my eyes.

"Isn't it great?" Jenna hugs me. "We're going to be sisters! I've always wanted a big family."

"Great." I back away, then turn to Mom. Tears run down her face. I collapse in her arms.

"God, be with Danny," she quietly prays. "Send your angels to guard and protect him. Keep him from freezing to death."

"Amen." I wipe my tears on her shoulder. "I'm so scared for him, Mom."

"I know, baby," she whispers. "Me, too."

"This calls for a toast!" My dad fills cups with cider.

Mom dries her face, then hands me a glass.

"To the happy couple." Dad raises his glass. "May they have a beautiful life together. And give us lots of grandkids—in time, of course."

There's laughter, clinking of glasses, and cheers. I choke down the cider and try to pretend my heart isn't broken.

# CHAPTER 12

## DANNY

*I SURVIVED*, I THINK WHEN I OPEN MY EYES THE NEXT MORNING.

It's bright, yet it feels super early. My face hurts from the cold. A deep breath causes me to cover my nose and mouth. I might puke. Maybe from the stench. Perhaps from the liquor. Or because my stomach is empty. I force myself up to find a restroom and food before I start a day of panhandling.

Day after day, that becomes my life. Figure out where to sleep to avoid the crazies, the best fast food places to clean up, get cheap meals, and charge my phone. My power cord was left by Mrs. Crews' desk, which means I carry around a computer I can't use. Maybe she'll mail it to my fictitious Grandma in LA.

The west coast will be more expensive. I probably need a minimum of three thousand to buy a car and have cash to live on until I sell my screenplay. Every day I try to charm people out of their money and tell myself it's worth almost freezing to death to achieve my dream.

My cash goes further when I get things for free. I'd rather use money on drugs than food. Food is necessary to live, but drugs make life livable. By nine and noon each day, orders pile up in the mobile order section of restaurants. Sometimes I simply swipe one. Other times I wait until a male name is called. If no one approaches in three seconds, I grab and go. Oh, the beauty of mobile orders.

The rest of my day, I panhandle and write. Inspiration for Joe's story isn't there. Sketches of potential characters now fill my notebooks. Mothers, kids, lovers, musicians. Whoever seems interesting. Their physical descriptions, tics, even random conversations I imagine or overhear.

The dealers who service street people have ridiculous prices. When I attempt to bargain with one, he laughs in my face.

"You're the addict, not me. Pay up or get sober."

When I make it to California, I'll get my life in order. Until then, it's about survival.

The people have started to look familiar in this city. They walk by without a glance in my direction. The money I collected yesterday barely covers my alcohol. Homeless Harry doesn't mind purchasing a bottle as long as I give him a full glass. It's kind of an ingenious way to not pay for your stuff. You know, take advantage of strung out teens like me.

Today the workers at the fast food restaurants I enter point to the door because I'm so dirty. I resort to something I never wanted to do. Trash picking.

Once past the layer of random receipts and empty fast food cups, I stumble upon banana peels and pastry crumbs. A few inches deeper uncovers bags with half-eaten pastries or breakfast sandwiches. Since people are idiots and pour their coffee straight into the trash, most of the food is soggy. Sometime around the fourth trashcan, I jam my hand in puke and lose what little nutrients I had left in my own body.

The grocery store bathroom is a safe place for me to clean up unnoticed. Now my arms aren't black and sticky. A flyer on the community board by the exit door of the store catches my eye.

"Free food boxes on Sunday" it reads, with today's date and an address. Maybe my luck is changing.

It's a quarter to one when I arrive. Men carry boxes from a room to women and teens who unload produce, bakery goods, and boxed items onto rows of tables. A long line of people various ages and ethnicities runs perpendicular to them. Some look like they showered this morning, others are filthy like me.

"I came for a food box," I say to a guy who walks by. A heart tattoo with *Love 1 Cor. 13* scrolled across it is on his massive bicep.

"Yeah. Go ahead and get in line. At one o'clock we hand out numbers. When the line opens, you'll come along here." He points to the tables. "There's plenty for everyone." He takes off in the opposite direction.

I scan the tables. Don't know how I'll walk away with all that food, but I'm willing to try.

At one o'clock, a woman makes her way down the line with numbers. A guy with a goatee strums on a guitar. The tune is familiar. I can't place it until he sings. Worship music. Guess I should have expected this since I'm in a church's parking lot. I allow my stomach to make the decision to leave or stay. It growls, so I stay. As long as the line is, it shouldn't take more than twenty minutes to get my stuff. A box full of food will set me up for at least a week. The song ends. A short chubby bald man steps up to the mic.

"We want to thank you for being here today. It's our privilege to be Jesus's hands and feet. We are thankful for God's blessings that allow us to provide for you. Before we open the food line, I want to share a story in the Bible about Jesus feeding a lot of people. Over five thousand actually."

I glance around. Everyone is paying attention to him. My face heats up. I came for food, not a sermon. The flyer said come get a food box, not come meet Jesus.

"God didn't barely provide," the preacher says. "He provided in abundance."

God provides in abundance? Where was He all those years I asked Him to take me out of baseball? Where was He when I needed to catch that ball to make it to state championship? Where is He now as my stomach growls?

"He's always there for you," the pastor says, "and He wants to pour out His blessings."

That's when I bolt. Since I have to walk in front of the tables to get out of this place, I snag a loaf of bread.

"Excuse me," some lady says. "You need to wait in line. We're not giving out food yet."

I throw my number at her. "Here. I just want a loaf of bread."

"We're not handing out food yet. No one gets food until after the message."

I stare at this middle-aged chick with glasses down her nose and arms crossed. Has she ever been hungry a day in her life? "It's more important that I listen to the Bible than eat?" I toss the loaf at her chest. "Keep your food."

"Hey, wait up!" I'm at the bottom of the driveway when I hear someone yelling. "Stop!"

Mr. Big Biceps has a loaf of bread in one hand and a box of granola bars under his arm.

"I don't need that crap." I stop. "The flyer said free food boxes. It didn't say we'd be subjected to a sermon."

"Hey bro, I'm sorry. Here." He reaches out the loaf. "Take the food."

"I don't want your food. And I'm not your 'bro.'" I walk away again. "You're hypocrites."

"Not really. She's new and trying to follow the rules." He jogs ahead of me. "We need to keep some order. But what matters is that you get food." He extends the bread and granola bars. "Please. Take it."

"I don't need it."

He looks me over. "I think you do. Besides, if you don't, I'll feel awful for the rest of the day. You'd be doing me a favor."

Setting my bag on the sidewalk, I unzip my backpack.

"What's your name?" he asks.

I place the food on top of my copy of Don Quixote. "Don."

"How long have you been on the streets?"

"Long enough." No way I'd tell this guy my story. He couldn't care less. He's simply doing the Christian thing.

"Well, Don, I know you're not much into sermons, but would you mind if I prayed with you?"

"Actually, I do." I put on my backpack.

"Okay, I respect that. I will be praying for you, though."

I chuckle. "Pray all you want. God isn't going to answer. He doesn't want anything to do with me."

Two blocks away is a fast food burger place. I decide to get a glass of water to go with my bread.

A mother with three little kids walks up behind me. The youngest, a boy, is in her arms. Her two girls hang on to her pantlegs. I hold the door open for them.

"Thank you." She smiles a genuine smile.

Every minute I grow more hungry as the kids chat about what they want to order, and the smell of French fries drifts out to us.

"Mama," the oldest says, "can I get a big kids meal? You told me I could when I was six."

"I did." She pats the girl's head. "I guess it's time."

"Yes!"

I laugh at her fist pump.

"But mama, what about me?" the younger girl asks.

"Two more years."

The younger girl sticks out her bottom lip. "But four pieces isn't enough."

"Hambuga, hambuga!" The boy pumps his fist in the air.

The six-year-old sees me smile at her brother. "He's pretty cute, isn't he?"

That totally makes me laugh.

The mom turns. "Sorry."

"No, it's fine. You have cute kids."

She glances to my bag, board, and backpack. "Can we buy you dinner?"

"I'm good. I was gonna grab a glass of water."

"You should let her," the oldest says. "She just got paid."

"It would be my honor." The mom wraps an arm around her daughter, maybe an attempt to quiet her. "How about a quarter pounder? That's what my husband orders."

"Sure. Thanks."

"Mama, should I go get a table?" the oldest asks when her mother steps forward to order.

"That would be fine."

"Come on." The girl motions to me. "You can come with."

The mom nods at me before going back to order. I follow the girl, confused. It's nice that they want to buy me food, but why would they want to have dinner with a complete stranger?

"This looks perfect." The girl runs to the largest booth in the restaurant, scoots to the middle, then fold her hands. "What's your name?"

"Thomas." I do have my doubts about this. "How about you?"

"Mandie. Do people call you Tommy?"

"No."

"Oh." She thinks for a minute. "Well, I'd like to call you Tommy."

"Whatever, kid." It's my turn for a few questions. "Does your family buy dinner for strangers often?"

"Depends on if we have the money. Dad couldn't come tonight cuz he has a meeting. Guess we have the money."

I examine her clothes for the first time. Faded jeans and T-shirt. The younger sister wears a dress that seems a little small. The boy's pants have a hole in the knee. Mom is wearing jeans and a T-shirt.

"We feed the homeless with our church every month. Go out to the parks with food and stuff. Daddy used to be homeless. He always says it's important to help others."

A once homeless dad, not a lot of money but will buy a stranger a meal? I don't get it. "What church do you go to?"

"The brown one by our house." She straightens. "Daddy's the helping pastor there. He doesn't get paid for it. He does construction for money."

"What grade are you in?"

"I homeschool." She smiles at her mom and siblings, who are now at the table. "I'm in Kindergarten, right Mama?"

"Yes, you are." She hands me a soda cup. "Here you go."

I slide out of the booth and the other two slide in. When I return with my drink, there's a seat on the end for me next to the youngest girl.

"My name is Ellie." She averts her eyes.

"Tommy." I glance at the boy. "And who are you?"

He buries his face in his mom's arm.

"Jonah." Mom smiles. "And I'm Crystal."

"Nice to meet you." I nod. "Thanks for dinner."

"Absolutely." She sips her soda. "Where are you from?"

"East." I hate to disrespect her by not answering, but she doesn't need to know my business. "Your husband's in construction?"

"He is. And assistant pastor of our church."

I nod.

"Why don't you have a home?" Mandie asks.

"Mandie, we don't ask questions like that," Crystal says. "Tommy might not want to talk about it."

I shrug. "My dad's not a nice guy. Sometimes the best place to be isn't at home."

Mandie presses her lips together. "My daddy used to drink alcohol and do drugs. But then he met Jesus. And Mama."

"We all have a story," Crystal says. "My husband's seven years clean and sober. We met in Celebrate Recovery."

"What's that?"

"It's a recovery program for various addictions and hurts." She thanks the worker who sets two trays of food to the table. "Sometimes the biggest blessings come from our darkest times."

Mandie hands out the food. Everyone takes hands. Ellie coughs into hers then takes mine.

"Tonight, it's Ellie's turn," Crystal says.

Eyes close, except mine.

"God is great, God is good. God, we thank You for this food."

"Amen," the entire table, including myself, says.

"So," I say to Crystal, "you homeschool?"

An hour later they hug me goodbye. Even shy Jonah. I walk away with a full belly and a less bitter attitude against Christians.

Crystal hands me her husband's business card. "I'm sure he'd be happy to talk anytime or just listen. He knows how hard it is."

That's it. No mention of God or quoting verses. They must be the small percentage of Christians who live their faith. I drop his card in the trashcan I pass. While they're nice, I still don't want to have anything to do with them.

---

## *LYDIA*

I stare at the box of donuts Dad buys Sunday morning. They're covered with frosting and smell of sugar. Twelve donuts for the four of us is such a waste. *God, I pray Danny is eating. Please, make sure that he gets the food he needs.*

Anna scoots onto the kitchen bench beside me with her computer. "We need to look at bridesmaid dresses. If we give Mary suggestions, we won't be stuck wearing something hideous."

I pray Danny's jacket keeps him warm while Anna discusses the pros and cons of sleeveless and off-the-shoulder. Mary texted us yesterday that they decided to marry next spring after she graduates. Danny would almost be a senior. I'm sure he'd look handsome in a tux.

A text arrives from Katie. *I'm a little over my family. How about a movie this afternoon?*

*Love to,* I reply. I need to be with someone who'll let me be me.

The youth room is half empty at ten 'til nine. Though I usually sit in the front row, I find a seat near the back. I don't want to be seen; I simply want to be fed. I'm trying to focus on breathing when I overhear the conversation of two girls behind me.

"Did you hear about that kid, Danny?" the first one asks.

"Is that the cute one who always wears a baseball hat?" the second says.

"Yeah. I heard he went psycho. Wrecked his family's house, stole their money, and ran away. Guess he was totally on drugs. He might have been a dealer."

"No way," the other girl says. "He was totally hot."

Closing my eyes doesn't hold back the tears. The worship leader asks us to stand as the band begins. I cry through worship, thinking the words, sometimes even lifting my hands, but not singing. If I open my mouth, I won't be able to stop weeping.

By the last song, the burden in my heart is less. When we're told to greet those around us, I turn to the girls behind me.

"Hi, I'm Danny's sister." I say. "Yes, he ran away. No, he didn't destroy our home. I'd appreciate you praying for him rather than gossiping about him."

Their eyes go wide, but their mouths remain closed. I grab my purse and Bible and go to the front row where there are less distractions.

"Today I wanted to share an encouraging message, something every one of us could attempt to live out in the next year." Pastor Mark opens his Bible. "Regardless of what your New Year's resolution is, I think by the end of this message, you'll agree this is an area to work on. Turn with me to Matthew chapter fifteen."

Pastor Mark explains how the Pharisees are always trying to trap Jesus. Though they talk about following the law, they're hypocrites through and through.

"They were more concerned about what they ate than how they treated people. This is seen in verses 10 and 11. 'Then Jesus called to the crowd to come and hear. 'Listen,' he said, 'and try to understand. It's not what goes into your mouth that defiles you; you are defiled by the words that come out of your mouth.'"

I lean my head down to hide my tears.

"The disciples ask Jesus if he cares that he insulted the Pharisees. I love his response. 'Don't you understand yet?' Jesus asked. 'Anything you eat passes through the stomach and then goes into the sewer. But the words you speak come from the heart—that's what defiles you. For from the heart come evil thoughts, murder, adultery, all sexual immorality, theft, lying, and slander. These are what defile you. Eating with unwashed hands will never defile you.'"

Pastor Mark walks around to the front of his pulpit. "Guys, it's time to realize that what comes out of our mouth represents our heart. Do you find yourself using profanity because it's cool?" He shakes his head. "That shows you're more caught up in the things of the world than the things of God. Are your comments cutting and filled with sarcasm? If they are, God's love hasn't touched your heart."

I think of Danny. Both continued to get worse over the past year.

"Do you gossip about people rather than cultivate relationships with them? That displays a heart full of jealousy and envy. Look at verse 20 again. 'For from the heart come evil thoughts, murder, adultery, all sexual immorality, theft, lying, and slander. These are what defile you.' I challenge you this year to watch what comes from your mouth. Evaluate it to see where your heart truly is. When our hearts are filled with filth, we spread filth to the world. If we want to spread truth and light, our hearts need to be filled with God's Word. They need to be filled with compassion, grace, and most of all, love. We can help turn the wicked from their sins if we choose to live this way."

The worship leader takes his place behind his keyboard. He plays the last song we sang.

"If you're ready to make a change this new year, come up for prayer. Let's not leave this place the same as we came. Let's not become the hypocrites the Pharisees were, people who knew the Word of God but didn't live it, didn't allow it to change their hearts. Today you have the opportunity to start over. Will you take it? Will you heed the Lord's words and realize it's what comes out of your mouth that defiles you?"

I kneel at the front of the room. I don't suppress my tears—I'm broken, and God knows it. I have nothing to hide.

*God, I don't want to be like the Pharisees. Let Your Word touch me and change me. Regardless of how others speak about Danny, regardless of how their words and actions hurt me, let me glorify You with my words and actions. Give me the courage and strength to follow You completely.*

A hand rests on my shoulder. One of the girls who was talking about Danny kneels beside me.

"I'm sorry for what I said."

"I forgive you," I say.

"I'll pray for him." She hugs me. "And not talk about him."

"You okay?" Pastor Mark approaches after he dismisses everyone.

"I will be." I hold my Bible to my chest. "Thanks for the message. It was great."

"Your authentic faith is a witness to others. Don't let anything change that."

I think about what Pastor Mark says on the way to the sanctuary. It might not get easier, but God is with me. *Continue to help me through this, God. I need You.*

A list of movies and times comes from Katie toward the end of service. I decide I'd be doing myself a favor if I miss lunch.

"I'm going to meet Katie at the mall instead of lunch," I say to Mom as we exit church. "We're going to a movie."

"You need to come to lunch," Dad says.

"Chris, she hasn't seen Katie her entire break—"

"It's Sunday. We go to lunch as a family."

"Actually, I need to grab my stuff and get on the road," Anna says. "You know, to beat traffic. Classes start tomorrow. Plus, there's a Bible study I want to attend on campus tonight."

Mom looks up from her phone. "Mary texted. They can't stop for lunch on the way back. They have too much to do."

Dad narrows his eyes, then waves his hand. "Go. Be home by eight. You start school again tomorrow too."

Katie's sitting at a table in the mall's food court when I arrive.

"Talk about cabin fever." Katie hugs me. "My siblings are literally climbing the walls."

Katie is the oldest of five, three of which are under the age of six. She can't wait to share a bathroom with college girls instead of toddlers.

"Better than looking through bridal websites. The dresses all start to look alike after a while."

Her eyes widen. "Oh my gosh! Mary and Dylan? They're getting married?"

"Sure are." I scan the menu board at the Italian place. "He proposed in front of us on New Year's Eve."

"How romantic!"

"I don't know about romantic. It was in our dining room—"

"Aren't you happy for her?"

"I guess. It's just hard, you know."

She stares at me.

"With Danny gone."

"Oh." Katie presses her lips together.

I search her face. "What?"

She avoids my gaze and takes a deep breath, as though she's working up the courage to say something. "Lyd, don't take this the wrong way, but you need to get past this."

I shake my head. "What?"

"If Danny doesn't want to be found, you won't find him, and if you don't find a way to move on and begin enjoying life again, it'll ruin you. I don't think that's what Danny would want, do you?"

We've been friends forever. I've helped her through every family, boy, life crisis she has had. How could she—

"What do you want for lunch? Pizza? Pasta?"

"I'm not hungry," I say.

"Yeah, maybe I'd rather have popcorn. Which movie do you want to see?"

I blink to stop the tears. "How about the one that starts the soonest?"

We are settled into our theater seats when Katie starts her play-by-play of her family's Christmas drama.

"Andrew was so mad Santa didn't give him the dart gun he wanted for Christmas he locked himself in his room. Olivia cried that she didn't get a horse. A horse! I totally blame my mom for not setting her straight on that one." She scoops up a handful of popcorn. "How was your Christmas?"

I put on a smile. "It was fine." I nibble on one kernel of popcorn. A text from Jason arrives.

*Happy New Year. I got home a bit ago from my dad's. Wanna hang out? Go to a movie?*

*I'm at one with Katie,* I reply. *But I could come over after.*

*Cool. See you then.*

"How's Jason?" Katie reads over my shoulder.

"I haven't talked to him since the twenty-seventh." I slip my phone into my purse. "He spent the week at his dad's."

"When are you two going to start dating?"

Thankfully the previews begin, and I don't have to answer.

The movie is a tearjerker, so it's acceptable for me to cry during it. I try to not think about Katie on the way to Jason's. The praise music, no matter how loud, can't drown out her words.

*"If Danny doesn't want to be found, you won't find him, and if you don't find a way to move on and begin enjoying life again, it'll ruin you."*

Danny's been gone three weeks. He's my brother. How can I get over it and move on?

I sit in my car in front of Jason's house, unable to stop the tears. I was a mess before he left. I can't see him this way now.

Not more than two minutes passes when Jason comes out of his house. He stares at me for a while. When I don't return his wave, he crosses the lawn to my car.

"When you said you'd come over, I thought we'd hang out inside," he says climbing in the passenger seat of my car, "but your car is comfortable enough."

I wipe my eyes on my sleeve. "I don't think Danny's coming home."

He frowns.

"And my sister got engaged."

He sighs.

"Dylan proposed on New Year's Eve. His family came over, and he made a big deal about how important it was for the entire family to be there—"

"But Danny's wasn't."

I raise my eyes to him. "Katie said I need to enjoy life again. But I'm so broken inside, I don't know how I can."

"Empathy is definitely not Katie's strength. I'm not saying she's an awful person. I mean, you guys have been friends forever, right?"

"Yeah." I drop my gaze to my steering wheel.

"She does care about you; she's just not thinking about how hard it is for you."

"How are you smart about things like that? You're a guy."

"Divorce is a type of loss. It wrecked me when my parents divorced. The past several years I've learned it's important to figure out who you can talk to about what. I talk to my mom about school and relationships. My dad can handle sports and health issues. I mean, I can never tell Mom if I think I'm hurt. She'll freak out. I call Dad. My youth pastor, Kellen, gives me good faith-related advice. I talk to Henry from baseball about sports-related stuff."

"And me?" I ask.

"I can talk to you about anything." He rubs my shoulder. "I hope you feel the same about me."

"I do."

"Because you're such an empathetic person, having someone who will just listen can make it hurt less. Your mom is a good person to talk to about Danny, but Katie's more of a problem solver than a shoulder to cry on. She doesn't want to see you hurt, so her solution is to move on with life. You shouldn't stop living your life, like we talked about before I left, but you don't get over it." He moves his hand down my arm to take mine. "How about coming in? Did you have dinner?"

I shake my hand.

"Did you have lunch?"

"No." I start my car. "I should go home. I didn't mean to bug you."

"You're not a bother." Jason leans over to turn off my engine. "Come inside. Have dinner. Cry or talk or listen to details of my visit with my dad and his new twenty-five-year-old live-in girlfriend."

"You're kidding."

"Wish I was." He laughs. "I actually caught her checking me out when I left the bathroom door open while I was brushing my teeth without a shirt on."

That makes me laugh. I love that even when I feel awful, Jason can make me laugh.

## CHAPTER 13

### DANNY

It starts with a random cough. Enough to make me remember that kid who held my hand a couple days ago while we prayed at dinner. It doesn't help that I laid my jacket over my sleeping bag one night instead of putting it on. The next day, it was gone. But I'm halfway to my goal with over fifteen hundred dollars. I try to focus on that. Maybe by the end of January I'll be on Malibu beach.

By Tuesday night, my throat is on fire. I drink alcohol instead of eating. It goes down smoother than water. I sit outside the grocery store at the dinner hour in hopes of a little extra pity.

"Can you spare some change?" I ask an old lady. "I really need some orange juice and cough drops."

"Sorry," she says. "I don't have any cash."

I cough into my sleeve. "That's okay."

Ten dollars comes in an hour, and that old lady sets a bag of orange juice, cough drops, and a pre-packaged turkey sandwich next to me when she exits the store. "God bless," she says.

I repress my laughter. Sure, 'cause He's blessed me so far.

"Do you have a jacket?" she asks

"Got stolen."

She frowns. "It's freezing out. You shouldn't be on the streets—"

"Thanks for this." I lift the sandwich from the bag. "I appreciate it."

After forcing myself to eat despite the pain swallowing, I hang out at the drugstore. The same line about juice and cough drops only gets me five bucks in an hour and a pack of cough drops that don't work any better than the last batch. I switch up my plea.

"I'm pretty sick. Any way you can spare a couple bucks for cold medicine?"

"I'm sick too," is the popular response. Sick people are exhausted, not empathetic. No one even tosses cold meds my way.

The chills start when I crawl into my sleeping bag. I have four layers of clothes on but can't stop shaking. I position myself in the doorway of a closed business, boxes in front of me to cut the wind chill. I'll feel better tomorrow if I get sleep.

*I'm on a ledge surrounded by fire. Everywhere as far as I can see there's fire. Sweat drips into my eyes. I take off my clothes and toss them into the flames to cool myself but also to stop the flames. I don't know why this will help, but I need to try something.*

*Screams echo through the canyon. Is that where I am? The screams vary in words, yet all are filled with pain and urgency.*

*Help!*

*Save me!*

*No, no, no!*

*I glance around to find figures, people, I guess. Their skin is charred. I don't recognize any of them until I look closer. There's Willow, the atheist I dated, and her entire family above me to my right. Mikey, the guy who sold me weed, is across this fire engulfed canyon. Armano, the cocaine dealer, is below him.*

*There's nowhere to look to escape this nightmare. I'm afraid of who I'll see next.*

*"Danny? Danny Boy?" A familiar voice drifts from below.*

*"Brett?"*

*"Danny Boy!" Brett is on a ledge beneath me to my left. "Get down here. I got something for you." He holds up a beer can.*

*Just the thought of the cool liquid eases my burning throat.*

*"I'll be right there." There has to be a way down. Maybe if I hang off the side of my ledge, I can swing myself over to his. Even if he doesn't catch me, he's big enough to break my fall. I squat and begin to climb down the ledge.*

*"Go, Danny! You got this!" Brett cheers.*

*"You gotta catch me!" I yell.*

*"Sure. I'll catch you. You know I'm here for you."*

*It's just a small drop, I tell myself. No big deal. You can handle it. The fun is worth the fall. You need to escape—*

*I'm about to release my grip when Brett starts screaming. Fire has consumed his clothes. He beats on himself wildly.*

*"Help me, Danny, help me."*

*I watch as his face melts. The beer can explodes. I cover my ears at the noise.*

*And I fall. Right into the flames.*

*The heat is more unbearable the deeper I go. It's like I'm walking on the sun. There's no breeze, no relief, yet I'm not burning. I don't want to die. I was stupid and selfish, but I don't want to die. God, help me, I don't want to die.*

I wake gasping for air. I pull my arms from my sleeping bag. I'm sweating like crazy. My face burns though I'm shivering. The cough that crushes my chest starts. A swig of OJ almost makes me puke, which is not a good thing since I can barely move. My water bottle is dry. Tomorrow it's off to urgent care. All the cash in the world will be useless if I'm dead.

---

*LYDIA*

"We are going to begin this semester by reading *Wuthering Heights.*" My English teacher, Mrs. Dapper, passes books to the first person in each row. "What do you know about this classic?"

I try to focus, but my heart is full of anxiety. It was six degrees last night. The weather report says to expect negative numbers by Thursday as another cold front is coming in.

Instead of thinking about Danny freezing, I think about his love for literature and writing. I found his journal from his freshman English class in his room last week. I read it cover to cover. He wrote about baseball, his wins, even the pressure from Dad in a fictionalized story. I loved his honesty, though I wish he had been honest with me. My favorite part was how he started the journal—*Top Ten Things You Need to Know About Danny Morton.*

I flip to a clean page of notebook paper and write *Ten Verses to Cling to in Hard Times.* Next I scroll through my highlight history in my Bible app. With each verse I copy, I lift a prayer.

#10: Matthew 6:30—"And if God cares so wonderfully for wildflowers that are here today and thrown into the fire tomorrow, he will certainly care for you. Why do you have so little faith?"

*I trust you to provide completely for Danny, Lord. More than the lilies of the fields and birds of the air, take care of my brother's physical needs.*

#9: Proverbs 18:10—"The name of the Lord is a strong fortress; the godly run to him and are safe."

*God, I pray Danny will seek refuge in You. Show him that You are His strong fortress.*

A chill comes over me, reminding me how cold it is outside. My stomach turns until I remember Philippians 4:6

#8: Philippians 4:6—"Don't worry about anything; instead, pray about everything. Tell God what you need and thank him for all he has done."

*I'm thankful You're with Danny, watching over Him. Keep him safe and warm. Remind me to continue to have a heart of thankfulness and lift my anxieties to You.*

I return to scrolling, pausing on my highlights of Psalm 139.

#7: Psalm 139:16—"You saw me before I was born. Every day of my life was recorded in your book. Every moment was laid out before a single day had passed."

*God, none of this is a surprise to You.* Tears fill my eyes. *You know all the days of my brother's life, including the day he will return to You. Let it be soon.*

Jason massages my shoulders from behind. I realize how incredibly tense I am. When my father comes to my mind, I search "stony heart" in my app.

#6: Ezekiel 36:26—"And I will give you a new heart, and I will put a new spirit in you. I will take out your stony, stubborn heart and give you a tender, responsive heart."

*Lord, that's what my father needs. A heart for You and a heart for Danny. Give him a tender heart that responds to Your Word.*

Next, my mom comes to mind. I smile at James 1:12.

#5: James 1:12—"God blesses those who patiently endure testing and temptation. Afterward they will receive the crown of life that God has promised to those who love him."

*God, bless my mom as she endures this trial. Bless her for continuing to love You. Help her to cling to You through this.*

I think of my sisters. Definitely need a verse for them. I'm convicted at 2 Timothy chapter two.

#4: 2 Timothy 2:24—"A servant of the Lord must not quarrel but must be kind to everyone, be able to teach, and be patient with difficult people."

*Lord, I hate this feeling of frustration that comes every time I think of my sisters. You want us to get along, so give me patience for them. Help me to understand how this is affecting them.*

My eyes prick with tears as I remember their attitudes toward Danny when they were home. Sometimes it feels as though we're not even a family anymore. An old favorite comes to mind.

#3: Jeremiah 29:11—"'For I know the plans I have for you,' says the Lord. 'They are plans for good and not for disaster, to give you a future and a hope.'"

That takes me to another favorite.

#2: 2 Corinthians 4:8—"We are pressed on every side by troubles, but we are not crushed. We are perplexed, but not driven to despair. We are hunted down, but never abandoned by God. We get knocked down, but we are not destroyed."

*God, You do have good plans for us. Even though things are hard, You are here. You won't allow this to destroy our family.*

Jason drops a piece of paper with a verse address on my desk. I smile as I write the verse from memory.

#1: Romans 8:28—"And we know that God causes everything to work together for the good of those who love God and are called according to his purpose for them."

I underline EVERYTHING and GOOD.

*I love You, God, and I trust You to work this for our good and Your glory. In Jesus's name, amen.*

"Quiz on Wednesday covering my lecture and this study guide." Mrs. Dapper passes the study guides down each row.

"We can go over it tonight," Jason whispers in my ear. "What you're doing is more important."

I nod and return to the top of the page to read my verses through again until the bell rings. I'll get through by holding on to His Word.

"Lydia!"

I hear my name when I step out of English. A teacher with short brown hair waves to me from across the hall.

"I'll call you after practice." Jason pats my shoulder.

I walk toward the teacher.

"Lydia, I'm Mrs. Del Pizzo." She extends her hand.

I smile. "Nice to meet you. Danny loved your class."

"Well, he's a great student. An exceptional writer." She sighs. "Is it true that he hasn't come home?"

"He hasn't." I bite my lip.

She takes a deep breath. "I heard teachers talking before break and thought for sure he'd come home. I know he and your father didn't see eye to eye, but I hoped whatever happened would resolve itself."

"You knew from his journal?" I ask.

She nods. "If I'd seen Danny's struggle with other things, I would've done something. I want you and your family to know that."

Drugs, she means. Yes, the entire school knows my brother is a drug addict.

I swallow the lump rising in my throat. "I know. The best thing you can do is pray for him. It's freezing out, and the thought of him on the streets—"

She hugs me. "I will. I'm worried too. If there's anything else I can do, please let me know."

"Thank you." I wipe my tears and head quickly down the hall reciting my last verse in my mind. *"And we know that God causes everything to work together for the good of those who love God and are called according to his purpose for them."*

*I trust you, God. I trust You to work it out for good.*

# CHAPTER 14

## DANNY

A SHARP PAIN IN MY TEMPLES FEELS LIKE SOMEONE STUCK A KNIFE through my head. The boxes I surrounded myself with the night before are gone. The sun is high. My backpack is several feet away. Crawling in a straight line is impossible thanks to my spinning head, but I manage to get to it. Only my notebooks and novels are in the main compartment. Computer—gone. Drugs—gone. The small bottom pocket? Empty. That's when I scream. My money's gone. All fifteen hundred dollars. I pack up and reach for my skateboard. It's nowhere. Seriously? They took my skateboard?

I head across the street to the pharmacy to pee, change clothes, and purchase some cold meds with yesterday's take that's in my pocket. The only cash I have left.

"Cold remedies" fill three shelves four feet long. Liquid or pill? Cough-cold, cold, or severe cold? Daytime, nighttime, runny nose with or without fever. My head continues to spin. I squint to read the prices. Do I even have twenty dollars?

"Do you need help?"

I face the woman next to me. She looks my mom's age. Her blondish hair is in a ponytail.

"There's a lot of choices." I scratch my head.

"What are your symptoms?"

"A lot of sinus pressure." I cough. "And there's that." I cough again. "My chest hurts. My throat feels like it's on fire."

"It sounds like what my son has." She grabs the box from the shelf. "This one will take care of the sinus pressure and cough."

I scan the box. Severe daytime and nighttime cold medicine. I glance back to the price. Twenty-nine dollars.

"It's daytime and nighttime. The nighttime is long lasting."

"Is there a cheaper form?"

She looks at me and then the price. "Oh. Let me get it for you."

"No." I put it on the shelf. "It's okay."

"Please. Allow me." She takes the box.

I stare at her, in no condition to argue.

"What else do you need?"

"A bed." I realize the words came from my mouth when she laughs.

"Do you live around here?"

"Medicine would be great." I smack my dry lips. "Maybe some water."

"Sure." She spins to scan the items behind her. "How about cough drops?" She snags two bags from the shelf. "These soothe sore throats too. Do you have a fever?"

"Yeah." I close my eyes when I see two of her.

"When's the last time you ate?"

"Yesterday. Maybe. I can't remember."

Her hand rests against my arm. "There are chairs by the pharmacy. I'll bring everything once I check out."

When my eyes open, I find her inches from my face. There's something that feels safe about her.

"Back there." She points. "Go sit down."

Although the plastic chair is hard, I'm thankful to sit. My elbow on the arm rest, I lean against my hand and focus on breathing. Every four breaths I cough. The tightness in my chest grows. I close my eyes and think of home. A warm blanket, soft pillow, and Mom's homemade chicken soup. The smell drifts from the kitchen to the family room. My favorite soft, brown blanket covers me on the couch-bed Mom's made. On the coffee table there's 7-Up mixed with orange juice with a bendy straw next to the package of Saltine crackers. A comedy is on TV. Lyd sits at the opposite end of the couch. She rubs my feet, and we laugh at the corny jokes. I hold my chest when I laugh because it makes me cough. There's a fire in my chest.

*"Lots of fluids, Danny."* Lyd hands me my drink. *"To get better you need to drink lots of fluids."*

I'm at my first baseball party, and Logan places the shot glass in my hand. The gold flakes float in the clear liquid. Everyone chants my name as I shoot it, fire rushing down my throat. It burns while the kids laugh.

Brett sits next to me on the floor. He talks while he prepares the bong. I can't hear his voice over Bob's whimpers in the hallway. Brett lights up, takes a drag, and passes it to me. My chest hurts. I shouldn't. I gasp for breath. The crowd calls my name. I inhale and cough, grab my chest. I can't breathe—

"Take a drink."

My eyes open to a water bottle in front of me. I take it and guzzle. The water is cool, soothing.

She places two pills in my hand. "Take these."

I do and drink another fourth of the bottle. The lights are bright. I can't keep my eyes open.

"What's your name?"

"Danny." I rest my head back on my hand. It won't matter that she knows my name if I die.

"I'm Layla. I'd like you to come with me."

I force my eyes open. The woman has two bags in one hand and offers me her other.

"Will you come with me?"

She pulls me up from the chair because, although I want to move, my body is too exhausted to get up. Once I'm on my feet, I grab my backpack. I lose balance when I lift my duffle.

Layla takes it from my hand. "Come on."

I follow her through the store to the parking lot. She opens the door to the backseat of a high-end SUV.

"Come sit down."

I climb onto the leather seat. It's soft and cool. I sink into it and close my eyes.

"Where do you live?"

"I can't go home." It's fine with me if Rich Mom kidnaps me. I'd totally live with her.

"I'd like to take you, wherever. You can't stay on the streets."

"I can't go home. It's not safe." I lie across the entire seat.

"You're terribly sick. If you stay on the streets in this weather, you'll end up with pneumonia."

"A couple hours in your backseat and I'll be good." I drift off to sleep.

I wake to a cough that's not my own. My vision focuses slowly. I'm in the back of the SUV. Layla is driving on the freeway. A teenage boy is asleep in the passenger's seat, a blanket over him. Eighties music plays on the radio. Michael Jackson, maybe.

With a yawn, I sit up. A plaid blanket is on me. I pull it around me, trying to think of something to say when I start to cough.

Layla peers in the rearview mirror. "You okay?"

I nod.

"There's water in the door beside you."

I grab the bottle and drink. "You drive around picking up sick teens on the street?"

"This is my son, Jameson." She nods to the boy next to her. "I found a shelter where you can stay. They have an open bed. We'll be there in about twenty minutes. A sandwich is in the bag on the floor if you're hungry."

"Thanks." Once the water is in the cupholder, I pull out the foot-long sandwich. Turkey and bacon with all the fixings. It feels like Thanksgiving.

"How old are you?"

"Eighteen."

She purses her lips at my response. "I would have guessed fifteen."

"Is that how old your son is?"

"Yes."

I eat staring out the window at the cars.

"You said it's not safe at your house?"

"My dad and I don't mix. It's best that I'm gone." I catch her eyes in the mirror. "Thanks for the food and medicine. You don't need to—"

"I'm sorry. I don't mean to pry." She focuses her gaze forward. "I can't imagine my son out on the streets alone. I'm sure your mom is worried sick."

Mom's face comes to my mind, her smile. I hope she's smiling, grateful that I'm free. Hopefully she can enjoy the last few months of Lyd at home. Maybe Mom will run off with her to the Ozarks.

I start coughing, almost choke on the food in my mouth. After a few minutes and a long drink, it subsides.

"The flu strand this year is awful. Jameson has been sick for four days." She glances at her son as he stirs. "Took him to the doctor today. His turned into bronchitis. Do you have siblings?"

I shake my head. It's easier to lie. The warm sun pouring through the window drains me of my energy. I rewrap the other half of my sandwich before closing my eyes.

"We're here."

I rub my eyes. The building looks like a large single-story house. The bluish paint needs a fresh coat. There are a couple of cars in the parking lot. Industrial buildings and warehouses surround it.

A white sign is above the door. "JumpStart" is written in blue letters.

"What is it?" I ask.

"A men's shelter. Hopefully a warm place to sleep and cold medicine will get you well. Maybe even help you get on the right track again." She opens the back to take out my belongings.

A complete stranger thought through my situation and found a way to help. Not only did she buy me medicine, she drove miles out of her way to find me a place to stay. The story of the good Samaritan comes to my mind. I remember what Pastor said that Sunday over a year ago.

*"When you see a person hurting and in need you have a choice—judge them like the priest, look down on them like the Levite, or be the Samaritan and show kindness."*

"Thank you." I climb out with my bag of medicine when she opens my door. "You didn't have to—"

"I did." She shifts her gaze to her son, asleep in the passenger seat. "I would want someone to do the same for him."

My cough prevents my words, but I nod. I take my things from her.

"Here." She drapes the plaid blanket over my shoulders. "To keep you warm." Her eyes are filled with compassion. "Take care, Danny."

"You too." I nod.

The door seems to magically open when I reach the welcome mat.

"Ya must be Danny."

I look up, up, up. A man with a dark-brown wrinkle-free face greets me. It's ironic his face looks young, because his hair is more gray than brown.

"Been waitin' for ya. My name's Ben."

"Nice to meet you." I cough in my arm.

"First things first. Do ya got any drugs or alcohol?"

I hold up the bag from the pharmacy. "Cold medicine."

He takes the bag from me. "We'll keep those for ya an' giv' 'em as directed. How's about the good stuff? Marijuana? Cocaine? Heroin?"

I place my duffle on a chair. "Have at it."

Big Ben digs through my duffle then my backpack.

"When's the last time ya used?"

I'm a bit taken back by his question, but too sick to care. "A couple days ago."

"Fair 'nuff." He hands my backpack to me. "Thanks for yer honesty. Use of illegal drugs and alcohol in the shelter is pro-hibutted and'll lead to ex-pellsion." He sets a paper in front of me. "Need yer name and signature that ya understand."

I scribble both.

He lifts my duffle. "Follow me."

We walk through the center. He talks about the men and the program; I focus on not falling over while keeping up with his long strides.

"That there's the dinin' hall." He motions to a room that resembles a cafeteria. "We serve three square meals a day."

"Water?" I'm out of breath. My throat burns. "Could I get some water?"

He flashes his big, crooked teeth, and with a "wait here," he weaves through the tables towards the kitchen.

Now when I breathe, I wheeze. The room seems to have a slight tilt to it.

"Here ya go." He places a bottle of water in my hand.

I drink a quarter of it before we continue down another hallway, then into a room with a couple dozen bunk beds.

"I made ya a bunk when Ms. Layla called."

He takes me to the corner of the room, points to a bottom bed with sheets, a blanket, and a pillow. I've never been so thrilled to see a pillow.

"Thank you." I drop my backpack.

"How 'bout a shower and clean clothes first? It'll help ya sleep. If ya need clean clothes, I could find ya something in wardrobe."

I sigh. "Clean clothes would be good."

He points the way to the showers and goes to find me an outfit that doesn't reek. The water on my skin hurts because of my fever. As I scrub the grime from my body and hair, I feel better. It's been weeks since I've showered. I forgot how good clean feels.

Big Ben brings sweats that are only a little loose and a long sleeve shirt. I take cold medicine and Tylenol before crawling into bed, exhausted.

"Here's another pillow for ya." Ben slides it under my head. "It'll help yer breathin if ya sleep with two."

"Thanks." I cough.

"We have a laundry facility on campus. If ya'd like, I'll wash everything in yer duffle."

"Knock yourself out." I close my eyes.

"Rest up, Danny. When ya wake, I'll have food for ya."

---

## *LYDIA*

I pray the entire way to work. *God, I know you don't want me to just sit at home and be sad. Help me to not focus on myself and my feelings. Help me to be a blessing to others.*

A man with tattered clothes sits at a table two doors down from Super Subs. He rocks back and forth, a small Styrofoam cup between his filthy hands, his brown hair covering his eyes. I think of that homeless guy I saw the first day I passed out flyers about Danny. Guilt filled me over not stopping. I won't make the same mistake, even though my shift starts in five minutes.

"Hi," I say when I'm beside him. "My name's Lydia."

"I'm George," he says without lifting his eyes.

"I was wondering if you're hungry? I work at the sandwich shop and would be happy to get you a sandwich if you are."

His expression doesn't change. He doesn't look at me, just continues to rock. For a minute, I wonder if he heard me.

"I like roast beef," he says. "No mayo."

I smile. "White or wheat bread?"

"Wheat."

No one is in line, so it only takes a minute for my co-worker to make my sandwich. Since employees are allowed one free sandwich per shift, I only have to pay for chips and a large hot coffee.

"Here you go." I place the bag and beverage in front of him.

"Thanks." He stares at the bag.

I start to turn and pause. "Do you mind if I pray for you, George?"

He raises his face to get a glimpse of me, then lowers it again. "I'd like that."

My prayer is for George's health, safety, and that he would know Jesus' love. A warmth comes over me. The heaviness that has built in my chest all day lifts. I no longer feel like the day has been a disaster. It's been redeemed. God answered my prayer that I could be a blessing to someone. Meeting George and helping him has been a blessing to me.

George lifts his face when I say amen. "Can I ask, why'd you do this? Most kids don't stop. If they do, it's to laugh at me."

"Because I want someone to do the same for my brother." I smile though tears fill my eyes. "God bless you."

Mr. Dannenberg is wiping a table by the door when I walk back in.

"Sorry, Mr. D. I didn't mean to be late."

"You're fine, Lydia. You're fine." He straightens. "In fact, if you want a sandwich for yourself on your break—"

"I'm good." I smile. "I'm gonna fast and pray for my brother. I'll eat after my shift."

I think of Danny and George my entire shift. Not in a sad way. In fact, the other employee comments on how good it is to see me smile again. All these years I've ignored the homeless. Now I see them as people who are loved by God, by parents, by siblings. It makes me happy that George will sleep with a full stomach tonight. I pray Danny will also.

A great idea comes to me during my shift. I don't need to give out sandwiches to make someone's day. Jesus said if we give a glass of water to others, it's like we're giving it to Him. After work, I stop at the grocery store down the street to purchase a case of water and boxes of protein bars. No longer will I judge those on the street. The Bible says we will be judged as we judge others. I can give the homeless a bottle of water and a protein bar, in Jesus's name.

On the way home I pull over twice. The first is for an older woman huddled by the door of a business. She asks for money after I hand her water and a bar.

"I don't have cash, but I'd like to pray for you."

"Well, okay then," she sighs.

The next person is on a bus bench. I hope for a peek at his face to confirm it's not Danny, but it's covered with a black scarf. The guy is much heavier than Danny. I set the bottle of water and protein bar on the sidewalk next to the bench, then say a silent prayer for him.

"Where have you been?" Dad is in his chair in the family room in front of the TV with his tablet in his lap.

"Work." I hang up my jacket, hat, and scarf.

"The store closes at seven. It's quarter to nine."

"I stopped along the way."

Dad raises an eyebrow.

He's going to freak out. I don't want a fight, but I'm not ashamed of what I've done. I take a deep breath. "I bought water and protein bars to give homeless people on the way home."

Mom glances up from her book, a smile on her lips.

"That's idiotic." Dad shakes his head. "Do you want someone to rob you? Or kill you?"

"Chris!" Mom stands.

"Really, Margaret. You know that's not safe." He turns back to me. "I forbid you—"

"Tonight, was the first time I didn't cry." I glare at him. "I was actually happy. It filled me with hope that someone might be doing the same for Danny."

"You don't know why they're on the streets. They could be psychotic."

"Or they could be lost, like Danny." I purse my lips. "This is what God has called me to do. I need to be obedient." I run up the steps.

"Lydia," Mom calls. "Did you want dinner?"

"I'm not hungry." Dropping my backpack on the floor, I collapse on my bed.

*I shouldn't hate him. I don't want to, but God, he makes me so mad. Please, please, help me.*

My list of verses comes to mind. I pull my notebook from my bag and read each one aloud to stop the negative thoughts from coming.

Mom knocks on my door five minutes later carrying a plate with a sandwich. "I made this for you." She sits on my bed, runs her hand over my hair. "You did a good thing. I'm proud of you."

"I worry about Danny." I set the plate on my nightstand. "I pray and try not to, but I do."

"Me too." She kisses the top of my head. "We need to pray God will keep him warm and safe." She looks down at my notebook. "That's a lot of verses."

I stare at Jeremiah 29:11. "Do you think he'll come home?"

"Even if it's not God's will for him to come home, we can pray that he gives up drugs and returns to God." She circles the verse with her finger. "That prayer aligns with God's will."

A tear rolls down my cheek. "Will you pray with me?"

"Yes, baby." Mom wraps her arms around me. We pour out our hearts, and our tears, to the Lord.

# CHAPTER 15

## DANNY

A cafeteria tray is beside my bed when I wake. Meatloaf, potatoes, and corn are under the domed lid. Though it's lukewarm, I eat every bite. The room is empty, the lights are dim. I stand with a stretch. My duffle and sleeping bag are underneath my bed. The clothes in my duffle smell spring fresh, as does my sleeping bag. It still hurts to breathe, but the world is no longer tilted. I head off with my dishes to find the kitchen and more water.

"Danny, right?" A blond guy in his late twenties stops me in the hall. "I'm Chad. Ben told me about you. I work the night shift."

"Hi." I shake his hand. "Thanks for the food."

"Ben hooked you up before he left." He takes the tray. "Are you still hungry? The kitchen is closed, but I could get you some fruit."

"Sure." I follow him. "What time is it?"

"After seven. Most of the residents are in the entertainment room. It's probably best you stay away, being sick."

"I just need more water and cold meds. Then I'll get back to bed."

"We have a doctor visit twice a week. He'll be in tomorrow. The flu has been nasty this season. I'm glad you made your way to us. Sounds like a total God-thing."

I clamp my mouth shut to avoid an argument.

"A little about our program. When you're better, you'll take a career assessment. Then we'll place you in a work program. After thirty days, we do an evaluation to see if it would be best for you to stay or move on. Our hope and prayer is rehabilitation. Counselors are on site three days a week, Bible studies take place Wednesdays and Fridays, with church on Sunday. Our desire is to meet all your needs—physical, mental, and spiritual."

I'm in no condition to argue. I'll lie low until I'm better. Enjoy the bed, free food, and warmth. Especially since my money is gone. Not-so-nice words come to mind for the jerk who stole my money, drugs, computer, and skateboard. Though my plays are safe in the cloud, I won't be able to afford a new computer for a long time. I understand the need to steal to survive, but to steal from those who are barely surviving is wrong. Very, very wrong.

"What do you feel like? Grapes, apple, orange?"

"An apple would be great."

"I'll be right back." Chad disappears through the door we are in front of.

My head throbs. I rub my temples. Why am I sweating? My stomach turns. Suddenly I regret everything I ate for dinner.

"Here you go, an apple and water."

I'm doubled over when Chad appears. "I need a bathroom."

He gets me to the one across the hall before I mess my clean clothes.

"How's your head?" he asks through the stall door.

"It hurts. Real bad." My entire body shakes. "It's super cold in here. Could you turn up the heat or something?"

"How much alcohol do you drink, Danny?"

"I don't know." Another wave of nausea comes over me. "I'm gonna puke."

The door to the restrooms opens and closes. Then it opens again. Chad pushes a large bowl under my stall.

"You drink every day?"

"Yeah." No sense in lying about it.

"What drugs are you on?"

I like Ben's bedside manner a lot more than Chad's. "Weed, coke." That's when I lose my dinner.

When I finally come out, Chad greets me with a toothbrush and toothpaste. That kinda makes up for his questions.

"I'll show you where the closest bathrooms are to the sleeping hall. I'm here awake all night long. If you need anything, there's a button you can press in your room. You don't have to go through this alone."

Go through this. Detox. Oh joy.

Chad hooks me up with more blankets and a clean bowl. "Alcohol detox can be intense. Tremors is part of it."

"How long will it last?" I wrap the blankets around me.

"Depends on your level of addiction. If it's not severe, less than twenty-four hours." He hands me cold meds and Tylenol. "Hopefully you'll sleep through it. Breakfast starts at six-thirty. If you don't wake up in time, I'll make sure Ben gets you something from the kitchen."

"Thanks." I take the meds.

"No problem, kid. We've all been there."

"You?" I lie back down, my head pounding.

"Clean and sober five years. Decided to make a career change to help others. Get some sleep, Danny. You'll feel better in the morning."

I don't sleep peacefully, but I sleep. And I sleep some more. I puke once more during the night. At six a.m., guys start getting up. An envelope with my name on it is on a tray next to a bagel in a ziplock bag. The envelope holds more cold meds. I manage two bites of the bagel after I swallow the meds. Then I sleep more.

The taste in my mouth when I can finally keep my eyes open for more than five minutes is raunchy. I brush my teeth and head off to find some food.

The cafeteria is locked. I follow the noise down the hallway to the entertainment room. A poker game is underway with about half a dozen guys. At the table beside them, an old guy and a younger one sifts through puzzle pieces. The rest shout from the couch at the basketball game on TV. A huge sign on the front wall reads "This is the first day of the rest of your life."

Shoot me now, please. If the next month is full of pep talks and lame clichés, I'd rather take my chances on the street.

"How ya doin'?" Big Ben towers over me.

"Better. Hungry. Any chance I can get something? I'll try not to puke it up."

Ben's chuckle makes his belly shake. "Oh, I'm sure I can smuggle something out for ya. I'll get ya meds too." He nods to the tables. "Have a seat. I'll be right back."

I sit at the puzzle table. Those guys seem more subdued. Don't know that my head can handle much action.

"Hi," I say. "My name is Danny."

"Nice to meet you, Danny," the older guy says. "I'm Graham."

The other nods. "Matteo."

"We'd love your help." Graham scratches his head. "We barely put a dent in this thing the past two days."

"I'm waiting for my food. Got in yesterday and haven't kept much down."

"Isn't detox fun?" Matteo smirks.

"Yeah, not really."

"Third time around for me." Matteo reaches for a puzzle piece. I see the track marks on his arm. "Maybe it'll stick this time."

"You'll make it." Graham pats his back. "For your baby girl, right?

"You have a kid?" I ask.

"Gabrielle." He lifts his sleeve to reveal a heart tattoo with the name written in cursive. "Six months old. Her mom kicked me out. Said I couldn't see her until I was sober. Been here five weeks. I'm workin' and stayin' clean."

"Here ya go, Danny." Ben places a turkey sandwich on wheat bread and a bottle of water in front of me. "Sandwiches are all we can get between meals."

"Looks great." I open the water. "How about my cold meds?"

"Doc's here. Down the hall to the right." He points. "When ya finish, he'll take a look at ya, to decide whatcha need."

Dr. Paulson is prepared with his lecture on the dangers of drugs and alcohol. Chad has let him in on my favorites, because he has all the stats on marijuana and cocaine. He places a picture of a healthy liver on his desk next to one of an alcoholic.

"Looks like it was left on the barbeque too long."

He doesn't laugh.

"You may think you're young and have it under control but talk to any of the guys in here." Doc points his glasses at me. "They'll tell you it started in their teen years. The choices you make now will affect the rest of your life."

"You're right." I nod. "Were you going to examine me?"

Bronchitis is his diagnosis. "Antibiotics with a week of bed rest should help. Continue cold medicine as needed, no more than every four hours. Discontinue the use of any pain meds now that your fever is gone."

"My head is killing me."

"It'll pass in a day or two." He stands. "I recommend you stay in the facility the full three months. If you leave in thirty days, you will relapse."

I nod like I care. My plan is to be gone as soon as I'm well.

I find Big Ben, share the doc's prognosis, and collect my meds. He tells me the antibiotics will arrive in the morning. He starts in about how great their program is. I can learn a trade, even be placed in a job. I open my mouth to object when I look out the window behind him. Snow. White, powdery snow. I have no coat. Nowhere to go.

"Sounds good." I rub my eyes. "Doc also said a week of bedrest. I'm gonna lie down now."

"Absolutely. Chad can tell ya more about it when yer feeling better."

"I'm sure he can." I force a smile.

---

*LYDIA*

Half the time my notebook paper is blank at the end of the class. Sometimes there are words I don't remember writing. When I feel like crying, I draw a happy face to remind myself to smile. I need to be here right now, yet conversations seem petty when I think about Danny on the streets.

Katie is oblivious to what I'm going through. Apparently, I smile at the right times when she talks, because she doesn't get on me again for being worried about Danny.

When she leaves lunch early, Jason puts his arm around me. "We can study together, when you're ready. Don't worry about notes. I'll make copies of mine."

I massage my temples. "I need good grades this semester or I lose my scholarship."

"Give yourself some grace. It'll take time."

"I don't have time."

"This isn't something you can control, Lyd. It's something you get through. One day at a time. One hour at a time. That's as far as you need to look. We'll finish lunch and go to fifth period."

I run my hands through my knotted hair. I didn't even blow dry it before coming to school. "I got out of bed this morning and showered. That was a huge accomplishment."

"It is." Jason rubs my back.

"I can't shake this feeling that something is very wrong." A chill comes over me to admit it.

"Then pray for God to change Danny and direct him to the people who will make a difference in his life. I'll keep praying for you to make it through."

I bump into Robyn on the way to fifth period English. "How did you keep going to school after losing your brother? It seems to get worse every day rather than better."

"It does for a while. I'm so sorry." She rubs my shoulder. "Keep showing up, copy notes. At some point you'll be able to think clearly again. You're always welcome to my notes."

"Thanks." We go to our seats on opposite sides of class. Thinking clearly is my issue. When I'm not battling my emotions, I feel like I'm in a fog.

The class starts off with me keeping up on taking notes. Then a kid comes in from the office. He looks familiar but not old enough to be a senior. I can't figure out how I know him until Mrs. Dapper says, "Thank you, Mr. Rodriguez."

Rodriguez, the new varsity baseball pitcher that Danny hated. One thought after another pulls me into a dark place.

*He hated baseball. Your dad shouldn't have made him play. You have every reason to hate him.*

I'm close to tears when I think about what Jason said. I need to get through this hour—and pray.

*God, show me what I should pray for Danny,* I write on my paper. *Show me what he needs.*

A vision of Danny forms in my mind. He's shaking uncontrollably and holding his stomach. Is he cold? Is he crying?

*God, take away the pain. Be with him, wherever he is. Make him well again. Bring people into his life right now who will show him Your grace, love, and the truth of Your Word. May his heart be open to accept it. Please, God, bring him back to You.*

As I finish, the burden in my heart lifts. My mind clears. I understand every word the teacher says. I turn to a new page to take notes.

"You took a lot of notes," Jason says when we leave class.

"I did. Maybe we can get together this weekend so you can help me fill in the gaps?"

"Absolutely." He wraps an arm around me. "I'm proud of you."

I breathe deeply all the way home. I might actually be able to study tonight.

"Mom," I call when I walk through the door. There's no response, so I head to the kitchen. I push open the door to find her feet parallel to the floor and only sticking out a few inches from the island.

"Mom!" I run towards her, expecting to find her unconscious on the floor. Instead she's on her hands and knees scrubbing with a toothbrush. "Mom?"

"Hi, sweetie." She doesn't break her rhythm. "How was school?"

I kneel beside her. "What are you doing?" I wrinkle my nose at the strong bleach smell.

"Cleaning the grout. I've meant to do this for years. The dirt bugs me. It was a shame we didn't seal it when we moved in." She pushes hair from her face, dips the toothbrush in a cup of liquid, then scrubs more vigorously. "I told him we should. He complained about the cost."

*She's lost it. She's really lost her mind.* "How long have you been doing this?" The grout between the surrounding tiles seems pretty dirty.

"A few hours, since before lunch I guess." She rubs her forearm. "I've made progress. A square or two."

At this rate, it'll take months—and a hundred toothbrushes—to finish.

"Mom, I don't think you should do this."

"No, I'm fine." She switches the brush from one hand to the other, increasing the pressure between the tiles. "Really."

"You can pay someone to pressure wash it."

"I can do it." Her voice is agitated. "I have the time. I mean, I don't have anything else to do."

"Mom." I rub her arm.

"I can do this." She jerks away, and a tear slips down her cheek.

My embrace stops her. "Please, Mom. Don't." Now I'm crying at what the stress has done to her.

"I have nothing to do during the day except think about him," she sobs. "I miss him more every day."

"I know, Mom. I do too." I hold her while she cries.

"I feel so lost. I thought if I kept myself busy, I wouldn't feel so bad."

"You can clean my room." The sound of her laugh, even between sobs, lightens my heart. "I miss him too. It's hard to concentrate on what the teachers are saying." I kiss her cheek. "Maybe you could start small. Organize the pantry? Change the sheets?"

"I did the pantry yesterday." She sniffs. "The sheets last week."

"Well, there's always my room. My laundry."

"That's in the dryer."

We both laugh. What we are going through is awful; however, I'm glad we have each other.

"I love you." I stand, offering Mom my hand. "How about we start dinner? We could watch a movie while we do."

She stands. "Thank you."

I flick on the kitchen TV. Mom sets the potatoes on the counter.

"Snow is coming to Indiana," the newscaster says.

We both turn to the TV.

"The storm is coming through the north. Expect several inches to stack up tonight before making its way south."

The five-day forecast scrolls across the bottom of the screen. The lows are less than zero all week.

"God, protect Danny," Mom says. "Take him someplace safe and warm."

"Amen," I whisper.

# CHAPTER 16

## DANNY

Five days in bed, two weeks pretending to better myself, and I'm no closer to California. It's mid-February. By now I should be basking on the beach. Instead, I sit around with a lot of time to think about how crappy it is that my computer and all my money were stolen. More proof that God is against me. One day, in an attempt to escape the mediocre life of puzzles and poker without money, I look up the word for man-hater. Misanthrope. That's my new term for God. I figure if He hates me, I might as well hate Him.

Yet here I am, surrounded by Jesus freaks. The religious stuff isn't required. I figure that out when I leave Sunday service, and no one follows me. However, the next week the preacher comes to visit.

"I wanted to stop by to encourage you," he says.

"How?" I ask.

"These troubles that you experience on earth are temporal. The Bible says with Him, all things are possible."

"Yup. Jesus said that, right?" I go back to my phone.

"So, you know God?" he asks.

"Sure do. He's a misanthrope."

The preacher narrows his eyebrows.

"Look it up. I feel the same about Him. You coming to visit won't change that."

The second week, the counselor, Teresa, tries to get me to talk about my childhood. Rather than tell the truth, I make up stories about my dad beating me, withholding food, and most of all, love. She offers me a tissue with every hardship I highlight.

"What a strong young man you are." Tissue Teresa wipes her tears. "I'm looking forward to working through things with you, Danny."

"Me too." I leave with a smile on my face. I was born to make up stories.

Job interest surveys tell Chad I'd make a good criminal or an author.

"Do you like to write?" he asks.

"Love to."

He breathes a sigh of relief.

"I'm headed to California to sell my screenplay."

"That's a great plan." He flips through his papers. "We could extend your stay to three months. A deli in town needs help. The pay is minimum wage plus tips. You'll go to work five days, live here, and continue therapy. Teresa says you would benefit highly from it."

No doubt she does. Since it's still freezing at night and staying means a guaranteed wage, a hot shower, meals along with a bed, I decide to stick it out. I can be in LA before the summer. Might be warm enough to live on the beach.

The center hooks me up with new clothes for my first day of work at Ricci's. Black pants, long-sleeved collared shirt, new tennis shoes, and a black jacket. I feel like a nerd, but I'm clean and warm. I take my backpack, some of my clothes in case I want to change after, my notebooks, and a couple novels. That's all I have of value. No way will I take a chance of losing them.

It's a thirty-minute walk to the deli. After a month of no activity, my feet are sore when I arrive. I tell myself it'll be worth it.

"You must be the kid from the homeless place. I'm Mr. Ricci."

I blink twice. It's eerie how he resembles my dad. His belly is larger and arms are thicker, but he's the same height with brownish-gray hair. The scowl he wears matches my dad's exactly.

"Come in. I'll show you the store."

I follow him to the back.

"This is where we make sandwiches. You piece together orders, deliver them to the tables or to-go customers. Every sandwich comes with potato salad, pasta salad, or chips." He takes out a small cup of potato salad with a lid on it from the fridge. "You scoop fifty of each in the morning. Fill it up below the top. We don't want it to stick to the lid or overflow."

I stare at him. What have I gotten myself into?

"You got that?"

The smell of stale coffee on his breath makes me gag.

"Yeah."

"So, you can talk." He slams the fridge door. "Sweep three times a shift. Eleven thirty, one thirty, three thirty. Mop after three thirty. Restock the bathrooms at twelve thirty and two. The janitorial supplies are in this closet."

He sizes me up after the tour. "Nice that they gave you clothes. Get a haircut before you come back tomorrow."

"I don't have money." I'm over this jerk. "That's why I'm here."

"You're a smart aleck, huh?"

"Nope, being honest." I do have twenty bucks in my pocket, but no way I'd use it on a haircut for this jerk.

"Figure that out with your people. You need to wear a hairnet. I'm not getting shut down because of you. What's your name? Dennis? Dwayne?"

"Danny." I force a smile.

The other employees are as cheerful as Mr. Ricci. Everyone assumes that because I don't talk much, I'm stupid.

"I can't work with this!" the cashier yells toward the kitchen in the middle of the lunch rush. "This kid's completely ignorant! He can't even answer me!"

I carry the two lunch bags I prepared to the register. Everyone in line stares at me.

"I heard everything you said." I drop them next to her. "I didn't respond because you talk so much, I knew you wouldn't hear."

"Hey, don't talk to my girl that way!" Mr. Ricci says.

I chuckle. "Oh, that's why she's rude."

A couple of customers laugh.

Mr. Ricci is suddenly in my face. "Listen to me, you good-for-nothing drug addict—"

Instead of punching him, I cuss him out. Then I throw my apron and hairnet at him, grab my backpack, and take off.

I half expect him to follow, but he's probably glad to be done with me. I walk the opposite direction of the shelter. I know Ricci will call them. I'll get a lecture from Chad tonight. Really, I don't care. I didn't run away for someone else to tell me what to do.

A grocery store is down the street. A loaf of bread and peanut butter will make perfect meals for today. I'll panhandle for a few hours before I return to the center. If the next job is a strikeout, I'm back on the streets.

"Danny?" Someone calls as I walk from the store.

I turn. A boy, around nine, runs at me. He wraps his arms around me.

"Michael." I recognize him as a student from Mrs. Debbie's class last year. "How are you?"

"People said you left." He steps back when his mom places her hand on his shoulder. "What happened?"

"You're Danny Morton?" The mom stares at my long hair.

"Yeah." I face Michael. "I went away for a while. I'm headed home."

Michael's mom wraps a protective arm around him. A year ago, I helped teach her son. Now she's afraid of me? She pulls out her phone.

"Good to see you, buddy." I hurry into the parking lot. "Take care."

I frantically scan cars I pass. I don't know what I want. Maybe a person nice enough to give me a ride out of this god-forsaken place. Maybe keys in the ignition. That's when I see it. A decal in the back window of a red commuter car. Moody Bible College. Chicago. A city I could get lost in. Even though Anna goes to school there, I'm sure she never leaves the safety of her dorm room.

"Can I help you?" A guy behind me asks. He's in his early twenties, dark-brown curly hair. "This is my car. Did you need something?"

"You go to Moody?" I point to the sticker.

"Yeah, I do," he says.

"In Chicago?"

"Yep. I'm headed back. I went camping with my parents over the long weekend."

"Could I hitch a ride? I was going up there to visit my mom." I glance behind me to find Matthew's mom staring while she's on the phone—

"Absolutely." He opens the trunk. "Wanna throw your stuff in here? Probably be more comfortable. There's not much room in the front."

Matthew's mom starts into the parking lot as I climb in the passenger seat. I quickly buckle up.

"I'm Nate. What's your name?"

"Jo-nah." I'm surprised at the name that comes, but then again, maybe not. Jonah was a runaway.

"Nice to meet you."

"Thanks for the ride." I glance over my shoulder as he backs from the spot. Matthew's mom is on the phone about ten feet away.

"Always happy to help a brother out." His cheerfulness is a little sick. "You're going to see your mother?"

"Yeah. She left my dad years ago." I sink into the seat and breathe easier when we pull out of the parking lot. "Dad's abusive. She said last month if I could make my way to her, she'd let me live with her. I left Georgia four days ago. Have you always lived here?"

---

*LYDIA*

Mom and Dad have been married almost thirty years. He has never taken her out on Valentine's Day. He argues the same meal the day before or the day after is twice as much on the fourteenth, yet he doesn't take her out the day before or the day after. That leaves us cutting vegetables for her Valentine's chicken pot pie.

"Your father loves homemade chicken pot pie," she says that morning when I ask why she's going through the trouble. "I'm honoring him."

*Because he cares so much about honoring you?* is the sarcastic comment that comes to my mind. Danny could get away with saying it. If I say it, I'll hurt her feelings. So instead, I honor her by cutting vegetables.

The pastor calls while we're on carrots. Pastor Raul has called every week since the new year. After her initial greeting, she sets down the knife. Her knuckles go white from gripping the counter. Her face turns pale. I hurry to her side, wrap an arm around her to hold her up.

"At what store?" Her hand is shaking. "Where?"

I lean closer to hear. It has to be about Danny. *God, let us find him. Please.*

"Why didn't she stop him? She could've offered to take him home or buy him a meal and called us."

Tears gather in her eyes. I rub her back as the first slips down her cheek.

"Well, thank you, Pastor." She places her phone on the counter. "Mrs. Jeffreys and her son spotted Danny at a grocery store."

"Let's go." I wipe my hands on the kitchen dish towel and grab my keys from the dish on the counter. "I'll drive."

"In Lafayette."

I shake my head. "Lafayette? That's over an hour away."

"They were visiting family. Her son recognized Danny from Debbie's class."

"Where did he go? Did they follow him?"

"No. He got in a car with a young man. She doesn't know where they went." Mom rubs her forehead.

"Why didn't she stop him?" Someone from our church saw him and didn't do anything?

"She said she was scared. He was skinny and didn't look like himself. He was so close. My baby was so close, and we didn't even know. Now we've lost him again."

Dropping my keys on the counter, I hold Mom. We stand in the kitchen and cry.

*God, why won't You stop this pain? Why won't You bring him home? He was so close. Please, God, please bring him home.*

"God, keep him safe," Mom whispers. "We don't know where he's going, but You do. We pray the person he got in the car with will help him, not harm him. Let him know we love him. We want him home, God. Please somehow bring him home to us."

"Amen." I squeeze her. "I love you, Mom."

"I love you, baby." She kisses the top of my head. "We need to keep praying and believing God will bring him home."

My phone rings. It's Jason.

"Answer it." Mom rubs my back. "It's okay."

"Hi." I walk from the kitchen to the family room.

"You busy today?" Jason asks.

"I don't know." I sit on the couch.

"Let me guess, you're sitting around waiting for Prince Charming to call. Well, wait no longer, Cinderella. Here I am."

I close my eyes as my tears come again.

"Lyd, you okay?" he asks when I don't speak.

"Someone from church called. They spotted Danny at a grocery store in Lafayette."

"That's great. Do you need a ride? If we leave now—

"He took off in a car with someone. They don't know where he was going."

"But we could hang up flyers. Talk to the people. Maybe someone—"

"They're long gone." I wipe my tears.

Mom enters the room, sits by me on the couch, and motions for my phone.

"Hi, Jason," she says. "It's been a hard afternoon, but Lydia needs to get out of the house. It would be great if you picked her up."

"Mom!" I try to grab my phone back.

She sticks out her hand. "Okay. I'll tell her. Thank you." She hands me back my phone. "He'll be here in thirty minutes. Dress casual and warm."

I shake my head. "I don't want to go out."

"Dad will be home later."

"Yeah, and if you say anything about Danny, he'll be mad all night. You know he will. You need someone here with you."

She lays her hand against my cheek. "What I need is to know my daughter is having a good time. Please. This will make me happy."

"I don't want to leave you."

She kisses my cheek. "I'm going to finish the pie, then call your aunt so I can cry with her."

I nod. The only decent thing that has come out of this is that Mom is closer to her older sister. They talk almost every day, sometimes cry, occasionally laugh. *God, thanks for bringing them closer. But please, please bring Danny home.*

For ten minutes I work on my hair. The third braid I try fails. The brown hat with a cross that Danny gave me two years ago catches my eye in the mirror. I pull my hair into a ponytail and put on my hat.

*God, I want things the way they were. I miss my brother. Why would you let someone see him if we couldn't get to him? I'm tired of the hurt.*

No verses come, no reassurance that things will be okay. For two months everything has been upside down. I'm exhausted mentally, physically, and emotionally. What I want to do is crawl into bed so this awful day will end.

A new song comes on my playlist. I recognize it but don't remember the words. Lifting my phone, I read the lyrics as the singer begins. It's in the middle of the first chorus that the words melt my heart.

*Remember the truth—He is deeply in love with you.*

I breathe it in. Regardless of my doubts, in the midst of this mess, God is deeply in love with me. If that's true, He's deeply in love with my brother, my mom, my sisters, and my dad. That's when I tear up again. Though I hate my father for what he's done, God is deeply in love with him.

I don't understand so much right now, but I feel like I need to get this. I think if I can, maybe—maybe things will be different. If God's love can't change things, nothing can.

"Lydia, Jason's here," Mom calls up the stairs.

I brush away the tears as I tie my shoes. Jason doesn't mind that I'm a wreck, but I'm tired of being one. Ozarks sweatshirt in one hand and a box of tissues in the other, I head downstairs.

## CHAPTER 17

### DANNY

Every time the Bible student asks me a question, I fire one back, and he talks for at least twenty minutes. He's so much like Anna I want to tell him to look her up at Moody. Course, I suppose all Bible thumpers are like that. The school is full of them.

"Tell me about your mom," he says when we pass a sign saying twenty-five miles to Chicago.

"She's a strong woman. Put up with my dad's abuse for years. Finally got fed up and left."

"And left you?"

"She wasn't in a place where she could care for me. I get it." I stare out the window at the cars. "She tried for years. He wore her down. Now that she's settled, has a job and a place, she sent for me. She couldn't afford to send me money, but that's okay. I'll get there eventually."

Nate smiles. "In about a half hour. You can text her with my phone." He nods to his phone, the latest and greatest, in the compartment under the radio.

"I want to surprise her." I smile.

"That's cool. Do you know Jesus?"

Here we go. He saved the best for last.

"Sure do. We were buds once."

"Once?" He raises an eyebrow.

"I lived that fairy tale for years. It gets to a point that you've seen enough hypocrites you stop going to church. Enough of your prayers go unanswered that you stop praying. And your father spends enough years abusing you that you don't want to have anything to do with the god he serves."

The Bible guy is speechless—for a few minutes.

"Regardless of how your biological father treats you, your heavenly Father loves you with an everlasting love." Nate glances my way. "If you've attended church, you know that."

"Actions speak louder than words."

"We aren't promised an easy life, but that God's with us."

I chuckle. "Don't need easy, but civil would be good. Like I said, I was buds with Jesus. He proved not to be someone I want to devote my life to."

Now it's Nate's turn to chuckle. "Good thing He didn't feel that way about us sinners, or He never would have gone to the cross."

"But He didn't have a choice, right? That was God's ultimate plan. For Him to die. Kinda sucked for Jesus, don't you think? God forcing all man's sin on Him."

"Jesus chose it. He wrestled with His mortality—"

"In the garden."

"You have gone to church."

"For too many years." I face Nate. "Look, bro, you have your beliefs built on your experiences and I have mine based on the hell I've lived. Judge me all you want, but I'm done with God. And if you judge me, you'll be judged for that."

"Jonah, you are a prophet." He laughs. "I think you need to come to Moody."

"Don't think they take high school dropouts. Or God haters."

"Wouldn't be hard to get your diploma. You seem like a smart and driven guy. You could do school online. Community college to finish up high school faster." A half grin appears on his lips. "I don't think you hate God. You're a prodigal. One day you'll come home."

I open my mouth to argue, then think better of it. I'll let this guy enjoy his fictional reality, even that of my life.

"Would you mind if I borrow your phone?" I ask.

"Go for it."

I search "where do I buy cocaine in Chicago?" A few streets downtown are named. I pick one close to a grocery store and ask Nate to take me there. I don't even have twenty bucks. Maybe in a couple hours I'll make enough for an eight ball.

"You sure I can't take you to your mom's house?" He pulls into the parking lot fifteen minutes later.

"I want to pick up a few things first."

We get out of the car and he opens the trunk.

"Do you need your sleeping bag?" I ask when I see it. Now that I'm finally out of Indiana, I don't want to freeze to death. If this guy is authentic, he should give me the shirt off his back. "I think my mom's in a one bedroom. I might be on the floor."

"It's yours. Do you need another jacket?" He holds up a black hoodie. "It is pretty cold here in the windy city."

"Yeah. Thanks."

He extends his hand to shake mine. When we're done, two twenties are in my palm.

"God bless you, Jonah. I'll be praying for you." He pulls a business card from his wallet and hands it to me. "If you need anything, let me know. Or call when you start at Moody." He pats my shoulder and leaves.

*Nate Fitzgerald*

*Bachelors of Music in Music and Worship*

*Emphases Composition and Performance*

Social media info and a phone number follow. I pocket the forty bucks and card, then head to grab dinner before I connect with a dealer.

I spend an hour in front of the grocery store. I walk people to their cars to unload their groceries. Most give me a couple-dollar tip, but what I'm more interested in is any alcohol I can grab. A bottle of beer from the six-pack of an old man, wine from the mom with three children, who's distracted. That alone is worth the time and energy. I score a bottle of wine and two bottles of beer along with the lunch meat and rolls.

It takes a few hours to find a dealer. A sleazy guy with missing teeth and greasy hair tries to take me for too much. I stand my ground and walk away twice. Toothless Tom comes down enough, even tosses in a few free joints. Drugs might be easier to get in the big city, but they're more expensive. I'm broke again, but well-stocked for a week.

The streets of Indiana reek, yet Chicago is worse. The underpasses are lined with tents. After getting all my crap stolen, I'm done with the other homeless people. It's a clear night. I make my way to the closest park. I'd rather have the smell of pine surround me than the smell of pee.

I kick it beneath a tree with my wine and marijuana. The star filled sky takes me back to the nights in my backyard when I'd smoke out. I didn't realize how much I missed this over the past month. They say you smoke out to lose yourself, but I lost myself before the drugs. My dad's face comes to my mind, hard, demanding in the workouts I despised.

"I hate you." There's a sense of release saying the words aloud. For years I lacked courage to say those three words. If I had it to do over again, I would say them to his face. After all the crap he put me through, he deserves to know he's not the great man everyone, including himself, thinks he is. Maybe now he realizes his family is as screwed up as he is. Of course, he's probably too conceited to care.

I pull up a Pink Floyd video. They remind me of Brett. I chuckle, thinking of how smart he is in math and how dense he is in everything else. Maybe he doesn't care about anything else. Another example of how a father can ruin his son's life.

The night goes on in a haze. I finish my smoke and the entire bottle of wine. The wind picks up, drops the already cold temperature. It's definitely not LA, but it's a new beginning. I'll get there, someday. Tonight, I just need to be.

---

## *LYDIA*

Thankfully, Jason's good with silence in the car. I don't have it in me to be social. That overwhelming feeling from the day Danny left is back, like a weight crushing my chest.

"Don't you want to know where we're going?" he asks when he exits the freeway.

"Where are we going?" I fail to show excitement.

"It's a surprise." He smiles.

I have to chuckle. "Whatever."

"Sorry it's been a hard day." He massages the knots from my shoulder with his right hand. "How was the rest of your weekend?"

"I worked." I close my eyes, relaxing at his touch. "How about yours?"

"Pretty miserable. We played our first pre-season tournament and were destroyed. Danny was right. Rodriguez is an awful pitcher."

I open my eyes at Danny's name. Rodriguez's face from when he walked in our class a few days ago comes to my mind. *God, Danny was so miserable playing baseball. If only Dad hadn't pushed him...*

"The third baseman is still adjusting to shortstop. He'll never be as good as Danny, but he's coming along—" He pauses, looks at the tears rolling down my cheeks. "Sorry, Lyd. I didn't mean to hurt you." He slips his hand back to the steering wheel. "Part of what made it hard was I missed Danny. I had fun with him on the field."

I grab two tissues. The rest of the drive we listen to Christian radio.

When he pulls through the gate of the national park, peace mixed with anxiety comes over me. I love the mountains and the fresh air, yet I'm far from home and Mom needs me.

"Your mom's okay," he says when I check my phone for reception. "I told her where we'd be. She has my number. I have service." He lifts my chin. His eyes remind me I can trust him. His smile tells me he cares. "Grab some Kleenex and let's go."

The path is damp, and the air is crisp. It's warm with the sun on our backs. As we move deeper into the forest, there's less light and heat.

"You didn't tell me to bring gloves." I put my jacket on.

"I did grab your jacket. Gloves were implied." He takes my left hand in his right, lifts it, and breathes warm air on it. "That better?"

*He'd do anything for you.* "It is."

We continue to walk hand in hand. He points out critters in the bushes and trees, I make him pause at the rustle in the bushes.

"It could be a rattlesnake," I say every time, half because that's my biggest fear and half as a joke.

"I'll protect you," is always his response. Then he slips his arm around me.

Thirty minutes later we make it to the top of a hill. A stream down below is barely visible through the thickness of the trees. We sit on a patch of grass. There's so much to take in—the lush green trees, pretty yellow wildflowers, the tiny swallows and blue jays. I close my eyes, inhale the cool, crisp air. The chirps and whistles of the birds quiet my heart.

The song I listened to earlier plays in my mind.

*Remember the truth—He is deeply in love with you.*

I'm taken back to my fifth grade Sunday school class.

"Do you know how much God loves you?" the teacher, Mrs. Danielle, asks. "It says in Luke, 'What is the price of five sparrows—two copper coins? Yet God does not forget a single one of them. And the very hairs on your head are all numbered. So, don't be afraid; you are more valuable to God than a whole flock of sparrows.' You are important to God. Never think He misses anything. He sees all your hurts. He knows all your successes. You mean the world to Him."

*God, thank You for loving me so deeply. Let Danny know how much he means to You. Bring someone into his life to show him his true worth. And be with the rest of my family. May they experience Your love in life-changing ways.*

"I bet when you woke up this morning you didn't think you'd climb a mountain, but you did." Jason wraps his arm around my waist.

I settle against him. His arms feel warm, safe—

"I want you to remember this, Lydia. You're stronger than you think. With the help of God and your friends, you'll rise above every obstacle that comes against you."

"No weapon turned against you will succeed." I say the verse that comes to mind.

"Exactly." Jason brushes his thumb across my cheek. "You're pretty amazing, you know that?"

Instead of the words encouraging me, they pierce me. I raise my face to his.

"That's what I love the most about you. Your heart for God and His Word."

He's great, everything I want in a guy. He's a spiritual leader, sensitive, smart, and so stinking cute. I'm honored that he cares about me.

*God, what's stopping me from loving him?*

His breath is warm as he leans in. I don't know if I want him to kiss me, but I don't want to stop him. Our lips meet naturally, like we were made for each other. For a moment, nothing else matters. Then we part, and I'm still a broken mess with tears in my eyes.

"I'm sorry," I whisper. "I have nothing to give you. I'm…so…broken."

"I don't want anything from you." He wraps those huge, strong arms around me. "Except for you to let me love you."

It's a beautiful thought, but that's not me. I'm not the romantic one; Danny always has been. I'm about equality in a relationship, not needing a man to take care of me. Needing a man has turned my mom into an anxious, unhappy mess. But I give Jason this time, me in his arms, because I know he needs it. It's on the walk down the hill that I bring him back to reality.

"Did you sign with Texas Christian yet?" They offered him both baseball and academic scholarships. Last year he went for a visit, and he loved it. I won't let him give that up for me.

"I'm waiting to hear back from Lindenwood in St. Charles, Missouri. They have a decent team."

I stop. "Don't do this, Jason."

"What?"

"Don't give up your dreams for me. I know you want to go to Texas Christian. You've talked about it for years."

"Have you ever been to Texas? The weather is hot and humid. There are thunderstorms, floods even. Remember that huge one several years ago?"

"Missouri is the same, minus floods. God is calling you to Texas. You said that yourself last year."

He frowns. "Maybe I want to be closer to you. Four hours is a lot better than four states—"

"You need to follow your dreams. I need to follow mine."

"Do you even know what your dreams are anymore?"

"No, but I trust that at some point God will bring them to me." I take a step toward him. "We can write, talk, video chat. If God brings us together again, we know it's meant to be."

He slips his hands in mine. "What if Danny never comes home? You know that's a possibility."

I bite my lip. "I can't see that far. Day by day, remember?"

"Yeah." Jason squeezes my hands. "I won't give up on my dreams if you don't give up on yours."

His words take me back to Danny's fifteenth birthday. He convinced me to go to College of the Ozarks with the same statement. I hate that Danny is gone, but maybe he's headed to LA to achieve his dream. Perhaps one day he will sell his screenplay.

*Lord, if he doesn't come home, at least let him seek his dreams. Help him to leave the drugs behind and pursue the life he's dreamt of.*

I squeeze Jason's hand. "I'll keep living my life as long you continue to live yours. In Texas."

He nods with a sigh. "What do you feel like for dinner? Your pick."

"Chinese." I smile. "Chinese would be perfect."

# CHAPTER 18

## LYDIA

"Hey, how are you?" Robyn approaches me at my locker.

I sigh. "It's been over a month since the person from church saw Danny on Valentine's day. Three months since he left home. We don't have any new leads." I slide my English folder and books in my backpack. "He's my first thought every morning and my last thought at night."

She frowns. "I still think about my brother every night. It's like when the day is over, I miss him the most." We start to walk toward English. "Does he still text you on Mondays?"

"Only *I'm alive*. It's even harder to get that text knowing that if he was ten minutes away, I'd have no idea." I take a deep breath. "The exhaustion I felt a month ago is one hundred times worse."

"That's how the entire first year was for me. What are you doing to take care of you?" Robyn asks. "You do need to take care of you."

"I read my Bible every day. I memorized my top ten scriptures, so I can quote them to myself."

Jason comes up beside us one door from our class. "Hey, Robyn. Hey, Lyd." He squeezes my shoulder as he passes us.

"He's great at checking in on me," I say.

"Good." Robyn smiles. "You need people who understand."

Robyn heads to her seat at the far end of the classroom when we enter. I take my seat in the second row over in front of Jason. We haven't talked about our Valentine's kiss, nor have we kissed again. After-school practice and pre-season tournaments take up his time. I'm happy to see him at school and text at night.

When I'm home, I focus on helping Mom. I make dinner with or for her. She told me several weeks ago she prefers not to leave the house, so I take care of grocery shopping. Most weeks she only gets out on Sunday for church and lunch after. Lunch is the restaurant of Dad's choice. He never asks our opinion.

When Mom's around Dad she shakes constantly—sometimes her knee, her foot, or her hand. A lot of times she silently stares at nothing. That's when I start a conversation to distract her, even if only for a minute.

Toward the end of English, Mrs. Dapper receives a phone call. She hands me an office slip. "Mr. Carter wants to see you, Miss Morton. You can go now."

"Thanks." I shove the paper in my pocket and gather my books.

"What's that about?" Jason asks.

"I have no idea. I haven't seen our guidance counselor since he approved my schedule last spring."

"Maybe it's a grad check. You'd have yours before me." He nods. "I'll text you after practice."

"Mr. Carter?" I stop outside his open door.

"Ah, Lydia Morton. Come in." He motions to the two chairs in front of his desk.

I find it slightly odd that he refers to students with their first and last name. Most teachers use our first names. Mrs. Dapper loves to call us Mr. or Miss. The combination of both first and last in regular conversation outside of the doctor's office is strange. Then again, his long, braided, grayish-white hair and the large cowboy hat prove he's odd.

I set my backpack beside the chair I sit in. "Mrs. Dapper said you wanted to see me."

"Yes." He leans back, hands linked behind his neck. The bookshelf behind him is so packed with books on counseling, psychology, and human behavior I doubt any of them could be removed from the shelf. "Your teachers have communicated concern to me about you. Your academics are stellar, but several commented that you haven't been the same since your brother—well, since he left."

His words take me aback. "I'm not the same since Danny ran away?"

Mr. Carter stares at me, then lifts a yellow pad of paper from his desk. "'Lydia used to be an outgoing student. Since December, she rarely participates in class discussions.'" His eyes scan down the paper. "'Lydia is known for her cheerfulness and fun-loving attitude. Nowadays I am more likely to catch her crying rather than laughing.'" He looks to me. "See what I mean?"

I always thought a counselor's office was a place you could go to find help. Isn't it their job to guide kids showing empathy? Instead I feel a guilty verdict has been passed down on me.

"Do you have any siblings, Mr. Carter?" My heart races as frustration grows.

"I do." He drops the paper on the desk.

"Are they living?"

"Why, yes."

"Do you have contact with them?"

He leans forward. "I don't see how this has anything—"

I lift a hand. "I mean no disrespect. I see your degrees on the wall. I know you've been trained to help others, but if you've never lost a sibling, you can't understand what I'm going through."

"I do." He folds his hands on his desk.

"You've lost a close loved one?" I ask. "A parent? A spouse? A child?"

"Well, no."

I lean forward. "I love my brother deeply. Every day I don't know where he is feels like a nightmare."

"I understand that, Lydia Morton, but you can't stay in this negative place. You need to live in the present."

"The present situation is that my brother is missing, possibly living on the streets. Half the days in January were below freezing. February was better with temperatures in the fifties and sixties, yet nights were in the twenties." I stand. "I'm sorry I don't smile as much and am not the outgoing girl I used to be. I'm doing my best to focus on my schoolwork and not be distracted by thoughts that my brother may die, but some days it's a little overwhelming. Feel free to share that with my teachers."

I walk out the door, suspicious as to which teachers reported me to Mr. Carter. Now I know what I need to do—smile until my face hurts. Never have I wanted to be considered fake, but apparently me being genuine is making people uncomfortable.

On the way home I loop my song about God's love and cry out my frustrations. When I park in the driveway, I dry my face. Mom doesn't need the stress of knowing how I've disappointed my teachers.

"Hi," I greet her with a smile when I enter the kitchen.

"Hi, baby." She pats the chair next to her at the table. "Come sit."

"Is everything okay?" I hurry to her.

"The counselor called today." She takes my hands in hers.

I shake my head. How dare he add more stress on her by calling. "I'm sorry, Mom. Don't worry. It won't be an issue anymore."

"They don't understand," Mom says.

"I'll make sure to smile more..." I pause. "What'd you say?"

She squeezes my hands. "They don't understand."

The tears rise inside me. "No, they don't."

"I've come to the conclusion that we may be broken the rest of our lives, but that's okay." She swallows hard. "It's because we love Danny.

All we can do is pray for his safety and salvation. We need to believe God can save him and bring him back to us."

"What if it's not God's will?" I speak my fear. "I want to believe it is, but the longer it goes I wonder."

She cups my face in her hands. "We pray. Until we find out he's gone to heaven or he comes home. That's what love does. 'Love never gives up, never loses faith, is always hopeful, and endures through every circumstance.'"

I can't stop the tears that began as she quoted 1 Corinthians 13. "I still miss him every day. I think of things to tell him. Sometimes I look for him in the caf during lunch. At night I want to go to his room and talk with him about our days."

Mom wraps her arms around me. "I know, baby. Every night I go to his room and cry. Then I pray for him. We need to pray. Danny needs us to keep praying."

"I will," I whisper.

---

*DANNY*

Chicago is a city known for its bold architecture, fine arts, and street crimes. Sure, some people say they feel safe in the city. But they don't sleep on the streets. They don't wake to sirens three to five times a night. They haven't heard shots fired a few blocks away. They cruise through the museums, attend the plays, and walk through the parks. They also ignore the homeless unless they perform. Yup, the people who make the most money are the street performers. I fail miserably at juggling. I'm great at writing, but can't draw. My attempt at magic includes stealing a guy's wallet. That doesn't go over well. Telling sad stories about my family at the gas stations and grocery stores brings in decent money the first couple weeks. Once my long hair is the length of a girl's and I'm filthy, the handouts slow down. People give me more food than cash. That helps, but since I spend most of my money on drugs, there's no saving to get to the west coast. Each day I'm further from my dream.

Since weekends are the slowest, I make an agreement with the busboy at Francisco's Italian Restaurant off 6th. Friday and Saturday nights, he sets forgotten leftovers in their to-go bags beside the dumpster rather than in it. My cost? One joint a week. It works out great. I do enough coke during the day that I'm not hungry until night.

After nine on Friday I pass by to find clams linguine. I'm on the sidewalk, fork in hand, when Old Man Fred stumbles by.

"Whatcha got there?" His breath reeks more than his BO.

"Pasta with clams." I twirl the linguine.

"Been two days since I've had real food. Stale crackers 'n' hard bread was all I got yes'erday."

I sigh. If I take one bite it'll be more difficult to give up. "Enjoy." I hand him the box and head back to the alley.

There's another package. I tear into it to find a forkful of chocolate cake. It's good but not filling. Now that I've thought about food, I'm hungry. I scale up the dumpster of a breakfast place across the alley. Sometimes at the end of their day, they toss out their donuts, muffins, and other pastries. I reach for the closest trash bag. With any luck they should be on top—

"Hiya."

I let go of the bag then drop to the pavement. The silhouette of a woman, one heel against the wall as she smokes, is at the entry of the alley.

"Looking for something?" Her top is short, her skirt even shorter.

"Yeah." I rub my hands on my jeans. I shouldn't be nervous. Obviously, she's not a cop or a restaurant owner, yet the sultriness of her voice causes me to flounder.

She takes another hit of her joint. "Looking for dinner?"

I push my knotted hair behind my ears. "Maybe."

She saunters toward me. "What's your name?"

"Danny." I'm shocked to hear myself say my own name. But like I said, my mind is in a fog.

The closer she gets, the more I see of her. The jean skirt barely covers her thighs. The red top emphasizes her cleavage. The way her hips sway, there's no doubt she's a prostitute. Which leads me to wonder why in the world she's talking to me.

"You hungry, Danny?"

She's less than a foot away. Her skin is a beautiful shade of brown. Her hair cascades over her shoulders in small braids.

"Getting there. Wasn't the productive day I hoped for." Her perfume makes my heart race until I catch a whiff of myself. I'm totally self-conscious now.

"I got an hour before my next appointment. How about you let me buy you something?" She offers me the last of her joint.

I accept it. "Thanks, I'm good."

I try to walk around her, but she grabs my sleeve. She releases it quickly, probably because it's sticky from some unknown substance.

"I know a place down the street."

"It's okay—"

"I'd like the company." The corners of her mouth lift.

This hot girl wants to have dinner with me? Only someone stupid, or blind, would say no. I motion for her to lead the way. The head of every guy we pass turns. A few whistle, one makes a crude remark. She slows to allow me to catch up to her.

"How long you been on the streets, Danny?"

"Too long." I shrug.

She sizes me up. "How old are you?"

"Eighteen." I stare into her face. Too much makeup, but gorgeous, nevertheless. "How about you?"

A smile spreads across her face. "The same, actually."

No way she's eighteen. She must see the doubt on my face because she chuckles.

"It's the makeup and heels. Do you like tamales? I know a guy who makes the best tamales."

"Never had them." The click of her heels draws my attention to her legs, which pushes my already raging hormones over the edge.

"Never? You don't know what you're missing." She links arms with me. "Where you from?"

"Indiana." Again, why am I compelled to tell her the truth when I've lied for months?

"And what do they eat in Indiana?"

"Anything fried or smothered in a sauce or gravy. Not quite the fine cuisine you find in Chicago."

"You find fine cuisine in dumpsters?"

"Had some great overcooked steak last week alongside some rubbery asparagus. Passed on clams and linguine today to a guy worse off than me."

"Been a while since I had steak. Maybe I need to let you get me dinner." She winks.

This hot girl winked at me. Wow.

"How long have you lived here?" I figure that's a safe question. I don't know her situation and don't want to pry.

"Two years. Came out when I was about your age." Her sly grin makes me chuckle. "Although I guess I was eighteen then, too. Funny how you don't age on the streets. Almost like time stands still."

I ponder that truth as we pass the nightclubs. Swarms of twenty-somethings dressed in trendy styles litter the streets to meet up with others. All are loud and obnoxious. No one gives us a second glance.

"He's always out on the weekends. He makes a bundle off the drunk idiots." She points to the right. "There he is. Carlos!" She waves.

"Kit Kat!" A middle-aged Hispanic guy returns her wave. "How are you?"

I repress my laughter. She's named after a candy bar?

"I'm good." She lets go of my arm to hug Carlos and kiss his cheeks. "I brought my friend Danny to meet you. He's never had tamales."

"Oh, Dios mío!" he exclaims. "Then Danny's are on me tonight."

"No, Carlos, I have money." My candy bar sidekick pulls a wad of cash from her small purse. A serious wad.

"Put that away." He motions to her, then turns to me. "Cheese, chicken, or pork?"

"Chicken?"

Carlos seems satisfied. He pulls two bags from his cooler, hands one to her and one to me. "Green or red?"

Now I assume he means salsas. "Red."

Carlos laughs, takes out two of each color. "She always has green." He places the red in my hand, then faces Kit Kat. "Done for the night?"

"On a break." She accepts the green-filled containers. "It's a busy weekend. Some convention in town."

"Isn't there always?" He smiles again. "Good to see you, Kit Kat. I worry when you don't come around."

"I'll try to do better. Say hi to your family." She stuffs a ten in his tip jar. "There's a bench this way." She nods toward the left and I follow. "I met Carlos my first week out here. Great guy. His wife and daughters cook during the day, and he sells at night."

We settle on the bench. I watch her take one of the tamales from her bag.

"Peel off the husk before you eat it." She demonstrates. "It's pure goodness inside."

I imitate her. This hot, spicy, stringy chicken is snug inside a corn blanket. Absolutely delicious. She's silent while eating. Must be as hungry as I am.

"So, you're named after a candy bar?" When the words escape my lips, I realize how rude they sound. I'm relieved when she laughs.

"Katrina Katherine is my real name. My mom liked both and didn't want to pick one. Most of my friends call me Kat, but when I'm working—"

"You go by Kit Kat." Now I get it. "How long have you been...in this profession?" Since we're on the subject, I figure it's not rude to ask.

"Too long." She shrugs.

I shake my head at her imitation of me. Think I've made a friend.

The rest of the dinner conversation is about our favorites. She asks the questions first, I answer.

"Favorite color?"

"Blue."

"Place?"

"The mountains." I think of hikes with Willow's family. The lush trees and chirping birds are quite the contrast to skyscrapers and sirens.

"Person?"

"My sister, Lydia," I say without pause.

"Painting?"

I think for a minute. "Monet. Water lilies."

She smiles. "Book?"

I purse my lips. "Hunchback of Notre Dame. Or Wuthering Heights."

"Drug?"

"Depends on the day."

Her smile widens. "How about favorite sport?"

I stare blankly at her. The image of myself on the field in my white and blue uniform, ready to be a hero, is in my head. "Don't have one. What about you?"

Her eyes roll up as she thinks. "Purple. The beach. My friend Viv. Sunflowers by van Gogh, Sense and Sensibility, cocaine, and football."

"Football?" I raise an eyebrow.

"Oh yeah. What's not to love about a group of buff guys pushed up against each other while they chase a ball?"

I laugh. For the first time in months, I feel alive. I feel normal. I forget who I am, what I've become. I'm a guy, hanging out with a beautiful girl. It feels amazing.

"Thanks for dinner," I say on the way back to where we met.

"My pleasure. You busy Sunday night? There's this great pizza place in Lincoln Park."

"You don't need to. I do okay—"

"Obviously, or you wouldn't be on the streets still." She examines me. "How long's it been? Four months?"

How did she nail it?

"I like the company." She bites her lip. "It's a nice break to hang out with someone my age."

"I'm only sixteen," I say.

"Close enough." She takes out her phone. "There's a shelter in Lincoln Park. It's not that I'm embarrassed by you, but it's best to shower before you go into a restaurant. And you'd probably feel better. I know I always did. Do you have a phone? I'll text you the address."

I rattle off my number.

"If I remember right, they open at one thirty. They have clothes, toiletries, even free laundry facilities." Her face is down while she types. "There's usually a line. I should be done by four o'clock. Maybe we can meet at four thirty?"

My phone chimes with a new message.

*Great meeting you Danny*, the text reads. *Thanks for a memorable night. See you Sunday. XO Kat*

An address follows. When I look up, she's down the street.

"Thanks again for dinner," I call.

She spins with a wide grin. "Looking forward to Sunday." She blows me a kiss before she climbs in the passenger seat of a silver Lincoln.

## *CHAPTER 19*

*LYDIA*

"I DON'T UNDERSTAND WHY YOU INSIST ON BEING SO WASTEFUL," Dad is saying to Mom when I walk into the kitchen on Sunday morning. She's pouring him a cup of coffee, he's beside her buttering his toast. I hurry to the refrigerator to grab my yogurt and leave.

"What do you mean?" she asks.

"It's stupid of you to make coffee on Sundays. We can get a cup before service at church."

I pause in front of the open refrigerator. Did he really call Mom stupid? His behavior has been getting worse every day, but still, to call her stupid is wrong. Mom and I make an effort not to talk to him, yet he picks fights with us constantly. Yesterday he told me I was wrong about my registration date for college. When I showed him the email, he screamed that I didn't need to be a know-it-all.

"You never want to go early to church to socialize." Mom's wide eyes show she's as shocked as I am.

"That doesn't mean we can't go get coffee. They give it away for free. We can show up ten minutes early to drink a cup before we go in. We don't need to talk to anyone." He glances to me, then my mom. "We tithe. We have the right," he mumbles, carrying his toast and coffee to the table.

Pure insanity. There's less oxygen when he's in the room.

The morning continues to play in my mind during Sunday school. I hate that I'm so distracted that I miss most of the teaching. I want regular church service to be different, but it's crazy how claustrophobic our pew feels though there's only three of us. It's not until after worship that I shift my focus with prayer.

*Speak to me, God. I want to hear from You,* I pray when Pastor tells us to open to Philippians 3.

I start underlining in verse seven.

"I once thought these things were valuable, but now I consider them worthless because of what Christ has done. Yes, everything else is worthless when compared with the infinite value of knowing Christ Jesus my Lord. For his sake I have discarded everything else, counting it all as garbage, so that I could gain Christ and become one with him. I no longer count on my own righteousness through obeying the law; rather, I become righteous through faith in Christ. For God's way of making us right with himself depends on faith."

I circle verse nine, "For God's way of making us right with himself depends on faith."

Before Danny left, my focus was attending church and Bible study. I totally loved God, but I put more time into my friendships than I did my relationship with Him. I'd read the Bible every morning, sometimes only the verse of the day. Now I read God's Word when I wake and before I sleep. Ten minutes quickly turns into twenty without feeling like it. It's the breath in my lungs that gives me energy to keep going. I pray fervently Danny truly knows Christ and surrenders his life to God. I don't want to spend eternity without him.

Dad stares at his phone. I watch long enough to find out he doesn't have his Bible app open. He's checking sports stats. Negative thoughts overcome me.

*No wonder Danny left.*

*You have every right to be mad.*

*He'll destroy you next. He's already destroying your mother.*

Out of the corner of my eye I see Mom twirl the side of her skirt. The paint is chipped from her usually beautiful nails. Long gray hairs grow among her brown ones. The circles under her eyes make me wonder if she sleeps at night.

Pastor reads verse ten.

"I want to know Christ and experience the mighty power that raised him from the dead. I want to suffer with him, sharing in his death, so that one way or another I will experience the resurrection from the dead!"

"Many have a distorted perception that good Christians don't face hard trials. I want to tell you today, that's a lie from the pit of hell."

I lift my eyes from the scripture to the pastor.

"Mountain top experiences encourage our souls. They remind us of the beauty in life. We have a view of all God is doing." Pastor shifts his eyes towards our pew. "But in the valley, we grow. That's where the soil is rich. It's where roots can go deep. Though it's dark and the view is limited, we can thrive." He continues to scan the congregation. "Paul understood that it is in the valley we identify most with Christ because of our hardships. It's through suffering we're reminded of our Savior's suffering. He suffered to experience our pain and comfort us in our time of need. That was the only way He could be an effective high priest."

I take Mom's hand. She brushes away a tear.

"Christ didn't only suffer; He rose from the dead to give us power over sin, death, and every trial. Your circumstances don't define you—Christ's victory over death does. I know your troubles can feel overwhelming. Sometimes they seem impossible. It's your job, Christian, to align yourself with the Lord. Fix your eyes on Him. You are saved by faith. No amount of work can make God love you more, just as no sin will make God love you less. Pursue a right relationship with Him in every season. By sharing in His suffering, one day you will share in His glory. Let's pray."

*God, help me to keep my eyes on You,* I silently pray. *Thank You that this suffering will somehow, in Your time, lead to glory.*

Dad chooses the wings place for lunch for the second week in a row. I'm frustrated, but I pray for him as I follow them in my own car. I pray that in this dark valley God will grow my dad's faith like never before.

"I believe, Lord," I repeat over and over. "You can do it."

I think of safe topics to talk about on the way into the restaurant. When none come to mind, I pray, "God, please give us a peaceful lunch."

"The wait is fifteen minutes," the hostess tells us. "Did you want to put your name in for a table?"

"The burger place didn't look crowded," Mom says. "Maybe we should—"

"Yes," Dad tells the hostess. "Morton is the name."

Mom moves against the wall next to the benches filled with people waiting. Dad looks past the hostess. "I see Fred Tiller." He points to a man across the restaurant. "I'm going to say hi."

I join Mom and we wait there until they call our name. Dad waves to us when the waitress finally seats us yet doesn't come to our table for several more minutes.

"That was Fred. His son, Ricky, played on my minor team years ago. The boys were ten." He carries the conversation until the food comes, all about baseball minors. I'm amazed that he manages not to speak Danny's name the entire time.

"Did you tell Fred what's going on now?" Mom stares into her salad, pushing the lettuce from one side of the bowl to the other.

Dad works through the last of the wings in his basket, buffalo sauce all over his hands and face. "We just talked about the good ol' days."

I stir more ranch into my salad. *God, please, there's got to be something else we can talk about.* I take a deep breath. "Prom tickets went on sale last week."

Mom turns to me with a smile. "They did?"

"A couple guys from work are purchasing baseball season tickets." Dad licks his fingers. "I told them to count me in."

Season tickets? Four years ago, Dad bought them for himself and Danny. He complained they were overpriced and would never do it again.

"Really?" Mom looks to him.

"I told them I'd prefer the Sunday games. We'll share two tickets among the four of us. It'd be twice a month at most."

"Did you hear any part of the sermon today?"

Mom's bluntness shocks me. She never talks to Dad this way.

"Of course. It was about trials. Being like Christ."

"You always said they were too expensive." She folds her arms across her chest.

"For two. With it only being a fourth—"

"You'll do what you want. Obviously, you don't need my permission." Mom shifts her attention to me. "Today is a good day to go shopping for your Easter dress." She rubs her thumbs over her nails. "We could get manicures too. I've needed one for a long time."

Dad starts to open his mouth, then takes a drink of his soda.

Mom is silent on the way to the mall. I pray that God will comfort her. I'm frustrated and he's only my father. I can't imagine how my mom feels. It's not until I park that she speaks.

"I'm sorry your father is so selfish."

I turn off my car. "Me too."

"A shift occurred in him about five years ago. The year before Mary went to college. I thought it was stress. I thought once Mary got into college and he saw we could afford it; things would get better. They obviously didn't. You and Danny have gotten the worst of it."

"No, Mom, you've gotten the worst of it. I'm sorry for what you've had to endure."

"We said 'til death do us part..." Her voice fades. She shifts her eyes down to her hands twisting her skirt around her finger.

I want to tell her no one should have to put up with constant criticism. Yet I don't know how to say it. She's my mother and she loves him—even though he has become the man he is.

"I pray for Danny to come home every night, but only if it would be good for him. The way it is now, I'm afraid—" She stares out the window. "I want him alive and well more than at home."

The question of whether home is an okay place for Danny crosses my mind often. I don't think he'd survive with the way Dad is.

"I pray for his salvation," she says. "For him to quit drugs and alcohol. For him to follow God's call on his life." Half her mouth rises in a smile. "I want to believe he's in California, enjoying nice weather." She faces me. "His play—was it good?"

"It was." I smile. "God gave him a talent for writing."

"He'll be okay." She wipes her eyes. "He's better off not being here."

---

*DANNY*

A line about ten people long is outside the center when I show up at one o'clock. Good thing I came early. I don't want to be late for our date.

Date.

My pulse quickens at the thought. Her face comes to mind. I smile. She's gorgeous, despite the makeup and revealing clothes. Something about her personality, the way she looks at me. It took me forever to fall asleep last night. I thought of her, our conversations Friday, the meal we shared. And now I get to do it again. Maybe my luck is about to change.

At check-in, a lady with a gray bun and a schoolteacher-type dress hands me a hotel-thin white towel, small bar of soap, and shampoo along with a number.

"The wait is about a half hour," she says. "Feel free to visit the clothing department. Toiletries and vitamins are also available in the south center as well as laundry."

I head in the direct she points. I find a large room full of racks. A sign by the door reads *On your first visit you may choose two outfits. Only one every visit after, please.*

Racks fill the room. Men's, women's, and kids' clothes. It's like a clothing store.

I guesstimate my size since I've lost weight. I never thought I'd fit size small shirts, but since I've lost most of my muscle I probably do. It feels like Christmas walking away with two pairs of jeans, a blue t-shirt with a faded logo, a flannel shirt, a pair of black tennis shoes, and two pairs of socks. Why did I ever complain about getting socks?

My fifteen minutes in the tiny cubicle of a shower are glorious. Seriously, I never thought I'd miss a shower until six weeks without one. I scrub my hair and body, watch the dirt wash down the drain. My new used clothes fit. I feel, and smell, like a new person.

While my laundry is washing, I head to a different room to fill my backpack with toiletries I once took for granted.

"How are you?" a man with a brown, bushy beard asks.

"Good." I nod. "Thanks for all this."

"Anything else you need?" He reaches under the table for a bottle of water. "Water?"

"Sure. Do you guys have books?" I've reread the two I have several times.

"Out that door." He points to my left. "The library is down the hall on the right."

It's four o'clock when I exit the shelter. New and clean clothes are in my backpack, Moby Dick in my hand. I've heard about it but never read it. Now is the perfect time to start. An empty bench under a tree across the street calls me over to lose myself in the fictional world.

"You look good all cleaned up. Shaved and everything."

I raise my eyes at the sound of Kat's voice and smile at what I see. Tight jeans, purple t-shirt, black zip-up sweatshirt. No eye makeup or lipstick. She's a sharp contrast from the night before. Her hair is not in braids but curls that frame her face. I wouldn't believe she's eighteen if she hadn't told me.

"You do too." I stand.

"No work clothes. I'm done for a few days." She nods at Moby Dick. "You found the library?"

"I did. Not a great selection, but I haven't read this one yet."

"Me either. Dropped out before they made me." She heads down the street. I follow. "Maybe you can catch me up during dinner. We can read together after. If you aren't busy."

"I had plans." I grin. "But that sounds better."

She glances at my shirt, then hers. "We're wearing our favorite colors."

I chuckle. "We are."

Next she runs her fingers through my hair. "You have great hair when it's clean."

"Doesn't smell quite as bad, either."

"That's for sure. Is pizza good?"

"Sounds delicious."

She asks about the center, the names of people who helped me.

"I went my first year in Chicago. Still go back sometimes to see the doctors." She shifts her gaze down. "They can prescribe medications when I get infections. It doesn't happen often, but when it does, they're cool about it."

"Where do you live now?"

"I share an apartment with some of the girls." She raises her face, still doesn't look at me. "There's five of us right now."

"How big is it?"

"Two bedrooms."

"Wow. Kinda crowded, huh?"

"It's a dump in the worst area. I had to step over a dead body at two a.m. to get to our apartment. Luckily the cops let me pass. It's awful when I work all night and they make me wait until the scene is clear. I guess it's a place to shower and hang up my clothes. I don't get much sleep because the walls are paper thin. How'd you sleep last night?"

"Not bad." The sleep I got was good. The rest of the time I thought of her.

The mom-and-pop pizza place is on the edge of a neighborhood. The aroma of garlic and tomato sauce greets us when we open the door. Tables are decorated with red-and-white checkered cloths. Candles in small chianti bottles flicker. I'm surprised the restaurant is only half full on a Sunday night.

A restaurant. I'm in a real restaurant. It's only been four months, but it seems like forever.

Opening the menu reminds me why I eat peanut butter and dig through dumpsters.

"I usually get the meat lover's pizza with Caesar salad. We could share."

I close my menu. "Perfect."

"And garlic bread. I love their garlic bread." She shuts her menu. "Thanks for meeting me. I tend to eat dinner alone. It's good to have the company."

"I feel bad with you paying. I mean, I could have picked up the tab at the shelter. They had some funky smelling chicken tonight."

"I remember their chicken. It tastes funky too."

The waitress returns with water and a plastic basket of French bread. Kat orders a glass of wine with the food. When the waitress asks for ID, she slips one out of her wallet.

"Tonight, I feel twenty-one," she says once the waitress is out of earshot. "That's one benefit of the job. Along with clothes, money, and free rent."

"Did you work today?" There's no reason to avoid the topic if she wants to talk about it.

"I had two jobs. Shaun knew I was out until two a.m. Now I'm free until Wednesday night." The waitress places the garlic bread and salad between us. "If you aren't busy—"

"We could read Moby Dick?"

Her eyes shine along with her smile. "You read my mind."

Deep dish pizza is my new favorite. Sausage, pepperoni, and Canadian bacon—it's more meat than I've had this month. I also polish off half of the large Caesar salad. I never thought I'd crave salad, but months without fresh produce can do that. She has two pieces of the garlic bread. I devour the rest. Kat grins the entire time I'm stuffing my face. Yup, she understands what it means to be homeless.

I tell her about the first several chapters of Moby Dick. Then she talks about Elinor and Edward in Sense and Sensibility like they're old friends.

"How many times have you read it?"

"Stopped counting." She sips her second glass of wine. "I was twelve the first time my grandma read it to me. She read aloud to me almost every night. Books she had when she was a kid. We started with Little House books before I even went to school, then Anne of Green Gables. We even read Nancy Drew mysteries for a while."

"Did you like mysteries?"

"No." Her ringlets bounce when she shakes her head. "I'm not a patient person. I always needed to know who did it. 'You gotta wait for the story to unfold, baby girl,' she'd tell me. 'Appreciate each chapter and the new revolution it brings.' But I couldn't. When Grams was out of the room, I'd flip to the end."

I can't help but laugh. "I don't like mysteries either." I crunch ice from my drink. Another thing you don't realize you miss until you don't have it. "I like to watch the story unfold, figure out what the author is doing. Most of the time there aren't enough clues to figure it out until the very end. By then I've guessed wrong at least five times."

"Right?" She glances at the bill, then drops three twenties on the tray. "Finally, someone who understands me."

I can tell this is going to turn into a great relationship.

# CHAPTER 20

## DANNY

"White or red?" she asks as we wander through the wine aisle at a liquor store three blocks from the restaurant.

"Either is fine."

"Do you like wine?"

I think of the first time I tried it, how bitter it seemed. Now I can down a whole bottle regardless of the type. "I'll drink anything."

A bottle of red, a bottle of water, a corkscrew, and two cups later we're headed down the street towards the park.

"Grams loved red wine and chocolate. She gave me my first sip at thirteen to kill my curiosity. Think she worried when I asked for more."

I chuckle. "She sounds like a great woman."

"She was. Her mama was an elementary school teacher. Grams didn't love little kids but got her degree for junior high. Her first job was at Grover Junior High. Fell in love with the principal." Kat links arms with me. "At the end of the school year they married. She never worked again. She talked about that year, the students, all the time. Think it was the best year of her life."

"Why didn't she keep teaching? Did they have kids right away?"

Kat shakes her head. "Not 'til she was thirty. Then it was only my mom." The corners of her mouth shift down. "He was controlling. Told her what she was allowed to do, who she could be friends with. That's why my mom ran at fifteen."

She drops her gaze. I can't tell if she's ashamed or sad. And I can't stand the thought of either.

"That's why I ran," I say. "My dad wouldn't let me make any decisions." Her eyes make their way to my face. "I told him I was done with baseball at twelve. He said I didn't know what I wanted. I told him in August I wanted to take drama, not be on the team. He refused. Even told me what college I'd go to. That's when I realized I'd never get to California if I stayed. My dreams were more important than being a part of the family."

"My grandpa told me I'd be a lawyer when I grew up. He always said what we need is strong black women in leadership. Said I should be a lawyer, then district attorney, and one day president. Wanted me to go to Stanford."

"What happened?"

"Grams died of a stroke. It was a month before my fifteenth birthday. She was fine one minute, then suddenly..." She rubs her eyes. "He went through a bad depression. Started to drink. My mom came home for the funeral. He told me I had to go with her. I don't think he knew Mom was using again. Or if he did, he didn't care."

"I'd been using nine months. They had no idea until that last day."

"What'd you start with?"

"Pain pills after a baseball injury. Then marijuana. Added coke a few months later."

We walk in silence. The reds, oranges, and yellows mix across the sky as we enter the park. Her hand slips down my arm into my hand. It's beautiful, more beautiful than anything I've ever experienced. I not only see the beauty but feel it surround me, build up in my heart. I've spent my entire life around people who act like they have it together, yet I've felt broken. To hear her admit her brokenness and come to terms with my own, I feel whole.

"Isn't it beautiful?" She pauses under a great oak tree.

I shift my gaze from the sky to her perfect face. "Pretty impressive."

"With a view like that you can't help but believe in God."

Her statement takes me by surprise. I don't know why. It's not like a person in her profession can't believe in God. Some of Jesus' best friends were prostitutes. But it seems an odd statement to make here, tonight. I drop my sleeping bag to the ground.

"Wanna sit here? Read a while?"

She opens the wine and hands me a Styrofoam cup. I lean against the tree with Moby Dick. My heart races as she leans against my chest. Then there's the extra pressure to not spill my wine on her while I turn the pages.

"I can turn the pages, if you want," she says after a while.

"That would be great."

I read until the colors in the sky fade to black. She pours us each a second glass. Her hair is soft and smells like lilies. I caress her arm with the back of my hand. Her entire body relaxes against me. We stare at the stars, and for the first time in a long time, all's right with my world.

"If I could live anywhere, I'd live away from the city," she whispers. "Somewhere that the only view at night is stars."

"We camped when I was a kid." I run my hand over her hair. "The view was always spectacular. Didn't appreciate it as much though."

"We never appreciate what we have until it's gone. I feel that way about Grams. She was always there and then one day, she was gone." Her hand slides over my chest. "I try to be thankful for what I have now. I remember how hard it was on the streets. That's why I'm glad you had dinner with me. It's nice to share it with someone who appreciates it."

"I don't want you to think I'm taking advantage of you."

"I get taken advantage of every day. The money isn't enough for what they do to me." She leans back to gaze at my face. "You make me laugh. I feel like me again. Before everything got crazy and I ended up on the streets. Is that weird?"

"Nah. I get it."

We share stories the rest of the night. We don't ask each other questions about who's who or when things happened. We just let one another talk. I can be transparent with her. What matters is I'm with her. Truly the best night of my life.

"Did you tell me how many siblings you have?" she asks.

"Three sisters."

"And you're—"

"The youngest."

She pulls a joint from her purse.

"First there's Mary, super intellectual. Anna's super spiritual, and Lydia is the super sweet one."

I watch while she lights up, inhales. She closes her eyes and holds it in. Once she exhales, she opens her eyes and passes it to me.

That's when I go silent. I thought we'd be different, escape this life. Reality sinks in. Drugs are my escape.

"And there's Danny, the rebel." She winks as I take the joint. "First time you smoked out?"

I inhale, remembering the night. The cheers when I nailed it. "April last year. I was fifteen."

"With?"

"Brett." I pass it back to her. "A stoner who had a locker next to me. He bugged me for a year to party with him. I finally gave in."

"Why?"

"I lost the game to get us into the state finals. My dad was such a jerk about it I decided I was done with the way he treated me. Nothing I ever did was good enough."

Kat eyes me while she takes another drag. "You were a good boy before that, weren't you?"

"Drank at baseball parties. And my girlfriend's house."

A sly grin creeps over her lips. "Bet the girls loved you."

"Nah." I take it back from her. "Baseball was my life, even though I didn't want it to be."

"And when did coke come in?"

"One of my dad's employees—"

She chokes. "You bought from someone who worked for your dad?" Hysterical laughter follows. "Bad boy Danny."

"Grant hooked me up with his dealer."

"Wow." She hands me the joint and lies facing me. "Let me guess the end. Your parents tried to put you in rehab and you ran."

"You got it." Like that, it's out. My entire life story while smoking one joint.

"Did you love her? Your girlfriend? What was her name?"

"Willow."

"Like the tree?"

"Yup." I lie beside her. "Not really. She was cute. Appreciated my sense of humor. I think the appeal was she was against everything my parents were for. And she helped me in math."

"What position did you play? In baseball?"

"Shortstop."

"Ah. Where's that?"

"Between second and third base."

"Did you like it?"

My first instinct is to answer no, but I pause. "I loved it until I was twelve. Loved playing it and loved going to major league games. Last year I liked the games when we worked as a team. There was this one game we were on fire. Made a triple play in the fifth." My adrenaline races at the thought. "It was the beginning of freshman season. I have a video." I open my YouTube app.

"You're on YouTube?" Kat moves closer to me.

"Dad had me start a channel for recruiters. I was on the fast track to success." There are close to thirty videos on my page, yet I go straight to it—home game against the Patriots. "My dad thought he'd guarantee me a spot in the big leagues."

Kat leans her head on my shoulder. I push play. The batter is up, Logan winds for the pitch. *Click.* A high line drive. I run back with a leap. I feel the stretch in my arm, remember my reach. I thought it was beyond me but *BAM!* In my glove. I toss it to third, he sails it to second.

"Easy as one, two, three."

"Wow." Kat takes my phone to bring it closer to her face. "That's you?" I hug the second baseman and wave my glove in the air.

"Yup." It was all about me. I thought I was the best. Maybe I was, but that was a long time ago.

"Man, you were cut." She smiles.

"Worked out six days a week, several hours a day. Told you. It was my life."

She returns to my home screen, scrolls through dozens of baseball clips of my own personal highlights. Views are in the thousands, higher than before I ran. That used to be important to me.

"Who's this?" Kat clicks on a video that brings up Lydia. Lydia, sitting on the sofa in our family room. Her blonde hair is in a ponytail, her eyes red. She's wearing a sweatshirt and jeans.

"My youngest sister, Lydia." I look at the date. December 18. Three days after I ran.

"She's cute." Kat presses play before I can object.

"Hi everyone, I'm Lydia, Danny Morton's youngest sister. I'm making this video to let you know, well, Danny left home. He ran away December 15. We believe he's on the streets in Indiana." She bites her lip as it begins to quiver, then holds up her phone. There's a picture of me from my sixteenth birthday dinner. "This is his most recent picture. If you have any information about where he is, please contact us. We appreciate your prayers for God's protection over Danny and for his safe return." She sets her phone on the coffee table, leans forward, and stares straight into the camera. "Danny, we're sorry for pushing you and not being there for you. We love you. We want you to come home." A tear rolls down her cheek. "Please. Come home."

Lydia's cell number appears at the end of the video along with my name and physical description.

Kat's eyes widen. "You need to go home. They want you back."

"Never." I grab my phone from her hands. "I'm never going back."

Her eyebrows shift down. "They love you."

"I can't live the life I want if I go back."

"A life of drugs? That's not worth it. I'd leave it in a second for the love of my family."

"Baseball was my dad's passion. He made it my life." I drop my phone on the grass. "I couldn't be my own person. I had to be who he wanted me to be."

"Who do you want to be?"

"An author. A playwright."

"Really?"

I unzip my backpack to show her my notebooks. "I've learned the elements of a story, the formula of a successful screenplay. I want to write authentic stories that'll make people consider their values, actions, and beliefs. It's time our generation became their own people rather than allow previous generations to spoon feed us their garbage." I drop my notebooks beside me. "I'm not going back. If I do, I sacrifice myself and all I am."

She's inches from my face, close enough I smell wine on her breath. "Are you writing a love story?"

I laugh, not sure if it's at her seriousness or the question. "It might be. Now that I've told you my life story, it's your turn to tell me yours."

"Mom took me to live with her before I turned fifteen. She worked as a waitress to make the rent, pay for her habit. I was fifteen when her dealer boyfriend moved in. I decided I'd rather get paid to have sex with middle aged men than do it for free, so I left home at sixteen."

My stomach turns.

"She knew what he was doing when I ended up pregnant. Took me to have an abortion and then put me on birth control. I hoped he'd grow a conscience. Six weeks later he sneaked into my room at night again. I hitchhiked from Nevada. I freelanced for a while, then decided the protection of a pimp was worth it." She picks up her empty Styrofoam cup with a sigh. "I've been with Shaun two years. He knows my habits and keeps me supplied. Got me a fake ID last year. Now I can hang out at bars with his affluent clients. I want to move out of the apartment, but he says I'd have to pay my own rent. Don't think I'm ready for that." She takes a deep breath. "There you go. Now you know my story."

"Sorry for pushing."

"I pushed first." Kat slips her hand into mine and closes her eyes. "This is a good place to spend the night, don't you think?"

"You don't want to go home? To your own bed? I'll walk you."

"It's quiet and comfy." She rests her head on my shoulder. "I'd rather stay with you."

I grab my now clean sweatshirt to lay over her, then my jacket for myself. "It still gets cold at night. Sometimes in the 30s."

She nestles her face into the hood. "You washed it."

"Yeah. It doesn't smell like garbage."

"Even when you smell like garbage, you're not repulsive." She yawns. "Goodnight, Danny. Thanks for hanging out with me."

"My pleasure." I replay every moment of the night in my head until I drift off to sleep.

---

## *LYDIA*

"The problem with zombie movies is the humans act like they don't have a brain either."

I laugh at Jason's comment. "Oh, is that the problem?" Balancing my phone between my ear and shoulder, I grab a handful of popcorn to munch on while we talk.

"Yeah. I mean, check this guy out," he says as a human character races toward a run-down hospital. "He heard the news report that the zombies took over the downtown hospital. Why would he be going there if he had a brain?"

"Maybe he's in shock from witnessing the zombies eat his best friend's brain."

"Which is another problem with zombie movies." Jason is chewing, probably his favorite movie candy, licorice. "They're full of inconsistencies. You know, in the first pop-culture zombie movie they actually ate flesh, not brains?"

"You do know they aren't real, don't you?" I pick the chocolate candies out of my popcorn. Danny used to make fun of me for dumping them in since I eat them separately.

"I do. But I forgot, why aren't we watching this together in person? It's a lot more fun than on the phone."

"Because it was a super long day. I wanted to get on my jammies and crawl into bed. You wanted to watch a zombie movie, so we compromised." I stretch, set my popcorn bowl on my nightstand and laptop on the other side of my bed. Lying down, I roll on my side to face it.

"Was your dad a jerk today?" Jason asks.

"Yeah. I think Mom is starting to realize it."

"Is that good or bad?"

"I really don't know." I turn my face from the zombies attacking the poor idiotic guy. "Did you know your parents were going to get a divorce?"

"Looking back, I should have...OOOHHH!" Jason screams, causing me to glance to the screen in time to see blood splatter everywhere. "Sorry, I'm turning it off."

"No, it's fine," I say.

"We both know it's going to end with the building exploding and zombie parts going everywhere."

"It is?" I laugh.

"Of course." Jason yawns. "Now I realize my parents couldn't have made it. They fought all the time."

Closing my laptop, I move it under my bowl on my nightstand. "My parents don't fight because she never says anything. Even when he said he was purchasing season tickets with some employees for Sundays."

"Seriously?"

"Yeah. I don't want to hate him, Jason, but he keeps making it harder and harder."

"I hated my dad for years."

"What changed?" I switch my light off and pull my blankets over me.

"I started doing discipleship with my youth pastor. He challenged me to pray for Dad every day. At first praying for him made me mad."

"That's how I feel sometimes." It's a relief to be able to admit it to someone who understands.

"I started by praying God would show him how awful he was," Jason says.

Chills come over me. Those exact words came from me last week.

"Then after a while I prayed I wouldn't hate him."

"I've said that, too."

"It took several months before I could pray that we'd get along." Jason sighs. "It wasn't easy and didn't happen overnight, but now we have fun together. Except when his twenty-five year-old girlfriend is around. Then I just feel awkward. Guess I need to pray for her."

I chuckle. "Maybe you can pray for my dad, too."

"I can. I will right now if you want."

"Are you sure? I mean, the zombie building is going to blow any minute."

"Is it really?" Jason pauses, then laughs. "You totally made me look. Let's pray."

He says all the words I know I should but find hard to vocalize. He prays for my father's heart to be softened, and then he lifts up my parents' marriage and my relationship with my dad.

The past four months have been a rollercoaster of emotions. Tonight is overflowing with peace and hope. A renewed faith builds within me that our family can be whole. It may take a miracle to change my father, but God is into miracles.

# CHAPTER 21

## DANNY

I WAKE AT SUNRISE, KAT IN MY ARMS. DURING THE NIGHT SHE was shivering. I pulled her closer to wrap the sleeping bag over her.

"Thank you," she whispered.

I stare at her now, peacefully at sleep. My heart races to be close to her. The past forty-eight hours have been like a dream.

*God, I don't want this to end.*

I pause. Did I pray? I close my eyes. Did I really ruin this by praying?

"Good morning." Kat nestles her hair under my chin.

"Good morning." I run my hand down her hair, which is now twice as big as last night. "You stay warm enough?"

"Mmmm. Once I snuggled up to you." She leans back with a yawn, quickly snapping her mouth shut. "Sorry. I have raunchy morning breath."

I laugh. "Can't smell it. I promise."

"That's good. I can taste it." She sits up with a stretch. "What d'you say we find a bathroom and breakfast?"

"Sure."

Fifteen minutes later our teeth are brushed and we're in a warm cafe, phones charging. I grab our order when they call out the name of my now favorite candy bar.

"Say it's your birthday." Kat glances from her phone. She leans forward.

"It's not my birthday." I place the bacon breakfast sandwich and cinnamon dolce latte in front of her. "My birthday's in—"

"Pretend." She holds up a hand. "Say it's your birthday."

"It's my birthday," I say.

"I knew it." She taps on her phone a few times before she pulls out a credit card. "I have the perfect birthday gift for you."

I take a bite of my bagel sandwich. "My birthday isn't for another eight months."

She enters the number from her card. "Today is your birthday."

We spend the day walking around, hanging out, and talking. Sometime around five p.m., she casually pulls up GPS on her phone and keeps the conversation going in an effort to distract me.

I know we're close not only because the sea of people thickens but because as the stadium comes into view, the number of blue caps with Red Cs increases. The coolest part? She's oblivious that I know her surprise. I also love that when we turn the corner, she skips like she's a little kid.

"This is it." Kat throws her hands up in a "ta-da" motion once the "Wrigley Field, Home of the Chicago Cubs" sign comes into view.

"Wow! We're going to a baseball game?" I ask with the same amount of excitement she shows. "I never would have guessed."

She slaps my chest. "You've known for miles. I'm not a fool." She grabs my hand. "Are you a little excited? I mean, you said you used to love going to games."

"Very. The last time I saw the Cubs I was eight."

"I've never been to see the Cubs. I thought it would be fun. Since today's your birthday, we're doing it right. I couldn't get field seats, but terrace isn't too bad, is it?"

My heart sinks when I think of the money she spent. Dad complained about how expensive tickets were every time we went. "That's great. You didn't have to—"

"It's your birthday." Her eyes widen. "Of course, I did. I'll even get you hot dogs, beer, peanuts, the works."

"That's thoughtful, but I don't have an ID like you do."

"You don't need one. Act like you know what you're doing. No one checks. Besides, if they do, I'll distract them." She pulls me into the nearest line to get our bags checked.

First stop is the merchandise store. Shirts and caps for both of us and a sweatshirt for her.

"I'm not going home tonight either." She grabs a blanket on the way to the register. "I need some things to keep warm."

She must like me. I mean, people don't drop several hundred bucks and spend the night on the street for someone they don't like, right?

We exit the bathrooms with our new shirts on about the same time. The small men's fits me fine. Hers is tight in all the right places.

"What d'ya think?" She twirls. A group of guys pause to whistle.

"Looks better than mine."

Yeah, she's completely out of my league.

The last time I went to a Cubs game with my dad, everything was exciting. The songs, the fans, and, of course, the game. Now my favorite part is to watch her. She shouts at the umpire along with the rest of the crowd and is one of the first on her feet when it's time to sing.

My eyes drift to the shortstop each play. I critique his moves, watch his precision, and wonder, *could I have done it? Could I have done what my father failed at? Could I have had a career in the big leagues*? Pride rises, realizing I could have. I was better than him. But that's in the past. I'm never going back.

"Wish you were on the field instead of up here?"

I gaze into her face. Unfortunately, she put makeup on in the bathroom, so her true beauty is hidden. "Nah. The view is better from up here."

"Were you good enough to make it?" She throws a handful of popcorn in her mouth.

"Probably."

"You really wouldn't consider going back? If you were that good, wouldn't it be worth it? Think of all the money these guys make. Millions!"

"I'd hate myself for it." I sit back in my seat. "Being home was miserable. Being on the streets is hard, but I'm free. I'm content 'cause I'm who I want to be."

"What's that like?" She laughs. "Because I have no idea."

"You could get out." I grab some popcorn.

"And be homeless again?" The left corner of her mouth rises. "No, I can't. Hanging with you is fun, but I like money."

"You could do something else. Get a different job—"

"Shaun would kill me. Literally hunt me down and kill me. Besides, if I did, we couldn't do fun stuff like this on your birthday." She lifts her beer cup. "Cheers."

I clink mine against hers. "Cheers."

"Oh, we need a picture." She pulls her phone from her pocket.

"No, we don't."

"Yes." She holds her camera high and leans against me. "It's your birthday!"

I laugh as she snaps the pic.

The third baseman is up to bat. He has the highest batting average on the team. Two guys are on base, first and third. I lean forward. The second pitch is fast and low. The bat meets it with a click. It sails over the wall. I jump to my feet with the rest of the crowd. When Kat doesn't rise, I turn toward her. Wiping her nose, she holds up a small glass container of white powder. The metal top of the container has a small scoop at the end.

"You're determined to make this my best birthday, aren't you?" I slide into my seat and take the cocaine from her.

"Stick with me, kid." She runs her fingers through the back of my hair that sticks out from my cap. "I'll take good care of you."

After my hit I lean back to enjoy.

She chuckles. "It's meant to excite you, not relax you. Has it been that long?"

"I wanna enjoy it." I gaze at her, hat over her puffy hair, her V-neck that shows more than I should see. "Taking it all in."

"It is a lot to take in." She scans the stadium. At the click of the bat, everyone is on their feet again. Kat tugs my hand. I spring up to cheer with her.

I've been to several games over the years, but this is the best. Not because of the drugs, alcohol, or even the action on the field. It's the best because I'm with her.

We're exiting the stadium with the mob when she starts texting. She links with me. I guide her through the crowd. I kinda want to know who she's texting about what. Then again, it's probably best if I don't know anything about her business.

"You had a great time?" She pockets her phone a couple minutes later.

"The best." I tug on the bill of her hat. "Thanks. For everything."

Her hand takes mine. "I never had any siblings. I always thought it would be neat to have someone to hang out with who didn't judge you because they came from the same messed-up family." She laughs. "You know?"

"Yeah," I say, but my only sibling who fits that description is Lyd. Although, I doubt she'd ever understand the drinking and drugs.

"I feel like you could be my little brother. I mean, we come from different families, but they're equally messed up."

"True." I straighten our arms to compare my pale skin to her dark skin. "We totally resemble each other."

She laughs. "I love hanging with you. You're funny and witty. I feel—safe." She squeezes my hand. "Will you be my honorary brother?"

Brother. Not boyfriend. Though it's not what I want, it'll keep her in my life. I've only known her four days, yet I can't imagine life without her.

"Yeah." I squeeze her hand back.

The winds kick up when we break from the crowd at the street corner.

"Let's ride the L." She tugs on my arm. "You can read me Moby Dick, and we can people watch. It'll be warmer than the park. Then I know this row of shops downtown on the outskirts that are pretty clean. Might be warmer to sleep there. The cops only patrol at eleven p.m. We can head down after that."

"Sure."

Another night together. I'll take it, even as her brother.

---

*LYDIA*

"I went online to check your grades," is Dad's greeting Monday morning when I enter the kitchen.

"You what?" I'm surprised he knows how to do such a thing, until I remember he checked Danny's frequently to make sure he remained eligible for baseball.

"You have an eighty-two percent in Precalculus. That's awfully close to a C."

"It's honors." I grab a yogurt from the fridge. "Bs count as As."

"But you're three percent away from a C." He narrows his eyes. "That's too close."

"We had a test last week. I can redo the problems I missed to bring up the grade."

"You need to spend more time studying. I'll tell Mr. Dannenberg you can only work Friday and Saturday evenings."

"Did you check all my grades? I have As in the rest of them."

"Economics is only ninety-one percent. If it starts to slip—"

"I'll turn in an extra-credit assignment next week. Mr. Knott didn't include our notebook checks yet—"

"Don't argue with me!" He slams his hand on the table. "You need to maintain your GPA. If you continue to let things slip—"

"Things aren't slipping," I snap. "I study and constantly do my best. My overall GPA with a B in Economics would still be 3.78."

"So, it's okay to settle for less? It's not important that you do your best? Did you learn that from your good-for-nothing brother?"

I slam my yogurt on the counter because I really want to throw it at him.

Mom walks into the room, her eyes bouncing between us. "Everything okay?"

"Fine." I kiss her cheek, then glare at Dad. "I'd appreciate you not messing with my work schedule. I will get all As and a B in Precalc." I'm out the door before he can respond.

It's not until I pull into the parking lot at school that I realize I left my yogurt on the counter and didn't bring a lunch.

*I didn't need to eat;* I think on my way to the library. Yet I also hear Jason's voice telling me I need to.

*You still at home?* I text him.

*About to leave,* he replies. *What's up?*

*I was wondering if you can bring me breakfast. I might have forgotten to eat.*

*Sure! Where do you wanna meet?*

I sigh. *I'll be in the library studying since I'm on the verge of failing.*

*Since when?* I can hear the surprise in his text.

*Since Dad checked my grades.*

*Ahh. K. See you soon.*

The library is empty except for one kid watching videos on his phone. The back tables next to the reference books seem to be the best place to do my work. No one uses the reference section anymore, so there shouldn't be distractions.

I'm watching a video to figure out why I got the fifth problem on the test wrong when Jason places two bags in front of me.

"I didn't know if we were going for healthy or sweet." He puts a water bottle in between them. "And I didn't figure I could smuggle coffee into the library."

"You're the best." The first bag has a donut with chocolate frosting. The second is a breakfast sandwich that's still warm. "I'll have the sandwich now and save the donut for a snack."

He sits. "That was my other thought. Sorry he's being a jerk."

"Me too. I'm dangerously close to a C in Precalc since I have an eighty-two percent. And ninety-one in Econ is as good as a B."

"Mrs. Jarson won't give you a C." Jason laughs. "She likes you. You're the only one who compliments her. If I remember correctly, Econ is graded on a curve."

"Dad doesn't care. I think he checks my grades daily. It's like he has nothing better to do—" I stop myself.

"Now that Danny's gone," Jason says.

"Yeah." I take a bite of my sandwich.

"Gives you a better understanding of the pressure Danny felt."

I think about the evenings they went to the backyard to practice. I could hear Dad yell at him from inside the house. Once Danny made the team and had after school practice, Dad made him workout in the morning. Danny would pass me in the hall, fuming, on his way to the shower.

"It was never enough," I say. "No matter how hard Danny worked or how well he played. It was never enough."

"Use that realization to pray for Danny in a new way. Let it remind you to keep praying for your dad too."

I take another bite. I'll start to cry if I speak.

"Thanks for texting me to bring you breakfast. I'm proud of you for not skipping it." His eyes tell me he really is proud.

"How could I?" I cover my mouth as I chew. "All I heard in my head was you saying I had to eat."

Jason grins. "I'm here for you. To hold you accountable, pray for you, even bring you unhealthy food."

As the stress builds through the day, I remind myself of the truth. I am doing well in school. God will provide for college. In three months, I'll graduate, head to college, and leave Dad and his craziness behind. No wonder Danny left. Three months feels like a long time. No doubt three years seemed like an eternity to him. That makes me pray for Dad like Jason suggested.

*God, change his heart*, is all I manage to say, but I know it's enough. Prayers don't need to be long, simply heartfelt. I do want my dad to change for my mom's sake, for his sake, for everyone's sake.

Listening to my favorite worship song on the way home sets a new prayer in my heart—*God, let Dad know You're deeply in love with him, and help me to carry the banner of Your love in our family regardless of what is said or how I'm treated.*

I greet my mom with a kiss. "How was your day?" I rub her back, focusing on her answer. She tells me about pulling weeds and making a shopping list.

"I can go to the store for you tomorrow. Let me know when you want to start dinner—"

Mom gives me a hug. "I know you have studying to do. I can take care of dinner. Please don't let your father stress you out. You're a good student. I know you'll end the school year fine."

"Thanks, Mom." I grab a water from the fridge.

Precalc requires an hour of time along with a ton of brain power. I move to my bed to read for English. The sun is setting with four pages left of my reading. Stretching, I grab my phone to check the time. There's one new text from an unknown caller.

My heart stops when I open it. It's a selfie of a girl with a guy, both wearing Cubs hats and shirts. The girl has beautiful brown skin and dark brown hair. The boy is skinny with long, dirty-blond hair. I recognize him by the tilt of his head as he laughs.

"Danny!" I run downstairs. "Mom! Mom!"

"What, Lydia?" Mom rushes to me with Dad close behind.

"Look!" I shove my phone into her hand.

She stares, then her eyes widen. "Danny?" She hands my phone to Dad. "Is that Danny?"

"Looks like it." Dad strokes his chin. "Ask her."

I take back my phone. What do I say?

*I guess you know I'm Danny's sister, Lydia, but I don't know you*, I reply.

A smiley face comes at the beginning of the reply. *My name's Kat. I'm Danny's friend.*

It really is Danny. *Thank You, God, thank You—*

"Where are they?" Mom asks.

"Obviously at a Cubs game." Dad points to their hats.

*Are you at a Cubs game tonight?*

The response comes quickly. *Sorry, can't say. Just wanted you to know he's okay.*

My parents both sigh. Dad pulls out his phone. I scroll back to look at the pic again, thankful she sent it.

*Thank you*, I type. *We appreciate it.*

*No need to worry*, Kat replies. *I promise to take good care of him.*

I pass the phone to Mom. She runs her hand over Danny's face. "Ask her to tell him we love him and want him to come home."

*Please tell Danny we love him and wish he'd come home.* I pause before sending. *And you're welcome, too. Any friend of Danny's is a friend of ours.*

"He looks too skinny." Mom stares at the picture.

"He's strung out." Dad glances up from his phone. "There's a game in Chicago tonight. I'll call Anna and see if she can search for him." He leaves the room.

"He's laughing." Mom's eyes meet mine. "He's okay."

"And not alone." I hug her.

# CHAPTER 22

## LYDIA

"Hiya."

I rotate from my locker at the sound of Jason's voice. My heart stops to see him in his home uniform. It's not his face I see, but Danny's. I slam my locker door and run in the opposite direction.

"Lyd!"

Dodging to the right, I duck inside the girl's restroom.

"Lydia!"

The cold water on my face washes away my tears and brings me back to reality.

*It's okay. It's Jason. It's only Jason.* Drying my face, I repeat the truth silently as I stare into the mirror. But my mind doesn't accept it. Now I envision Danny in his uniform, his head hung and shoulders slumped walking from the field that last game. Jason runs up beside him, places a hand on his shoulder. Danny shrugs it off, brushes his sleeve over his eyes.

*God, he was crying. It was too much pressure. He couldn't handle it—*

"Are you Lydia?" A girl who looks no older than a freshman asks when she enters the bathroom.

"Yeah." I blot my face with paper towels.

"Jason wants me to let you know he's outside. He said he won't leave until you talk to him. I think he's pretty serious." She smiles. "And totally hot. Is he your boyfriend?"

I shift my eyes to the door. He's stubborn enough he won't leave. I don't want him to be tardy for class.

*It's okay.* Deep breath. My feet are like lead, but I force myself out the door. *It's Jason—*

The white jersey, blue sleeves, Dillinger scrolled across the front is too much for my heart. It's what destroyed my brother. I frown.

"Lyd." He places his hand on my arm. "What's going on?"

I jerk my arm away. His eyebrows shift down with his frown.

"It's not you. It's just—" I cover my face with my hands.

"You saw Danny," he says.

I peek through my fingers at his eyes. The eyes that see what a mess I am. Why is he still here? Why does he care? "I'm sorry. It's too hard." I hurry past him.

"Lydia!" He catches my arm. "That's it? You're going to avoid me all day because I'm in uniform? I don't have a choice. Coach wants us to wear them to promote the game."

"I know." A tear falls again. "I get it, Jason, but it hurts too bad. Baseball destroyed him. I can't be around it."

Jason stops. "You can't be around it, or you can't be around me?"

My back is still to him. I can't look at him.

"I don't expect you to come to the game, but please don't push me away." He places a hand on my shoulder. "I'm not the bad guy. I'm on your side."

*God, why is it this hard?* I wipe the tears. *Why does it continue to hurt?*

Jason steps in front of me. Though I resist, he cups my face in his hands. "I love you, Lydia."

In that moment, I know the truth. I love him, too.

"There's nothing to freak out about." His thumb caresses my cheek.

I want to believe him and let go of this anxiety that gnaws at me. I remember the peace on Valentine's Day when we kissed. My fears melted when I was in his arms. I love how we laughed together on the phone watching the zombie movie. He takes care of my needs like no one else does. My eyes drift from his blue cap to his cleats.

*He's a baseball player. Always will be. It'll only cause you pain. You'll be constantly reminded of Danny. You're not strong enough to handle that.*

"Jason." My head pounds with the conflicting thoughts. My heart races with the flood of emotion. I want him to hold me. I want him to pray over me to make it all better. *God, I just want to be better.*

"It's okay." He wraps his arms around me. "I know it's hard. We'll get through this."

I melt in his arms until the next thought comes.

*He'll leave you, too, in six months to go to college. Then the pain will start over again.*

Breaking from his arms, I run from the building.

Jason sits in the back row of Precalculus and English. He doesn't come around at lunch. Katie asks what's going on. When I tear up, she drops the subject. I probably made the stupidest mistake of my life, but I can't continue to feel wrecked. I need to keep it together if I'm going to college next year.

Someone calls in sick to work, which leaves me alone to make sandwiches and ring up customers at the rush.

"You need more help!" an impatient old man yells at me because he waits in line ten minutes.

"Yes, sir, I do," I say, slathering mayo on the bread in front of me.

It's eight o'clock when I enter the house tired and hungry. I meant to eat, I should have eaten, I just didn't. The only light on in the house is the kitchen light. I flick on the family room light on my way through.

"Hi." I walk to Mom, who's sitting at the kitchen table in silence. "You okay?"

I glance to where she's staring at the center of the table. An unorganized stack of the missing flyers I made are in front of her. Some have pin holes at the top, some tape.

"What's this?" I lift one.

"That's what I'm wondering." Her eyes meet mine. They aren't filled with sadness but fury. "Your father took my car today because it needed an oil change. I took his to the grocery store. When I went to put bags in his trunk, I found these."

My face heats up. There are dozens of them. For a month I hung up flyers in an attempt to find Danny, and he went around town taking them down?

"Hello." Dad enters from the garage. He walks straight to the fridge and opens it. "What's for dinner? I'm starving."

"I didn't make anything," Mom says.

"What?" He shuts the fridge. "Why not?"

"Because I've sat here for hours trying to figure out what kind of man does this." Mom lifts the papers. "What kind of man undoes all his daughter's work in trying to find his son?"

He stares for a moment, then snatches them from her hands along with the one in mine. "I was saving us from embarrassment and my daughter from being contacted by psychos." He crams them in the trash can. "Seriously, Margaret, do you want the entire city to know our son is a drug addict runaway? I know Lydia meant well, but there's no way I'll allow Danny to destroy this family's reputation."

"Destroy our reputation?" Mom's voice shakes. "What about our son? Our *actual* family?"

"Excuse me?" He straightens.

"You've been destroying this family for years. You pushed our son into a sport he hated. You refused to allow him to follow his dreams. Now you're riding our daughter." She balls her hands into fists. "Get out."

I'm shocked. I've never seen Mom this furious or seen her stand up to Dad—

"What?" he chuckles.

She points to the door. "Get out! You've been bullying us for years, although I was too blind to see it for a long time. But to go around and take down the posters that gave us hope to find our son?" Her finger shakes as she puts it in his face. "I don't know who you are anymore, and I won't allow you to continue to bully me or our daughter."

"Margaret, stop this! You know I love you—"

"No, you don't. You love your business. You love your success. You love your daughters' success in college. You love baseball. You haven't loved me in any way that counts for years." She points again. "Get out."

"You're insane!"

She runs her hands over her skirt. "For the first time in years, I'm rational. What's insane is how I've allowed you to treat me and our children."

I walk beside her, slip my arm around her waist.

"This is my house. I will not leave." Dad's eyes narrow. "I'm the one who works long hours to provide for this family. I'm the one who pays for the girls' college. I've made it possible for you to stay home all these years!"

"And I'm the one who keeps peace in this house, who encourages our children after you rip them apart and who teaches them to respect everyone, even bullies like you. God tells husbands to love their wives like Christ loves the church. If this was how Christ loved the church, there would be no Christians!"

"And wives submit to their husbands—"

"I have done what you said for years! Dinner on the table by six. No church on Wednesdays so we could eat together. Quit Thursday Bible study to chauffeur the kids because you were tired. Make Danny steak if his team wins but give him the meal he dislikes the most if he doesn't." Tears rise in her eyes. "I will leave right now with Lydia, but if I do, you will never see me again."

"Me either." I say.

"Margaret." He rests his hand on her arm.

She jerks away. "When you learn how to treat us with love and respect, you may come home. Until then, you've lost your privilege to be here."

He lets out an incredulous laugh. "What do you think your precious pastor will say when you tell him you kicked me out?"

"When I explain the circumstances, I think he'll agree I waited too long." She wraps her arm around me. "I made an appointment with him for tomorrow. You're welcome to come. He has agreed to do marriage counseling with us."

"I haven't done anything wrong."

She shakes her head. "Get out, Chris. Get out."

The fury distorts his face, but he doesn't speak. He grabs his car keys from the dish on the counter. The door slams behind him.

Tires screech. He's gone, along with the hurtful remarks and criticism. The silence is a relief. Mom wraps both arms around me. Air slowly fills my lungs as I relax in her embrace. We're safe from his rampage. Maybe this insanity we've lived for months is ending.

"I love you," she whispers. "I'm sorry."

"I don't blame you, Mom."

"I'm sorry I didn't do that sooner. If I had, Danny would still be here."

The truth of her words break my heart. "It's okay, Mom. We'll be okay."

---

*DANNY*

*You busy?*

I smile at Kat's text. It's seven p.m. She's been on my mind since she left after lunch. Her laugh, her beautiful face, invade my mind.

*Never too busy for you.*

My phone rings after I send the text.

"Hey," she says. "I was between clients and thinking of you."

"Yeah?" Her statement is kinda creepy, but I'm honored to be on her mind.

"That was fun at the baseball game Monday, wasn't it?"

"It was. And the museum yesterday. And dinner. And breakfast."

She giggles. "And peanut butter sandwiches in the park for lunch. I haven't had peanut butter for years."

"It's very nutritious. Peanut butter on wheat bread is the meal of champions. The ingredients don't go bad in your backpack either."

"I might need to get some for my apartment. Seems like food grows mold extra fast around here. What are you doing?"

"Found a copy of *Sense and Sensibility* in the used bookstore. Thought I'd read it."

"Really?"

"Yeah. How about you? Almost done for the night?"

"Two more." She sighs. "Wish you were here. I miss you."

That makes my entire life. "I miss you, too."

"I know I said I couldn't see you until Friday, but maybe we can meet for coffee tomorrow? Around nine? I'm not out too late on Wednesdays."

"Sure." Score. Another morning with her.

"K, I gotta go. I need to finish redoing my makeup." She takes a deep breath. "I'll see you tomorrow?"

"Text me where. I'll be there."

I pull up the picture she took of us at the game to make it my screensaver. People talk about love at first sight. I didn't believe in it until now. I was physically attracted to Willow. The sight of her made my pulse soar. It's different with Kat. Our conversations stimulate me. I want to get to know her. I love to listen to her talk. She fits perfectly in the crook of my arm. Our hands meld together. Yeah, she's gorgeous enough to make my heart race, but the attraction goes deeper.

Oh, the irony. I wouldn't sleep with my last girlfriend. Now I'm in love with a prostitute.

I read in my sleeping bag until my eyes start to close. She's the one I think of as I drift off to sleep.

My ringtone wakes me. Kat's number is on the screen. "Hey, you okay?"

"I want you to come over." Her voice shakes. "Can you? Come to my place?" A woman is shouting profanity in the background.

"Yeah." I sit up, run my fingers through my hair. "Where are you?"

"14th and State."

"Are you okay?" I'm out of my bag. It's not easy to roll when on the phone, but I do it.

"It was a bad night. I need to get high. I want you here." Now a guy cusses.

"Are you sure you're okay?" Hooking my bag to my backpack, I start down the street. "Sounds like there's a lot going on."

"It's my bipolar roommate and her boyfriend. Think it's her time of the month. She's a little over the top."

"Oh." I don't know what to say to that. "I'm on 4th and Elm. It'll take a while."

"K. Hurry. I need you."

She needs me? All night I've thought of her, I've wanted to talk to her, and she asks me to come to her. She needs me. Unreal.

An address with an apartment number arrives in a text with *Hurry!*

I quicken my pace. Definitely don't need cops or gang members hassling me tonight. I just want to find Kat.

The bus shows up at the corner of 5th a couple minutes after I arrive. It's packed. Women in the same uniform fill the front seats. Their voices are loud and their gestures big. I pass a guy with a dark-blue hoodie hunched over behind them. His lack of movement makes me wonder if he's alive. The couple across from him, I think it's a guy and girl, apparently only had enough money to ride the bus, not to rent a room.

I slide into the only open seat on the aisle toward the back. The girl in the seat by the window is in jeans and a sweatshirt with holes. Her long brown hair is knotted. The lack of teeth tell me she's on meth or heroin. She's in the middle of an animated conversation—with herself. It entertains me, although the amount of profanity is a little over the top. I don't cuss that much in one day let alone in one conversation. I wonder if someone will win the debate. Does she know who wins?

At the next stop the couple attached at the lips pauses long enough to leave. A family gets on. Dad, Mom, two boys, and a girl. The kids' eyes are wide. The mother has the youngest boy on one side and the girl on the other. The father leads the oldest boy down the aisle. The two with Mom squeeze into the seats across from me and she hovers over them. I stand, motion to the dad.

"Thank you." He has the son sit, then stands beside him.

The boy's eyes widen even more when schizo's not-so-nice half starts on a rampage again. The dad grips the son's shoulder, speechless.

"Did you go to the Cubs game?" I asked.

The boy looks at me. I tap the bill of his hat.

"Yeah." He swipes the brim. "Tonight."

"How was it?"

"They won." He smiles. "My name's Wyatt."

"Danny." I extend my hand. "How old are you? Ten?"

"Eleven," the boy says. "I play baseball. I was supposed to be in a tournament, but there was a hurricane—"

"Tornado," his dad says.

"Something like that." He pauses when crazy lady screams unintelligible words. Once her voice becomes a mumble, he speaks again. "They canceled the games. We decided to come see one here."

"Where you from?" I ask.

"California. We get earthquakes. After a couple seconds they're done. Not like stupid hurricanes."

"Tornadoes," his mother says.

"Whatever." Wyatt rolls his eyes.

"I want to go to college in California," I say.

"Which one?" his dad asks.

"USC."

He nods. "I work for the UC schools."

"Oh. You're a professor?"

"No. Police officer. My wife is the teacher in the family."

She smiles when he turns to her.

The muscles in my neck and shoulders tense. I tell myself he's far from home, out of his jurisdiction, but the thought of a cop in front of me freaks me out.

"Did you play ever play baseball?" Wyatt stares at my Cubs hat.

"I did. I was on the varsity team my freshman year in high school."

His jaw drops. He glances to his father.

"What school?" Cop Dad asks.

"Dillinger High, Indianapolis."

Now his eyes widen. "Good school. Amazing baseball team. Last year was the first year they didn't make it to state finals."

"Yeah, I know." I rub the back of my neck.

"What position did you play?" Wyatt asks.

"Shortstop."

"That's a hard one. I play center field mostly."

"That's an important position."

The bus stops. Two ladies in front of the other kids leave. A girl in her twenties, skirt above her thighs and tank top cut low, stumbles down the aisle. She kicks off her heels, almost falling when she attempts to pick them up. One moment she laughs, the next she clamps her hand over her mouth like she's going to puke. The mother faces her kids when the girl plops down in the seat in front of them. The daughter and mother immediately cover their noses. I understand when the smell of alcohol mixed with BO wafts across the aisle.

"Mom, I think she's going to throw up," the younger boy whispers.

I bite my lip, so I don't laugh.

"You live around here?" Dad's focus is on the sleeping bag connected to my backpack.

"Passing through."

"On your way to California?" Wyatt smiles.

"Something like that."

"You graduated last year?" Cop Dad slips into interrogation mode.

"December. Early grad." I nod to his wife and other kids. "Looks like you have a nice family."

"What are you going to major in?" Wyatt's eyes are fixed on the drunk girl. Her moans increase as she lowers her head between her knees.

"Communications. I write scripts for movies and plays."

"That's cool. Maybe you can name one of the characters after me. And my siblings. Abby's the oldest." He points to the girl. "Carson is younger than me."

I grin. "The dreaded middle child, huh?"

"Yeah, but I'm the oldest boy. It has its perks."

"14th and State," the driver says when the bus stops.

"You guys be safe while you're here." I head down the aisle.

"Bye, Danny." Wyatt waves. "Maybe I'll see you in California."

"Maybe." I wave as I step off the bus.

The empty lot on the way to the five-story apartment building is littered with trash. I pass a broken toilet someone used, a smashed TV, and a filthy mattress two teens are making out on. I walk quickly in hopes that I don't step on feces or a decomposing body. That would be a bummer.

Stairs seem safer than the elevator. I double time it up two flights. I'm overwhelmed by noise the minute I open the door. Screaming and yelling, groaning and moaning, laughter and singing come from all directions. I see why Kat chose to sleep on the streets with me.

A redhead, who's maybe eighteen, answers the door. Her black lace lingerie shows everything it's supposed to cover. Her short hair is disheveled. Overdone eye makeup is in streaks down her face. I assume she's the bipolar one.

"Hi. I'm here to see Kat."

"Are you?" Her eyes wander from my baseball cap to my shoes before she opens the door wider. "Down the hall. Second door on the right."

I knock twice before I crack open the door. "It's Danny."

"Danny. Come here, Danny."

The room is lit dimly. My heart races as soon as I see her. She's laid out in the middle of her bed. Her shorts barely cover anything, and her thin T-shirt is almost see-through.

"Danny. I knew you'd come." She scoots to the far side of her full-size bed and stretches out her arms. "Come lie with me."

That's when I see them for the first time. Track marks on her arm. I also see a drop of blood on her right arm. "What'd you do?"

"Come here, Danny."

I glance to the nightstand. An empty syringe teeters on the edge of it. "What'd you shoot up?"

"Heroin. I got another. Wanna try?"

I drop my pack beside her bed, step over the clothes spread on the floor, and sit beside her. "Why'd you do that?"

"I told you, it was a bad day. I need it."

I shake my head. "No, Kat, you don't."

"Yes, I do." Her eyes open. Her pupils seem incredibly small. "He looks like my mom's boyfriend. He smells like cigarettes and beer. The way he stares at me..." She sets her hand on her forehead. "Tonight, he paid for two hours. I didn't know until I showed up. It was awful. I told Shaun I hate him. I told him the guy makes me want to throw up. He says this takes the edge off. And it does." Her eyes close again.

"But heroin—"

"There's one in the top drawer. I saved it for you."

I feel like I could hurl. I've heard how addictive the drug is, seen people on the streets who use it. Gnarly teeth, chunks of hair gone, eyes sunken, faces covered with scabs. I have my own issues with coke and weed. I don't need this. I should walk away. I want to but can't. I can't leave her here in this mess. I can't leave because—I love her. I want to report her mother's boyfriend who raped her. I want to confront these middle-aged men who have sex with a girl who's only eighteen. Most of all, I want to track down Shaun, who made prostitution her life and gives her an addictive drug to cope with it. I've never wanted to hurt someone so much.

"You get an amazing rush, the highest high you've ever felt. Then you don't feel or care about anything. There's no regret or shame. Nothing. Only escape." She reaches in the drawer, pulls out a syringe with an amber-colored liquid. "Escape with me, Danny. Come escape with me."

She's right. It's a phenomenal high. But after that, the room spins. Not around like it does when I smoke pot, but upside down. Sideways. I'm on a roller coaster without wheels. Or a seatbelt.

"I'm gonna lose it." I drop to the floor, try to focus my eyes to find a trash can.

"Are you going to puke?" Kat calls from the bed.

I continue to crawl. To where, I have no idea, but I don't want to get sick on her clothes. My hand hits a fast-food bag. The smell of stale French fries when I open it brings forth everything that's within me.

"I got sick my first couple times. It gets better."

"Did he barf in our room?" bipolar redhead screams. "He better not get sick on my clothes."

"Only on your dinner," Kat says.

We both laugh as her profanity starts up again.

Kat kneels beside me, runs her fingers through my hair. "You okay?"

"If I don't move." I open my eyes to a somewhat tilted room. "Are these all her clothes?"

"Pretty much. She's a slob."

"The walls are thin," she says. "I can hear you!"

"Then why are you yelling?" I ask.

More cussing comes as we laugh. We lie beside each other on the floor, talk about stuff that doesn't make sense. I hear the TV of the people who live next door, the music of the people below, and the evening pleasure of the couple above. Mix in sounds of the distant train and occasional sirens. There's no quiet.

"How do you sleep?" I ask.

"With earplugs most of the time." She sits up. "Can you move now? Come back to bed?"

"I'll stay down here. I'm quite comfy on these fine garments."

"C'mon. Here's your chance to sleep in a bed." She tugs my hand. "How long has it been?"

"February, when I was in a shelter." I say.

"Bet that was fun." She walks me to the bed.

"Not at all." I take my hand away when she drops on the mattress. "I can't sleep with you." I know how it sounds but can't think of another way to say it.

"You're sleeping by me." Kat flicks off the light on the nightstand and pulls me to her. "Like your sister. What's her name?"

"Lydia." It hurts deep inside my chest just to say her name.

The glow of the streetlights outside shines through the thin curtains. I close my eyes and see Lydia, kneeling beside her bed.

*Come back to Jesus*, she says. *He loves you. He can help you and make your dream come true.*

"I'll be your sister." Kat wraps her arm around me. "Don't you miss her?"

A flood of emotions comes over me. "Yeah. I do."

"Does she have a nickname for you?"

Tears fill my eyes. "Danny Boy."

Kat runs her hand over my hair. "I love you, Danny Boy. Everything's going to be all right. Just sleep."

# CHAPTER 23

## LYDIA

My alarm goes off at seven o'clock. I should get up, shower, and go to school, but I don't want to. My head is pounding from being up with Mom until eleven p.m. crying. Then I woke in the middle of the night worried about Danny. This awful feeling came over me that he was hurting himself with drugs. I prayed, cried, and prayed until I fell asleep. The guilt over how I treated Jason when he was in his uniform yesterday is also overwhelming. Much more so than the guilt over the idea of skipping school.

Today's devotion is on Psalm 46:10—"Be still, and know that I am God!" More confirmation that today should be a day off.

"Good morning." I shuffle into the kitchen in my pjs and slippers.

Mom is at the bar in her robe. The mug in her hands was a gift from Danny two years ago for Mother's Day. A portion of Isaiah 62:4 is on it—"the Lord delights in you."

"Oh." She checks the microwave clock. "Don't you need to get ready for school?"

"I'm not going today." I head to the fridge for a yogurt.

"Lydia, I don't want what happened last night to affect you or your scholarship."

"I'm entitled to a senior ditch day." I grab a spoon and sit beside her. "Maybe I want a day to shop with my mom. Besides, there isn't much going on since spring break starts tomorrow. The teachers are already checked out."

She purses her lips. "I don't want you to—"

"Something happened last night with Danny. I woke in the middle of the night and prayed for a long time." Tears gather in my eyes. "I can't do school today."

Mom nods. "What did you have in mind?"

"The Fashion Mall at Keystone. Shopping and Cheesecake Factory for lunch?"

"Will you actually eat food or just cheesecake?"

I stir up my yogurt. "Both. I think we deserve a whole cheesecake with the week we've had."

"Maybe." Her smile fades. "I need to be back by two thirty. I'm meeting with Pastor Raul at three o'clock."

"Do you think Dad will show?"

"Only God knows. I pray he does." She stares at her coffee. "I do still love him. I just hate what he's become." She lifts her gaze. "I won't allow him to continue to bully us. It's not okay."

"It's very brave of you, Mom." I take her hand. "I know it's hard."

"That's what I want to teach you. God calls us to hard things. Like Pastor said last week, things aren't easy when we're in God's will, but He'll help us through." She wipes her tears. "I want you to know that no one has the right to disrespect you. The right man will love God and will love you like the church."

Jason's face comes to mind.

"I pray your father will come to that point."

"Me too, Mom. I have been praying God will change his heart."

She stands. "I guess today is a good day to shop for a prom dress. Before we eat cheesecake."

"I don't think I'm going."

"Of course, you are. I assumed you and Jason—"

I shake my head. "I was kinda mean to him yesterday."

Her frown returns. "Please don't allow this thing with me, Dad, and Danny to mess up your happiness."

"I'll go shower." I swallow back my tears. "How about we leave in an hour?"

It feels like an almost perfect day. Mom and I hold hands through the mall, which is something we haven't done in years. We each pick out a new outfit. I help her choose a new tablecloth and napkins for the dining room. I even humor her by trying on prom dresses. My favorite is a dark-blue, off-the-shoulder swoop back.

*What are you doing?* I sigh as I look myself over in the mirror. *You aren't going to prom.*

My phone chimes with a text from Jason.

*Hey, you okay? I was worried when you weren't at school.*

I was the jerk and he's worried about me?

*I'm good,* I reply. *Decided to use my senior ditch day to shop with Mom.*

*Good for you. Pick out a prom dress?*

I think of what Mom said this morning about continuing to live my life. Like Jason has told me for months. Danny could come home tomorrow or maybe he never will. Regardless, I need to make my own memories.

I angle my phone to snap a pic of the entire front. *Appeasing my mom,* I text with the photo.

First arrives a smiley face. Then the words of his complete forgiveness.

*If you don't have any better offers, I'd love to take you. Friends don't let friends go to prom alone. I even promise not to wear my baseball uniform.*

I laugh out loud as I respond. *LOL. I'd be honored to go with you. I promise not to hide in the bathroom all night.*

*Then it's a date,* he replies with a winky face.

Mom leaves for the church shortly after we get home. Even though we had a big lunch, I decide to make her dinner. I pray for Mom's peace, strength, and comfort while I chop up tomatoes and veggies for a new pasta recipe. I pray Pastor Raul will have compassion for us and see Dad for who he is. And I pray conviction on my father for what he's done and who he's become.

When I have no more words, I listen to the Psalms. David's pleas become my own pleas for Mom until I get to Psalm 13. That plea becomes my own.

"O Lord, how long will you forget me? Forever? How long will you look the other way? How long must I struggle with anguish in my soul, with sorrow in my heart every day? How long will my enemy have the upper hand?"

I repeat the words over and over. "How long will you forget me? How long must I struggle with the sorrow in my heart?" There's a strange release when I speak them, yet the reality of them crushes me.

*You're broken.*

*Destroyed.*

*Things will continue to get worse.*

*The pain will NEVER end—*

"God, why do you look the other way?"

I replay the psalm from the beginning. When I get to verse five, the tears of joy come.

"But I trust in your unfailing love. I will rejoice because you have rescued me. I will sing to the Lord because he is good to me."

"Yes, God, I trust you." My smile grows with the proclamation. "You rescued me from sin and death. I trust you to do the same for my brother and father. You are good to me."

I'm at the kitchen table writing out Psalm 13 on sticky notes when the garage door opens at five o'clock.

"Something smells delicious." Mom drops her keys and purse on the kitchen counter.

"I found a new pasta recipe. Thought I'd make it for us tonight."

"Great. How about some of that cheesecake first?" She grabs the cheesecake from the fridge and two forks.

"He didn't show?" I accept the fork from her.

"Oh, he showed. According to him, it's all my fault." She sits beside me. "I put the kids' needs above him. I'm selfish in every area—" She pauses before she crams the bite into her mouth.

Mom is the most unselfish person in the world. I'm sure it transfers to every part of their relationship. Dad has always been her top priority.

"What'd you say?"

"Nothing." She wipes her mouth. "The longer he talked, the angrier he became. Pastor Raul asked for my side when he finished. I didn't get out two sentences when your father began to yell it was lies. Pastor told him it was my turn and he needed to listen. That's when he accused Pastor of taking sides. He screamed at him before he stormed out."

I frown. "He didn't stay?"

Mom shakes her head. "This didn't happen overnight, baby, and it can't be fixed overnight. It'll take time. I'll put forward the effort. The question is, will he?" She forks another bite. "Pastor shared a lot of scriptures and resources with me. He gave me names of places I can call if we don't feel safe at home." She stares at her bite. "I pray it doesn't come to that."

"I read Psalm 13 today. I liked verses five and six." I pick up the sticky note with the verses. "'But I trust in your unfailing love. I will rejoice because you have rescued me. I will sing to the Lord because he is good to me.' He is good to us. We still have each other."

"I'm thankful for that." She places a hand on my cheek. "I know I have your support."

"I pray God will rescue all of us. You, me, Danny, and even Dad."

"Amen, baby. Amen." She eats her bite. "I wasn't going to call your sisters just yet."

"Good." I dig into the other side of the cheesecake. "That's more drama than I can handle right now."

"I'm glad we agree. Since they both called a few weeks ago to tell me they weren't coming for Easter, we should be good for a while. They only call once a month, if that."

"If you need me to, I can tell them," I say. "They can't hurt my feelings."

"You and your brother have always been the tough ones." She pushes the cheesecake toward me. "Where's that picture of Danny? Why don't you pull it up and we'll pray for him."

---

*DANNY*

Sunlight wakes me at seven o'clock. Kat is in my arms, face nuzzled in my chest. Best feeling ever.

I stare at the track marks in the crease of her elbow. How long has she been shooting up? I'm in love with a heroin addict prostitute. I think of the absurdity. A good Christian boy—

*You haven't been a good Christian boy for over a year, Morton. Don't try to fool yourself.*

What am I? A washed-out ball player like my dad? A screw-up teen? An alcoholic, coke-snorting, high-seeking, homeless bum? My eyes shift to the needle prick in my own arm. A soon-to-be heroin addict? I'd prefer to be a young writer who experiences life on his road to success. That's how Kat would see me. And funny. Maybe cute. She told me she loved me. Granted it was in context of being like my sister, but she said it.

She begins to stir. I kiss the top of her head.

"Good morning," she whispers.

"Good morning," I say when her eyes open.

"You sleep?" She rolls to her back and stretches.

"Yeah. You?"

"Better than usual." She traces my cheekbone.

I wonder what's on her mind. Should I bring up us? Is there an "us"? I want to tell her how I feel. I lean closer to her, feel her breath on my face—

"I could use some cocaine and caffeine. How about you?"

I force a smile. "Sounds good."

She dresses while I'm using her restroom. A different roommate is passed out on the sofa. We do coke on the table inches from her without waking her.

Kat on coke is hilarious. Her natural speech is fast, but after two lines of powder, she averages three hundred words per minute. She also sprints half of the way to the coffee place. By the time I sit across from her with our breakfast sandwiches and drinks, I'm exhausted. I should've got a double shot to keep up with her.

"What do you think about me dying my hair purple?" She unwraps her sandwich like she hasn't eaten in days. "Or silver? Red might be hot. It's the thing now."

I sip my coffee. "I like your hair—"

"Curly or straight?" She braids it. "Or braided? Minis, or havana twists? I do cornrows on Friday, then I don't have to deal with it over the weekend. It makes life easier. Sometimes I can do a fishtail—"

I snag the baseball cap from her head. Instant poof. "Like this."

She grabs my cap from my head and forces it over her own. "Stop."

"Really." I put her hat on my head. "It's cool braided too. I don't know the different kinds. My sisters and Mom have always had long hair but don't do fancy braids. Dad freaked when Mary cut hers last year."

"And you?" She leans forward. "Have you always had long hair?"

"Nah. Once upon a time I was a clean-cut guy." I take a bite of my sandwich. "This is my four-months-of-living-on-the-streets look."

"Let's get our hair done today. You can get it cut, dyed even. I'll get mine braided."

"You don't braid it yourself?"

She laughs. "What they can do in twenty minutes takes me hours. And it'd be crooked. Shaun pays for my salon visits." She plasters a fake smile on her face. "Because it's important."

"You're beautiful with big hair and no makeup."

"You think so?"

"It's what's inside that counts." I wink.

She rolls her eyes. "Inside I'm a total mess."

"You're kind, thoughtful, generous. After all, you bought the coke. I only paid for breakfast."

"That's what siblings are for." She switches hats with me.

The salon is on Walton Street, among fancy clothing and purse stores. I've never understood how a purse store could stay in business, especially when they cost hundreds of dollars. Kat threatens to take me in one after.

"I think going to a salon is torture enough. Couldn't we just go to a barber shop? It would cost like twelve bucks."

She laughs. "No brother of mine is getting a twelve-dollar haircut." She opens the door. "Lashawn will take care of you."

"Beautiful Kat." A black man in skinny jeans and a silk shirt greets her with a kiss on the cheek.

"Lashawn, this is Danny. I thought you could work your magic on him while I get my hair done."

"Danny." He sizes me up. "For sure. What are we going for?"

"I was thinking shave the back and sides, leave the top long? But not quite that long."

He walks around me, running his fingers through my hair. "Like one of those handsome white movie stars?"

"That's what I'm going for." Kat winks at me before she sits in some six-foot lady's chair.

"Fabulous," he says. "Let's get you shampooed."

I follow the guy to his station past several ladies, most at least twice my age, getting their hair done. Each stare at me, and my pack, a bit too long. Will I ever feel like I belong in Kat's world?

"You live around here?" Lashawn asks while he shampoos my hair.

"Kind of."

"Kat has a soft spot for the down and out. Definitely an example of someone who didn't forget her roots."

"How long have you known her?" I'd love to learn more about her from someone who knows her.

"Two years. Since Shaun took her in. She was a wreck. A skinny, homely mess."

Kat's laughter fills the salon.

"It's gotta be a hard life, you know." He glances her direction. "But at least she's living. Looked like death that first day. Took her almost a month to talk to any of us."

That's what I ponder the entire time he cuts. How being forced to give herself away could somehow give her life. It kinda shows God is not engaged in our lives. He couldn't care less about us except for his own amusement. That's the only explanation for why such a beautiful person would be put through hell.

"You look hot!" Kat says an hour later when Lashawn is finished. "If you weren't my brother—"

"You're siblings?" her hairdresser asks.

We laugh. She runs her hand over the back of my hair. "You like it?"

"Yeah." I stare at her in the mirror. "I love it."

# CHAPTER 24

## LYDIA

*DANNY'S GONE,* IS STILL THE FIRST THOUGHT WHEN I WAKE EVERY morning. Now it's followed by *Mom and Dad are separated.* Mom's heart is broken, and Dad's is hardened. *God, I know You're here, but my family is falling apart. We need you.*

I take my phone from my nightstand. Each day I hope to find good news on it. A text from Danny with his location or that he's on his way home. Another picture from his friend. Something. The only good news I find is in my Bible. The verse of the day is from Isaiah 53. I open the entire chapter and start to read.

"He was despised and rejected—a man of sorrows, acquainted with deepest grief. We turned our backs on him and looked the other way. He was despised, and we did not care. Yet it was our weaknesses he carried; it was our sorrows that weighed him down."

Jesus does understand my grief. It's okay that I hurt. I close my eyes, the truth washes over me before I continue to read.

"But he was pierced for our rebellion, crushed for our sins. He was beaten so we could be whole. He was whipped so we could be healed. All of us, like sheep, have strayed away. We have left God's paths to follow our own. Yet the Lord laid on him the sins of us all."

*God, we've all sinned. My entire family.* My pillow catches my tears. *Help us to understand that reality and remember there aren't different degrees of sin. Danny's use of drugs, Dad's pride, Mom's anxiety, my lack of faith, it's all sin. Thank You for dying to set us free. Set us free, Jesus, once and for all.*

"Good morning," Mom greets me from the coffee maker when I make my way downstairs a little while later.

"Good morning." I reach to get a cup from the cupboard and notice her left ear lobe is swollen. I lean in to see a large red lump in the middle. "What's wrong with your ear?"

"I don't know." She runs her index finger over it. "I noticed it yesterday. I thought it was a pimple but it's bigger today and more red. Maybe it's infected. Does it look bad?"

"Kind of." Truth is it looks awful. "I think you should go to the doctor."

She sighs. "What if you take a picture to send to Mary? Ask for her opinion. I don't want to go to Urgent Care, especially on a Friday. I'll wait for hours. Maybe it's an ingrown hair."

"On your ear?" Now I realize she's not rational. I snap a pic and text it to Mary. *I think something's wrong with Mom's ear. Any ideas?*

I sit at the table with my yogurt. Mom joins me with her coffee.

"You work today?" she asks.

"Yeah. Eleven to six."

*Does she have any other spots?* Mary replies.

Mom feels around her ear.

*One, maybe two above her ear in her hairline,* I type as Mom tells me.

My phone rings. "Hey, Mary."

"Lydia, I think Mom has shingles."

"What's that?"

"It's related to the chickenpox virus. It's brought on by a weakened immune system and stress. It's extremely painful. Is she in pain?"

"Are you in pain?" I ask.

"No."

"She needs to go to the doctor right away," Mary says. "It's going to get awful."

"Okay. I'll take her now."

"I'm at work, but call me when you get home," she says.

I stand. "Mary thinks you have shingles. We need to go to the doctor. I'll get dressed and take you."

Mom shakes her head. "You can't. You have work."

"Mr. Dannenberg will understand. I'll get my shoes on."

"But—"

"We leave in five minutes," I call on the way up the stairs.

We wait in the Urgent Care for two and a half hours for the doctor to confirm Mary's diagnosis. "It's shingles. Are you in pain?"

"Not really. It itches a little."

"It's going to get painful."

I shift my eyes down as I see tears in Mom's. *Why, God? Hasn't she suffered enough? Why give her this, too?*

"Antiviral medication will hopefully shorten the length of the virus." The doctor types away on his laptop. "Stress can be a trigger for shingles. Is there something specific going on that adds stress to your life?"

"My son ran away from home before Christmas."

I raise my eyes, surprised that she admitted it.

"Things haven't been well in my marriage for years. They've escalated since my son left. I asked my husband to move out yesterday."

Pride rises inside me at my mom being honest. It seems like for years we have hidden what a mess my family is. It's a relief to hear her speak the truth.

The doctor sighs. "That's a lot of stress."

"Is shingles contagious?" She wipes tears from her cheeks.

"The virus is in your nerves, so not technically, but it's best no one touches any of your open sores. You do need to manage your stress in a healthy way. Do things you enjoy, watch comedies, light exercise when you feel better." He glances to me. "Help around the house would be great, along with lots of hugs."

I nod.

He scans the computer screen. "Are you Lydia?"

"Yes, sir."

"How old is Danny now?"

"Sixteen."

"Is he on drugs?"

"Yes, sir," I manage to say, though my heart is in my throat.

"Do you have an idea where he ran to?"

"Maybe California. LA." I wipe away a tear as it falls.

"Call ERs. It's a long shot, but addicts, especially the homeless, usually end up in the ER at some point. If they aren't hurt, they seek prescription drugs. Notify your health insurance in case he uses it in another state. They can track him that way." He takes a card from the pocket of his white coat and hands it to me. "Email me his picture and description. I'll send it to local hospitals."

"Thank you, Doctor." I rub the card between my fingers. "Thank you."

Mom takes her first dose of the antiviral medication before she settles on the couch bed I make her.

"What about a comedy?" I'm scrolling through the guide on TV. Suddenly both her hands shoot to the left side of her face.

"You okay?" I ask.

"It feels like someone is pulling my ear." She squints her eyes shut.

"Did you take Advil like the doctor said?"

"Yes. It's radiating up my face." Her face twists as she moans.

"What can I do?"

"My eye!"

"What?" I kneel by her side. "What's wrong?"

"It's like someone is ripping my eye from the socket." She weeps, shoulders shaking.

I pull the blanket over her and rub her arm. "The doctor said a cold compress could help. I'll get one."

Racing to my parents' room, I run a washcloth under cold water. About the time I turn off the water, Mary calls.

"How's Mom?"

"It's bad. She's in a ton of pain."

"When did it start?"

"Just now." I hear Mom whimpering in the other room. "I gotta go, Mary. She's crying."

"Lydia, what's going on? Why's Mom stressed out?"

"Oh, let's see. Maybe because her son is addicted to drugs and on the streets. Or maybe because her husband is a selfish jerk."

"Lydia! Did Dad take her to the doctor?"

"No. She threw him out Wednesday night."

"She what?"

A muffled scream comes from the other room.

"I don't have time for this, Mary." I end the call and sprint to the family room. "Sorry." I gently set the washcloth over her ear and face. "Breathe, Mom. Try to breathe."

"I'm sorry," she mumbles between cries. "I'm sorry."

"You have nothing to be sorry for. It's not your fault."

Mary calls again. I silence my phone, then open my Bible app. "What if I read to you? Maybe from Psalms?"

"Okay," she whispers.

After the fourth Psalm, she breathes easier. I put the worship music channel on TV.

*God, give her rest. Let her rest in You.*

My phone vibrates. I flinch at the word DAD on my screen. I reject the first call, but he calls again. Mary must have talked to him. If I don't answer, he'll call Mom.

"Hi." I go to the office, shutting the door behind me.

"What's going on?" he screams.

"Mom has shingles, which is from stress. Any guess how she got that?"

He cusses. "Because your good-for-nothing brother—"

"No, Dad, because of you! You started all of this. If you hadn't—"

"Don't you blame me for your brother's sin!"

"Goodbye, Dad."

I'm about to hang up when he yells. "Lydia, please!"

I pause. Has my father ever said "please"? I return the phone to my ear.

"Please don't hang up." He sighs. "I love your mother. And you."

"Well, you have a crappy way of showing it."

"I'm sorry."

I shake my head. Did he say sorry? He probably thinks I'll let him—

"Please put your mother on."

"No. She can't take any more stress."

"Please." Frustration returns to his voice.

"No. She's in a lot of pain. She can't talk."

"Did the doctor give her pain meds?"

"Only an antiviral medication. She won't take narcotics after everything with Danny." Tears fill my eyes.

"I'm coming over."

"No!" I shouldn't talk to my father this way, but right now he's the man who forced my brother to run and broke my mother.

"I'll bring dinner. Help take care of her. You can't do it all."

"Yes, I can. I'll call in a few days to let you know how she is." Pressing end, I take deep breaths on my way to the family room.

"Was that Dad?" she asks when I sit at her feet.

"Yeah. Mary called him." I rub her foot. "How are you?"

"The cold helps."

"Should I get it wet again?"

"Maybe." She hands it to me. "I don't want to see him."

"I told him."

"Will you call Mary and tell her what happened? Ask her to talk to Anna. I don't want them to only hear his side."

"Sure. I'll get you water to drink too."

Once I've taken care of Mom's needs, I go to my room to call Mary.

"What's going on?" she asks. "I called Dad—"

"He called. I'll tell you, but you need to listen without interrupting."

"I will."

"Promise you won't freak out or defend Dad."

"I promise."

Starting from the day Danny left, I share the details of Dad's downward spiral ending with Mom's discovery of the posters in his trunk.

"I don't understand why he'd do that. There must be a reason."

"He's ashamed, too prideful to admit any of us are a mess." Yet we all are, I want to add. "They met with Pastor Raul on Thursday. Mom said Dad blamed her and left when Pastor asked him to let Mom share."

"I'm sure—"

"Mary, stop. Please don't stand up for him. Think about how he used to talk to Danny, how he always talks down to Mom. When's the last time he showed her any physical affection?"

"Well, I'm not there that often."

"Exactly. You haven't been here for years," I say. "It doesn't happen. His heart is too hard for anything to get through."

Mary sighs. "It's that bad?"

"Yeah, it is." I lie on my bed.

"I should come home."

"You can't. You have classes and work. I can help Mom through this. I have been for months."

"I'm sorry, Lyd. I'm sorry I didn't see it. I'm the oldest. I should have stepped up, at least been more supportive after Danny left. I guess I was wrapped up in myself."

Several responses run through my mind, none of them very nice. "I forgive you," is what comes out. I inhale deeply. *I forgive her God, I do.*

"What can I do for you guys? I want to help."

"Can you call Anna? Try to help her understand. It's probably best that she not call unless she can be supportive."

"I will. Is Dad coming home?"

"No. That's not what's best for Mom. She doesn't want him here." The doorbell rings. "I gotta go."

"Okay. Call me tomorrow. Or sooner if you need something. I'm praying."

A takeout bag from Mom's favorite restaurant is on the porch next to vase of a dozen red roses. I lift the vase. A small card reads *I'm sorry for the pain I've caused you. I love you.*

"It's a step in the right direction." Mom picks up the bag of food. "How about you put them in the office."

"In the office?" I ask.

"That way I don't need to see them. It's probably nicer than throwing them away."

I kiss her cheek. "Go sit on the couch. I'll get us drinks."

---

### *DANNY*

All morning I stare at my phone in hopes Kat will call or text. I'm eating my morning PB sandwich in the park when she does.

*Good morning.*

I smile. *Good morning.* What else do I say? I don't want the conversation to end, but I don't want to ask her about work. *You sleep okay?*

*Would have been better with you here. :) Plans for today?*

*Make a couple bucks helping old ladies across the street. Or carrying out groceries. Fun stuff like that. You?*

*Work from 5pm-2am. Blah. Meet for tamales around 10?*

*Sure. See you then.*

She sends a cartoon graphic of herself throwing a kiss. Seriously, how can even a cartoon of her be sexy?

The laughter of a little kid grabs my attention. A young boy is on the swings. He pumps his legs while his mom pushes him.

"Higher?" she asks.

"Yes!" He grips the chains. Laughter increases the higher he flies.

Are they the perfect family? Is there a father at home—well, at work—who comes home every night excited to spend time with them? People judge others by one moment or by one picture on social media. If their hair is combed, their clothes free from rips, we peg them as good. But if they're dirty with overgrown hair, we label them losers. I made three times as much as I have in a week in two hours last night. People smiled at me rather than hurried past me. All because of my movie star haircut.

I think about that mom and kids who bought me dinner at McDonald's in January. Sometimes people hand me half-eaten food or purchase something for me at a store. They were the first to buy me an entire meal and invite me to eat with them. That meant a lot. Funny, her husband was homeless and a drug addict. As was Kat. Maybe only people who've been here can understand. Guess you need to feel the struggle to grow the empathy.

My own family flashes in my mind, shoulder to shoulder in that church pew. No doubt my dad still greets the pastor with a smile after every sermon like nothing's wrong. Pastor used to compliment my parents because their teens came to church. He even called us a beautiful family.

*"People judge by outward appearance, but the Lord looks at the heart."*

In my mind, I'm in second grade. Mrs. Debbie teaches the story of Samuel when he went to Jesse's house to find the son to anoint.

"Then David came in." Her gaze falls upon me. She motions for me to come forward.

I walk timidly to the front. I'm the shortest in the class and self-conscious because of it.

She rests a hand on my shoulder. "He was the youngest, the shortest of all the brothers."

The class giggles, but she places her other hand on my right shoulder so I can't bolt.

"But the Bible says, 'He was dark and handsome, with beautiful eyes.'" Mrs. Debbie leans forward. "'And the Lord said, 'This is the one; anoint him.'"

The entire room is silent.

"This was the boy who would fight and defeat Goliath. He would survive the persecution of Saul and become one of the best kings to rule Israel. And, most importantly, he would be called a man after God's own heart."

I knew she meant David, but in that moment, the words felt like they were for me.

I shake my head. I've learned my lesson. It's fairy tales and sweet sentiments. People aren't how they appear, and God will crush your dreams in an instant. My family is another example of hypocrites who pretend to have it together and fail miserably.

The streets outside the clubs are wall-to-wall people when I show up at ten p.m. I'm wondering how I'll find her when she slips her arm around me.

"Miss me?"

My heart races at her touch and the sound of her voice. "Yeah."

There's an awkward pause in which I don't know if I should hug her, kiss her cheek, or ask her the same. Thankfully she walks toward the tamale guy.

"I'm starving. How about you?"

"Getting there."

She's impressed, as is Carlos, that I pay.

"It's the haircut," I say when we sit at the bench with our dinner. "Evidently people give more to a clean-cut homeless kid than one with long unkempt hair."

The laugh that follows makes me grin.

"People are about appearances." She tugs at her short skirt when two college guys gawk at her as they pass. "The looks and comments I get when I'm dressed for work are nasty. Like I don't deserve respect or have feelings."

"Why do you dress that way? I know you have other clothes."

"It's like my uniform. The more skin I show, the better." She runs her hand up her bare thigh. "Intriguing, right?"

I cram my tamale in my mouth, shift my eyes from her in an attempt to calm myself.

She laughs again. "I bet clean clothes helped too. Maybe you should go to the shelter every Sunday to do laundry. We could meet after for dinner like we did."

"Sounds good. Both clean clothes and dinner with you."

"Saturdays are rough because I'm tired from Friday and work even longer hours. It's probably best we stick to Friday nights and Sundays."

I nod. I don't want to be disappointed but being with her on her days off was awesome.

"Of course, I'm free Mondays and Tuesdays." It's like she read my mind. "And I'd like you to come over Wednesday nights to shoot up with me. I hate doing that alone."

"Do you think you'll ever quit?"

"Drugs or prostitution?"

"Both."

She unwraps her second tamale. "I make great money. Drugs come with the territory, I guess." She pulls an eight ball from her purse, slips it under my leg. "Got you a little something. I needed more to get through the weekend. Thought I'd share."

"Thanks." I shove it in my pocket, thankful, yet hurt at the same time. Am I only a strung-out friend to her? "Maybe we can go to a movie on your day off. It's been a while for me."

"As long as we get popcorn. And M&Ms."

"I'm more of a sour candy kind of guy."

"I bet you drink root beer, too."

"More like rum and Coke nowadays." I lift my can of Coca Cola.

"Is there rum in there?" She snatches it from my hand. After a sip, she sets it beside me. "Such a disappointment."

I laugh. "It's easier to swipe wine and beer. Rum bottles are big and awkward."

"You're funny." She passes her fingers through my hair. "You look hot with your hair cut. If you weren't my brother—" Her hand lingers for a moment. I almost think she's going to kiss me, but then she stands. "Wanna walk me to my pickup spot?"

Yup, that's how life is when you're in love with a prostitute.

# CHAPTER 25

## LYDIA

Friday night Mom wakes every couple hours crying in pain. It's a constant cycle of cold washcloths, back rubs, scripture reading, and Tylenol. At six a.m., when she's finally sleeping soundly, I hurry out to get her favorite sundried tomato bagel. Dad only goes to the donut store on Sunday mornings when the girls are in town, because that's what he likes. It's time to change that.

The entire way to the bagel shop, I pray God will reduce her stress level, take away the pain, give her comfort and peace. I pray He will give her wisdom and strength to continue to stand up for us.

Us. Me, her, and Danny.

Though Danny's not at home, he's still part of the family. If God loves him despite his sin, why shouldn't we? I think of the flyers Dad took down. Rage grows inside me. He deliberately destroyed my hard work. Did he skip work one day to drive around town, or was it a gradual thing, a different place every day?

"God, I...I..." The word hate is on my tongue, but the word love keeps coming to mind. "God, I know you want me to love him. It's just so hard."

*Things aren't great at home*; I text Jason when I get to the bagel shop. *I could use your prayers that God will change Dad's heart and help me love him.*

His response comes when I'm paying. *Sorry. Wanna talk?*

*I can't.* I know if I do, I'll be wrecked. *Thanks though.*

*I'll pray. Call me if you need anything.*

The worship music I play on the way home reminds me God will never let me down. The circumstances might be beyond my control, but I can control my response. I can control my emotions. *God, help me to stay focused on Your goodness. Help me to have faith that You can work miracles through this mess.*

Mom is on her side reading on her phone when I enter her room with our bagels and her coffee.

"You okay?" I set the tray in front of her before I remove my plate.

"Your father called."

I frown. "You didn't have to answer it."

"I was so angry, I prayed for him a lot last night. I figured maybe I should. He'll be by tonight with dinner and to pick up clothes for the week." She sits up, moves the tray over her. "Thank you, sweetie."

"Do you want him to come over? If it's too hard for you, you can say no."

"In twelve years, he's made or picked up dinner less than a dozen times. Two nights in a row is a step in the right direction. Besides, he asked to pick up clothes. That means he understands he can't come home. I'm impressed that he's accepted that." She takes a bite of her bagel. "Maybe you should put the flowers on the dining room table."

"Sure. How's your pain?"

"Not awful. It's a dull throb."

"Maybe we could play cards after breakfast." I take a bite of my cinnamon raisin bagel.

"I'd like that." She sips her coffee. "But I am sick. You need to let me win."

I smile. "Yes, Mom."

My day is all about taking care of Mom and answering texts. Mary checks in with me, then Mom's sister. Right before five o'clock, one comes from Katie.

*Hi. Missed you at school Thursday. Is everything okay?*

For months I've been hiding my feelings from her. That's not a friendship, especially if I consider her my best friend. I don't know that she can handle the full truth, so I throw a little her way. *Not really. Things are a mess with my family. We could use prayer.*

*I'm sorry, Lyd. I'll be praying. We're home during the break. Maybe we can go to lunch?*

The doorbell rings. I take a deep breath. *God, be with me.*

Dad's on the porch with two bags from my favorite burger place in one hand and a bouquet of mixed flowers in the other.

"Your favorite tonight." His smile makes my stomach flip.

I step back. "Come in."

He walks to the dining room with the food. After he admires the roses, he hands me the bouquet. "For you. I'm sorry for the way I've acted."

"Thank you." I force the words out. Is he trying to buy my love?

He heads straight to the family room. "Oh Margaret," I hear him say. "I'm sorry."

I can't hold back the tears. I want him to be deeply sorry. *God, let this change him. Show him how much we're hurting.*

Dad takes his seat at the head of the table when I call them in for dinner. Mom sits beside me on the right side of Dad.

"Don't you want to sit across from me?" he asks.

"No." She places her napkin in her lap.

For a moment, it looks like he's going to say something, and I brace myself for an argument, but then the moment passes, and he reaches for his burger.

My burger says no tomato, add onion which is how Anna orders hers. I guess I should be impressed that he remembered Mom prefers turkey burgers.

"How's school?" he asks as he lifts his burger.

"Fine." I take Mom's hand. "Should I pray for the food?"

"Yes, dear." She bows her head.

Dad pauses, burger midair. I don't wait for him to put it down.

"God, thank You for this food. Bless it to our bodies. Thank You that Mom's pain is less today. Please continue to heal her. Be with Danny and provide for all his needs according to Your riches in Christ Jesus. In His name we pray, amen."

"Amen." Mom squeezes my hand.

Dad clears his throat. "You're not in pain today?"

"It's less. Manageable." She unwraps her burger. "It hurts when I stress."

"Mary said there's a medication—"

"Hopefully it'll shorten the course of the virus. There's no guarantee," Mom says. "The doctor said the most important thing is to eliminate stress and get lots of rest."

He looks at me. "How's school?"

"Fine." I drop the onions on the burger wrapper.

"You're keeping your grades up?"

My hands ball into fists. *Here he goes—*

"Lydia is an excellent student, Chris." Mom places her hand on top of mine. "You don't need to ride her about school. In fact, I think it's best that we not discuss it tonight."

"I got a call Thursday about her absence. I wanted to make sure—"

Mom lifts her hand. "We spent the day together. That was more important than her sitting in classes."

My pulse begins to decrease. I'm in awe of how calm Mom is.

Dad shoves fries into his mouth. "I deserve to know what's going on in my daughter's life. I'm her father."

"But you have no right to run it." Mom rests her left hand on the side of her face and closes her eyes. She takes a deep breath. "A father encourages and leads his children in God's Word. He doesn't rule their lives with an iron fist."

"Is that what you think I've done all these years?" He leans forward. "Been some nasty tyrant?"

"Since Danny made all-stars. And since you started spending less time in God's Word."

"Excuse me?"

I put my burger down. *God, please let him hear Mom out.*

"First there were small signs, like when you'd use profanity. Then came the obsession with money. That's when your job became more important than us. You insisted I not attend Bible study because it was too hard on you to drive the kids." She presses her hand against her ear. "You started to yell at the kids, demand perfection from us all. I tried to encourage you in the beginning by asking if you were in the Word. You told me you were too busy, and it wasn't my business. You insisted you got what you needed from Sunday mornings."

He drops his gaze to his plate.

"Attending church Sunday mornings isn't enough to build a personal relationship with God, like Sunday lunches aren't enough to build a Christian family." She stands. "Thank you for dinner. I'm going to lie down. Please take enough clothes for the week. I'll see you at Pastor Raul's office Tuesday afternoon if you decide to come." With that, she's gone. I'm so proud that she spoke the truth with such calmness.

I want to leave too but continue to eat. I can't look at him, so I stare at my food.

"I didn't mean to," he says.

I bite a French fry.

"I don't know what to do. I don't want her to divorce me."

The tone of his voice captures my attention more than the words. He almost sounds humble. I raise my eyes to see tears in his.

"I know I've messed up. Pastor and your mom tell me I need to show my love. I don't know how to do that. We had a good marriage years ago. I don't know how to get back to that."

"You don't need to go back, Dad. You need to move forward."

He rubs the back of his neck. "How do I do that? Everything's a wreck."

The chapter of the Bible I listened to with Mom last night comes to mind. "Philippians 2."

He shakes his head. "What?"

*God, let him receive it.* I open my Bible app to Philippians 2. I start reading with verse one. "Is there any encouragement from belonging to Christ? Any comfort from his love? Any fellowship together in the Spirit? Are your hearts tender and compassionate? Then make me truly happy by agreeing wholeheartedly with each other, loving one another, and working together with one mind and purpose."

Since he hasn't left, I continue to read. "Don't be selfish; don't try to impress others. Be humble, thinking of others as better than yourselves. Don't look out only for your own interests, but take an interest in others, too."

His forehead is pressed against his folded hands. Is he praying?

I put my phone on the table. "I know it's hard, but if you want to change, God will help you. He can break your pride if you surrender to Him."

"I don't even know what that means," he says.

"You need to admit that you don't know everything, that He is God and does have the answers. Tell God you want Him to be in control of your life, then ask Him what He wants from you. Instead of worrying about what others think, read the Bible to find out what God thinks. Like in verse three, it says to think of others better than yourself. You've done that by getting our favorite food."

"I am trying." He raises his eyes to me. "I want to do better."

"The more you read the Bible and pray, the more you'll change. When you taught me to ride a bike, you told me it would take time. I needed—"

"Patience," he says. "And practice."

"Building a relationship with God like that. Every morning I read the Bible and talk to Him in prayer. I try to confess my sins immediately and repent. It's not easy, but it's worth it." I swallow back my tears. "We're worth it."

He wipes his sleeve over his eyes. "I need to get my clothes. Can you send that to me?"

"Sure."

He kisses the top of my head. "I love you. Thank you for taking care of your mother."

I hold back my tears until he leaves the room.

We don't talk about Dad once he's gone. Mom doesn't even acknowledge that he left. She keeps her eyes fixed on her TV show. A half hour after he's gone, she tells me she's ready for bed.

As I rub her back, I pray she'll sleep through the night. We decide to stay home from church tomorrow. Hopefully we'll both sleep in. Tomorrow will be a jammie day while we cry our eyes out to our favorite love stories. She says that's exactly what she needs.

I stay with her until she falls asleep, then head to my own room like I promised. Four verses into Philippians 3 my eyelids struggle to remain open. I check the time. Eight thirty. *God, I'm so exhausted. It feels like it's been one thing after another for months. Will it continue to get worse? I can't handle any more—*

*Keep reading,* I feel the Spirit whisper to my heart.

I dry my face on my pillow, then go back to the home page of my Bible app. The verse of the day is Habakkuk 3:19. "The Sovereign Lord is my strength! He makes me as surefooted as a deer, able to tread upon the heights."

I read it three times. The exhaustion is replaced first with peace, then with comfort, and finally with faith. I don't need to be strong. I need to lean on Him. He'll continue to take me where I need to go to overcome these hardships. My hike with Jason on Valentine's Day comes to mind.

*"You're stronger than you think. With the help of God and your friends, you'll rise above every obstacle that comes against you."*

"I trust You, God," I whisper. "I don't like this, but I trust You."

---

## *DANNY*

It's a busy Saturday in the park. Fifty-two bucks is my take for five hours. Reminds me of my beginning days of panhandling. Time to start saving again for my trip west. Only this time, I may have a traveling partner.

The homeless camp Kat told me about is a good walk from the park. Definitely not looking to relocate there; however, I'm hoping it will spark some creativity within me. While I have notebooks with character sketches, I lack story ideas. The best stories are somewhat based on reality. Maybe the average person would be less judgmental toward homeless people if they see a story, or several stories, played out. It'll be great research to talk to people. The camp holds endless possibilities.

I pass a couple of inhospitable women, one man who mumbles to himself, and a woman with gnarly teeth offers her "services" for the low cost of ten dollars. I'm at the peak of my frustration when I find Rudy.

Rudy claims he was once 5'10" but being on the street has shrunk him to 5'8". He offers me a crate and soup. My stomach turns as I watch him heat the mysterious liquid meal in a tiny pot over a small fire. Think he said it was tomato, but there are green chunks in it. I can't refuse it because I'll offend him.

"How about a PB sandwich to go with the soup?" I pull out my half loaf of bread and my peanut butter.

"Perfecto." He flashes his front gums at me. The thing about the homeless is you don't quite know if they lost their teeth to the overuse of some drug or a lack of dental care. Makes me remember to brush twice a day.

"I grew up in New York." He sips the soup after he stirs. "Lots of family. The cousins and me could find trouble anywhere." He snorts when he laughs. "Like the time I was thirteen. Frankie was the oldest. Fifteen. He didn't have his license, but he always wanted to drive." He chuckles, stirs the soup again. "This one night, his parents were out, left us alone. Went to a movie. Some shoot 'em up. You know, a good ol' Mafia flick. That guy was in it. You know, the one with the face and the nose?"

"Al Pacino?" I ask.

"That's it."

I wonder by the way he talks if he was a gangster himself.

"Frankie found the keys for his mom's Mercedes. It was topless with all the gadgets. 'Let's go for a drive,' he said. Well, his brother Tony and I were bored, so we went." He removes the soup from the flame and pours some in the "I heart Chicago" mug in my hands. "We drove for hours. Almost ran out of gas. Wouldn't have got caught if we hadn't passed his parents goin' back home." He laughs as he fills his own cup. "His dad broke the wooden spoon on poor ol' Frankie's backside. Like spankin' an almost sixteen-year-old works." He shakes his head. "One of the funnest nights of my life. There's something about bein' free."

"Yeah, I know what you mean." The soup tastes remotely like tomato, but not really. I follow with a bite of sandwich to offset the sour kick to it. "That's why I left home. To be free."

"Thought I lost my freedom when I got married." He bites into his sandwich, smacks his lips the entire time he chews. "Told myself

I was missin' out. Workin' too hard. No time to go drinkin' with my friends. I took to drinkin' every night in my garage. For almost twenty years I thought she was destroyin' my life."

"Then what happened?" I take a long drink of my soup. Figure it's better to shoot it and get it over with, like whiskey. It only burns a little on the way down.

"Car accident. Don't suppose it was her fault. She was a good driver. But it was late. She was comin' home from our younger daughter's college. Medical examiner said his best guess was she fell asleep. They found pills in her purse, said she mighta been abusin' them. The other person got this lawyer. I was already using coke; the debt was pilin' up. Took me for everything we owned. I felt guilty for the years I didn't treat her like I should. My daughter says I had one of those psychotic breaks, you know, like when you can't handle any more." He drinks his soup.

Everything Rudy says plays out like a movie in my mind. It has it all—drama, drugs, deceit, devastation. "Could your family help?"

"My youngest was still in school. She had to pay her own way. My oldest, well, she's a lot like her old man. Likes her freedom. She told me I needed rehab, but nobody was gonna lock me up. I got all I need right here." Rudy motions behind him at the two-person tent and clothes hung out to dry. "My social security checks pay for my food, so I don't hav'ta beg. And keeps me healthy when I'm sick. Lotsa people die on the streets 'cause they don't got money for medication. Every time I'm sick, I'm able to go to the doctor."

"That's good. You ever talk to your daughters?"

"I visit on holidays. They like that." He nods. "Sometimes I stay with the youngest and her family a few days. Had her second baby last year. Said I could move in with them, but that's okay. I've been here seven years. It's like home to me now."

I glance around. This is home to a sixty-some-year-old man? Pathetic is the word that comes to me. My condition is worse since

I don't have steady income, yet I can't imagine this being my life. It's a season. A detour on my way to make my dreams come true. I've been on the streets four months longer than I wanted to be. I'm grateful now that I met Kat; however, there's no way I'll call the streets "home."

Rudy rinses the mugs when we finish dinner. Then he fills them with scotch. The more I drink, the easier it goes down.

"What's your story?" He reclines in a tattered lawn chair. I'm on the ground on my sleeping bag, back against the crate.

"I was a baseball star. Hated it, so I left. I'm headed to California to sell my first script."

His already curved eyebrow rises. "You a writer?"

"Yup. Plays, movies." I raise my glass. "You'll be a great character in my story."

"That's hilarious." He does his snort laugh. "Me in a movie?"

"Sure. People want real stories about real people. That's what sells. You're an interesting person."

"No." He shakes his head. "People want to escape. They don't wanna be reminded about life." He lifts his cup. "They wanna forget it. Ain't that why you ran? Ain't you out here tryin' to forget?"

"Sure, but they want real stories as evidence that their lives aren't the only messed up ones."

"That's what this camp is about. We stick together and look out for others."

We talk until the glow of the fire is out. He invites me to stay until breakfast. I agree, since I can't get to the shelter until the afternoon.

It's not Kat I think about as I drift off to sleep but Brett and his brother. The summer nights I hung out at their house. The conversations we had around their disgustingly dirty kitchen table. I never had to pretend with them, explain myself or my motives. There was laughter, acceptance, friendship. Though Brett was an idiot when it came to reading and writing, he was a great guy. He was a good friend. It took me being completely miserable to find a real friend. Can't help but wonder how many people go through life without finding someone like that. If I hadn't been miserable, I could've missed him.

I turn Jim Morrison on low to serenade me to sleep.

# CHAPTER 26

## LYDIA

"Hey, beautiful."

I'm cleaning the lobby in Super Subs when a familiar voice causes me to turn my head. Jason is beside me wearing jeans, a T-shirt that defines his muscles, and a huge smile.

"Hi." I give him a quick side hug.

"Figured I'd find you here this week. Have you had your break yet?"

I shake my head. "About an hour. Can I get you something?"

"I'll wait until your lunch." He sits at the table in front of him and raises his novel. "I have a little reading to do."

"Our paper is due next week. You haven't read yet?"

"I'm a couple chapters in. That's what vacation is for, right?"

I continue to clean tables. It seems he glances my way after every page he reads. The other sandwich specialist, Mackenzie, notices.

"Are you guys dating?" she asks.

"No." I stuff the lettuce in the bin. "We're friends."

"C'mon. He has the hots for you."

Our Valentine's Day kiss comes to mind. I quickly push it out. "We're just friends."

Jason insists on paying for both of our meals. Mackenzie has an I-told-you-so grin on her face when she rings it up.

"So, how are things?" Jason asks once we pray for our food.

I stare at my meatball sandwich. Mary's the only person I've told. Just thinking about it brings tears to my eyes.

"Lyd?" He puts down his roast beef sandwich. "What's going on?"

"Mom kicked Dad out Wednesday." I whisper. "Now Mom has shingles."

"What? Are you kidding?"

I shake my head. "She found a bunch of the Missing posters we'd put up lying in Dad's trunk. He was awful, Jason. I took Mom to the doctor Saturday. Her pain that night was over the top. She was sobbing." I wipe the tears with my sleeve. "Things keep getting worse. I don't understand what God's doing."

"Oh, Lyd." He takes both my hands. "I'm sorry."

I frown. "I'm sorry I was mean to you."

"You don't need to apologize. I get it."

"But I keep hurting you."

Half his mouth turns up in a grin. "If I couldn't handle it, I wouldn't be here. I can take care of myself." The back of his hand grazes my cheek. "I'd take care of you, too, if you'd let me."

"I can't—"

Jason sits back, folds his hands in front of him. "I'm okay with being friends. I didn't mean to pressure you with the kiss, but, well..." His cheeks redden. "I wanted to do that for years. I gotta say, it was the best."

Now I feel my cheeks heat up.

"'There are "friends" who destroy each other, but a real friend sticks closer than—'" He stops with a sigh. "I'm here for you, Lydia. You don't have to go through any of this alone."

I shade my eyes to cover my tears. Jason moves his chair around the side of the table to be beside me. He wraps his arm around me.

"Dear Lord, take ahold of Mr. Morton's heart." I feel his warm breath on my neck as he prays. "Let him see how he hurt his family and walked away from You. We pray he'll repent and turn back to You. We pray the same for Danny, that he would repent and come home. Let Danny know not only how You love him but how much his family does. And be with Lydia." He gently squeezes me. "Heal her hurt. Help her feel Your peace. We trust that You'll work this out for good in her family. In Jesus's name, amen."

"Amen." I wipe my face with my napkin. "Thank you."

"Anytime. You'll let me walk with you through this, right?"

"Yeah. I will." I lift my sandwich. "I've started feeding the homeless."

"You have?"

"Yeah. I carry water and protein bars in my car with me. I leave for work a half hour early to stop when I see someone. Most of them let me pray with them too."

"That's awesome, Lyd."

"It's just a small thing, but hopefully it makes a difference in their lives, and hopefully someone does the same for Danny."

"Tell me about some of the people you've met," Jason says.

I tell him about George, then a guy I met last week and a lady I prayed for this morning who offered to give me her scarf. The time passes quickly. Before I know it, my break is over.

"I get off at three and need to go to the store after." I gather our trash. "I've been cooking for Mom, trying new recipes. She seems to like it."

Jason smiles. "I'd love to go with you."

Chicken cordon bleu is in the oven at five p.m. and I'm reading at the table when Mom enters the kitchen after. "How was counseling?"

She sits at the table without a word.

"Mom?" I put down my book. "Are you okay? Did he show?"

"Oh, he came." She hands me a piece of white paper from her purse.

My hands shake when I unfold it to my father's handwriting.

*Dear Margaret,*

*I am extremely sorry for what I have put you and the children through the past several years. Baseball had become my god. Ever since Danny's team won the finals when he was ten, I've chased a dream that one day he would be the professional ball player I wanted to be. My injury seemed unfair, like God cheated me from becoming what I should be. I found contentment in our marriage, in our kids, but harbored bitterness against God. That kept me from building a relationship with Him. I had such big plans for Danny, and I held the girls to a high standard as well. I thought if my kids were successful, it would make me feel accomplished, rather than like a washed-out failure.*

*Danny told me he wanted to quit baseball, but I couldn't let him. I was already planning what college he'd attend, saving money for our travel to his college games. I even started a CD for him in case he wanted to play minors, so he wouldn't struggle financially like we did in the beginning. I loved going to his games with you, watching your excitement when he did well. It reminded me of when I played. I've missed that look of admiration you once had for me.*

*Knowing you were in such pain opened my eyes to what a monster I've become. I cried when I left the house Saturday because of how I've failed. I don't deserve your love and forgiveness but I'm asking for it. If you can find it in your heart, I'd like to start again to build the marriage we should have. I do love you more than anything. More than my job, baseball, even my life itself. I'm sorry it took you being in pain for me to realize that.*

*I don't want to continue to hurt you. You can let me know when you want to see me. I won't pressure you. I want to come home, but it is your decision.*

*I love you, Margaret. Can you find it within you to forgive me?*

I stare at the letter. Can it be real?

"His assistant, Neil, came in early Sunday morning and found out your dad is sleeping there," Mom says. "He told Neil the truth of what's going on."

"You're kidding."

She shakes her head. "They went to breakfast and talked. Neil voiced everything I've told your dad over the past week—how mixed up his priorities are, how all he talks about is Danny's baseball." Mom pauses for a moment. "Neil pointed out he didn't even talk about Danny but about his baseball. He shared scripture with your father, talked about his own struggles with pride and how he turned around." Mom rests her hand on the letter. "Not only did your father write this, but he's taking time off. Two weeks. Maybe three. He said we could go to California to look for Danny. Or Chicago. Wherever I feel led to search."

Her words give me chills. "What? Dad hasn't taken a vacation in years."

"He said he'll walk the streets with me, check homeless shelters and hospitals. He wants to help find Danny."

"Wow." I'm amazed. "This almost feels too good to be true."

"I see a change in him, sweetie." She lifts the letter. "I thought it was too late. It's not that I doubted God's ability, but your dad's pride was out of control."

"Is he—coming home?"

"Not yet. I invited him for dinner Friday and church on Sunday." She places her hand over her ear. "I can't handle more."

"You okay?"

"Exhausted." She rises, gives me a kiss. "I think I need a little nap."

"No problem." I smile. "Dinner will be ready in an hour."

I text Jason. *Dad apologized. He seems to have repented.*

*Praise God,* he replies. *I'll keep praying. I was going to come to your youth group tomorrow night if that's okay? Maybe we can grab dinner before.*

*I'm making tacos. Wanna come over?* I start to push send and pause. *Thanks for your prayers.*

*I'd love to. Anytime. I'm here for you.*

I set my phone on the table. "God, be with Dad. Continue the work You've started." I sigh. "I know if You can do a miracle and change his heart, You can help us find Danny. Please bring him home."

---

*DANNY*

Spring break means crowds of people in the streets from day until night. It also means more cops. We get chased out of three different locations Monday night.

"Tonight, we sleep underground," Kat says Tuesday morning over coffee. "Last night was ridiculous. I do need some sleep."

"Will you be super busy this week?" I hate the thought of not seeing her as much.

"Not at all. As crowded as it is, it'll be slow for me."

"More people doesn't mean more money?"

"Too many families. Summer is big because of the conventions." She glances at the line of people that extends out the door. "Spring break means a crowded mess without extra cash."

Her gaze wanders to the husband, wife, and their two kids a few tables away. The kids, probably under five, watch cartoons on a phone while the couple talks.

"Do you want kids?"

I sip my coffee. "Maybe after I make a movie or two."

Her eyes widen and shift back to me. "Movie?"

I shrug. "Writing movies is like writing plays—only intensified. I figure start small, get bigger."

"Will you go back to school?" She takes a bite of her croissant.

"Not unless I have to. It's about your talent, writing a story that sells, and finding someone to buy it. Some pretty big-name writers and directors dropped out of college."

"You have that story?"

"Got a good one to start with."

"Where does it take place?" She leans forward.

"In America's second home." I raise my hands to motion around me.

"In a coffee shop?"

"Yup." I glance around. "Look at these people. In thirty minutes, they'll be a whole new crowd. Everyone can relate to life in a cafe."

Kat laughs. "It's about coffee?"

"It's the meet ups, the conversations between customers and baristas. Joe is the experienced barista. He's been at the cafe for six years. Everyone knows him. Amanda is the rookie—"

"Is there a girl named Kat?" Her eyes widen.

"No." I smile. "I wrote this before I knew you."

"Ah." She sips her coffee, deep in thought. "Are you the barista?"

I shake my head. "I'm not in it."

"Of course, you are." She rolls her eyes. "Read the biography of any author. You can find their story or some part of it in at least one of their books."

"Guess you might find hints of my life here and there."

"Like baseball? Is there a baseball player?"

"I'll never write about baseball."

"Because you hate it or because you hate your dad?"

"Both." I sip my drink. This conversation is going in a direction I don't want it to. "What about you? You want kids?"

"I'll never have a family." She stares at the table.

"C'mon." I gently push my foot against hers. "You won't do this forever."

"I knew what I gave up when I started two years ago."

"What?"

"A husband, kids, the house in the suburbs. I'll never have that."

"You're only eighteen."

"People don't marry prostitutes." She smirks. "Not unless they're a pimp. There's no way I'd marry a pimp."

"But one day—"

"You can't live in someday, Danny Boy. You gotta live in the here and now." Crumpling her pastry bag, she stands with her coffee. "I know a park on the north side. How about we go there to escape the crowd?"

I pick up a frisbee on the way to the park. We spend a good amount of time tossing it around. That's when I discover how competitive Kat is and how out of shape I am. She insists on keeping score. Her wild launches have me running and diving like I'm playing ball.

"Good Danny Boy!" She laughs when I do a faceplant to save the frisbee.

"What? Now I'm your dog, not your brother?" I send the blue disc sailing ten feet over her head.

Her laughter increases. "Bad Danny Boy!"

That's when I charge her. We land on the ground. I tickle her until she laughs so hard, she says she's going to pee in her pants.

Next we have a tree climbing competition. Who can climb the highest the fastest.

"You only won because I didn't want to break a nail," she says when she stops halfway up the tree.

"You're just scared of heights," I tease.

"Keep it up and you won't get any wine tonight!"

Our last game is swing jumps. I don't tell her I could out jump all the kids in elementary school except Patty Russin. I heard she went on to do the long jump in high school.

A few kids gather around as we begin to swing.

"Watch out," Kat says. "My brother isn't very coordinated. He might end up landing on you."

By the time we leap from the swings, the boys are chanting my name and the girls are cheering for her. I fall six inches farther than she does. That's when Kat says you lose if you don't land on your feet. Whatever.

In the shade of the tree I climbed, we prepare our PB sandwiches. The half dozen kids come running. She sends them all to wash their hands while she makes them lunch. The bread is low, so they only get a half each, but they're grateful for the food. The girls compliment Kat on her hair, the boys admire my baseball hat. She shines with joy in the afternoon sun.

"That was fun today." She links arms with me as we walk down the Pedway.

"Yeah, it was." I want to tell her she'll make a great mom but know she'll disagree. After a day of fun, I'm not in the mood for a fight.

"You ever been in the Pedway?" she asks.

"A couple times. I got so turned around I thought I'd never get out."

"It connects over fifty Loop buildings, from City Hall and the Thompson Center, to shopping centers and residential buildings. I'll show you all my favorites."

She does. Macy's, Starbucks, Dunkin' Donuts. I've never seen anything like the stained-glass windows.

"They're gorgeous, aren't they?" She stands beside me admiring one that resembles fall trees through a window.

"They really are."

"They remind me of church." She walks on to the next, making me wonder how many churches she's been in.

We ride the train when the main Pedway closes to a place where she says there are no cameras or cops.

"How do you know?" I ask as we step off.

She shrugs. "Common knowledge."

I chuckle at the amount of homeless people that fill in the shadows. We find our own portion of darkness and settle down for the night.

By the time the bottle is empty, Kat is asleep against me. I think of what she said earlier. There's no someday, only today. I get it but don't agree. As messed up as my life is, I have to believe there's something more. I have to believe that maybe, somehow, someday, I will be a screenwriter of blockbuster movies with a beautiful bride at my side. Kat, if I have my way.

I want to tell Kat that life comes in seasons. This is her season to work the streets, like it's my season of homelessness, yet it doesn't define the rest of our lives. It doesn't determine who we are.

"You may think you're too broken to love," I whisper as I run my hand over her hair, "but everyone's broken. Anyone who says they aren't lies. And I'd marry you." A lump rises in my throat. "I don't care what you've done. I love you."

# CHAPTER 27

## LYDIA

"Lydia, dinner time."

I'm on the last paragraph of my English paper when Mom yells for me. The doorbell never rang, so I guess Dad decided not to come.

The dining room is set with Mom's good china. The plates we only use at Thanksgiving. Dad is busy transferring Mom's food to her plate. Is it shrimp alfredo?

"I thought we could try the new seafood restaurant," he says. "Mom picked the crusted mahi-mahi for you. If you don't like it, you're welcome to my pan-seared ahi."

"It looks good." My stomach growls at the smell.

There are garlic mashed potatoes, grilled vegetables, and warm sourdough rolls. There's even a slice of a seven-layer chocolate cake for dessert.

"Maybe I should've gotten two slices," Dad says when he opens the container.

"No," Mom and I say.

"This is great, Chris." Mom smiles. "Thank you."

Dad asks me to pray for the food. He doesn't ask about school, only work, church, and Jason. I'm impressed that he mentions Jason, not the baseball season.

"How's work?" I don't care about his answer, but Mom is silent. I don't want her to feel pressured to make conversation.

"I promoted Jon as second assistant. He trains this week. Then Neil will have support when I'm off the next few weeks."

"Didn't he only start in February?" Mom asks.

"January. After Grant left." Dad stares at his plate.

"Did you ever figure out why Grant left?" Mom asks. "It was right after the new year, wasn't it?"

"When I told Neil about Danny, he said he suspected Grant was doing cocaine. He didn't have proof, so he never brought it up." Dad sets down his utensils. "I wonder if he was Danny's supplier, and when he found out Danny left; he was afraid the truth would come out."

"I didn't think you told anyone." My words come out a ruder than I mean.

"I didn't. My wonderful daughter made sure to get the word out. The entire store has known since January."

I frown.

"You did the right thing. I didn't." He wipes his hands on his napkin. "I'm sorry, Lydia, for how I've treated you and your brother through the last several years. There's no excuse. I hope someday you'll forgive me."

"I forgive you," I say barely above a whisper without making eye contact. Maybe I'm afraid to trust him completely because I don't want to be disappointed.

"Have you thought about where you want to go?" Dad asks Mom.

"Since Anna can't come home for Easter, I think we should drive to Chicago to visit her and spend some time looking there. Then I'd like to go to see my sister in Nebraska."

"Oh. I didn't think you were on good terms with Michelle."

"We talk every day. She's been a great support."

Dinner continues with Dad asking genuine questions, sometimes making wrong assumptions, but he seems supportive. He's slower to speak—maybe because he knows he's on thin ice. But I pray it's the change God is working in him.

After years of verbal and emotional bullying, tension still comes over me every time he opens his mouth. Mom twists her napkin the first half of dinner and then rests her hand over her ear during the last part. That's why I'm shocked she asks if he'd like to stay to watch a movie.

"Sure." He stands, lifts his plate and mine. "How about you two pick one while I do dishes?"

Mom and I exchange a glance.

"Has he ever?" I whisper when he leaves the room.

"When I was pregnant." She stands. "I think it's jammie time."

We're on the couch in our pajamas with our favorite blankets when Dad enters the room. He sits in the armchair beside the sofa.

"You can sit here." Mom pats the couch. Once he sits, she lays her pillow in his lap. "Do you mind?"

"No." He clears his throat. "Not at all."

She settles with her head in his lap and stretches out her feet on my footrest. From the corner of my eye I see him rest a hand on her shoulder.

"Is this okay?" he asks.

"Yes," she whispers. "But don't touch my ear. That's where my spot is."

"How's your pain?"

"Not bad."

"Good," he says softly. "I'm glad."

He watches her more than the romantic comedy. When she moves her hand from under her blanket to hold his, Dad brushes away a tear from his eye. Our family is broken, yet God is gracious to bring us to this place of trusting Him. That's where we'll find healing.

I snap a picture of my parents' hands without them knowing. I need it to remember God is good and He'll carry us through.

---

*DANNY*

On Friday night I go to where Carlos is a couple hours before Kat. I people-watch, take notes of interesting conversations. Pick-up lines, and the responses to them, are my favorite.

"My friends and I have a bet—"

When the brunette with short hair says, "Let me help you lose," I laugh until I cry.

"You have the best hair." This was especially great when the guy said it to a girl who then took off a wig.

"I seem to have lost my phone number. Can I have yours?"

After a blonde rambles off hers to the guy, she says, "I hope you find it."

"Aside from being sexy, what do you do for a living?"

Miss Long Boots and big breasts smiles and says, "Put up with jerks like you."

Complete awesomeness. I could write an entire play that takes place outside the nightclubs of Chicago. I begin to write up a sketch of my main character when a group of girls passes by. Their laughter makes me lift my gaze. A blonde, hair pulled back in a braid, about the same build as Lydia, walks by. I tell myself it can't be, but I call out her name. All the girls turn.

Her face is longer, yet her eyes are crystal blue.

"Sorry," I say. "I thought you were my sister."

The rest shake their heads and continue down the street. She whispers to a girl before coming toward me.

"My name's Becca."

"Danny. Sorry. It's just—" I stare into her eyes, at a loss for words.

"It's fine." She smiles. "Does your sister live around here?"

"Indianapolis." I rub my hands on my jeans. "My older sister goes to school out here. I thought maybe she was here to visit."

"I'm here from Pittsburgh with friends for spring break. You live here?" She glances at my backpack and sleeping bag on the ground.

"I'm between places."

"Would you go see your sister, if you had the money?" Becca sits beside me.

"I'm not welcome at home." I know what she's thinking. I'd love the money but can't lie to her. "Maybe in the fall. She'll be going to college in Missouri."

"Does she know—" Tears form in her eyes. "Does she know you're okay?"

"I text her on Mondays. To say I'm okay."

"Good." She rubs her eyes. "Sorry. I lost my oldest brother in an accident last year. I know what it's like to be without your sibling. I still miss him every day."

*I still miss him every day.*

A pain pierces my heart. I see her mouth move, know the words came from her, but I hear them said in Lyd's voice.

"Let me buy you dinner tonight." She pulls a twenty from her purse.

"No." I hold up my hand. "It's okay."

"Please." She crams the bill in my hand.

I start to argue but have this feeling she needs to do it for herself. "Thanks."

She starts to stand, then pauses. After a sigh, she places a hand on my shoulder and closes her eyes. "God, be with Danny," she whispers. "Protect him. Provide for his needs. Ease his sister's breaking heart. Bring them together soon. In Jesus's name, amen." Becca wraps her arms around me. "God bless you." Then she runs to catch up with her friends.

I don't believe in super spiritual things, yet I feel like I've been with my sister. If angels walk on the earth, there's one who looks like Lyd.

"Hi." Kat plops down, kicks off her heels. "Whatcha doing?"

"I saw a girl who looked like my sister. Only older."

"Like Lydia?" She rubs her feet.

"Yeah." I open my hand to reveal the twenty. "She's buying dinner."

"Cool." Kat pulls her phone from her purse. "I think we should take a picture to send to Lydia. I bet she'd like that."

"No." I know Lyd would, but I can't have communication outside my Monday text with her. It'll make this pain worse.

Kat leans close to me with her phone raised. "Well, then take a selfie with me. We need a new one now that you got your haircut." Before I have the chance to object, she snaps a picture. "Chicken, please. Green sauce."

Don't think I'll ever understand girls' obsession with taking pictures. I head over to Carlos. "Hey, Carlos."

"Hola, Danny. The usual?"

"Yeah. How's the family?"

"Rosaito got her license this week." He crosses himself while he mumbles something in Spanish.

I chuckle. "How many kids do you have?"

"Six. Two teenagers. When the others get to be teens, I'll need to expand my business to afford them. You got siblings?"

"Three sisters. All older."

"So, you know." He nods. "Girls are drama."

"Yes, they are." I hand Carlos my twenty in exchange for the food. "Put the change toward your daughter's car."

"Gracias, Danny. Tell Kat to take care of herself." He nods toward her. "She looks too skinny."

---

## *LYDIA*

I'm halfway through reading Ephesians chapter ten before bed when a text arrives. My heartbeat increases at the name: Kat, Danny's friend.

It's another picture of the two of them. I smile at his haircut. Danny's bangs are combed to the left and the sides are very short.

Except for his face being super skinny, he looks good. His half smile tells me he didn't want to take a picture. It's like when Mom or I insisted he be in a picture. Oh my. He's in love.

Her braids cascade over her shoulders. Her makeup is overdone, her tank top doesn't cover much, but she must be a great person if Danny likes her.

*Hi Lydia! He talked about you tonight. I can tell he misses you. I'm sure you feel the same. Thought this might make your night. :)*

*Thank you.* After I send the reply, I upload the picture of Mom and Dad's hands. *Please tell Danny things are changing for the better. Here's proof. Let him know I love him.* I exhale as I press send.

"God, I don't know what You're doing." I can't take my eyes off Danny's face. "But I trust You. Work all this out for our good and Your glory."

---

*DANNY*

Kat's on her phone when I come back.

"Carlos says you're too skinny. Guess you need to eat one of my tamales too."

She runs a finger over the screen.

"What's up?" I hand her the bag with her tamales and a soda.

"Nothing." She sets her phone beside her and takes her dinner. "Tell me about your sister's twin."

"Becca was her name." I unwrap my first one. "Her brother died this year. Think she would've given me bus fare home."

"Maybe it's time for you to go. I got the cash. You could leave tomorrow."

"I'll never go back."

"What if your dad changed?" She lifts her phone. "What if—"

I laugh. "Are you high? I've known my dad my entire life. Every year he's gotten worse. He won't change. Ever."

She stares at her phone. "Maybe you leaving changed him. He could have realized—"

"How's work?" I ask.

She frowns. "You don't want to know."

I pour hot sauce on my tamale. "I'd rather listen to you talk about your clients than talk about my dad."

"Point taken." She pockets her phone. "But Lydia loves you. And misses you."

"One day when she moves out, I'll find her."

"You should." Kat nods. "Maybe you should call her this week. I'm sure she'd love to hear your voice."

I roll my eyes. "How's your night?"

Kat unwraps her tamale. "You really want to know?"

"Not at all." I take a bite.

## *CHAPTER 28*

### *LYDIA*

*DANNY'S GONE, AND IT'S EASTER,* IS MY FIRST THOUGHT. *It should be getting easier*, is my second thought. But it's not.

My beautiful blue dress with tiny daisies hangs on the back of my door. It's one of my favorite days of the year, yet everything is a mess. On this day that's about the hope of the cross, the resurrection of Christ, I'm empty. I'm grateful for the picture Kat sent on Friday, but I want my brother home.

Dylan had to work at the hospital all weekend, so his parents were driving out to celebrate with him and Mary. Anna had a big children's ministry play in Chicago. Mom asked me last night if I wanted to dye eggs, but I couldn't. That was Danny's thing. I think he still did it because it would make Mom smile. I would dye one or two eggs, but I loved watching the two of them decorate together. When he was fourteen, Mom found directions on how to swirl the eggs. Danny accidentally launched a green and yellow one across the room. Mom laughed until she cried.

I read the verse of the day in John 20 and keep reading that chapter along with the next. Jesus meets Peter on the beach. He shows His forgiveness by asking him three times to feed His sheep. God forgave Peter's doubt. He can forgive mine as well.

"God, forgive my lack of faith," I pray. "Thank You for being the Good Shepherd. Bring Danny to You today. Let him consider Your sacrifice and all You've done for him. Let him feel Your love."

Mom's in a lavender spring dress, her hair down to cover her ears. The kitchen smells of fresh baked banana bread. She smiles at the sight of me. "You look beautiful."

"Thanks, Mom." I run my hands down my dress. "I love it."

She offers me a piece of bread from the cutting board. "Dad will meet us at service."

Her eyes tell me she feels the same way I do inside. Anxious, exhausted, overwhelmed.

"He said we could go out to eat after."

I nod.

She kisses my cheek. "It'll be a good day. After all, He is risen."

"He is risen indeed." I hug her.

Pastor Mark greets us in the foyer. Mom smiles, then continues into the sanctuary.

"Hey, Lydia. Nice dress. Is it new?" he asks.

"Yeah. It's kinda an Easter tradition."

"Are your sisters in town?" He glances toward the door.

I shake my head. I want to say something, to tell him how awful it has been. Instead, I just sigh.

He pats my arm. "I've been praying for your family."

"Thank you," I whisper.

"I'm going to a local shelter to feed the homeless after service today. I understand if you can't, but if you'd like to—"

"I'd love to," I blurt out. "I can ask my parents if they want to come, too."

"That would be great." He smiles. "He is risen."

Joy fills my heart. "He is risen indeed."

I hurry to our pew in the sanctuary. Dad is on the end; Mom is about a foot away from him. "Pastor Mark invited us to feed the homeless after service," I say to Mom. "I want to go. Will you come?"

Mom purses her lips as tears come. "I think that would be great." She turns to Dad. "Don't you, Chris?"

He frowns at first, then forces a smile. "Sure, that would be fine."

Worship is a mixture of Easter hymns and choruses. I can hear Dad singing, which I seldom hear. At the end of worship, Mom has moved closer to Dad. When Pastor begins to read the Easter story, he follows along with Mom in her Bible.

"'Then the angel spoke to the women. 'Don't be afraid!'" Pastor Raul reads. "'I know you are looking for Jesus, who was crucified. He isn't here!'"

*He isn't here.* My heart races. I think about when Dad burst into my room that first morning.

*"Where's Danny?"*

That was the day the nightmare began.

I think of Mary from the Bible, on her knees outside the tomb. She cried from her brokenness because her Savior was gone. She didn't see God's bigger plan, only felt the pain, the disappointment, the despair.

But Jesus was there. He said her name—

*Lydia.*

Mom's focused on Pastor. She didn't say my name. Dad is still reading the Bible. I glance beside me to an elderly couple. It couldn't be them.

*Lydia.*

I fix my gaze on the cross high on the wall in front of me as a verse comes to me.

*"I am leaving you with a gift—peace of mind and heart. And the peace I give is a gift the world cannot give. So don't be troubled or afraid."*

*So don't be troubled or afraid.*

Jesus calls my name, reminds me to focus on Him, not the circumstance. None of this makes sense, just like the ladies' first glance into the empty tomb. It hurts like the thought of someone stealing their Savior's body. But God has a plan beyond my comprehension. He is beside me—if I will only look up.

*God, I'm sorry for not seeking You. My eyes are open. I know You're here and have been. Show me Your glory.*

Dad slides his hand from following along in the Bible to Mom's hand. He lifts it to his lips. She closes her eyes and smiles.

*He has risen indeed.*

We follow Pastor Mark to the center in one car. Dad attempts conversation as he drives. Neither Mom nor I say much. By the way she wrings her hands, I guess she's as nervous and excited as I am. Today we get to love on hurting and lost people, like our Danny.

The food line is a steady stream of people for almost an hour. We each serve a different part of the meal to the homeless people—ham, green beans, scalloped potatoes, rolls. Some people have filthy clothes and reek of BO and dirt. Others look pretty normal. Pastor Mark, Mom, and I greet people with a smile and "God bless" or "He is risen." Dad doesn't look at them.

"You're welcome to fill a plate yourself," Roger, the head of the kitchen, tells us after everyone has been served. "Some volunteers like to visit with the guests." He smiles. "Always a blessing for everyone."

"There's a guy I need to talk to about discipleship," Pastor Mark says. "I'm glad you came. Hope to see you Wednesday, Lydia."

"I think we should go," Dad says to Mom. "I'll take you both out—"

"We should stay." Mom wraps an arm around me.

"I'd like to stay," I say.

Dad hands us both plates with a sigh.

One table in the dining room has an older man, a young adult, and four empty seats. The two men are eating silently when we come up.

"Hi, I'm Lydia." I extend my hand to the young man.

"Jeff." He shakes my hand.

Albert, the older man, greets my parents and then me.

"How long have you been here?" I ask.

"Five weeks." Jeff cuts his ham. "My dad threw me out when he found my drugs."

My father's knife freezes mid-cut.

"He never understood." Jeff forks potatoes. "You know, all the pressure."

"What kind of pressure?" I ask.

"To fit in. To be perfect." He laughs. "I have an older brother in medical school who lives a wonderful life. I found even better parties in college than high school. Cocaine, heroin, for free even. It was the break in reality that I needed."

"You're clean now?" I ask.

He nods. "Have to be to live here."

"That's a good thing?" I mean it as a statement, but it comes out as a question.

He shrugs. "I miss my friends and the life I had. But I'm out of money. This is the only way to survive."

My mom brushes away tears.

Dad sets his silverware on the table. "Is there anything your father could say to get you to come home?"

"It's too late for that. My old man is a—" He clears his throat. "There are some things you can't take back. I'd rather go back to partying than be at my parents' house." He looks to me. "You in college?"

"I graduate from high school in June."

Dad wipes his eyes with his sleeve. Mom slips an arm around him. I continue to chat with Jeff, praying Danny doesn't feel the same as he does.

My parents talk to Albert, but I can tell they are both exhausted. When we go to leave, Dad hands me the car keys.

"Can you drive?"

"Sure."

They climb into the backseat. We're down the street from the shelter when Dad speaks.

"I'm sorry. I'm so sorry."

Mom opens her arms to him. Leaning his head on her chest, he begins to sob. The only time I've seen Dad cry in my life was the day his mother died. He didn't even cry at the funeral.

"I pushed him too hard. I told him to do whatever he needed at the team parties to fit in. I told him whatever it took—"

My stomach sinks at his words.

"I was awake when he came home from that first party so drunk, he could hardly walk." Dad pauses. "That night he ran out of the house after the last game, I smelled marijuana on him when he got home. He told me he did it because of me."

A tear escapes down my cheek.

"I told myself it was his choice, but it was my fault. If I had been the father I was supposed to be, the father God calls me to be—"

"I love you, Chris."

I glance in the rearview mirror. Mom kisses the top of his head as she rocks him. "I forgive you. God forgives you."

"I can't make it better."

That's when Mom sighs. Finally, after all these months, Dad understands how we feel.

"You can pray," she whispers.

I hear his breathing steady, see Mom in my peripheral vision run her hand over his head and arm.

"I need to tell you, I got a call, the end of the first week," he says. "Danny used the credit card you gave him. Ran up hotel and food bills around Bloomington."

My heart sinks.

"That's only an hour away," Mom says.

"I know."

"You never told me."

"It was thousands of dollars. I told the credit card company I didn't realize it was stolen so we wouldn't be responsible for the charges."

My heart races. My brother was only an hour away from home for a week, and when Dad found out, he did nothing?

"I'm sorry," he whispers. "I'm so sorry, Margaret. I wish I could change things. I was so angry. It hurt my pride that he stole from us. I understand if you can't forgive me."

"I can forgive you." Mom's voice is gentle. "But you need to search your heart to forgive our son."

"When that boy—" Dad takes a ragged breath. "I could imagine Danny saying those words. I realized how awful—" There's a pause. "I do forgive him. I want a second chance to become the father I should be for him."

I can't see my father's face, but I hear the sincerity in his voice.

"Then we'll pray God gives you that chance," Mom says. "I think it's time for you to come home."

"No," Dad says, "It's okay—"

"It's time." I hear her kiss him. "It's time we become a family again."

Dad's the one to suggest we play cards when we get home. He tries so hard I want to laugh. He knows nothing about Canasta, which is great because Mom loves to win. He laughs when she demolishes him.

"You've always been the best at games." He takes her hand in his. "Guess that's why I never played with you and the kids."

She clears her throat. "You were too busy."

"That's about to change." He leans back in his chair. "We leave for Chicago next week?"

"Yes."

Dad turns to me. "You'll be okay alone?"

"Yeah. I have lots of studying to do."

Dad frowns. "I'm sorry for being such a jerk. Your grades are fine. You're a great student, Lydia. Please don't stress about your classes."

I don't want to cry, but I do. Maybe from the release of the anxiety that's built for months, or perhaps the hope that things are about to improve. Or maybe because it's the first time in years my father has complimented me.

He takes my hand with his free one. "I want things to be different. I'd like you both to hold me accountable to that." He looks to Mom. "You're right that the only way to help Danny is to pray. Maybe we can do that every night as a family."

Mom and I nod. We take hands before bowing our heads.

"God, we don't know where Danny is, but You do," he says. "Thank You that he's alive. Thank You that he's not alone." He takes a deep breath. "Forgive me of my sins. Forgive me of the pressure I put on Danny and the harsh criticisms I threw at him. Please let him forgive me. Please bring him home."

It's not eloquent, but it's heartfelt. Mom and I each offer up a prayer for Danny's safety and return. After we say amen, I hug him.

"I do forgive you," I whisper. "For everything. I love you."

"Thank you, sweetie." He runs a hand down my hair. "I love you, too."

---

## *DANNY*

"C'mon, Danny. Hurry!" Kat waves to me from down the street. She's in a long sundress and her hair is in ringlet curls. Truly the most beautiful she's ever been.

I jog toward her. I didn't really get why she texted me this afternoon asking me to get a collared shirt and dress pants, but now I'm excited for our semi-formal date, although I still don't get where we're going. The address she sent was some business complex. "Why do I need to hurry?"

"We're late!" She snatches my hand. Glancing both ways, she pulls me across the street.

"Late for what?"

"Church, silly."

We run upstairs toward a brick building with huge arches and a steeple. I stop. Holy Name Cathedral the sign in front says.

"No." I break from her grasp.

"It's Easter." She grabs my hand again. "I have to go to church on Easter."

"You go. I'm not." Instead of going back down the stairs, I look into her face. The frown and downcast eyes tug at my heart.

"I don't like to go alone. Please go with me." She doesn't beg but asks in the sweetest way. "I promise you a great dinner after. It'll only be an hour."

"Better be a really good dinner." I walk hand in hand with her into the lobby.

The floor is high-quality tile, a sharp contrast to the multi-colored cheap carpet that's in the lobby of my church.

My church? I shake my head. I'm done with that.

Kat dips her fingers in the large marble bowl that stands in the center of the entry, then crosses herself.

"Did you want—"

"No, thanks." I lift a hand.

The first sight when we walk through the doors of the sanctuary is Jesus, the superstar himself, almost as large as life, hanging out on the cross.

Images of an empty tomb with a stone rolled away and the phrase "Hallelujah, He is Risen" shine on the wall on either side of the crucifix. Yet there's Jesus, sad eyes and pouty lips, between the pictures. Stuck on that cross for all eternity. The night is going to be full of irony.

An old man approaches the podium where a large book is open. At the rate he walks it's either going to be a short message or we'll be here more than an hour. Scripture from John 20 appears on the wall.

"Let us read from the book of John." His voice reminds me of my grandfather's.

The entire congregation stands as he reads. The inflection in his voice deepens instead of rising. There's no excitement as he reads about the angels, the cloth, the empty tomb. Even when Mary realizes who Jesus is, his deadpan voice doesn't change. When we get to the end of the scripture, everyone sits.

"There's a lot to grieve in this world," he reads from the book in front of him. "Not every cloud has a silver lining. Life isn't a bed of roses. It's not all sunshine and rainbows."

I chuckle to myself. Is the Catholic church one big cliché?

"But what you need to focus on is Easter."

The girl next to me giggles. No doubt images of bunnies and candy-filled eggs come to her mind.

"The glory of Easter drowns out the despair of Friday."

I lift my eyes to Jesus. He doesn't look like the superhero of Easter. He looks sad, broken, tormented, completely hopeless—

*"Therefore, it was necessary for him to be made in every respect like us, his brothers and sisters, so that he could be our merciful and faithful High Priest before God. Then he could offer a sacrifice that would take away the sins of the people."*

I shake my head as the verse comes. I don't believe the Bible anymore. I turned my back on that when I left home.

"Imagine if God treated us like He did His Son that first Easter morning."

And yet, He doesn't. He treats me like He treated His Son on Friday. Indifferent to my prayers, mocking my needs. He has turned His back on me, not once or twice but over and over again. I squint and focus on Christ's face. Are those tears in Jesus's eyes? Maybe since His last words were "My God, my God, why have you abandoned me?" I chuckle to myself. Jesus does understand. His Father was a hypocrite too.

"God loves you." The old man finally glances up from the book in front of him. "Do you know that? God loves you."

I wish I could bolt from the church. I actually consider it—until I see Kat wipe away tears. As bad as I've had it, it's nothing compared to what she's endured. The physical as well as emotional pain. The psychological pain of giving her body away five days a week, including Easter. She places her hands in her lap, smooths out her skirt. I place one of mine over them, which makes her attempt to smile.

Kat's silent when we walk from the church an hour later. I follow her lead, turning right on the street toward a row of restaurants.

"You okay?" I ask though I can tell she's not.

Kat frowns. "It makes me sad that I won't go to heaven. I want to see my grandma again."

"Who says you won't go to heaven?"

"What I did was awful." She glances around before she continues. "I took a life—"

I shake my head. "You didn't have a choice. They made you—"

"I could've run."

The firmness in her voice causes me to pause.

"I thought about it." She wraps her arms around herself. "On the way there I thought about running away, going to my grandpa or the police. I convinced myself Gramps didn't want me, and the police wouldn't believe me. I felt like I should've stopped it somehow. Or that I deserved it. He always told me I was too pretty for my own good."

Listening to Kat blame herself for being raped crushes me. I know there's no way I can change her mind. This is something she's held on to for years.

"God doesn't love me. How can he forgive something like that?"

"The Bible says there's no condemnation in Christ." Her face tells me she's as shocked as I am at my words. I lead her to a bench. "If you believe in your heart Jesus is Lord and confess with your mouth, you'll be saved." The phrase I've heard a million times comes quickly. "He's faithful to forgive those who ask Him to."

Her eyes narrow, wrinkles gathering on her forehead. I sigh. This is what I want to walk away from. This is what I want to be done with. The talk of sin and redemption. The idea of Jesus the superhero. But I see the hurt in her eyes. I hear the condemnation she has placed upon herself. I can't handle the thought of her continuing to beat herself up. She needs this to move on. If there's one thing I learned going to Sunday school for twelve years, it's the sinner's prayer.

"Do you believe Jesus is God?" I ask.

"Yes." She nods.

"Do you believe Jesus died for your sins?"

"Yes. He died for everyone's sins on the cross."

"Have you ever told Him that?"

"What do you mean?"

"Have you prayed the sinner's prayer?"

She shifts her eyes up in thought. "Is that the one that starts 'O merciful God…' "

I shake my head. "You don't have to repeat some big long prayer. You tell God you believe in Him. You accept what He did on the cross."

Kat stares at the people as they pass. "I don't understand."

"You say something like this. Dear Jesus."

"Dear Jesus." She shifts her eyes to me.

"Thank You for dying for me."

"Thank You for dying for me." Kat searches my face.

"Please forgive me of all my sins."

She takes my hands in hers. "Please forgive me of all my sins."

"Come into my heart."

A grin spreads on her lips. "Come into my heart."

"Make me a new creation."

"Make me a new creation."

"And help me forgive myself for all I've done."

Kat squeezes my hands when she shuts her eyes. "And help me forgive myself for all I've done."

"Amen."

"Amen." She opens her eyes. "That's it?"

"Yup. Most people say the entire thing with their eyes closed, but you did fine."

She nods, bites her lip. "I kinda feel different. Better."

"Good." I smile.

"Have you said that prayer?"

I stand, begin to walk in the direction we were headed. "I did."

"When?"

"At six."

"Wow." She giggles. "Did your mom teach it to you?"

"Nah. It was at Vacation Bible School." My heart raced from excitement while the kids around me prayed. I finally understood. Jesus didn't only love me—He died for me. He was beaten and crucified so God would forgive my sins. That was a long time ago—

"One of the things I love about you is you're smart."

"You must have me confused with someone else."

"I'm serious. You read. You write. You know a lot about God." She frowns. "I wish I knew more. I only went to church on holidays with Grams. She was raised Baptist, but there wasn't a Baptist church close by, so we went to a Catholic one. I didn't understand much of what they said. And now." She looks around. "I don't feel like I belong."

"Church is full of sinners." I laugh at her shocked expression to my statement. "The Bible says we're sinners saved by grace. You don't need to go to church to learn about God. You can read the Bible for yourself. There's even an app for your phone."

"Will you help me find it?" Her mouth turns up in a grin.

"Sure, after dinner. My treat. The tourists were generous this weekend. Where do you want to go?"

"Italian's my favorite. There's a good one down the street." She pulls out her phone. "I better make sure it's open."

*There's a party in heaven,* I hear Lyd say.

I take in Kat's beautiful face. I'm thankful I met her.

"What else did you learn in church?"

"How to make paper airplanes. How to pretend to listen while I wrote my screenplay in my head."

"You're awful." She leans against me.

"You're pretty wonderful. Guess we balance each other out."

I entertain her with stories of tourists. She glows in a way I've never seen before. True to my promise, once we've settled down with a bottle of wine in a deserted doorway after dinner, I install the Bible app on Kat's phone.

"What does NIV stand for?" She stares over my shoulder the entire time.

"New International Version."

"How about NLT?"

"New Living Translation." I point underneath to the entire name. "Lyd likes that one the best. She says it's easiest to understand. Anna likes NIV."

"What's your favorite book?"

"Used to be the book of Daniel."

"Because Daniel is your real name." She laughs. "Well, maybe I'll start there."

"Maybe you should start to read tomorrow." I replace her phone with a full glass of wine. The last thing I want is for her to read how Daniel refused the king's food and drink because it would defile his body. I've dreamt about our wine time since sliding in the church pew.

She picks up her phone. "Why are some of the words red?"

"Those are the ones Jesus said."

"Oh." Her eyes get wide.

"They're mostly in the Gospels."

She frowns. "What are the Gospels?"

"Matthew, Mark, Luke, and John," I say. "New Testament books written specifically about Jesus' life and ministry."

"Jesus said all this?" She scrolls through the Book of Matthew.

"Yup, pretty much."

"'Love the Lord your God with all your heart, all your soul, and all your mind. And love others as yourself.'" She shifts her eyes from the screen to me. "Do you love God?"

I take a drink. "This is a good one. I like the reds you choose."

"Do you love God?" The pitch of her voice rises.

"I don't know, Kat. It's not that easy."

"You love your mom? Your sister, Lydia?"

I nod. "Yeah, I love them."

She settles beside me with her wine. "I hate my mom for what she allowed her boyfriend to do to me, and that she chose him over me. I hate him even more. But I don't hate God. It's not like God made them do it."

I run my hand over her hair. "I hate my dad. He thinks he's a good person who has this great Christian family. A real Christian doesn't act the way he does." I take another drink. "It's cool that you want to read the Bible. Lyd always said everyone needs their own faith. We're not supposed to be cookie cutters."

"But isn't there a right way and a wrong way?"

I shrug. "You read that verse. It says to love. Guess how you do it is up to you."

"Why are you mad at God?"

I stare into my glass. "You know when you count on someone and they don't come through?"

"Yeah." She chuckles. "I can't count on Jennifer for anything, but I continue to ask for her help. Then I feel like a fool."

"That sums up my last several years with God. I'm done with the disappointments."

We drink in silence. It's not awkward, kind of comforting actually.

"What are you most afraid of?" she asks as I refill my glass.

I don't think I've had enough wine yet to answer her. I remind myself she's several glasses ahead. "Haven't thought much about it. How about you?"

"Going to hell."

"You took care of that today." I clink my glass against hers.

Her giggle makes me smile. "Yes. Thank you. What about you?"

I take a nice, long drink. When I finish, the question still hangs in the air. "Losing you."

"Why would you lose me?" Her eyes look sad.

"My life hasn't gone the way I want it to."

"Guess we can both say that. How would it go, if you were in control?"

"You and me in LA. I sell my first screenplay—"

"And we live happily ever after?"

"Something like that." I set my empty glass beside hers and lie down.

"Hmm." She leans her head on my chest. "I've always wanted a happily ever after."

"Me too." I kiss the top of her head.

# CHAPTER 29

## DANNY

THE BANNER IN FRONT OF THE SHELTER PROCLAIMS IT'S MOTHER'S Day. For the first time in weeks I think about my mom. Her smile, the way she laughed at my jokes, how she came in my room every night to pick up my clothes and say goodnight. Yeah, I won the jackpot with my mom. Truly, her only fault is that she loves and has stayed with my father.

I want to text her, but what would I say?

*I love you, Mom, but I'm never coming home.*

*Get a clue and leave Dad, would you?*

*If you ever give the old man the boot, I'll come home.*

I decide I'll let go of the guilt and text Lyd *I'm alive* tomorrow.

"It's Mother's Day." Kat stands from the bench she's on when I walk up. "Every restaurant will be crowded."

"Not McDonald's." I slip my arm around her neck. "I got enough to treat. Or we can have peanut butter sandwiches in the park."

"The park will be overrun. Trust me."

"You're early." I lead her down the street.

"Mother's Day. My clients have wives they need to dote on."

"That's—sad."

"But true. It's okay. I slept in. I need to enjoy the calm before the storm."

"What do you mean?"

"Busy season is around the corner." She sighs. "Tourism. Conferences. Lots of lonely men with money. I make double my rate during the summer. Well, except at Christmas."

"Christmas?" I choke on the word.

"Sick, isn't it? Christmas Eve and New Year's Eve are my two busiest days of the year."

I shake my head. I don't understand this world or her profession. But I can't stop loving her. "You'll have to work more?"

"As of next weekend. Shaun gives me a bigger cut. It's worth it." She steps to the right to avoid a homeless guy with a cart who walks between the two of us. "Did you call your mom?"

"No. Why would I do that?"

Kat rolls her eyes. "Because it's Mother's Day. She's your mother."

"Did you call your mom?"

"That's different."

"Really?"

"Your mom didn't make you have an abortion."

She's got me there. "I've moved on."

"She loves you, Danny. They all do."

"I'm pretty sure my dad hates me. Anna probably couldn't care less. At best, Lyd, Mary, and Mom care about me, but Mary's debatable."

Kat lifts my phone from my back pocket. "Text her. She brought you into this world. You owe her that."

I take my phone back. "No drama today." I open the door under the golden arches for her.

After Big Macs and milkshakes, we go to the liquor store. Then we head one level under where there aren't families or cops.

"Best birthday party?" Kat asks.

"My tenth." I uncork the wine. "Dad rented a box at the baseball game. I invited five friends. There were unlimited hot dogs, popcorn, and nachos. The shortstop even stopped by with autographed balls for us."

"What teams?"

"Red Sox and the Orioles."

She takes her glass from me. "What made it the best birthday ever? The unlimited food, the game, or the ball player?"

"I think because my friends were there. Most of time it was me and Dad at games. He'd get serious, shout at the umpires, sometimes even the players. That night he hung out with the other fathers. We all enjoyed the game. How about you?"

"My fourteenth. Grams let me have an epic sleepover. Ten girls."

"Ten?" I almost choked on my wine. "You're kidding?"

She giggles. "Ten."

"My sisters were never allowed to have more than three because that would make six in the house."

"Grams sent Pops away on a guys' weekend. It started before lunch. Ladies came to help Grams do our hair, makeup, and nails. After we got fancied up, they served us a high tea. Then we went to an art museum, took pictures in a rose garden, and ate at my favorite Chinese buffet for dinner."

I can't help but smile. "You like Chinese food?"

"Love it. You?"

"My fave."

She grins. "Next week I'll take you to the one on Archer Avenue."

"Sounds good. What'd you do after dinner?"

"We had a scary movie marathon at our house. We didn't go to bed until two a.m." Her smile starts to fade. "That was the last birthday Grams was around for. Sometimes I wonder if she knew."

"My last birthday was pretty rockin'. This hot girl took me to a Cubs game."

Kat rolls her eyes. "I know it wasn't your real birthday." She sips her wine. "What'd you do on your sixteenth?"

"Got my license. Got grounded from buying a car. Ditched my last class and baseball practice to get drunk and go bowling." I think of how Brett hurled two balls down the alley at once. "You'd like my friend Brett. He's a cool guy."

"Did your family do anything for you?"

"My mom made my favorite meal."

"Which is?"

"Steak, homemade mac and cheese, and cornbread. No vegetables required. She gives me one day off a year."

"You going to call her?"

"No." I take another drink.

Kat takes my phone from my pocket. "Text her. It's not that hard. Happy Mother's Day, Mom," she says aloud as her fingers type. "I love you." She hands me back my phone. "That's it. Now send it."

"We talked about this—"

"If I had a mother who loved me, who wasn't strung out, I wouldn't be here with you. I'd be home with her instead of hating her each day." She runs her hand over mine. "I know your dad's a jerk. I totally get why you ran, but don't take it out on your mom. It's Mother's Day. She's loved you for sixteen years. She deserves to know you still care about her." She grabs my phone back, and her fingers glide across the keyboard. "I miss your steak and mac and cheese." She extends it back to me. "Now it's perfect."

I stare into her brown eyes. She's so beautiful, and so right.

I type Mom in the "to" section, push send, then down the rest of my wine. I hand Kat my glass. "Do I get a refill now?"

She giggles, handing me the whole bottle. "Good Danny Boy."

I shake my head, fill my glass then hers.

"Think she'll reply?"

"I blocked her." I take a sip. "So no, I won't hear back."

"You're terrible."

"Let's move on." I clear my throat. "Favorite animated movie?"

"Beauty and the Beast."

That makes me smile. "You're definitely Belle." I raise an eyebrow. "Am I—"

Her laugh widens my smile. "The good beast. Right before his transformation."

"The beast Belle falls in love with?"

She tilts her head. "Yeah."

If I was experienced in such things, this would be when I kiss her. I feel a magnetic pull towards her. I'm close enough to see the sparkle in her eyes. I feel her breath—

"It was the right thing to text your mom." The corners of her mouth shift down. "It was."

I lean back. "You should call yours. Maybe her boyfriend's moved on. Maybe she's changed."

"You think people change?" Her voice is now more like Eeyore than Tigger.

"Absolutely. For the better and for the worse."

She lowers her gaze. "Some days I'm afraid I'll turn into a nobody like her."

Placing my hands on her cheeks, I raise her face to mine. "You're everything to me." I gently brush away a tear that slips down her cheek. "You're beautiful, Kat. Inside and out. You'd never hurt another person the way she hurt you."

"But I did." More tears rise.

I set a finger on her lips. "Forgiven. Forgotten."

*"Instead, be kind to each other, tenderhearted, forgiving one another, just as God through Christ has forgiven you."*

I hate that the verse comes to mind, but maybe that's what she needs.

"The Bible says to forgive others as Christ forgives you." I lift her phone from the sleeping bag. "Hi, Mom," I read as I type. "I wanted to let you know I'm okay. I forgive you for everything that happened before I left. Hope you have a happy Mother's Day." I place the phone in her hands.

She stares at it. "You make it sound easy."

"It is. All you need to do is press send." I rub her leg. "I don't think you want to continue to hate her."

That makes her tears return. "I don't."

"Then forgive. After all, it is Mother's Day."

She wipes her face, types numbers in the "to" section, and quickly presses "send." With a big sigh she takes a long drink.

"Good Kit Kat." I pat her head in a playful way that makes her smile.

"Thanks, Danny." She kisses my hand. "You're a great friend."

The thrill of her kiss is drowned out by her words. Maybe I'm forever destined to be a great friend.

I reach in my backpack to pull out our latest read, *The Invisible Man*. "What chapter are we on?"

---

*LYDIA*

Mary and Anna stare at Dad as he makes breakfast on Mother's Day.

"Dad, we can help," Mary stands.

"You set the table. That's enough." He flips the pancakes. "These will be done in a minute. How about one of you get your mother?"

"I will." Anna leaves the room.

"Is he always like this?" Mary whispers.

"Cooking or nice?" I ask.

"Both."

I nod. "Kind of. She cooks on Tuesdays and Wednesdays. We go out as a family on Mondays. Family date night he calls it. Thursdays they both go to Bible study, so we have leftovers. He cooks all weekend, even does the dishes."

"He cooks? Like dinner?"

"I may help with recipes and tips here and there."

"Amazing." Mary's eyes widen at the mound of pancakes Dad puts in front of us.

"I have homemade strawberry syrup, too." Dad sets the gravy boat in front of us. It smells of warm strawberries and sugar.

"You made my favorites." Mom kisses him on the lips when she enters the kitchen.

"Nothing but the best for my beautiful wife."

Anna and Mary exchange a glance that makes me laugh.

"You had a good vacation?" Mary asks after we pray for the food.

"We did." Dad serves Mom two pancakes. "Your sister was a great tour guide in Chicago. We left flyers at some local businesses, hospitals, and homeless shelters."

"Your father spoiled me." Mom takes bacon from the platter he holds for her. "We stayed in the nicest hotel in Chicago and a beautiful bed and breakfast on the way to your Aunt Michelle's house. It felt like our honeymoon, only better."

"Much better." Dad raises his eyebrows.

"Chris!" Mom nudges him.

I giggle. Anna blushes.

"You two are the cutest," Mary says. "Good to see you both happy."

"Have you decided where we're taking you to lunch?" Anna asks.

Mom pours the strawberry glop on her pancakes. "I'd like to serve at the shelter like we've been doing."

"Shelter?" Anna's face scrunches up.

"We've spent every Sunday afternoon there since Easter," Mom says.

Anna raises an eyebrow. "Why would you—"

"Anna, stop," Dad says. "We can take Mom out for dinner this evening."

She glares at Dad. "You always said—"

"I was wrong. Jesus cares about the homeless. We should, too." He clears his throat. "You don't need to join us, but that's what we do on Sundays."

"It's a very noble thing," Mary says.

"We don't do it to be noble." Mom says. "We do it because we realize each person there is someone's son or daughter. We pray someone is loving on our Danny."

I've never been so proud of my parents.

Since I drive myself to Sunday School and the rest of the family comes in one car, Anna offers to go with me to the shelter after church. I've prayed for the opportunity to talk to her about Danny. This seems to be my chance.

"Why do you hate Danny?" It's not the most polite way to open the conversation, yet it's what's been on my mind for months.

"I don't hate him. He's our brother."

"Then what do you have against him?"

"I don't 'have something against him.' It does concern me that he doesn't respect the church, the Bible, or any of the leaders." She counts off a finger for each point. "I don't even think he respects God. Though he knows the truth, he chooses not to live it. I mean, he was raised in a Christian home and this is how he acts? He knew better than to drink."

I grip the steering wheel. "Dad forced him to go to those baseball parties. He told him to do whatever it took to fit in. Jason said alcohol was everywhere."

"He never should have tried drugs."

"It started with the painkillers." My heart races. "He was pushed too hard."

"If Dad trained him too hard, he should've said something. If he'd said he didn't want to play baseball—"

"Dad admitted he wouldn't take no for an answer."

"You can't keep blaming it all on Dad, Lydia. Danny still had choices, and he made the wrong ones."

How can she be so unsympathetic? We *all* make wrong choices sometimes. Or has she forgotten that? I inhale slowly. I don't want to attack her. I want to help her understand.

"You know, Anna, Jesus died on the cross for you."

"I know that."

"Do you remember why?" I stop at a red light.

"What?"

"For *all* have sinned and fall short of the glory of God." I stare at her pointedly. "That includes you."

"I didn't say I never sin."

"But you act like it. Where's your compassion for our brother? You only care that Danny learns his lesson. He's on the streets, probably not even eating three meals a day." I start to drive when the light turns green.

"I *do* care, Lydia, but you need to face the facts: Danny's run away from home and he's addicted to God only knows what drugs. He's rejected Dad's help, and he's rejected God. Those are choices he made!"

"Do you think you need to be harsh on Danny because Dad was? You know, he almost destroyed his and Mom's marriage."

"Mom told me they hadn't been close in years," Anna says. "And she pulled away too, which made things worse."

"She pulled away because Dad became a monster! He wrote a letter last month confessing his sins. He realizes he's not perfect. Why can't you see that?"

"I *can* see that! But I can also see Dad works hard to provide for our family. That involves sacrifice."

"Obedience is better than sacrifice." I say the verse that comes to me.

She rolls her eyes. "But obedience often requires hard work along with sacrifice. Look at me. I didn't get where I am purely by sitting around and waiting on God's grace. I studied hard. I put in the time doing menial tasks at church until I worked my way up."

"And that had nothing to do with God?"

She sighs. "You know, I could ask you the same."

I narrow my eyes. "Ask me what?"

"Why do you hate me? You've never liked me."

"I love you, Anna. It's just that you take the whole personal part out of a personal relationship with Christ. You make it about works. Not the work Jesus did on the cross, the work you do. That's one of the things that pushed Danny away from God. You've read the Bible enough to know it's about Christ's work of salvation. His sacrifice."

Anna nods. "You're right. I've also read my Bible enough to know that faith without works is dead. I don't work *for* my salvation, Lydia, I work *because of* my salvation. *Because* of my personal relationship with Christ. Danny fell away because he didn't have that firm foundation. He stopped going to youth group and Sunday school. He never participated in discipleship. Simply accepting Christ at VBS can't carry you through life."

The rest of the car ride is silent. Maybe Anna and I are too different to see eye to eye on this subject, but with every mile I pray God will give Anna greater compassion for Danny and help her understand the pressure he was under.

As I pray for her, God brings to mind what I'm holding against my sister. In middle school it took me days to work up the courage to ask Anna if I could eat with her and her friends. I was hurt, craving acceptance.

*"You need to make your own friends."* She literally pushed me away. *"Stop being shy. Go introduce yourself to someone."*

That's when I began to hide in a bathroom stall at lunch, not eating. I eventually started cutting. It quickly spiraled out of control. I understand that Danny is in a similar place of not being able to help himself. Maybe that's how we grow compassion—we remember the trap we were once in.

Out of the corner of my eye, I see her open her Bible app.

*God, help me to truly forgive her for hurting me when I was younger. Now I realize she was trying to help me make friends. Spark something within her today. When she sees the homeless people, move her heart toward compassion. Bring complete unity to our family again.*

Mom has a smile on her face the entire time we serve at the shelter. She welcomes each person as she hands them a pre-made salad, Mary shovels the mac and cheese with a grin, and Dad plops the pork on the plate with a "God bless." Anna is uncharacteristically quiet as she hands over rolls.

"Happy Mother's Day," I say to the older women as I hand them a piece of chocolate cake.

Once the line is gone, Dad makes each of us a plate.

"I don't understand why we're not taking Mom out," Anna says. "It is Mother's Day. We should be honoring her."

"This is how you can honor me today." Mom kisses her cheek.

"We can still go to dinner tonight." Dad follows Mom.

The dining room is close to full. I scan the room to find two chairs together at Jeff's table.

"Come with me." I nudge Anna. "I want you to meet someone."

With a sigh, she follows.

I place my tray at the seat beside Jeff. "Jeff, I'd like you to meet my sister, Anna. Anna, this is Jeff."

He wipes his mouth and stands. "Nice to meet you." He extends his hand to Anna.

She shakes, flashes a small smile, and sits by me.

"How was your week?" I ask.

"Good." He nods. "I started that book you recommended. You're right, it's pretty intense."

"I told you it's fun to read. How's Bible study?"

"Went over James chapter two this week. A lot to think about for sure. My brain hurts when it's over." He butters his roll. "You got finals soon?"

"In June. I have one more ten-page paper to finish for English and a project for Economics."

"You're going to prom next week?"

Anna's eyes move back and forth with each exchange.

"Yes, with Jason." I glance to Anna. "You and Jeff are close to the same age. He's twenty."

"Where are you going to college?" Jeff asks.

"Moody Bible," she says.

"That might have been a better choice than UIC." He chuckles. "Some people go to college to find themselves. Guess I went to find heroin and cocaine."

"What was your major?" Anna asks.

"Industrial and Systems Engineering." He takes a bite of mac and cheese.

Anna looks him over. I can't help but wonder what's on her mind.

"I've always liked to make things. I might go to a trade school. That way I can learn a trade without the pressure of college."

"That's a great idea," I say.

"What's your major?" he asks Anna.

"Biblical studies."

Usually Anna straightens a bit when she says that but not today. She stares at the tattoos that cover Jeff's arm.

"That's great. Going to college to study the Bible would be a cool experience."

Anna doesn't speak again until we're in the car headed home. "How long have you known him?"

"About a month. He was only in the center to get off the streets. The more we talked, the more interested he became in the Bible. I told him about Bible study, he shared about the study they do at the center. He and Dad begin discipleship next week."

"What?" Anna shakes her head.

"The facility has a discipleship program. Mom and Dad have both volunteered. They were trained last week. She'll meet with a woman named Victoria, he'll meet with Jeff."

"How does Dad have time for that?"

"His priorities have shifted. He's hired a second assistant for the business and works ten hours four days a week to have an extra day at home."

Anna stares out the window. "Jeff seemed normal."

"A sinner saved by grace. Just like all of us."

Dad picks up Chinese food to bring home for dinner at Mom's request. She orders every one of Danny's favorites. After we eat, Mom opens her gifts and Mary serves the cake she made.

"What if we read the story of the prodigal son?" Anna says while I collect empty cake plates. "We could read it, then pray for Danny."

Every eye is on her. Chills make their way up my arms. Did my sister really say those words?

"Why don't you get your Bible, Chris?" Mom places a hand on Dad's arm. Dad immediately gets up. "Let's go to the family room."

Mom and Mary sit on the couch, Anna in the chair. I kneel on the floor. Dad takes his place beside Mom with his black leather Bible.

"Luke fifteen," Anna says when he flips towards the concordance.

He takes a deep breath before he reads. "To illustrate the point further, Jesus told them this story: 'A man had two sons. The younger son told his father, "I want my share of your estate now before you die." So his father agreed to divide his wealth between his sons.

'A few days later this younger son packed all his belongings and moved to a distant land, and there he wasted all his money in wild living. About the time his money ran out, a great famine swept over the land, and he began to starve.'" Dad bites his lip. Each night when we pray for dinner, he prays Danny has food to eat.

Mom lifts God's Word from his hands. She continues to read about the young man longing to eat the pigs' pods. A vision of Danny as he digs through dumpsters comes to my mind.

*Please, God, don't let him starve. Provide him with safe and healthy food.*

Mary reads the son's journey home. Tears overtake her as she reads the prodigal's repentance. She hands it to me.

"'But his father said to the servants, "Quick! Bring the finest robe in the house and put it on him."'" My heart soars as I think of Danny coming home. What a great reunion we would have! I continue to read of the father's gifts, the party, and the father as he explains why he threw the party.

Anna kneels beside me and lifts the Bible close to her chest. "'The older brother was angry and wouldn't go in. His father came out and begged him, but he replied, "All these years I've slaved for you and never once refused to do a single thing you told me to. And in all that time you never gave me even one young goat for a feast with my friends. Yet when this son of yours comes back after squandering your money on prostitutes, you celebrate by killing the fattened calf!"'"

I rest my hand on her shoulder.

She wipes tears from her cheeks and continues. "'His father said to him, "Look, dear son, you have always stayed by me, and everything I have is yours. We had to celebrate this happy day. For your brother was dead and has come back to life! He was lost, but now he is found!"'"

Anna sets the Bible on the floor in front of her. "I've been jealous my entire life—of Mary for being the oldest, Lydia for being the youngest girl, Danny for being the boy. I was even jealous of Mom for a while because I knew Dad loved her more. I used to pray Dad would love me the most. I decided being the most spiritual would make me the best." She dries her face and raises her gaze to me. "You were right earlier, Lydia. I haven't been compassionate toward Danny. But it's not because I don't love him, it's because I've begun to take pride in being more spiritual than him." Her tears begin again. "I'm sorry for being awful to him."

I wrap my arms around her. "I forgive you. I realized that all these years I've been mad at you for pushing me away in middle school. It really hurt me and made me think you were uncaring. I'm sorry for judging you."

Dad joins us on the floor, wraps his arms around both of us. "I'm sorry for being a horrible role model. You learned that prideful attitude from me."

Anna shakes her head. "It's sin. I understand that now."

Dad kisses the top of her head.

Mom kneels beside Anna. "We've always loved you, Anna. Not because of the number of verses you know or how you serve in church, but because you're ours."

*Thank You, God, that You never stop loving Danny because he's Yours.*

Mary joins our huddle. She prays for Danny's safety and his return. We each take turns. We're a tangled mess, each somehow touching the others. The tears come faster, and my nose runs, but that's okay. The Holy Spirit is here. He's warming my heart along with igniting my hope.

Anna prays last. She repents from her sin, claims scriptures over Danny's life, for God to strengthen our parents' marriage and bless one thousand generations for their obedience to God. It's the most beautiful prayer I've ever heard. One thousand generations. I thought the idea impossible until a few weeks ago. Tonight, I have no doubt God will restore our family completely, which includes bringing Danny home.

We separate from our prayer huddle with hugs. When we stand, I see the message light on Mom's phone flash.

"Mom." I hand it to her. "I think you have a message."

She freezes once it's open, her eyes widen. "It's from Danny."

We surround her as she reads aloud. "Happy Mother's Day, Mom. I love you. I miss your steak and mac and cheese." She laughs at the last part. "Oh, my Danny Boy."

Dad wraps an arm around her. "I prayed this morning he'd reach out to you." He kisses the top of her head. "See? God is answering our prayers."

*Please, God, please continue to answer our prayers.*

## *CHAPTER 30*

### *LYDIA*

PROM PREPARATIONS ARE A SERIOUS THING ACCORDING TO MOM. Manis and pedis are scheduled for the morning, lunch will be at my favorite burger place, and we have hair and makeup appointments at a salon in the afternoon. I hate being fussed over, but Mom is like a giddy teen. She has six inches cut off her hair.

"Do you think Dad will like it?" Her hair bounces above her shoulders. The highlights bring out the red tones.

"He adores you, so he'll love it. It is gorgeous though."

Mom tells the makeup girl she doesn't want too much. The shadow and mascara make her eyes shine.

"Are you a prom chaperone?" the makeup lady asks.

"Oh, no." Mom laughs. "My husband made reservations at a four-star restaurant. He promised to wear a suit if I bought a new dress."

Not only did Dad make reservations, he purchased tickets to a play she's been dying to see. I believe it's his goal to make her smile every day. He's definitely succeeding.

The doorbell rings at five p.m. I exhale, check myself in the mirror once more. I'm beautiful on the outside. Inside, I'm a wreck. My spirit is very unsettled. Something must be going on with Danny.

"God, You know where Danny is. Protect him." I sigh. "And be with me tonight. Help me to have a good time. I don't want to disappoint Jason."

"You're headed to Texas Christian in the fall?" I hear Dad ask as I walk downstairs.

"Yes, sir. Signed with them last month."

"That's a great school. What area of study?"

"Kinesiology, majoring in Physical Education with a minor in Athletic Training."

"Physical education? Like teaching?" Mom asks.

"Yeah, I think I'd like that. You know, inspire high schoolers to greater heights. Maybe be a coach, too."

I pause on the bottom step when I catch a glimpse of him. He's Christian, respectful, smart, driven, and looks gorgeous in a tux. He's the perfect guy for me.

I hold my breath. Did I just think that?

"There she is," Dad says.

Jason's gaze shifts to me, making his smile widen.

"Hiya." He meets me in the entryway, a white rose corsage with navy-blue ribbons in his hand. "I showed them the picture of your dress. This is what they came up with."

"Thank you." I help him pin it to me. Mom hands me the white rose boutonniere. "We match." I run my hands down his jacket, which increases my heart rate.

"You're gorgeous." His eyes lock on mine.

"Pictures!" Mom announces. "You two in front of the fireplace for pictures."

I tell Jason he doesn't need to take me anywhere fancy, yet we end up at a four-star restaurant.

"This is a special night for both of us. It's prom and you agreed to go out with me, which means I get to spoil you." He opens the door. "No arguments."

He insists I order what I want, yet laughs when the waiter places a porterhouse steak in front of me.

"Do you have a problem with my meal?" I ask.

"No." He cuts into his chicken. "I love a girl who's comfortable enough to devour a hunk of beef in a formal dress."

"I thought the purpose of tonight was to have fun, not worry about appearances. I ordered what I wanted." Well, maybe I ordered what Danny would love.

"You're right." Jason nods. "I want tonight to be fun."

"So, if I decide I don't want to go to the dance, you'd be okay with that?"

He searches my face. "If that's what you want. I'm just not sure it is."

I focus on my meat. "Would you be terribly disappointed?"

"Not at all. It would be my most expensive date in which we didn't do what was planned, but that's cool. I'm sure Henry will accept prom king if I win."

That's right, he's on the prom court. I feel like a jerk. I lift my eyes to his. "I'm sorry. It's fine, really."

Jason takes my hand. "It's not a big deal. What's most important is that I spend time with you. And you're happy."

"I forgot you're on the prom court. Of course, we'll go—"

"It's not a big deal," Jason says. "I won't win. Guys from the team put my name in as a joke."

"I'm not sure about that." I stir my mashed potatoes. "All the girls love you."

"Do they?"

His sly smile makes my palms sweat. "I hear them talk."

"What do they say?"

"You're kind, polite. Gorgeous. Smart and funny." I bite my lip. "You're an amazing guy, Jason. You should've taken someone else to the prom."

"The night is perfect because you said you'd go with me." He squeezes my hand. "Even if we don't show for the dance, it'll still be perfect."

I take my hand back. "How about a walk after dinner? We'll be fashionably late?"

"Sounds like a plan."

On our walk around the pond, I talk about my family serving at the homeless shelter on Mother's Day, Anna's breakthrough, how our family read the prodigal son together and prayed for Danny. Jason tells me everything he's learned about the Ozarks, things I need to do and places to visit.

"Why all the research on the Ozarks?" I ask.

"Because you'll live there. I want to know what you'll experience."

"You're still going to Texas, right?"

"Yes." He sighs. "But I'll be back for Thanksgiving. You?"

"I'll come home every holiday. How was your season?" I didn't attend any of the games. Not only did he completely understand, he never came around me in his uniform.

"We had some wins after Coach trained Martinez as pitcher and moved Rodriguez to first." He faces me. "Though we'll be miles apart, I'll still be there for you. You can text or call any time. I pray for you every day." He brushes one of my curls behind my ear. "You have my heart, Lydia. I'm convinced there's no one else for me. You know that, right?"

"I do." There are a ton of reasons to love him yet only one not to. We'll be thousands of miles apart next year. We won't see each other. It'll hurt if I give him my heart now, but maybe it'll hurt regardless. I do deserve a season of happiness, even if it won't last. As scared as I am to lose him, I'll lose him anyway. Maybe it's time to take a leap.

A chill comes over me. He rubs my arms with his hands.

"You cold?" he asks. "I could give you my jacket."

That's when I kiss him. His timidity quickly gives in to passion.

"I love you, too," I whisper as we part.

He leans his forehead against mine. "Definitely the perfect night."

*We kissed. I told him I love him, and we kissed.* That's what's running through my head as we talk with friends at prom. Katie links arms with me after a half hour.

"We're going to get sodas," she announces. "What happened during dinner?" she asks on the way to the other side of the room. "You guys haven't let go of each other's hands since you walked in. I've never seen either of you this smiley."

"Well, I guess it started on Valentine's Day when he kissed me."

She stops. "He kissed you on Valentine's Day? Why didn't you tell me?"

I keep walking. "You know what a year it's been. It was great, but I didn't have it in me to love him."

"What about now?"

"We have three months 'til college. It's going to hurt either way. I might as well go for it."

Katie orders us both sodas. "Don't think that way, Lydia. Even though you guys are going to be in different states, it can still work."

"I don't want him to spend four years hung up on me. I want him to go without attachments. If it's meant to be, God will bring us together."

"You say you're not a romantic, but that's pure romance." She hands me my drink. "I'm excited for you. Jason is amazing. He told me where he took you. Marcus took me to that Italian place with the checkered tablecloths. I swear they microwave their food."

"I think Jason saved all year for prom in hopes that I'd say yes."

"Not only did you come to the prom with him, you said yes to being his girlfriend." Katie squeals. "I'd say he won."

*Girlfriend.* I'm his girlfriend.

Jason waves me over to a group of his baseball buddies.

*Oh God, what have I gotten myself into? I don't know that I'm ready for this.*

"Lydia, I'd like you to meet the guys."

Jason introduces me to each. I vaguely remember them by the position they play.

One guy, Zack, stares at me the whole time Jason does introductions.

"You're one of Morton's sisters, aren't you?" he asks.

"I am."

"Is it true he's living on the streets? That he stole your parents' money and trashed the house before he left?"

"Knock it off, Zack," one of the guys says.

"That's what I heard." He glances back at me. "Did he really get caught in the school bathroom doing a line of coke?"

Jason walks me to the dance floor. "I'm sorry, Lyd." He takes me in his arms. "I didn't think he'd be that insensitive."

"Not all guys are as great as you." I rest my head against his chest.

"We'll hang out with your friends the rest of the night," he says.

"I'm fine here." I run my hand over his chest, then through the back of his hair. "Just the two of us."

We do hang out on the dance floor until they announce the prom court. Then he humbly waves to everyone before taking my hand in his.

"And our prom king is—"

I squeeze Jason's hand as the drum roll plays.

"Jason Swanson!"

He shakes his head at his name before giving me a quick kiss on the lips. Along with cheers from the audience come moans. Jason accepts the crown then bows to Mia, the prom queen.

"You're so lucky," a girl says as she walks by.

The girl with her sizes me up. "Congratulations."

He chats with Mia as they dance. She flips her long, perfect dark brown hair over her shoulder. They're friends because she's the captain of the cheerleaders. Sports and people in sports are his life. Beautiful people who live beautiful lives—

*God, why shouldn't he be with her? If not her, he should be with someone who doesn't have so much garbage...*

My life this year has been a whole lot of drama, except for Jason. He makes me happy. He's been the silver lining on my cloudy year.

"May I have the next dance?" Jason approaches me after the song ends.

"Only because you're the prom king." I push his crown back from his forehead.

He places it on my head and kisses me. "You'd be done with me if I lost?"

I follow him to the dance floor. "Nah. You can't get rid of me that easily."

"Mmmm." He leans his head against mine. His lips are level with my ear. "I'm glad you feel that way. When you kissed me tonight it felt like a dream. I never imagined life could be this amazing."

I breathe deep. *Amazing. That's how it feels in Jason's arms.*

Jason walks me to my porch two hours later. "Prom down, graduation to go. Do you have family coming in?"

"My grandparents, probably my aunt and uncle."

"Well, that should be good." His arm slips around my waist.

"Yeah. Mom is closer to Aunt Michelle since Danny left. They talk almost every day."

"Another blessing that came from it, right?"

My heart sinks. I want Danny to be here too. I fumble for my key in my purse as the tears come.

"Lydia, are you okay? I didn't mean to upset you."

"It's great that my parents get along, but it still hurts that Danny's gone."

"I know." He rubs my back.

I open the door to my empty house. My tears begin when I step inside.

"I should get going since your parents aren't here."

"Please, don't." I grab his hand, my lip quivering. "I don't want to be alone."

The dam of tears bursts open. Maybe it's the talk of graduation or this feeling that Danny's not okay. Next come the negative thoughts.

*It's been five months and you're still a wreck. You'll never be okay.*

I stumble to the sofa. Jason takes me in his arms.

"What can I do for you?" Jason whispers.

"Nothing." I sob. "Everything's a wreck. Danny will never come home."

"You don't know that."

"It's been five months. Every week I wonder if it'll be the last time he texts me."

"We need to pray." He runs his hand down my hair. "Continue to believe God can change his heart. Look what he did with your father."

I can't answer. I want to, but I'm tired. Tired of hoping, tired of praying, tired of believing. Faith is hard work. I'm too exhausted to continue.

"Dear Father, calm Lydia's heart," Jason prays. "Help her see that You're in control. Remind her of the good You've done and the promises in Your Word. Have your hand of protection over Danny. I pray that with every step he takes, You would bring him closer to You, and closer to home. Nothing is impossible for You. In Jesus's name, amen."

"Amen." My faith was shattered, he prays and it feels whole again. How does he do that?

He squeezes me tighter, kisses me on the head. "I love you, Lydia."

Peace rushes over me. My head still on his chest, our breathing syncs. I focus on his heartbeat. He's here with me. He loves me. He'd do anything for me. I do love him.

I run my hand down his bicep, over his firm forearm. Our fingers interlace. I bring his hand to my lips. His heartbeat quickens. I sit up, run the back of my hand down his cheek.

*You deserve to be happy.*

*So much bad has happened this year, you need something good.*

*He's yours. It's time to show him how much you care.*

Jason closes his eyes when I lean in to kiss him.

*I do deserve to be happy;* I tell myself. *There's nothing wrong with feeling good.*

His fingers make their way up my back, caressing my bare skin. I move closer until I'm on his lap.

"Whoa." He backs away.

"It's okay." I interlace my hands behind his head, bringing his lips to mine.

"Lyd, no." He moves my arms to my sides. "Your parents aren't home—"

"I know."

"I gotta go." He lifts me to the couch before he stands.

"Jason." I reach for him.

He stops at the front door with a sigh. "It's wrong."

"But you love me." I don't know why I'm whining, begging for something I know is wrong, but I find myself going to him.

"I'll call you tomorrow." He kisses my cheek and walks out the door. "Lock the door behind me."

The door shuts. I'm alone and feel like a fool.

I switch off the light when I crawl into bed. If Danny were here, I'd tell him. We said we'd be accountability partners. He'd tell me it was wrong. I slip my phone from my nightstand, open the text from his friend, Kat, and stare into his face. *God, what is he doing? What is he thinking?*

For months I've wanted to text him, but I suddenly have an overwhelming feeling that I need to. That for some reason, I should reach out to him to tell him my struggle.

"He'll hate me," I say, maybe to God, partially to myself. "He told me not to."

The feeling grows. I know I won't be able to sleep until I do. Maybe he needs to hear from me. Kat did say he talked about me.

*I know you told me never to text you, but I had a bad night.* I pause. *Jason and I are dating. Tonight was prom. I almost went too far. I would have if he hadn't stopped me.* I brush away the tears of shame. *We said we'd be honest about our struggle and supporting one another. Please don't be mad or stop texting. I love you and miss you.* I take a breath before sending it.

---

### *DANNY*

*Meet me on the corner of 8th and H in 20 min. I got something for you!*

Business has ramped up since Memorial Day weekend. That's why I'm shocked Kat texts Saturday night. I check my GPS. I'm fifteen minutes away.

*Okay,* I respond.

There's a hot dog vendor two streets away. I grab a dog for Kat plus two sodas. I've been on the curb a couple minutes when she runs up. Her eyes are wild.

"You won't believe the night I've had." She's out of breath.

I hold out the hot dog. "Good or bad?"

"Well, I thought the last guys were pretty lame until one of them pulled out this." She removes a tiny white pill from her pocket. "You have to try it."

"Do you take random drugs from strange men often?"

She laughs, not her cute laugh, but her eerie, high laugh. "You gotta take it."

"I won't take something if I don't know what it is."

She sticks it in my hand. "It's ecstasy." She bites into her dinner like she just handed me a Tylenol. "I'm starving. Did you already eat?"

"A few hours ago. I didn't think I'd see you." I examine the tiny pill.

She pops open a soda and hands it to me. "You need to take it now. It won't kick in for about twenty minutes." A grin spreads on her face. "I wanna be here when it does."

I stare at the soda, then the pill. I hate that she can talk me into anything. I toss it in my mouth. I try to wash it down quickly, but the taste makes me gag.

"Nasty, huh?" She sits beside me. "Maybe you need a bite. You know I hate to eat alone."

I take a bite along with another drink.

"Shaun told me there would be several guys. He had to get someone to cover my second job." She grabs the soda back from me. "It was worth it. Not only did they tip well, he gave me one for you." Kat scoots closer to me. Our knees touch. "How was your day?"

I tell her about the people I met, the money I collected. After she finishes dinner, Kat creeps closer to me. My heart beats faster. And faster. And faster. She smiles when I scoot back. That's when her hand slides up my leg. My hormones shoot through roof. I jump to my feet.

"What the heck? What did you give me?" I walk backwards into the alley as she saunters toward me.

"Amazing, isn't it?" She runs her hands up my arms, which creates a whole new rush.

"Kat." I grab her hands. "Seriously."

"I wanna make you feel good." Her breath is warm on my neck. "Don't you want to feel good?"

She presses her lips against my neck. I feel like I'm about to melt and explode at the same time. Her hands find their way up my chest. Everything that's within me desires her. My hands slide down her hair to her neck, then over her arms. I kiss her shoulder, neck, cheek—

"Whatever you want, Danny. I'll give it to you."

Though my hormones are still over-the-top, I freeze at her words. Her voice has changed. She's in work mode.

"What do you want?"

I walk backwards to avoid her until I'm literally against the wall. A dumpster blocks the view to the sidewalk.

"We're all alone. No one can see. C'mon." She unbuttons my shorts. "Don't you wanna to have fun?"

I grab her wrist. "No, Kat. Not like that. I'm not like that."

She laughs, raises an eyebrow. "Like what?"

"I'm not going to use you."

Her hand slips into mine. "It's not using me if I want it too."

What's she saying? All these months she's called me her brother. Now she wants me?

She bites her lip when I lean in. She smells like roses. Pure goodness. I run my hand down her braids. She sways to music from a nearby restaurant. Her body is pressed against mine. My thoughts run to places they shouldn't go. I can't stop them. I lean my cheek against hers.

"I love you," I whisper.

When she backs her face away, there's a twisted smile. That's when I move in for a kiss—

She cusses, pulls her phone from her pocket. "I gotta go. I'm late." She grabs her purse and shoes from behind her.

"Think of me." She blows a kiss as she runs off.

I'm standing in the alley wondering what just happened, and what would have happened, had she stayed.

---

"Hey, how are you?" I hear Kat's voice before I realize I have my phone to my ear.

My head is spinning and pounding at the same time. "Um, well, a little while after you left I got a blaring headache. I thought the stars were meteors falling from the sky." When I talk, the feeling that I'm going to hurl returns.

"Oh no."

"Yeah. Then my head began to spin like the first time I did heroin, only worse. I puked for a long time." I open my eyes to the world slightly tilted.

"Oh." Kat sighs. "That's bad."

"Thankfully I made it into the alley for cover, so the cops didn't find me." I take a swig from the half empty water bottle beside me. "I'll never take that crap again."

"I wouldn't have given it to you if I'd known."

I believe her, but that doesn't make me feel better. "What time is it? You done for the night?"

"Almost midnight. One more to go. I called in hopes that you were thinking happy thoughts about me." She laughs. "Guess you were cursing my name."

Laughing would take too much effort. "It's not entirely your fault."

"I'm sorry I had to take off. I wanted to finish what we started."

I close my eyes. How do I respond to that?

"Danny? Are you there?" Kat asks.

"Yeah."

"Did you like it? I mean, when I was there?"

This feels like a loaded question. Is she asking if I liked the way I felt or if I liked the way she felt? I guess the answer is the same. "Yeah."

"We'll have to do it again. Only next time without the ecstasy." She pauses only for a second. "You should drink lots of water."

"Yes, Mom."

"I'll buy you dinner tomorrow to make up for it. Okay?"

"Okay. Be safe."

"Yes, Dad."

I pull my sleeping bag back over my head. As much as I wanted her, I don't want to be that guy who is totally hung up on sex. I like that we have fun together, that we can talk about everything and nothing, that we have so many of the same interests. Seems to me that's worth more than a few minutes of physical pleasure.

I'm about to fall asleep again when my phone chimes. My eyes take a while to focus. Lydia? My blood boils as I read it. I'm mad, not because she texted but because I'm not there for her. That I let her down again. I imagine her crying in bed with no one to talk to. It makes me angry at my dad for making me run and myself for not being man enough to stay.

It's ironic that tonight I struggled with the same problem yet didn't think to reach out to her. I mean, how could I? *Well, Sis, I took ecstasy and might have had sex with my prostitute girlfriend if she hadn't run off for a job.* Yeah, I'm sure Lyd wouldn't approve of that.

"I miss you too, Lyd," I whisper, "but I'm never coming home."

# CHAPTER 31

## LYDIA

*I BLEW IT*, IS MY FIRST THOUGHT WHEN I WAKE SUNDAY MORNING. *Jason ran out of my house. Yeah, I've totally scared him away.*

My parents told me not to worry about going to church because of prom. I figure it's better to get up and go than to dwell on my stupidity.

A text comes from Jason when I'm blow drying my hair.

*You going to church today?* Such a subtle way to tell me I'm a sinner needing to repent.

*Getting ready now*, I reply.

*How about lunch after?*

I smile. I'm an idiot yet he wants to see me? *I'd like that. Would you like to meet me and my parents?*

*Sure. What time does your youth meet?*

*9:30*. I check my clock. *With a little luck, I'll be close to on time.*

*See you soon. :)*

I toss my phone onto my bed. "God, I hope I didn't destroy our relationship before it started."

My longest dress that shows the least amount of skin seems most appropriate to wear to church.

The first half of my drive I pray for Danny. The last half I pray for myself to not be such an emotional mess.

The worship band is in the middle of a song when I enter the youth room. There on the end of the front row is Jason.

"What are you doing here?" I ask.

"Worshipping." He smiles. "I decided I'd rather worship with you today than alone."

He does worship. I smile at the sound of his voice. He's not the best singer but he's not ashamed. When the chorus comes, Jason closes his eyes.

*God, he's so great.*

I close my eyes, allowing the words to wash over me. God is good, so good to me. Not only do I sing them, I feel them deep in my soul. He is good, not because of what He does or what I have. God is good because of who He is.

*He is my counselor.*

*He is my strength.*

*He is the light in my darkness.*

*He is my Father.*

*He is my Savior.*

*He is the lover of my soul.*

*He is my everything.*

*Thank You God that You are so good to me.*

Half the teens in the room greet Jason after, the others stare at us holding hands. How I ended up with such a popular guy is beyond me.

"It's good to see you," he says on our way to the sanctuary.

"I'm glad you came, but don't feel like you need to—"

"I didn't feel like I had to." He squeezes my hand. "I wanted to."

My parents are even more excited to see Jason than I was.

"You'll come to lunch with us after?" Dad asks.

"I'd love to."

Dad slips his arm around Mom. "Did you two have a great time last night?"

"Yes," we answer at the same time.

Dad laughs.

"Jason won prom king," I say.

"Congratulations." Mom's eyes drift to our hands. Her smile spreads.

"Your daughter danced with me all night. It was perfect." Jason lets go of my hand to slip his arm around me. "How was your play?"

"Fabulous." Mom leans against Dad.

"The entire night was fabulous." Dad squeezes her.

Today is the first time since November that I've felt at peace in our pew. Even though my parents have restored their relationship, I still missed Danny terribly. With Jason beside me, I feel supported, like his faith is upholding mine. God has grown me through this. He'll continue to do so if I keep my hope and trust in Him.

Jason's handwriting is so messy I can't tell what he writes in the blanks when I miss the pastor's points. His random happy faces and hearts look like something a first grader would draw, yet they make me grin every time. A dozen different ways to apologize swarm in my head. I offer to drive with him to lunch to get rid of this guilt.

"You know last night, at my house—" I pause. What do I say? *When I jumped you. When I went too far. When I turned into a sex maniac—*

"Yeah?" He glances at me.

I sigh. "I'm not like that."

"I know." He squeezes my hand. "We've been friends for years. I know you don't give yourself away to guys." He grins. "I want to think I was so incredibly handsome in my tux you couldn't keep your hands off me."

I chuckle. "You were for sure, but I was also an emotional wreck. It's been such a horrible year, it felt good being with you." I frown. "I know it was a bad choice. I'm sorry."

"You're forgiven. Let's move on. Go to lunch with your parents. Maybe to a movie later."

I nod.

"I do love you, Lyd, but I won't have sex until marriage. That's a commitment I've made to the Lord and my future wife." He glances to me at the red light. "I like to hold your hand. A kiss at the end of the night is great as long as our parents are home and one of us is about to leave."

"Sounds like a plan." I smile. "You're so gorgeous it is hard to resist you."

"More like the other way around." He winks.

Jason and I head to a movie after lunch. The only kiss we exchange is when he takes me back to the church to get my car. Before I even open my eyes, he's safe in his own vehicle.

Mom is in Dad's arms on the couch watching a comedy on TV when I get home.

"I guess you two are finally more than friends," Dad says.

"Maybe." I sit in the armchair by the couch. We never talked about dating, so I have no idea how this will be received.

"He asked your mother and me if he could date you when you went to the restroom at the restaurant."

My eyes widen. "What'd you say?"

"That we support you in that decision." Mom smiles. "Something happened last night?"

"He's been great since Danny left. He understands what I'm feeling because of his parents' divorce." Tears come to my eyes. "He treats me so well, never judges me for my emotions. He makes me happy."

"And he'll go to church with you," Mom says.

"And lunch with your parents," Dad adds. "I've always liked Jason. Not only because he played baseball."

I think of how Danny hated him. Maybe he wanted to be like Jason—a good ball player, a real Christian, a nice guy. Danny didn't realize he was that until he turned from God.

*Bring Danny back to You.*

A text from Jason pops up.

*Thanks for the fun day. I like going to your church and hanging out with your parents. Spending time with you is my favorite thing to do. :)*

*Thanks for coming,* I reply. *I had a great time, too.*

*Text me if you're up early tomorrow. We could meet for coffee before school. Only three weeks 'til graduation!*

My heart sinks. Three weeks until the countdown to college, and life without Jason, begins.

---

*DANNY*

"Are you mad at me?" The past several Sundays Kat hasn't shown until after five, so I'm surprised to find her under the tree when I exit the shelter at three thirty.

"Not at all." I help her up. "You got me totally horny and ran away. It's every guy's dream."

She giggles. "Well, dinner's my treat. Where are we going?"

"You mentioned Chinese last week."

"Oh." She pulls up her GPS. "It's a twenty-minute walk. You up to that?"

"My head's not spinning." I glance up. "The sky isn't falling. I'm not puking. It's all good."

"For what it's worth, that's not how it played out in my mind." She crosses the street.

"How exactly did it play out?" I'm not sure I want to ask, but since she brought it up...

"We had a spectacular time." She raises an eyebrow. "You loved every minute."

"Yeah, not so spectacular puking your guts out."

"I know." She links arms with me. "Guess I kind of blew it."

"I forgive you. You off earlier makes up for it."

"I didn't get home until almost six a.m. I gave away my appointments to my roommates. Decided sleep and dinner with you was more important."

"Good choice." She chose me over work. That's gotta be good.

"I've been wondering..." She stares into my face.

"Yes?" My heart starts to race.

"Have you ever..."

"No." I sigh internally. It shouldn't surprise me that she asks. Her life revolves around sex.

She bites her lip. "Did you want to last night?"

*Heck, yeah* is the response that comes to mind. "I liked being close to you." I rub my sweaty hand on my shorts. "I just decided a long time ago never to disrespect a girl by doing something with her if I don't love her."

Now that it's out I feel lame. Did I really say that to someone who's disrespected by guys on a daily basis?

Half her mouth lifts in a grin. "You told me you loved me."

Deep breath. No turning back from that one. "I do."

"That means you wouldn't be disrespecting me."

"Did you want to?" I hate these games. I can't read her at all.

"I would've."

"But did you want to?"

"The drug made me want to. It felt good being close to you. But..."

In my mind I fill in her pause.

*...you're like a brother to me.*

*...I hate sex.*

*...I'd rather be with girls.*

*...you can't afford me.*

Yeah, the last one would hurt the most. Even more than her preferring girls.

Kat lowers her gaze. "I've never been with someone I wanted to be with."

"Really?" That takes me by complete surprise.

"My mom's boyfriend was my first time. Then I was on the streets. I was kind of a nerd in school. Got straight As. Gramps told me I didn't need a guy, only an education and connections. I believed him, so I didn't date."

Reality hits. I ran away to escape a life I felt trapped in. She ran away and got trapped in a life she never wanted.

"I'm sorry."

She shakes her head. "It's stupid."

"No, it's not." I slip my hand into hers. "It's supposed to mean something."

"And you're supposed to be married, right?" She laughs at the shock on my face. "I've been reading the Bible."

"That's what the Bible says."

"I know my profession is wrong, but I feel like I made the most educated choice I could at sixteen. I even researched the pimps in the area. Although Shaun can be a jerk, he gives me a high percentage, pays my rent, and covers salon visits. You saw how much it was to get my hair done."

"Yeah, that's quite a tip."

"I make about the same as a teacher without graduating from high school let alone college."

My eyes widen. "You're kidding!"

"It's pretty sick. People will pay a lot for money for it."

"Like drugs."

"I like those perks, too," she says. "You have to admit it's fun."

"Yesterday, not so much."

She laughs.

"I started to use when everything went wrong," I say. "I'd like to get back to a place where I feel good without them. To being satisfied with life."

"Is anyone ever satisfied with their life? I don't think that's possible."

"If I lived in LA. If I sold one of my scripts."

"Sometimes I think the point of life is to be happy where you're at. This is where I'm at." Kat shrugs. "I do what makes me happy."

"Then you might not want to read the Bible." I smirk.

"It makes you a better person, right?"

"Reading it, no. Living it, supposedly." My sister Anna comes to mind, so I know it's time to change the topic. "What do you get at this restaurant?"

"Love the pot stickers. And sake. The noodles are super good. What's your fav?"

"Mongolian beef, orange chicken, fried rice."

She smiles. "How long has it been since you had Chinese?"

"My birthday dinner. December."

"Lucky me. I get to celebrate your birthday twice this year."

I laugh. Maybe life *is* about the moment. This is the moment I love. This is the moment I want to last. This moment with her. It's not about drugs or physical attraction. It's about being together. Experiencing life. Enjoying one another.

# CHAPTER 32

## LYDIA

"ANOTHER GRADUATE." ANNA ENTERS MY ROOM AS I SLIP ON MY blue robe. She pulls my hair out from underneath. "Congratulations, Lydia."

"Thanks." I place my cap on my head.

She takes the bobby pins from my hand. "You okay?"

"Kinda sad. How's Mom?"

"She hasn't cried in about an hour. It's good Aunt Michelle is here."

My phone announces a new message from Jason. It's a picture of him in his unzipped robe, hat tilted down. There's a grin on his face as he winks. *See you soon!* the caption says.

Anna peers over my shoulder. "He's the perfect guy for you."

"I know, but he's going to Texas. We'll break up before he leaves." I toss my phone on my bed.

"You don't need to. You can totally have a long-distance relationship. Call, text, video chat—"

"I've already told him." I examine myself in the mirror. It's all I've thought about for two days. The dark circles under my eyes show it. "We can't stay together."

"Will you ever let yourself be happy?"

I turn at Anna's comment.

"As awful as it is that Danny's gone, you can't live the rest of your life depressed."

I thought she'd changed. "You shouldn't live your life like nothing happened."

"I pray for him every day. I serve at the shelter with you guys on Sundays."

"What if he returned tomorrow? Would you party with us or pout over him being welcomed home?"

"That's not fair. I admitted my sin."

"But did you repent?" My heart pounds. "I miss him every day. This morning was one of the few times since he left that I didn't think about him being gone as soon as I opened my eyes."

"That's great." Anna smiles.

"My first thought was 'I graduate today.' My second thought was 'Danny won't be there.'"

She frowns.

I sit on my bed. "When you and Mary were too busy as teens to hang out with me, Danny would play with me. He was the one who convinced me to go to Missouri for college. He promised we'd meet once a month. He sat in the front row of youth group last year when I gave my testimony, even though he probably hated God by then." I swallow hard. "We told each other everything until—"

She takes my hands in hers. "I'm sorry. You're right. I wasn't that close to him. I pray God will bring him home so that I can be a real sister to him." She sighs. "I just hate to see you this way."

"I'm thankful for what God's doing in our family. I'm happy for Mom and Dad. I do have a good time with Jason. You need to remember a huge part of my life is gone. It makes me sad to think I might not see him again."

She wraps an arm around me. "Mom wants pictures before we leave. You can't cry or it'll set her off. We'll do that tonight, after." She hugs me. "Slumber party in my old room?"

I nod as we walk down the stairs together.

---

"We did it!" Jason greets me in the line of graduates and sweeps me off my feet with a bear hug. "Did you check your final GPA?"

I smile. "Three point eight two."

"Nice. Knew I picked a smart one."

"And you?"

"Three point six. Not bad for a dumb jock."

"It's because we studied together, I'm sure."

"Definitely." He raises his eyebrows.

"I'm going to miss you so much!" Katie throws her arms around my neck.

I pat her back. "Katie, it's summer vacation. You live five miles from me. I'm here for two more months. I'll see you almost every day."

"Oh yeah." She straightens up. "I forgot. I'm in my goodbye mode."

"Sixty-two days." Jason wraps his arm around my waist. "Lots of time to make memories."

He's counted the days. This is going to be harder than I thought.

The procession seems to take forever. Jason entertains me while we walk at a tortoise's pace. Excitement and joy build as we take our seats. Then come the speeches.

*You can be anything you want to be.*

*The entire world is within your grasp.*

*With hard work and perseverance, you will succeed.*

I want to roll my eyes at the feel-good clichés. They sound encouraging and motivational until you line them up with reality.

*Unless your parents push you in a direction you don't want to go.*

*Unless you're suppressed for years and turn to drugs for an escape.*

*Unless that's not God's plan.*

I push the palms of my hands on my knees to still them. *I believe You have a good plan for him, Lord. A plan for him to succeed, not to fail. I just don't understand how this is part of it.*

"It sucks that Danny isn't here," Jason whispers. "But I'll be beside you for all your special events. Awards you win, college graduation, and, hopefully, at the end of the aisle on our wedding day."

He intertwines his fingers with mine. I stare at our hands. If only life could be that simple.

We emerge from the field to our families standing together, all smiles.

"We've invited Lydia's family over to the house," Jason's mom tells us. "There's plenty of food."

"Is that okay, honey?" Mom comes up beside me. "We can take you to dinner tomorrow."

"Sure." I smile. Jason's mom told me weeks ago she wanted us to come over after the ceremony. I politely declined. The last thing I want is my family to fall in love with Jason's before I break up with him in August. Looks like it might be too late.

"Hey, Anna." Jason greets Anna with a hug. "Good to see you." He turns to Mary. "You must be Mary."

"I am." She hugs Jason. "This is my fiancé, Dylan."

"Nice to meet you." Dylan extends his hand. "We've heard a lot about you."

Jason rides with me and my parents to his house. Dad asks him about Texas Christian University. They're chatting away when I feel like the wind has been knocked out of me. I gasp for breath.

"You okay?" Jason turns.

I shake, clenching my chest. "Something's wrong."

"With Danny?"

I nod. *God, what is it? What's going on?* "He's in danger," I say what comes to mind.

Jason grabs my hand. "God, be with Danny. Protect him. Send Your angels as a guard around him. Whatever situation he's gotten into, please lift him out of it. We pray that he sees Your protection and love for him. In Jesus's name, amen."

"Amen," my parents echo.

"Thank you." I dab the tears from my eyes.

"Yeah." He pauses. "Do you have those feelings often?"

"At random times. I sense that something's wrong, so I ask God what it is so I can pray."

"That's the gift of seeing, Lydia."

"Seeing?"

"It's kinda like an off-shoot of prophecy. God allows you to see things you couldn't otherwise, either in the natural realm or the spiritual realm. I learned about it when we studied spiritual gifts in church last year."

"Oh." I guess it's okay, but the way Jason describes it feels a little over-the-top.

"It's a good thing. Keep praying for him. If you let me know when it happens, I'll pray too."

I focus my attention out the window. *Please, God, keep my brother safe. Bring him home.*

---

*DANNY*

Kat shows up a few minutes after I buy our tamales. Her speech is fast, and the conversation bounces from topic to topic.

"How much coke did you do today?"

"Enough to get by." She rubs her nose. "The night's barely half over."

"Did you even sleep?" I can't tell if those are bags under her eyes or remains of her makeup.

"A few hours. This morning."

"Kat, this is too much."

She unwraps her tamale. "I told you. Busiest season. I need to take the business as it comes. Please. Let it go."

I do. For the rest of dinner, I tell her about the homeless people I've met. She talks of roommate issues. She downs whatever is in her flask before moving on to her soda.

"You don't seem okay," I say when we throw away our trash.

"One of the girls left. Didn't show up for her jobs yesterday. I heard Shaun found her apartment cleared out." She links arms with me on the way to the street. "He's totally on high alert. Stopped by my place before I left tonight."

I sigh. I want her out of this profession. I know saying that won't go over well.

"I'll be fine. Things will settle down soon."

"Well," a man's voice from behind us says. "Look who's here."

Kat yanks her arm from mine. The color drains from her face. As we turn, she forces a smile.

"Shaun, how are you?" Kat approaches the black man behind us. He's wearing tailored cream pants and a short-sleeve dress shirt with only two buttons done to display his six-pack and gold chains.

"Not good." He pushes her away when she tries to kiss his cheek. "You swore your loyalty to me this afternoon. Now I find you with some punk white kid in the middle of your shift?"

"This is my cousin." She motions to me. "He came in from Iowa. Offered to buy me dinner. I was headed back out—"

Clamping her arms to her sides, he lifts her off the ground. "Don't lie to me!"

"Let her go!" I rush him. I bounce off his side and land on my butt.

"Cousin? Right." He stares me down. "You think you can get some for free?"

"Really, Shaun." Kat's voice turns desperate, whiny. "He's like my brother. We just hang out. Go to dinner. Read books together."

"Books? You read books?" He laughs like Jack Nicholson from *The Shining*.

"Yeah." She glances at me. "Show him, Danny."

I dig through my pack, pull out the first book I touch. "Don Quixote."

"I love that scene with the windmills," she says.

Shaun's eyes bounce from me to Kat then the book. He lowers her to the ground with a firm grip still on her left arm.

"How old are you, boy?"

I'm offended at his tone and the term boy but can't do anything about it. Number one, he's holding Kat. Number two, I felt the butt of a revolver when I crashed into him. "Sixteen."

"You don't screw my girls." He sticks a finger toward me. "Got it?"

"Yeah."

"I see you with her again, you're done." He drags Kat in the opposite direction. "Time for you to learn your lesson."

Like that, she's gone. No fight, total submission. Not even a glance back. I know it's for my safety, but it hurts. A lot.

I run down my options. If I follow, he could kill both of us. Reporting him to the cops could still end with us dead, or me being sent home and her arrested. So, I decide to go to the park to wait for her there. That's the one consistent place we spend the night together.

*Where are you?* Her text arrives after one a.m.

*My Sunday usual,* I reply in case it's Shaun.

*K. b there soon.*

Reclined against our favorite tree, I stare at the stars. It's odd that I still have this impulse to wish on them. If I could, I'd wish for her freedom. My career as a screenplay writer. Her love. But I won't release my wishes. Not if they go to God. He's perfected the act of crushing my dreams rather than making them come true.

"Hi."

Her voice startles me. How long had I been asleep?

She's in baggy sweatpants and a sweatshirt I've never seen. When she sits beside me, I feel her entire body shake.

"Kat?" I open my arms to her. "Are you okay?"

"Ow, ow." She flinches when I wrap my arms around her.

"What's wrong?" I remove my hands from her.

She buries her face in my chest and weeps. I gently rest my head against hers, tell her it's okay, even though it's not.

"What'd he do?" The rage builds inside me with every tear.

"Hit me enough to hurt but not bruise." Her voice shakes. "Made sure I know I'm his property."

"Did you work tonight?"

"I can't work for a few days." She slips her hand in mine.

She's shaking uncontrollably. I pull my sleeping bag from me, unzip it, and wrap it around her.

"I—I need to lie down."

The way she squirms, biting her lip every time she repositions, tells me what happened, but I still ask. "He raped you?"

She places her hands over her face.

"Did he?"

"Not him. His friends." She wipes her tears, wraps her arms around herself. "I'll be okay. I'll be better tomorrow."

I kiss the top of her head. "I'm sorry. I'm so sorry."

"It's not your fault."

"If you hadn't been with me—"

Kat grips my shirt. "Don't say that. You're the only good in my life, Danny. I need you."

The silence of the night falls over us. As my body heat transfers to her, she stills. Her breathing steadies. I think she's asleep until she speaks.

"I listened to the Bible on the way over, on that app you showed me."

"Oh, yeah?" I run my hand over her knotted hair. It reeks of smoke and alcohol.

"Jesus talked about prostitutes. He said they would go to heaven before the religious teachers."

"Cause the teachers were full of themselves," I tell her. "Some of Jesus's best friends were prostitutes."

"Really?"

"Mary Magdalene was one of His favorites. She was a prostitute."

"Why, do you think?" Her voice is so insecure it breaks me.

"Because you've been abused, mistreated. You're genuine in your friendships. And loyal."

"I'd rather Shaun hurt me than you," she whispers. "Please don't ever try to attack him. He carries a gun. He'll use it."

"I figured that out."

She leans back to see my face. "I don't know what I'd do without you."

I gaze into her eyes, past the hurt and shame, into her soul. She's the most beautiful person I've ever known. I caress her cheek. Though I told myself I'd let go of the idea of God, somehow, I see Him in her. In her brokenness. In her innocence. In her love.

"Have you really never kissed a girl?"

I slowly shake my head.

"Have you kissed a boy?"

"No." I can't help but chuckle. "It's not that I don't like girls." The longer I gaze into her eyes, the more courage I gain. "I want it to be special. To mean something."

The corners of her lips turn up. "You're a hopeless romantic, aren't you?"

"Maybe."

"The world isn't a pretty place." She averts her eyes.

"It is when I'm with you."

A smile appears as Kat locks eyes with me again. "I feel the same about being with you."

She gently places a hand against my cheek. It's so soft. My heart races as her eyes close and she leans in. The moment our lips meet, I feel complete. I feel at home.

All these years I pictured it differently. On a moonlit path or a walk along the beach. At one point I even thought my first kiss wouldn't come until I slipped a ring on the finger of my bride-to-be. Instead it's here, in a park in Chicago. A homeless guy snores from a nearby bench. Groans come from the west end of the park. The cops could wander by in an hour. But none of that matters. Everything is perfect. Everything feels right. On this night, when she's been so abused, she gives me an amazing gift.

"Hope it wasn't a disappointment," Kat says when our lips part. "I'm not the best at that."

My hand slips from her cheek to her shoulder. "It was perfect."

"You're a great guy, Danny Boy," she whispers. "If I thought I could love someone, I'd want it to be you."

I close my eyes, so she doesn't see my tears. I've never wanted something so badly yet been so afraid. I kiss her again because I don't want this feeling to end.

# CHAPTER 33

## LYDIA

JASON SHOWS UP TO MY WORK BY TEN O'CLOCK. HE READS HIS Bible until my break.

"Will you visit me every day I work this summer?" I ask after we pray for our sandwiches.

"Maybe. Would that bug you?"

I smile. "Not at all. But if you want to work, I think Dad's hiring."

Jason pauses, sandwich in the air. "He is?"

"He mentioned it yesterday. Stop by and see him after we eat." I take a bite of my meatball sandwich.

"He won't care that I leave in August?"

I shake my head. "They do inventory in July and fill large team orders. He's always short-handed."

"That would be perfect. I can still have lunch with you." He wipes his mouth then takes out his phone. "I made a list of stuff to do this summer after work or on your days off."

There are about twenty things on the list. National parks and waterfalls he wants to visit, places to eat, museums to go to, even a couple service projects.

"Kissing Bridge?" I laugh.

He raises his eyebrows without a word. I choke on my sandwich.

"I'm open to suggestions," he says. "It doesn't have to be all my ideas. I just want to make a lot of memories with you."

Make memories because we leave soon. "Movies. I like movies."

Jason smiles. "How about tonight?"

After lunch, Jason returns with the great news that Dad's assistant, Neil, hired him.

"On the spot?"

"Yep. I filled out the application online, gave Coach and my youth pastor as references. He even did an interview. I start next week, if I pass the drug screening."

A change Dad made after he discovered Danny got cocaine from one of his employees.

"Your dad had nothing to do with it. Thanks for thinking about it. I'll be able to save up money for school, and I won't bug you all summer."

I laugh. "You can bug me anytime."

"Well, your dad did mention he does the schedule. I can work morning shifts, maybe have the same days off as you."

Jason follows me home from work when I'm done, then we head out for a hike. Two months is all we have left, is what's stuck in my mind on the way up the mountain. Two months ago, my parents were separated. Two months before that, Jason kissed me for the first time. Two months before that, Danny ran away. Crazy how much can happen in two months. So, I wonder, will I be able to let him go in two months? Can I move six hours from home, two thousand miles from his college after I've spent time with him every day this summer? Now I wonder why I was so stubborn. Why didn't I allow him to apply to the college in Missouri? Why didn't I apply to Texas Christian?

"You're awfully quiet," he says. "Everything okay?"

"Yeah."

"You thinking about Danny?"

"Kind of."

"We should save up money to meet in LA over winter break. You know that's where he's headed. He's such a determined guy, he'll end up there."

"You think?" My heart races with joy at the idea of him in LA.

"Yeah. He's a good writer, isn't he?"

"He is."

"Then he'd go. I bet if you went without your parents, he'd meet you. He still texts you every week?"

"On Monday." I think about how great it would be to see him. I'd run to him, wrap my arms around him. Tears build in my eyes. "You'd go with me?"

"I'd love to. Of course, we'd need a chaperone or separate hotel rooms. Or both."

I squeeze his hand. "I love you."

"I love you too." He smiles. "Don't give up hope, Lyd. I believe you're going to see him again."

*God, let him be right,* I pray.

---

## *DANNY*

Kat's screams in the middle of the night cause me to bolt straight up.

"It's okay." I run my hand down her hair.

She crawls away, sobbing.

"Kat, it's me, Danny." I follow her, wrap my arms around her. "You're okay. I've got you. You're safe."

"It hurts." She melts in my arms. "It hurts so bad."

I hold her, whisper that she's safe until she calms. Then I carry her back to our tree, wrap her in the sleeping bag, and hold her until she falls asleep again.

The rest of the night I drift in and out. When I'm awake, my mind reels with ways that I can get her out. Being with her has been my first priority for months. Maybe the safest thing is for us to go to LA together, to get her out of this horrific life. If Shaun has begun to unravel like she said he has, she could be his next target. Especially if he knows I'm still around.

Her eyes open shortly after seven.

"Good morning."

"Hi." She brings a hand to her head but pauses before she touches it. "My head hurts."

"Did he hit you there last night?"

"Yeah." She closes her eyes again. "Sorry to drag you into this."

"Don't be sorry." I gently kiss her lips.

She jerks back for a second, then she leans into my kiss. Last night wasn't a dream.

I run a hand down her cheek. "How's the rest of you feel?"

"Okay." She opens her eyes. "If I don't move." She bites her lip. "I need to go to the clinic."

"I'll take you. Whatever you need." I interlock my fingers with hers. "I think it's time. You need to get out."

"He'll kill me." She swallows hard. "He will. That's what last night was about. He wanted to prove he has complete power over me."

"LA is over two thousand miles from Chicago. It's a huge city. No way will he find us."

"I can't walk right now, let alone travel." She sighs. "And that would be expensive. I mean, we'd need a place to live and a car—"

"You'd consider it?" Excitement builds at her interest.

"You really love me?" she asks.

"Yes. Yes, I love you." I kiss her, amazed that somehow, every time we kiss, it gets better.

"You're only sixteen."

"You're only eighteen. We have our entire lives ahead of us. I'll write movies, you can be in them."

She giggles. "I'm not an actress."

"Sure you are. You act like a prostitute five days a week. I know that's not who you are."

"Eight weeks until summer is over. The first two weeks in August are the busiest. I should make enough to keep us afloat in LA for a few months."

"Yeah?" It seems too good to be true.

"Yes." Now it's her turn to kiss me. "But first, coffee and food. Then the clinic."

What should be a fifteen-minute walk to the clinic takes close to an hour. I'm amazed at how slow she is but don't mind. We drink our coffee and eat our bagels while we try to act like she's not in tremendous pain.

"They'll question you, too, because I won't give details," she says when a building with Clinic painted on the side comes into view. "Let's stick with you're my brother, we went to a party last night and got separated. You found me afterwards, passed out and naked."

"Why is that important?" I ask.

"It's rape. They have to report it. They'll want my clothes as evidence."

"How many times has this happened?"

She frowns. "My name is Lisa. Lisa Banks. I don't have ID because they stole everything."

*Eight weeks,* I squeeze her hand. *Eight weeks until I free her.*

"Promise that's the story you'll give."

I nod. "What's my name?"

"Lewis."

I chuckle. "Lisa and Lewis?"

"Kinda cute. Like the typical American family."

"There's only one problem," I say.

"What?"

"I'm white. You're black."

She laughs. "My mother's philosophy was 'the whiter the better.' "

I stay in the waiting room when Kat goes back. She's gone for about twenty minutes before the older nurse behind the window calls, "Lewis Banks." She calls three times before I remember that's my make-believe name.

She opens the door to the back for me. "Please have a seat in the office on the left."

The place is creepy with a skeleton in the corner and the model of a human torso on the desk. I hope those are the only body parts he has.

"Lewis, I'm Doctor Amir." He shakes my hand before he sits behind his desk. "I'd like to know what happened to your sister."

I rub my hands on my shorts. "We went to a party last night. She disappeared after a while. She does that sometimes, you know. I found her after. Passed out."

"Was she wearing anything?"

"No." I shake my head, avert my eyes.

"Did you see anyone?"

"No, sir."

"Why didn't you take her to the hospital?"

"She begged me not to." I wonder how many more questions the guy can come up with. "I convinced her to come in this morning."

"I'm glad you did." The doctor strokes his beard. "Do you have any idea who would have done this to her?"

I shake my head. "A lot of guys were checking her out."

He leans forward. "Do you feel safe at home, Lewis?"

"Yeah." I cross my arms.

"Your father. Has he ever—"

"No. Everything's cool at home." I stand. "Where's my sister? Can I see her?"

"She's getting dressed. I had to examine her. We need to keep her clothes for evidence."

"Is she okay?" Fear suddenly has a grip on me.

"She needed a few stitches. I'll give her antibiotics to fight against infection and the STD. It's best if she stays in bed for several days. She said she'd need a note for work, so I'll write her off through next Thursday."

Tears rise inside me. "Can I see her now?"

Kat's curled up under a blanket on the exam table. She looks super cute in her doctor scrubs.

"Lewis wants to see you," the doctor says when he opens the door. "The police should be here in about fifteen minutes. I'll get your antibiotics along with that work note."

"Thanks." She shifts. "You know, Doc, I'll take you up on the offer for stronger pain meds. Tylenol doesn't seem to be helping."

"You got it." He shuts the door behind him.

She frowns at me. "You still love me?"

"Yeah." I rest my forehead against hers. "I'm sorry."

"You didn't do anything," she whispers.

"I'm sorry you're in pain. I'm sorry you're going through this." I kiss her forehead. "I'm sorry I can't help you."

"You brought me here," she says. "I'll let you take me home."

I nod. "I'll even pay for the ride."

She takes a deep breath. "Well, it's not the first time. For stitches or an STD."

"But it'll be the last time."

"I hope so. I did score you some narcotics, though."

I shake my head. "You need them for the pain."

"They give me a gnarly headache. Stop at the liquor store on the way home. I'll get a couple bottles to numb me."

We're almost to her place when Kat shares her suspicions with me.

"I'm pretty sure my bipolar roommate told Shaun about you. He talked about rumors. She's the one in the apartment who can't keep her mouth shut."

"Oh." I know what's to come.

"You can't stay the night anymore."

I swallow my tears. I just want to be with her, take care of her—

"I'll figure out her schedule and text you. You can come after she leaves, maybe bring me food. I need to stay in bed for several days if I want to get better."

I nod. "Will Shaun be okay that you can't work?"

"When he reads the doctor's report about what his thug friends did to me, he will." She smirks. "Loss of two nights is huge for me—and him. I'm gonna fight him that I should get paid. I don't think he will, but maybe when he finds out I was loyal and didn't report them." She rests her head on my shoulder. "Eight weeks?"

"Yeah. It'll be here before you know it."

# CHAPTER 34

## LYDIA

"AM I ALLOWED TO ASK WHERE WE'RE GOING?" JASON ASKS WHEN he climbs in my car the morning of July 15.

"Since you're the birthday boy you can ask, but I won't tell." I purse my lips. "Well, except, did you have breakfast? Because I was thinking of coffee and pastries."

"Sounds delicious."

Conversations center around church, scripture, and work. It makes me smile to hear him talk about Dad as his boss. The stories of Dad's kindness toward his employees tell me the transformation has occurred at work as well.

"How's your mom with you going to Texas?" I ask when he brings her up.

"She called a real estate agent this week." He laughs.

"She did?" My heart sinks. If she moves, he has no reason to come back. His dad lives in Michigan.

"I tell her I'll come back for holidays, but that's not enough. She wants to be at my games." He shrugs. "Guess it's a mom thing."

"You can't blame her," I say. "It would be easier. Then you won't have to travel."

"I'll come back to see you." He rests his hand on my shoulder.

"I'll be in Missouri."

"But you'll be home for the holidays. I know you will."

It's true. I've grown so close to my parents the past four months; I'll want to come home as often as I can. Though they like to spend time alone together now, I hear them talk about not being ready to be empty nesters.

Jason's eyes grow when we pass the sign "Indianapolis Motor Speedway and Museum next exit."

"Really?" he asks.

"It was on your list."

"You said you don't watch racing."

"I don't, but you do. Today is about you."

"Have I told you lately you're the best girlfriend ever?"

"Not today." I grin.

"Well, you are." He kisses my cheek.

First is the guided tour. After we visit the press box to see how enormous the span of the track is, we pile on a bus to cruise around it. Our eighty-year-old guide has probably seen the Indie 500 every year of his life. He talks about the drivers like they're friends. Jason is on the edge of his seat the entire ride.

"How have you lived in Indiana your whole life, watched the races every year, and never done this tour?" I ask.

"I did it with Dad when I was like eight. I only remember kissing the bricks."

I raise an eyebrow. "Kissing the what?"

"Kissing the bricks at the start-finish line. The winners and their team do it at the end of the race. When the bus tour ends, they let you kiss the bricks."

I wrinkle my nose. "Gross."

He laughs. "It's awesome. The best of the best have kissed those bricks."

I shake my head. "Cars run over them. People and animals walk on them. No, thank you."

Once I've snapped a picture of Jason's lips on the dirty bricks, we head to the museum. He's like a kid in a candy shop rushing from one car to another, telling me about the races and the drivers. I take loads of pictures. Rather than complain, his smile widens.

"Was it everything you hoped for?" I ask him over lunch.

"More." He leans over and kisses me. It's all good until I remember the bricks. I jerk back.

"You need to wash your lips." I wipe mine on my sleeve.

He chuckles, tousles my hair.

The racing education continues on the way home. His excitement about the sport, if you can call it that, is equal to baseball. It's definitely easier for me to listen to him talk about racing.

"Perfect timing." His mom is slicing tomatoes at the kitchen bar when we walk in his house. "Everyone will be here in an hour. Did you two have fun?"

"It was awesome." He kisses his mom's cheek. "Lydia put up with me talking about cars for hours. But she wouldn't kiss the bricks."

"A girl has to draw the line somewhere," I say.

"That was your favorite part when your father took you ten years ago."

"Still is." Jason washes his hands with soap at the sink. He passes a sudsy hand over his lips before he rinses them. He does care about what I think.

"How about you grab the burgers from the fridge and tell your dad about it. He's in the backyard with Sophie supposedly preparing the BBQ."

"Sure." He pulls out hamburger patties. "Want a soda, Lyd?"

"Yes, please."

"Maybe you can also remind your father it's not appropriate to make out with his girlfriend in my house." His mom peers out the window. His dad's hands are all over twenty-something Sophie.

Jason hands me a Coke and kisses my lips. "Is it appropriate for me to make out with my girlfriend in your house?"

"Yes, because I'm your mother, not your ex-wife."

"Technically they're in the backyard, not your house." The screen door slams behind him as he heads out.

"That was great of you to take Jason on the tour," his mom says. "He's wanted to go for years. I never quite understood the excitement over those races."

"I wanted it to be a special day." I wash my hands at the kitchen sink. "What can I do to help?"

"The lettuce needs to go on a plate." She motions to a head of lettuce on the counter.

I grab a plate from the cupboard. We've spent almost as much time at Jason's house this summer as we have at mine, so I'm comfortable in their kitchen.

"You mean the world to him, Lydia," she says. "He talks about you constantly. Gets that smile on his face every time."

I grin thinking of the smile he reserves for me. It's one of admiration, joy, even peace.

"Next school year will be hard, but after that, at least you'll be in the same state."

I pause, lettuce in midair. "What do you mean?"

"He's decided to transfer to Missouri his sophomore year. I can't remember the name of the school, but they offered him a scholarship this year. He called the recruiter at the end of June. The coach said they'll keep an eye on him. If he plays well, they can probably offer him something." She glances up from the tomatoes. "He had told you, right? I didn't think it was a secret."

"No, but he mentioned you might move to Texas?"

"I'm done owning. I can rent a place out there during baseball season, then follow him to Missouri. He's my boy. I'll go where he is. Are your parents still coming today?"

"Yeah," I say. "They love Jason. They'll be here."

"They seem like wonderful people. I'm looking forward to getting to know them more."

At one point there are over fifty friends and family members at their house. If I'm not helping Jason's mom, I'm on his arm. My parents talk with both of his parents. Every moment of the night is—comfortable. I don't even mind that my father gives Jason a load of baseball stuff for his gift, because he loves it, almost as much as he loves the new Bible I give him.

"Thanks for everything." Jason walks me to my car after midnight when the last of his friends leave. "It was the second best day ever."

"Second best?" I lean against him. "It was only the second best?"

He stops in front of my car. "The best day was prom 'cause you told me you loved me."

What his mom said comes to my mind. I can't let him give up his dreams for me. "Jason—"

His kiss silences me. It's long and passionate, the kind that makes my mind fuzzy and my hormones crazy.

"Sorry," he says when we part. "You're so beautiful I couldn't help myself." His thumb brushes my cheek. "I've loved every part of the past two months."

"Even finals? Precalc was awful. I had a headache for two days after."

"But you were in front of me." He wraps his arms around my waist. "No day is awful as long as you're in it." Another kiss. "Thanks for being cool with my family and friends. I know they can be exhausting."

"I had fun tonight." I run my hands over his chest. "Eighteen. You're officially an adult."

"Yep. I can vote. And get married."

Married? My heart starts to race. "One month until we go to college."

"A whole month." He hugs me. "Still have several things on the list. Maybe we can go to that Thai restaurant for dinner after work tomorrow."

"Sure." I relax in his arms, shift my eyes upward. Stars twinkle in the clear night sky. If I had a wish, what would it be? If I had one wish—

I slowly exhale. *God, help me. I don't want to let him go, but I know I need to.*

---

### *DANNY*

The countdown is on. While Kat works too hard five days a week, I do my part to earn extra cash. The streets outside clubs are packed every night. A line of coke right before makes me an outgoing, sociable guy. Kat has a philosophy that our true personality comes out when we're on drugs. She tries to convince me that deep within is this guy who can strike up a conversation with anyone. I'm not buying it.

Since I write great dialogue between characters, I write myself a script. There's a set hook and wrap up. The middle depends on the person. It takes a few weeks to nail who I should approach. Turns out the biggest contributors are those dressed to impress. Usually the guys are in slacks, sometimes a tie, with a five o'clock shadow. They give the most because they're full of themselves.

Friday nights the streets outside the fancy restaurants downtown are jammed by six o'clock. I walk up to a guy who checks his appearance on his phone.

"Hey, I'm raising money to head to Hollywood. Can you spare a few bucks?"

He sizes me up. "To be an actor?"

"No way. A screenwriter."

"You write movies?"

"Movies, plays. A couple hundred bucks will get me a bus ticket."

The guy removes a five from his pocket and slams it in my hand. "You'll mention me in one of your movies?"

"Absolutely." I pull my notebook from my backpack. "What's your name?"

"Theo Green." He straightens.

"You got it." I scribble his name then walk away.

The rest of the night goes like that. Groups are the best. They one up each other with their contributions or sometimes throw in a couple twenties for the entire group. By the end of the night, I have lists of names. This is awesome because I have name-block when it comes to writing. Basically, I've been given permission to use them. People may be ticked when the character is nothing like them, but hey, I never promise that. Not even when they tell me their profession or how many degrees they have. Their name will be in it. Besides, no one asks my name, so they'll never know.

Another reason to approach the large groups is they know how to party. One offers me some of their powder. I ask them their life stories, take copious notes. They're excited, assuming I'll write a movie about them.

"We'll be the next *Friends,*" one of them says, "or *Breakfast Club.*"

"*The Night Club.*" The blonde who speaks laughs so hard she almost falls over.

"Definitely." I shake my head at the absurdity.

"We gotta get him to LA," Mr. Blue-Dress-Shirt-and-Skinny-Tie says. He walks around the group with his hands out. When he gets to the last person, he counts the bills before adding a twenty. "Here you go, man. A hundred bucks. Can you leave for LA tomorrow?"

"Absolutely. Thanks." I hurry out of sight before they change their minds.

Kat checks out my earnings while we eat tamales. "I think you brought in more than I did tonight," she jokes.

"I probably had more fun." I dip mine in salsa.

"I'm sure. I do have exciting news."

"What's that?"

She leans forward. "My second cousin works at a used car place in Colorado. He texted that they got a Honda in with decent mileage. It's only a couple thousand. He's offered to buy it, fix it up a bit more, and resell it to us."

"That's awesome."

"We can take a bus there, get the car, and drive the rest of the way."

I pat my pocket. "I can afford the bus tickets."

"I also researched apartments." She pulls out her phone. "I found these. They take cash for first and last month's rent without a credit check. Most of the reviews are decent. I mean, they talk about mice, but I've never had pets." She hands me her phone.

I scan the photos on the website. "When did you have the time?"

"I get paid by the hour. Some guys do the stupidest things, like spend twenty minutes in the bathroom. I got nothing better to do than be on my phone."

"Does this mean you're excited?" I hand her back her phone.

"Of course. It's our new adventure." She lifts her soda can.

She chats the rest of the time about her favorite places in California, things she can't wait to do. She's the liveliest she's been on a weekend in a long time. The minute we start to walk to her pick-up spot, she goes silent.

"You okay?" I ask.

"Payton will be gone tonight. At her boyfriend's. Will you come over?"

"Won't you be done super late?"

"Two a.m." She rubs the inside of her elbow, her track marks. I've learned she does this when she's stressed.

"What's wrong?"

"I need to unwind. It's been a hard week."

I frown. She shoots up three days a week now. Most of the time I'm with her, partaking.

"Meet me in the park. We'll have wine, relax under the stars."

She shakes her head. "I need to escape. Please come over. I like it when you're there."

"You don't need that, Kat."

"I do! Like you need coke to be outgoing, I need this to let go." She rubs her arms. "It gets harder every day."

"Then let's leave." I take both her hands. "Please. Let's leave Sunday night."

"No." She jerks from me. "We need more money. It's only July. I need one more month of pay."

"We'll be fine. If we can't get a car yet, that's okay. It'll come together when we get out there."

"I can't live on the streets again." She wraps her arms around herself. She's shaking.

"We won't live on the streets. You found a place that takes cash."

"They aren't available until August. I can't take the chance. Please, Danny." She pulls on my hand. "I need more time."

In thirty minutes, she's gone from excited to an anxious mess. There's something else going on—

"That guy, the one on Wednesdays?" The volume of her voice drops. "The one who reminds me of my mom's boyfriend?"

"Yeah?"

"He pays for twice a week now. Fridays, too."

"Tell Shaun you can't."

"I don't have a choice." She closes her eyes. "I try to not think about it. I try to make myself go to another place in my mind, but it doesn't work."

I wrap my arms around her. "Don't let them get the best of you. Not now. We're close to being free."

"That's what I'm afraid of."

"What?"

"That I'll never be free. I've wanted it so long it doesn't seem possible."

"It is possible, Kat. We're leaving. A month, or sooner if you will."

She wipes her tears on my shirt, then kisses my cheek. "I'll text when I head home. You'll come?"

"Yeah," I whisper. "I'll be there."

---

The truth about heroin is your first high is always the best. Still, you continue to use, chase the hope to achieve a more phenomenal high. But it never comes. The truth about Kat is, even though she tells me she wants to shoot up with me, she never waits until I get there. I show up at her place ten minutes after she texts. She's on her bed, enjoying her high.

"You always want me here but never wait for me."

"You're too slow," she laughs.

"I'm early. You said two. You only texted me a little while ago."

"Sorry." She removes the tie from her arm and hands it to me. "Catch up with me."

I can tell she's exhausted because she doesn't speak, only lies in my arms. I wish she'd agree to leave this weekend. I wish I could take her away from this.

"I have bad news," she says.

"What?" Has she changed her mind? There's no way we can stay here—

"I don't know how to cook."

I laugh. "Really?"

"Yes, it's true."

"Is that why, in the four months since we've met, you've never made me a meal?"

"You've found me out."

"Well, don't worry." I kiss her cheek. "I do know how to cook."

"I know. You make awesome peanut butter sandwiches."

I chuckle. "I can cook other stuff. I'm an awesome sous chef."

"What's that?"

"The person who cuts and preps ingredients for recipes. I do that every Thanksgiving. I also make Christmas cookies."

Her eyes pop open. "Like the little ones with the jam?"

"Peanut butter with kisses are my favorite."

She smiles. "Those are good. Can you make a turkey?"

"I'm sure we'll figure it out."

She's quiet so long I wonder if she's asleep.

"We're really doing this," she whispers.

"Yeah, we are."

"I've never had a guy roommate."

"I've always had girl roommates. If my sisters count."

She laughs.

"I'm actually a pretty clean person," I say. "I promise to shower daily. And I'll put my trash in the trash can and not dig through it."

That makes her laugh harder. "I remember my first apartment after being on the street. Three girls in a one bedroom. It was so cramped we could hardly move. But showering every day was a plus."

"It'll be great." I run my hand over her arm. "Because I'll be with you."

"I love you."

I close my eyes, take in her words. I can't believe I'm so lucky to have her in my life. There's only one thing I would change if I could. "I want us to get clean when we get there."

"We established that. You can shower every day—"

"Clean from drugs," I say.

She's silent again.

"Will you do that? For me?"

Kat sighs. "What if I'm boring sober?"

"You couldn't be boring if you tried."

"Can I still drink?"

"Only with me. Good wine with a good meal."

Her fingers dance across my chest. "I'm scared."

"You don't need to be." I squeeze her. "You have me. I'll take care of you."

"Because you love me?"

"Yes." I kiss her. "Because I love you."

# CHAPTER 35

## LYDIA

One week until we're off to college. Each item on our summer to-do list is checked off. I've never laughed so hard or learned such random things. It's been the best summer of my life, which is ironic, because it's been the worst year of my life. God's grace is how I see it. Now it's time for it to end. It's time to say goodbye.

The past three years I've joined Katie's family on their annual camping trip. We leave today when her dad gets off work. Every time I go to pack, I have this overwhelming feeling that I need to tell Jason now. When he invites me to go dorm room shopping with him, I see it as an open door.

"What do you think about this?" he asks for the entire hour we're in the store. I give my input on towels, sheets, comforters, and storage bins while I run through transitions in my head.

*I love you, but—*

*Things will change when we go to college—*

*I wish it didn't have to be this way—*

Then I gaze at his handsome smile, his gorgeous face. He does something sweet like wrap his arm around my waist. Why do we fit so perfectly together? Or he makes some ridiculously funny comment. How does he always know how to make me laugh?

The last aisle we go down is the camping gear. He fills the cart with everything I need.

"Don't forget warm jammies and socks. The nights are cooler."

That's my guy, always concerned for me.

At lunch he strikes up a conversation about the study he and Dad are doing on the book of Colossians. He's doing a Bible study with my dad? Ugh.

On the ride home, I open my mouth to drop the bomb, but he asks about Mary.

"She got a job at a teen rehab center near her college. She's specializing in addictions."

"Wow. That's great."

"Yeah, she loves it. She calls me every week with stories of the kids she helps."

"What about Anna? Your dad said she went back to Moody a few weeks ago. I thought she worked at your church over the summer."

"She actually took the rest of this year off from ministry to focus on her own relationship with God. We had a lot of heart-to-hearts this summer. Though she's memorizing scripture and studying it for school and to teach others, she stopped reading the Bible to discover God for herself. She's making that her top priority."

"Another prayer answered," he says. "Danny's been on my mind a lot. I've been praying for him a lot. Have you been thinking about him?"

*Not too much*, I want to say, *because I've been consumed with how to break up with you.* "I still think about him daily. I don't cry as much, but I wonder where he is." Kat hasn't sent pictures since the night months ago when she said he talked about me. I pray he's safe, well, and not alone. I can't stand the thought of him being alone.

Alone, like I will be in a week—without my family, without Jason. Somehow, I feel like that's how it's supposed to be. Then I can focus on school and what God has for me.

*What do you have for me, Lord?*

Jason comes to mind.

I shake my head. He shouldn't give up everything for me. It's not right—

"I'll walk you in." He's parked in my driveway and out of the car before I can object.

"Make sure to reapply the bug spray several times a day." He hands me my bags as we walk toward the porch. "It'll wear off if you hike for a long time."

"Jason." I stop on the first step. "We need to break up."

Not eloquent but it's out there. By the look on his face, he's crushed.

"What?"

"It doesn't make sense to stay together when we'll be so far away."

He's silent for what feels like forever, then takes my hand. "I love you, Lydia. It doesn't have to be this way."

I can't look into his eyes. If I do, I'll go back on what I promised myself.

"We can talk every day," he says. "We can text. I'll save money to come see you. I'll come home when you're home. Please." He raises my chin to force eye contact. "What are you afraid of?"

I try to look beyond him but can't. His gorgeous brown eyes beg for an answer. Can I tell him I'm scared God's going to take away another person that I love? It almost crushed me to lose Danny this year. What if I'm thousands of miles from home and Jason decides he no longer loves me? Or worse, he signs with a professional baseball team. I can't let baseball become my life. Not after how it almost destroyed my family.

"College will change us. We should wait. Let God decide if we're supposed to be together."

"I've prayed for you the past four years." He caresses my cheek. "For us to be together. We're supposed to be together, Lyd. I've never been so sure of anything in my life."

My decision needs to be rational, based on logic, not on feelings. Yet my thoughts run wild as I stare into his face. Then he kisses me.

*Why are you holding back? You love him.*

"You don't need to be afraid," Jason whispers. "I know you've been hurt a lot this year. I'll never hurt you."

I place my hand against his smooth cheek. I do trust him—

*But do you trust God?* The question pierces my heart. *Can you trust God to do what you want?*

My phone vibrates with a message from Katie.

*Be there in an hour!*

"I gotta go." I slide my phone into my pocket.

Jason's searches my eyes. "You do know how much I love you, right?"

I sigh. "I do." Nothing has gone like I planned. I thought it would be easier. I give him a hug. "I'll call when I get home."

He walks to his car with his head down. My heart breaks all over again.

My bag is packed an hour later when Katie's family shows up to pick me up. Her dad leaves Mom with our camping location.

"I downloaded movies for us," Katie says when I climb in the back of the van.

"Great. Any of them depressing love stories? I could use a good cry."

She narrows her eyes. "What'd you do?"

"Nothing yet." I put my backpack under the seat. "You can't talk me out of it, so don't try."

There are hot dogs for dinner and s'mores for dessert, along with meltdowns from her siblings.

"Girls, are you okay alone in the two person tent?" her dad asks.

"I'll sleep with you to keep you safe," her six-year-old brother Andy tells us.

"Me too, me too!" Four-year-old Olivia climbs in my lap.

"No," Katie says. "I get Lydia to myself."

I laugh.

"C'mon you two." Her mother lifts Olivia from me and takes Andy's hand. "I know you'll be up before with the sun, so you need to go to bed now."

"Are you okay?" Katie asks once we are zipped up in our tent.

"It was a long day." I yawn. "At least I should sleep well."

She yawns. "Me too. I had to keep the kids busy all day so Mom could pack. Have you started packing for Missouri?"

"Some. Anna helped me clean out stuff from my room before she went back to school. Mom's having a hard time."

"I bet. You're the only one left." She pauses. "Well, you know what I mean."

"Yeah. It's been hard."

"You ever wonder where Danny is?"

"Every day." I yawn again, my eyelids too heavy to keep open. "Every day."

*Danny is running through the streets. Though I call his name, he doesn't stop. He runs faster and faster through puddles, but the puddles aren't water. They're blood. With every step he takes, blood sprays into the air.*

*"Danny, Danny, Danny!"*

"Lydia, Lydia."

I wake to Katie beside me.

"Are you okay? You're moaning and rolling around."

I glance at her, then my sleeping bag. We're camping with her family. "I had a dream." I sit up, run my hands through my hair.

"Sounded like a nightmare."

"It was." I grab my phone. "I'm going outside for a while."

"Stay close," Katie says.

The dream comes back to me. Danny was running. Why? Was it just a dream or was I seeing something?

Pacing a few feet from the tent, I check my phone. No signal. I want to text Kat to make sure everything's okay. That's when it comes to me. Something's wrong with her.

I drop to my knees. "God, be with Danny and Kat. Protect them. Place Your hand upon them."

*Peace.* The word comes to me, followed by *love.*

"Let Kat feel Your peace and Your love."

I continue to pray fervently until she fades from my mind. A clear picture of Danny comes. He's alone, mad. And scared.

The rage inside him builds, as does the fear. He's so afraid. I pray for peace, that God's love and Word will surround him to bring him comfort. I feel a spiritual wrestle. Satan wants Danny dead. Danny feels so hurt, alone, and angry he wants to die. The air is sucked from my lungs. *Oh, God, he wants to die.*

But God is there.

I open my Bible app to Psalm 34.

"I prayed to the Lord, and he answered me. He freed me from all my fears. Those who look to him for help will be radiant with joy; no shadow of shame will darken their faces. In my desperation I prayed, and the Lord listened; he saved me from all my troubles. For the angel of the Lord is a guard; he surrounds and defends all who fear him."

I repeat it over and over. It's my plea for my brother's safety, for his life.

Tears of rage stream down Danny's face as he screams at God.

"Come home, Danny," I beg. "It's time to come home. Come back to God. Come back to us. We love you."

---

## *DANNY*

We leave tomorrow. I'm literally counting the hours. Tonight, Kat will meet me with her stuff.

"I'll sneak out before the others get home, so they don't see my bag," she said last night.

I purchased the bus tickets for eight a.m. tomorrow for Colorado Springs. We'll spend the night at her cousin's, then leave with the car the next day. This is it. Finally, we're on our way to LA. All my dreams are about to come true.

I did research today on the legal age to marry. Unfortunately, you need parental consent under eighteen. I wanted to surprise Kat and propose, get married on the way to California. Then she'd know the depth of my commitment. How much I love her. She'd know I respect her completely. That's the best gift I can give her. Maybe I'll get her a ring and we'll make plans for my eighteenth birthday. There are a lot of uncertainties, but I know we'll make it. After all, we've made it this far.

I shower, wash my clothes and sleeping bag at the center. In the clothing room I find slacks, a long-sleeve dress shirt, and a tie.

"Special occasion?" Roman asks.

"Need to look professional. I'll be interviewing next week."

"Awesome." He bags up the clothes. "I'll be praying for you."

*Don't bother*, I want to say. Instead, I smile and take the bag.

I head to our favorite Italian restaurant. That's where Kat wants to go for our last meal in Chicago.

The minute she catches sight of me, Kat runs towards me. I laugh at her enthusiasm. I'm excited too, but wouldn't run. That's what makes Kat, Kat.

"I'm done." She jumps into my arms. "I'm free."

"You are." I inhale her sweet smell. Sweet pea, she told me her lotion is called. Her hair is damp and in small curls. There's no makeup or work clothes. Jeans, t-shirt, and tennis shoes. This is the Kat I love.

Her grin never fades during dinner. Neither does mine. There's a bottle of champagne to celebrate. The waitress only brings one glass, but when we're alone, I finish what's in front of her before I fill it again. We don't talk of her clients or panhandling. Instead we make travel playlists, plan sights we'll see on the way, and talk about what we'll do first in sunny southern California.

"Disneyland!" Her eyes are huge. "We have to go to Disneyland! I went with my mom when I was fourteen."

"I thought it was for little kids."

"No way. I had a blast. My mom had fun, too. Of course, she replaced the water in her bottle with vodka."

I choke on my food. "You're kidding?"

Kat shakes her head. "She was that great of a role model."

"I've heard teens smoke out on Tom Sawyer's Island." I raise my eyebrows.

She giggles. "Bad Danny Boy."

"I bet Tom and Huck smoked out together a few times. Kinda like me and Brett."

"Maybe that's your next play. Like a parallel with some details from your life." Kat grins. "I'm Becky, right?"

"Of course."

After dinner, we purchase our bottle of wine. The park is surrounded by cop cars.

"Guess we go somewhere else tonight." I tug at her arm as she continues forward.

"What do you think happened?" She's on her tiptoes to see over the crowd of people.

"Nothing we want to see." I pull her away.

"Party pooper." She links arms with me. "How about that tunnel under the bridge? Since the activity is up here, it should be a quiet night there."

"Quiet sounds good," I say. "We have a busy day tomorrow."

"You got the tickets?" she asks.

I pat my backpack. "You got the cash?"

She pats her pink backpack. "Enough for the car and three months' rent. It was a good summer."

A couple women are clustered where we enter. Fast food wrappers with their day's pickings are in between them. Two old men share a cigarette at the far end. Someone in dirty, baggy clothes with short hair is passed out across from them.

"Think you'll be able to sleep?" I spread my sleeping bag in the middle of the openings.

"We'll sleep fine." She sets her backpack on top of her duffle and pulls out two syringes.

My heart sinks. "C'mon, Kat, we talked about this. Time for a new start. We don't need drugs."

"We aren't in California yet." She yanks me down on my sleeping bag. "Once more for old time's sake. Besides, we don't want to detox on the way. Let's wait 'til we get there and get set up."

"No." I can't believe the word comes out. By the look on her face, she can't either.

"For me." She kisses my neck. "Once more." Her lips find mine. "We'll sleep so good tonight."

Everything that's within me tells me not to, yet I can't deny her anything.

"I need to go to the bathroom." I stand. "It's hard to walk straight after."

She laughs. "Hurry or I'll start without you."

"You always do," I say on my way out of the tunnel.

It takes a while to find some privacy. First, I spot a guy hunched over something that resembles roadkill.

*Crunch!*

I start to turn, but I'll hurl if the woodland creature is his dinner. I stop at one bush that's being occupied by a woman. Next I pass an old man who shares his soup bowl with an even older dog. Definitely looking forward to a bathroom in our private apartment.

The thought of Kat at Disneyland makes me smile as I walk back. She'd look adorable in a pair of glittery Mickey ears. Then there's Kat at the beach. I should've grabbed a bathing suit at the shelter. It didn't occur to me—

The tunnel is complete chaos. People are gathered towards the center.

"Somebody help her," one lady says.

"She's ODing," a guy says.

The other lady shakes her head. "She's just a kid."

That's when I realize it's Kat.

I sprint like I'm headed to home base. The scene is surreal. Foam is gathered in the corners of her mouth. She flips from side to side. An empty syringe rolls down to the center of the tunnel.

"Kat! Kat!" I push my way through the crowd, scoop her into my arms. I hold her thrashing body against mine. "Kat, wake up. Kat!"

I glance to the woman behind me. "Call 9-1-1!"

"The cops won't come," some guy mutters.

"Call!" I scream. "She needs help."

Kat's face is pale gray. Her eyes are rolled back

"Kat!"

That's when it happens. She stops. Like in slow motion, her eyes freeze, her jaw drops, and she loses control of her bowels.

"Kat!" I wipe the foam from her mouth, press mine against hers. I don't know CPR, but she needs to breath. I need her to be okay. Tomorrow we're going to LA to start a new life. It's finally time. She's finally free.

"She's dead."

"Too bad. She was only a kid."

The skin around her lips and eyes is purple. Her body cold. She's gone. Forever.

We sat at dinner, talked, planned, laughed. What happened? I stare into her ghostly face.

"Why didn't you wait for me? For once, why didn't you wait?"

Then come shouts. "Cops! Cops!"

Kat's dead. The cops are here. If I get caught, I'll end up in jail. Or worse, back home.

"I love you." I kiss her lips, then lay her on the sleeping bag. My pants are a mess from her. It smears when I wipe them with the sleeping bag. There are sirens. Grabbing our backpacks, I run the opposite direction of the emergency vehicle lights. I sprint for blocks, miles, until I collapse breathless in a back alley.

Kat's gone. She's dead.

Hands on my knees, my whole body shakes as I gasp for breath. God did this, like He did everything else.

"How dare you!" I glare at the sky. "How dare you take her!"

*Come home, Danny. It's time to come home.*

I run my hands through my hair. Nothing turned out the way I wanted. Nothing has gone according to my plan.

*Come home, Danny. It's time to come home.*

"You crushed my hopes and dreams!" First with the epic baseball mess up. Then Dad forced me to be on the team and give up drama. Finally, my bank account was frozen so I couldn't get a car. "You took my passion, my money, now the person I love. Can't you leave me alone? For once, couldn't you let me be happy?"

I think of Kat and me on a bench outside the Catholic church. She's filled with condemnation. Holding her hands, I lead her in the sinner's prayer.

"She loved You. She believed in You even though You never protected her. She saw Your beauty everywhere though You forced her to live in filth."

Next I remember when we ran into Shaun on the streets. The look in his eyes is one I saw in my father's so often. Determination to control. He didn't want to lose Kat, so he killed her. He gave her the tainted heroin.

"Why couldn't You let things go my way?"

*"The Sovereign Lord is my strength! He makes me as surefooted as a deer, able to tread upon the heights."*

"No!" I say when the verse comes to mind. "You constantly tear me down."

*"Take delight in the Lord, and he will give you your heart's desires."*

"*She* was my heart's desire. I loved her and You took her—"

*"For this is how God loved the world—"*

"You didn't love her. You let her die. You've never loved me. You've proved that time and time again. Just like my father. You want me as a pawn in Your stupid game. You don't care about me or what I want."

*"My thoughts are nothing like your thoughts—"*

That's when I see it. The second syringe in the small pocket of her backpack.

*"—and my ways are far beyond anything you could imagine."*

"I can imagine what You have for me." I stare at the amber liquid as I roll the syringe between my fingers. "You want to strip me of my creativity and dreams. Force me into a life I'll hate."

*Come home, Danny. It's time to come home.*

The cold needle slides in easily. I see Kat's face in my mind. Not the beautiful face I fell in love with but the twisted one while she seized. Her gray skin, her eyes rolled back, foam around her mouth.

I loved her, despite her habit. I saw past that to the real Kat. The drugs destroyed her though I wanted to save her.

Then I see my family, not as they were before I left but as they were the previous Christmas. There's laughter, happiness, love. Lyd tells me I can start over again. That God has a good plan for me.

*Come home, Danny. It's time to come home.*

Next come shouts, anger, and hatred. I stand before my father. My hatred boils over as he closes his hand over my drugs.

*Game over, Danny.*

Profanity follows, along with destruction and pure rage.

My mom's face appears in my mind. Sadness plagues her eyes. *All we want for Christmas is for you to be clean.*

*C'mon Danny,* Kat begs. *Do it with me. It helps you forget. You won't care about anything.*

The drugs take effect. This is my life. I live in filth, wallow in sin, do anything to forget. But I can't. The pain grows. My mistakes haunt me when I close my eyes. I can't forget. There's no release. No high. Darkness surrounds me. Consumes me.

My stomach cramps. I break out into a cold sweat. Everything rises up inside me. I glance around for help but no one's there.

*Game over, Danny. You did this to yourself. You can blame me all you want, but one day you'll stand before God and you will be responsible for every decision you made. This one is huge.*

I've completely destroyed my life like my dad predicted I would.

*"The Sovereign Lord is my strength! He makes me as surefooted as a deer, able to tread upon the heights."*

Varsity. I made varsity baseball. The only freshman in five years to not only make varsity but the youngest shortstop ever. God took me to places no one that young had been.

*"Take delight in the Lord, and he will give you your heart's desires."*

I needed a friend, someone to understand me, and He brought me Kat. I wanted my first kiss to mean something. It meant everything with her.

*"For this is how God loved the world: He gave his one and only Son, so that everyone who believes in him will not perish but have eternal life."*

I was six years old, at Vacation Bible School. "I love You, Jesus," I prayed. "Thank You for dying for my sins to make me clean. Please come live in my heart and never leave me."

Never leave me.

*"My thoughts are nothing like your thoughts. And my ways are far beyond anything you could imagine."*

In my mind I see Mary beside a kid my age. He groans as he rocks. She wraps a blanket around him, dabs a washcloth on his forehead, and tells him to be strong and courageous.

"You can do this," she says. "I believe in you."

Next I see Anna. She holds her Bible in her hands, wipes tears from her cheeks. She underlines a verse. "God, forgive me," she says. "Forgive me for how I've judged my brother."

Then I see my parents in bed. My dad holds my mom. He prays for her. Peace, comfort, a sound mind. And he prays for me. *God, keep Danny safe. Provide for his needs. Let him know we love him and miss him. Please, Lord, bring him home.*

Lydia kneels on the ground. She prays for me and Kat, even though she doesn't know her. She prays so passionately tears roll down her cheeks, or sweat, or both. "Come home, Danny," she says into the night. "It's time to come home."

The world spins. There are spots in my vision. My stomach hurts so bad I'm curled up in a ball. My heart races. I gasp for breath. No longer am I able to hold my head up. I collapse on the cold, wet pavement. My body shakes uncontrollably.

"Come back to God," Lyd whispers. "Come back to us. We love you."

The encouragement, the compliments, the words of concern my mom and sisters spoke to me over the years flood my mind. They love me. Even though they're as messed up as I am and didn't always treat me great, my family loves me. I ran when they tried to save me from myself. Now it's too late.

*Game over, Danny. Game over.*

"God, what have I done to my life?" I whisper. "I don't want to die out here. Please help me."

*GET A SNEAK PEAK AT THE FIRST CHAPTER OF THE REDEEMED*

# *CHAPTER ONE*

*THE ENTIRE GAME HANGS ON MY SHOULDERS. IT'S THE BOTTOM OF the ninth. I'm on third, two outs, the score is tied. Martinez is at bat. As soon as he makes contact with the ball, I'm off. My first mistake is to slide too soon. I feel the sting of the sand along the top my arm. The second mistake is not lifting my face. It's completely raw, burning in pain. Now it radiates from my right eye when I open it.*

I'm lying in a blackish liquid.

Oil? Why does it reek of garbage and urine?

I raise my head. The world spins. Everything is blurry. This isn't a baseball field, it's an alley. The muscles in my arms burn when I push myself up. I stagger to my bare feet. What happened to my shoes? My arms are black and sticky. There's crap all over my pants, literal crap.

*What did I do?*

The memory hits me like a tsunami—Kat's dead.

Her pale gray face appears in my mind. I held her as she convulsed, foamed at the mouth. I screamed. When she went limp, I gave her CPR. There were sirens, and I ran. I grabbed my backpack, and hers, and ran.

I spin fast enough to lose my balance.

*Where are they?* I scan the area. *Where are they?*

Sprinting to the closest dumpster, I grip the side as the world tilts. Nothing's on top. Behind? Nope. I stagger to the next one. Faded black material sticks out the top. My backpack.

"Be there." I yank it down. "Be there, please be there."

I unzip the bottom pocket. Empty. The main compartment? Only my notebooks. Beat-up notebooks with fictitious names and character sketches. My wallet, my phone, our bus tickets, gone. ALL my money. Gone.

Profanities fly from my mouth as I throw it to the ground and heave myself into the trash pile. Garbage sails in every direction. Kat's backpack has to be here. It can't be gone. Not after all this. It took her months to save thousands of dollars. It must be somewhere.

The dumpster is half empty when I realize I'm a fool. It's gone. Everything we saved. Our hopes and dreams of a future are destroyed.

Gone, just like her.

It requires five times the amount of strength to climb out. My bare feet throb when I land on the asphalt. My clothes, legs, and arms are a black, sticky mess. My hands get stuck midway through my hair. I managed to untangle them. The stench causes me to gag, then dry heave.

I'm on my knees, head down when a flash of metal half under the dumpster catches my eye. The syringe I shot up with.

I crawl over, pick it up, roll it around in my hand. I wanted to die. I hoped my heroin would be tainted, too. I can't live without her. Rage builds inside me. I should've died. Instead I'm alive left with a backpack of failed dreams. Disappointments. I hurl the needle toward the wall.

The pain returns to my right temple. I feel something wet. Blood.

Nice. Some jerk stole everything, including my shoes, then bashed in my head. Definitely my best day ever.

My biceps scream as I pull my shirt off. I turn it inside out. After wiping my face and hands, I toss it in the dumpster. If I don't clean up soon, I'll puke again.

The sun shines brighter on the sidewalk. By the amount of people, I guess it's midmorning. It takes a while to get my bearings. My eyes only feel half-open; it's a chore to keep my head vertical. People stare as they pass. I'm sure it's not because of my ruggedly handsome body.

In the two blocks to a grocery store I step on glass three times, in animal poop, get gum stuck on my big toe, and almost burn my foot on a lit cigarette. At the far end of the parking lot is a donation drop box. Bags of clothes are piled beside it. Halfway down I find a pair of shorts that might fit, a faded T-shirt, and flip flops that don't fall off.

A guy is at the urinal in the bathroom when I enter. He gives me a once over, finishes his business, and leaves without washing. I understand why when I look in the mirror. My hair is black and sticking straight out. The right side of my face is covered with dried blood. There's a gash above my right eye with fresh blood.

Every movement exacerbates the pain. My head scraps against the faucet. The sticky substance on my hair transfers to the stupid water handle I have to continually push to get the water to trickle out. The soap doesn't cut through the gunk—it just runs into my eyes.

Whatever. I don't care. Nothing matters anymore.

Shaking my hair dry almost lands me on my butt. I run paper towels across my face to uncover a black eye. A nice souvenir from the worst day of my life.

I shove my soiled pants into the trash. Paper towels rub like sandpaper against my skin. Asphalt is embedded in my arms; they're red by the time I'm done scrubbing.

*She didn't really love you. Look at yourself. You're a scrawny kid. You didn't deserve someone as beautiful as her.*

"She did love me," I say aloud. "I deserved her. I loved her. I'd do anything for her—"

*But you didn't. You couldn't save her. You didn't even try.*

"I didn't want her to shoot up—"

*You didn't stop her, did you?*

Tears rise. I wanted to. I hated her heroin habit. I just couldn't tell her no. I thought when we got to California, everything would change.

*You were too weak to stop her. You've always been too weak.*

"Shut up," I say.

*Too weak to stand up to your dad, too weak to say no to drinking.*

"Shut up," I say louder.

*Too weak to make it to LA. You know you're too weak to survive this—*

"Shut up!" I hit the mirror with my fist. Pain surges up my arm.

*See, you're too weak to even break a mirror.*

A growl comes from deep within. I rip the lid from the trash can. "Shut up!"

*Bam.* The shockwave vibrates through my hands when I slam the lid into the mirror.

"I'm not weak."

*Bam.* It makes its way to my arms.

"You don't know—"

*Crack.*

The door swings open. Through the spidered mirror I catch the eye of a middle-aged man. He backs out of the restroom.

*Look at yourself,* the voices mock as I stumble to dress, *you're a strung-out addict. You should be dead. There's nothing left for you.*

The shorts sit below my waist. The shirt hangs like a tent. I race from the store, shirt bellowing and holding up the shorts. I won't get arrested. Not now. Not from this.

Hand pain now trumps head pain. I need alcohol, or cocaine. Since I can steal the first, I position myself around the corner of the store. I watch people exit, wait patiently for the right victim.

A mom with two kids comes out.

"I've told you not to wake your brother while he's sleeping!" the mom is yelling over the screams of the infant in the carrier at the toddler sitting in the cart. "Now he's going to scream all the way home!"

I spy two tall, slender paper bags in her cart. Wine. Yeah, she definitely needs it, but right now, I need it more.

She slows by a brown minivan. That's my cue to head down the row.

"Apple juice? Apple juice?" the toddler begs.

"Not until we get home." She grabs the baby as the side door opens. "Don't get up until I come back for you."

I quicken my pace when her back is turned and snatch one bottle from the cart. The toddler narrows his eyes at me. I place a finger to my lips. His pouty lips shift into a grin. Maybe it made the kid's entire day that I took his mom's fruit juice away.

Shoving the bottle in my backpack, I weave through the rows of cars out of sight.

Three rows over a thirty-something year old guy loads his car. A quick scan of his cart reveals nothing of interest. He turns. Suddenly, we're face-to-face.

"Hey, man. Got any spare change?" Maybe I can scrounge up enough by the end of the day to at least get a joint.

"I don't." He reaches into a bag and pulls out a banana. "How about a banana?"

"Yeah." I snatch it. "Yeah, that's good. I haven't eaten all day."

"What's your name?" he asks.

I peel the banana. My stomach growls. "Got anything else?"

"How about a granola bar?"

"Yeah, sure." I stuff it in my pocket and walk away. "Thanks. I appreciate it."

"You didn't tell me your name."

I glance over my shoulder. "Danny."

"Can I ask you something, Danny?"

"Sure." I don't want a conversation with a stranger but at this point he might buy me a meal if I entertain him.

"Do you know Jesus?"

How do I answer that? *Oh, yeah, you mean that guy who screwed up my life? The jerk who took the girl I love from me?* I stare into his face. What has he to gain from this? I'm thinking straight enough to realize sarcasm will only gain me a lecture. Ignorance could get me more food. "Heard of Him." I point to the case of water at the bottom of his cart. "How about a water bottle?"

He grabs me one. "Then you know He loves you?"

"That's what they say. Thanks." I start to walk away.

"I need some work done tomorrow. Weeding, mostly. Maybe some mowing. If you were interested, I'd pay you."

I pause. "How much?"

"Eighty dollars for the day. We start at seven, finish by one. I'll feed you breakfast and lunch."

Two meals and eighty bucks. That might get me an eight ball.

"I'm game." I reach in my pocket for my phone. "Some jerk stole my phone. Could you give me directions?"

"No problem." He pulls a card from his pocket, turns it over, and starts to scribble. "Seven isn't too early?"

"I'm up with the sun." Truth is, without a sleeping bag, I doubt I'll sleep at all.

"How long you been on the streets?" He continues to write.

"I don't know." At the moment, I don't know what day it is. "Long enough."

He hands me the card. "I'm glad we can help each other out. Thanks, Danny. See you tomorrow."

I laugh when I read the card. Pastor. Of course. I begin to crumble it up then stop. Eighty dollars is a lot now that I have nothing.

A few blocks away, I score three dollars and eighty-five cents at a coffee place, then french fries along with a dollar in change at a fast food restaurant. I'm walking toward the door when a girl Kat's complexion and height exits. The image of Kat, in my arms dying, pops in my mind. I dash to a nearby bush to toss the french fries I consumed.

I sit on the curb next to the bush I puked in. She's gone. Twenty-four hours ago, I met her for dinner. She ran to me over-the-top excited.

*I'm free*, she said when she leapt into my arms. *I'm free.*

*You took her,* I think to God. *You took the girl I loved.*

*"Yet what we suffer now is nothing compared to the glory he will reveal to us later."*

I cover my head when the verses come. She's dead, gone. That's all that matters.

The two of us on Easter on the bench outside the Catholic church comes to mind. She stared into my eyes as she said the sinner's prayer. She accepted Christ. When she said, "Amen," peace covered her face.

*"But to all who believed him and accepted him, he gave the right to become children of God."*

My face heats up. *You destroyed my life. Time and time again, You've destroyed my life, in Jesus's name.*

"Are you Danny?"

My eyes wander from the black snakeskin boots up the skinny jeans. The hispanic guy's maroon silk shirt is half open. Gold chains hang around his neck, a black cowboy hat is on his head.

"Danny? Kat's friend?" He helps me stand. "I'm Andres. We got mutual friends."

The pieces come together in my mind. Andres is Shaun's competitor. Kat talked about him a few times. He's pimp to women and men.

I grab my backpack.

"Whoa, whoa, Danny Boy. Hold up."

I freeze. There's only one way he knows my nickname. Kat's bipolar roommate—

"My condolences. Kat was class. I offered her a place on my team several times." He slips his arm around my shoulder. "I know how hard it is—"

"Get off me." I jerk away. "You don't know anything."

"I know you cared about her, 'n she watched over you. I know you're hard up for cash."

I stare into his sleazy eyes.

"I know you have habits 'n need a place to live." His grin reveals gold teeth. Gold. Is the word 'pimp' on his bottom row? "I put my guys in luxury, not crap holes like Shaun keeps his girls in. You'll have new digs. No thrift store toss outs. You'll clear more cash than Kat ever did." He glances to the track marks. "There's other benefits. Whatever you want. Whenever you want it."

There's four dollars in my pocket, useless notebooks in my backpack. I glance down at the clothes I got from the donation bin.

*You're a ridiculous mess.*

"You got potential." Andres eyes me.

*You know you can't survive on your own.*

"I can get you in shape." He runs his fingers over my shoulder and down my arm. "In a week you'll be on the market. A young kid like you'll make prime green." The onions on his breath make my eyes water. "'Course I'd set you up in the meantime. Tonight, you'll be off the streets. Have a steak dinner, get real clothes, sleep in a bed." He slips a syringe in my hand. "Get plenty of this."

The devil himself is in front of me, asking me to make a deal. As much as it makes me want to hurl, it's tempting.

"Fifth and State. 657 apartment D. Bodie's your roommate." Andres walks backwards. "He'll take care of you, show you the ropes. Offer expires in twenty-four hours. I only guarantee your safety until then." He climbs into a black BMW. "See you soon, Danny Boy."

I'm on the sidewalk, the drug that destroyed Kat in my hand. She was right. Shaun did kill her for trying to leave. If I stay in Chicago, I'll be next.

Once Lost Series

The Deceived

The Beloved

The Redeemed
coming fall of 2020 - excerpt in back

Other series by Kelly Harrel

Lauren Drake

Angel Discovered

Angel Defined
introduces adult Danny Morton

Angel Reconstructed

Angel Resolved

Walking the Walk

Freedom in His Love: Tasha's Story

Running in Such a Way: Josh's Story

facebook.com/kellyharrel.author.speaker
twitter.com/kellyharrel
instagram.com/kellyharrel
amazon.com/author/kellyharrel
bookbub.com/authors/kelly-harrel
goodreads.com/kellyharrel